# ALL THE
# TOMORROWS

## A Novel by
## Nillu Nasser

FIRST EDITION SOFTCOVER
ISBN: 1622537858
ISBN-13: 978-1-62253-785-3

*Editor: Jessica West*

EVOLVED PUBLISHING™

www.EvolvedPub.com
Evolved Publishing LLC
Butler, Wisconsin, USA

Printed in Book Antiqua font.

*For Jan,*
*who believed and was patient.*

# 1

**The sun hung** like a molten pendant on the horizon as Akash rolled away from his sleeping wife. He cursed as the bed creaked in protest, threatening to wake Jaya. He tiptoed across their bedroom, heavy with the Indian heat, and stubbed his toe in his eagerness to escape the confines of his marriage and reach his lover. In his arms he carried neatly folded clothes, and he eased through the door without a look back.

Safely on the other side of the threshold, Akash's heart rate slowed. He dressed quickly and headed out into the daylight, where honking rickshaws already jostled for space on the road despite the early hour. He threaded his way to university through littered streets, where rats the size of his forearm fought with street urchins for the right to scraps.

"Soraya." Her name felt like sherbet on his tongue.

Fifteen minutes later, he turned a corner into the university grounds, and there she sat on a bench nestled amongst roses, a woman secure in the knowledge of her own beauty and her hold on him.

The streets pulsed with people but Jaya paid no heed as she pushed on. Her husband was up to something, and today would be the day she unravelled his secret. The note she had discovered inside the door to their bedroom, the one that proved her instincts had been right, lay like a stone inside her shoulder bag. A stranger's elegant handwriting adorned its jagged form:

*7 a.m., the university rose garden*

Jaya passed street vendors blackened by the sun, selling sugared almonds and bright bags of turmeric and chilli. Thoughts tumbled through her head: how Akash stole away each morning from their marital bed, leaving her to wake alone in a house laden with silence; how he spurned her touch, making her question whether she knew how to please him; how even the liveliest conversation fell on deaf ears.

A year ago, they had been strangers; a brief introduction later, betrothed; now, husband and wife. She'd spoken to Akash only briefly before their marriage, with her mother watching intently from the sidelines. She'd searched him for a sign that everything would be all right, and had taken his silence for shyness.

*Did you ever want me, Akash?*

Her parents had ensured she understood the importance of the match for their family. Her father could no longer afford to feed them all, and if she wanted to complete her studies, the marriage was essential. She would live with her in-laws, two families would be one, and her father would no longer have to pay for her upkeep. The old way, to have a marriage arranged, suited her parents, and Jaya had agreed, determined to make it work.

The wedding had taken place in a marquee on the outskirts of Hyderabad in the height of summer. Hundreds of well-wishers had arrived in buses, dressed in sequins and bright hues, sweat-stained even before the first ceremony. Jaya's hands and feet were painted with intricate *mehndi* the colour of earth. It trailed up her arms, a tattoo proclaiming to the world that she was a bride. The mehndi artist, playful and coy, had hidden Akash's initials within the pattern in the crook of Jaya's arm, for her husband to find on their wedding night.

A good match, their families had said.

*Then why do I feel such distance between us?*

She wanted to hold him to account, but instead her anger ebbed and despair set in. She looked down at herself, wishing she had made herself more beautiful for him, wishing the city had not already left its mark. The dust from the Bombay streets mingled with her feet through her open-toed sandals. Chipped nails peeked from behind worn leather. At the university gates, she stopped to hand a few rupees to a street child holding a broken drum, all forlorn eyes and scraggly hair.

She forged on through the gates, her chest heavy. Her instinct told her not to question Akash, but to test him. What could he be hiding? Jaya knew one thing: she loved her husband enough to overcome anything. If even the smallest piece of him belonged to her, she could save them.

"I will find a way to make us work, Akash Choudry," she said. "Mark my words."

The lovers stood in the overgrown alcove in the rose garden. The heady fragrance of the blooms filled Akash's nostrils, competing with the scent of Soraya's newly-washed hair.

She curved her body into his, her pelvis pushing against his thighs. He closed his eyes, and she shook him, laughing lightly.

"We can't do this here. What if someone sees?" she said.

"I don't care. Let them see. This is the best part of my day."

He didn't feel guilty for his deception of his wife. He didn't care if he and Soraya received censure for their public displays of affection. Their illicit meetings brought him joy: Soraya's touch, her smell, the lilting timbre of her voice. To deny himself would have been too painful, and so, week after week, month after month, their affair had continued, wherever and whenever it could, with no regard for the vows he had taken or the damage he inflicted.

He tangled his fingers in Soraya's hair, still damp from her shower, and pulled her closer. Their lips meshed, and he savoured the plump moistness of her closed mouth, then pried it apart with his tongue.

She reached up to loop her arms around his neck, and then jerked suddenly, her fingers caught on a thorn.

"Ouch!"

He sat down on the worn bench and pulled her down onto his lap. Then he took her finger, drew it to his mouth, and gently sucked.

"Better?"

She nodded, kissed his ear, and rested her head on his.

"You know," he mumbled into soft swaths of fabric at her chest, "you are the only person I'd happily serve all my life. Did I tell you that myth I love about Arjun, the greatest archer in the world? He was equally proficient with left and right arm, trusted and loved by Krishna, a man cursed never to be king, always to serve."

Soraya groaned. "You've only told me that about a hundred times."

Footsteps sounded ahead of them, and Akash hesitated. Despite the risk of discovery, he remained reluctant to push Soraya away.

*Just a little more.*

"Akash?"

A voice he recognised.

It struck him like a whip, a note of discord on a perfect morning. He froze at first, then looked up, hoping his ears had betrayed him, that he would be able to laugh at himself for this moment of panic.

"What's going on?" His wife stood before him, eyes filling with tears. Her bag lay at her feet, its contents spilt across the pathway. Time slowed while she looked from him to the woman on his lap, her features twisted with distress.

Akash pushed Soraya off his lap, blood rushing to his face.

"Jaya...." He stood and reached out to his wife, but she flung his hand away and pivoted, stumbling on her strewn possessions before running through the gardens, away from him, towards the throngs outside the gates.

Panic marred Soraya's face.

"Oh God, Akash, I'm so sorry. Aren't you going to go after her?"

He sank back onto the bench. "What would I say?"

He hung his head in his hands, reeling, unable to ignore the consequences of his actions any longer. Jaya's pain was clear, and finally, after all this time, the consequences of his actions confronted him. How had these stolen moments with Soraya spiralled so out of control? He couldn't put an end to their affair, even if he wanted to. He was not capable.

"Find her," Soraya said. "Tell her you'll make it up to her."

He pulled her to him, the woman he had chosen, and his hands trembled as he framed her face. "I don't want her. I didn't choose her. I want you, Soraya. Us. This."

Soraya set her lips. "This? This is just fun, Akash, until it's not. Your wife *knows*. Why are you still here? We're from different worlds, Akash. Do you really think your Hindu family would accept a Muslim wife for you? What we have—what we *had*—was good, but it was never meant to be forever. Go after your wife. Save your relationship."

She gathered up her purse and cardigan, and reached up to kiss his cheek—perfunctory, as if they had never been lovers. As if he could fit the pieces of his life together without her as easily as a jigsaw puzzle.

Akash stood statue-like, listening to the clip-clop of her heels as she left him amongst the blooms.

"He was with another woman, Maa."

Tears streaked down Jaya's face in the cramped kitchen of her parents' home. She craved comfort, but her mother had other ideas.

"Just look at all these bills piling up, Jaya. I don't care what he has done. We cannot afford to have you back here." She flung her hand to her forehead. "Oh, the shame of it! I will not put any more pressure on your father. You sort this out. You will not dishonour our name."

"But Maa, I've been trying. For months I've been trying. I think he regrets ever marrying me. He's hardly home, and now I know why. I saw his face, the way he touched her. He has never shown me such tenderness. He doesn't want to sort this out. I just know it." She sobbed, grasping the toilet paper her mother pushed her way.

She thought back to her wedding, to the weight of the gold-embroidered wedding sari, which had suffocated her. Their future had lain ahead, resplendent, symbolised by the heavy jewellery that adorned her and the painted elephant Akash rode. She teased him about the red turban that struggled to contain his buoyant hair, but he remained solemn. Disappointment dampened Jaya's excitement.

The ceremony had begun, and her father, stern and upright in his *sherwani*, gave her away. *Kanyadaan.* They held their hands over the holy fire to signify their union. *Panigrahana.* Finally, Jaya followed Akash around the flames. Sanskrit washed over her as they traversed seven times around the fire, bound together, each round a promise. *Saptapadi.* After the ceremony, when the *dhol* player leapt to his rhythm, the crowd began their celebrations.

*I am yours,* she thought at that moment, *and you are mine.* She'd glanced shyly at Akash from beneath thick lashes, careful not to be bold, but his gaze had remained fixed at a point in the distance.

Even as newly-weds, Akash rarely touched her. On their wedding night, he made no effort to find his name hidden in the curl of her wedding mehndi. His lips remained downturned, his body rigid. She feared her overtures had come across as brazen, and that Akash would be perfectly happy if she did not initiate contact. Now she knew that the closeness she craved with him, the child of her own, would never come to fruition. He remained absent, even when they occupied the same space, even when she had caught him red-handed.

Her mother continued, determined to shape her daughter into the woman she herself was. "Don't you think we all have our problems, Jaya? This is the real world. Men cheat. It's your job to make sure he plays at home. Feed him, wash his clothes, let him have his way with your body. What else are women here for?" She scrubbed the floor by the cooker where spices had fallen. When she rose, her knees were red, her eyes accusing. "It's these studies of yours. Did you want to send us into ruin? I knew it was a bad idea, giving you ideas above your station. You don't have enough time for him."

"Maa, I promise you, I wait for him there. He never comes. Where is he now? I caught him in the act, and even now he is not here."

"All I hear are excuses, Jaya. Come what may, you are not coming back into this house. Your father would be furious. What would our neighbours say? We'd be the laughing stock of the community. I can hear them now, gossiping about how we raise our daughters, how they are not even able to keep their husbands happy. And you wonder why women long for sons." Her mother drove her finger into Jaya's chest. "You make this work."

Jaya shrank bank into the corner of the kitchen.

"I can't sit around here all day. I promised your father I would make him vegetable samosa, the tiny ones he likes. I need to go and get chilli and coconut for the chutney. Make yourself useful if you are here and fry the samosas, will you?" She pointed to the row of floured pastry pockets, perfect triangles filled with vegetables. "It's lucky you came. Your sister was going to do it, but the lazy girl is napping upstairs." Her mother patted her arm awkwardly. "And don't worry, you will get the hang of this."

Jaya's mother squeezed through the small archway on her way to the front door, and left without a backward glance.

Jaya followed her progress down the street, watching her mother's swaying hips through the open kitchen window. "Can I rescue us?" she asked, alone with her darkening thoughts.

She fried the samosas, watching the ghee spritz out of the pan as she worked.

*He looked so happy with her.*

Batch by batch, she continued.

*I am not enough.*

She poured more oil into the saucepan.

*Am I enough?*

After she fried the last of the samosas, she laid them out onto kitchen paper to absorb the excess moisture, and sat down heavily on a stool by the cooker.

*He still has not come to find me.*

Her bag probably lay in the rose garden where she dropped it. It would not take a great leap of faith for Akash to follow her to her parents' house. He should have come by now.

*He does not care.*

Next to her, the oil bubbled and spat.

Her eyes glazed as she took the pan off the cooker. Oil residue on the handle caused her grip to slip. The world continued to turn—men worked, women cooked, children played—as she poured the contents of the pan slowly on the hem of her sundress, first at the front, then each side, and as far back as she could reach. She cried out as her flesh seared, but still she continued.

*It is my fault.*

The sky-blue dress darkened with the liquid, and her legs became raw where the hot oil splashed against her skin. She welcomed the physical pain.

There she stood, thinking and unthinking, playing with a box of matches from her mother's drawer.

A knock on the window startled her. Akash appeared, peering through the crack.

"Jaya, can we talk?"

She turned to look at him, a flash of colour in the dingy kitchen, her movements robotic.

"You came," she said, her voice wooden. "Do you love me?"

"I...."

"Are you here to leave me?"

"I don't know," said Akash. "Can you let me in?"

"You love her?"

"Yes." He shrank from her gaze.

Jaya barely moved. *You don't love me.* A scratching sound, and then a brief flare. "Then what else is there to say?"

Akash screamed as fire swept around the hem of her dress and the orange flowers caught alight.

*Now you have an excuse not to touch me.* She stood in the midst of it all, her face contorted as she burned. Her flesh began to melt and the tortuous flames ripped through her until there was nothing else, only agony.

*What have I done?*

She gave herself to the pain. Her skin peeled, curling, and the fire spread upwards. Shouting somewhere on the periphery of her consciousness sought to anchor her in the here and now, but she paid no heed.

The fire cleansed her.

# 2

**Her skirt turned** a seething red and hung in threads around her calves. For a moment, she became a goddess, but Jaya's story did not follow Hindu legend. Sita's flames bloomed into lotuses; Jaya's blazed.

She burned—for hours or perhaps a few seconds—in a hell of her own. The flesh of her legs singed as if she were a newly slaughtered lamb lain over hot charcoal. Every nerve ending protested against the onslaught. She writhed in pain, her world dissolving into one moment: this trial. Fiery teeth raked her skin, blistering her once smooth limbs, branding her with their mark. The smell of meat cooking down to the bone rushed into her nostrils and she convulsed. A warrior cry, anguished and other-worldly, erupted from her smoke-filled throat that bore no similarity to her own voice.

By the time her sister Ruhi dashed into the confines of the kitchen, Jaya had collapsed onto the floor, her lower body ablaze. She lay in a heap as Ruhi froze, horror painted on her face as she took in the angry fire licking up Jaya's legs, her nose instinctively scrunched up against the pervading smell of oil and cooking flesh in the room. Too slow, Ruhi's reaction.

A scream erupted from Ruhi. "Jaya! Jaya!"

Ruhi snapped into action, jerking a towel from the clothing rack, sending it scattering in her haste. She wrapped Jaya in it.

Jaya's mind bled.

Her sister rolled her into the living room, away from the oil remnants and the oxygen flowing in through the slither of open window. Still the flames refused to be spent. The thin, frayed towel stuck to Jaya's skin. The flames raged, like Jaya's internal world, seeking vengeance where they touched, peeling back her skin like a deft chef skinning a vegetable.

*Would Akash be sorry? Would this shame him how he deserved to be shamed?*

Her sister shuddered and covered Jaya with her own body. Jaya moaned as they rolled together amongst the legs of furniture, in sight of the altar where they prayed together, one a burning rag-doll, the other sobbing with terror.

Ruhi cursed, smothering the flames, using her own hands to pat out the fire until it died.

The armour of Jaya's sundress had almost entirely disappeared save for a panel around her singed torso. Her legs had taken the brunt of the fire. The skin bubbled and stuck fast to the towel. Soot clung to her. Beside her, the pale blue statue of Vishnu watched. His arms encircled the room. Jaya closed her eyes, the shallow inhale-exhale of her breath a roar in her mind. She sizzled, and finally, mercifully, slipped into unconsciousness.

Akash banged the window. "Jaya! Jaya! Somebody help me!"

He ran to the front door, pounded it with his fists, and tried in vain to shoulder it open. The door would not budge, and nobody came. Her screams followed him, and the stench of cooking flesh filled Akash's nostrils until the horror became too much.

He ran, the images of his burning wife searing his brain. He ran past heaving market stalls and darting rickshaws, away from the Bombay that was familiar to him, until the phlegm built up in his throat. He ran—he ran until his lungs ached and his ribcage heaved, until he reached the cooling banks of the water, where he vomited.

He stopped to lean against a wall, shaking his head to free himself of the horrors lurking there. Then he sank down and cried. Shame hung around his neck like a medallion, heavy and cumbersome. Had Jaya really set herself alight? He squeezed his eyes shut. Perhaps if he took a deep breath and reopened them, the images would fade and he would realise it had been a nightmare.

*Is this a dream, Jaya? Did my mind play tricks on me?*

He opened his eyes as his stomach churned. Still, he could not escape the horrors of the present.

*Did I really run away from you while you burned? What kind of man am I?*

Her screams echoed in his head, and his shoulder throbbed from where he had tried to break down the door.

*I could have tried harder.*

Reality crushed him, so he retreated into hope, foolish though it was. Maybe Jaya was still alive. He could go back and try harder to make his marriage work. He could forget Soraya, but every fibre in his body protested against cutting Soraya out of his life. But neither could he forget his wife—his responsibility.

None of the blame for the disintegration of their marriage could be laid at Jaya's feet. They had both agreed to an arranged marriage. An aunt on his father's side, an insufferable woman with a hairy chin and protruding belly, had arranged for their families to meet. Jaya represented the perfect match, his father said: the right caste, elegant, unassuming, a good wife.

But Akash was not ready. Jaya's wit shamed him, as did her warm nature, so forgiving of his inadequacies. He felt as harassed by her faith as by her smiles. How could he tell his family he rejected their way, the old way?

So they married, dazed amidst excited relatives and clashing colours. Jaya became a dutiful wife; Akash an emotionally-absent husband. He went through the motions—waking up with Jaya, their bodies occupying opposing corners of the bed, attending lectures, returning home to have dinner with his wife and parents, touching his wife when the lights went out, but everything felt perfunctory rather than passionate. The foundations of their marriage had seemed irreparably damaged as his hope for the future seeped through the cracks in their relationship.

Not until he met Soraya did he realise he was capable of romantic love.

He jumped through his memories as if they were a yellowed film reel to 1980, the summer after he had married. He'd been slouching on a slow-chugging bus, seated next to Jaya, when he spotted Soraya the first time, tearing through the dusty streets towards the university gates, her hair drenched by the musty rain, her features obscured—a girl who took no prisoners. He couldn't pull his eyes away. His shirt stuck to his back in the sticky heat as Jaya's thigh pressed against his own, yet everything dropped away except for this stranger. He turned awkwardly, twisting his neck like a giraffe to watch until Soraya disappeared into a tiny speck in the distance.

From that first encounter, he'd never been able to shake the thought of her. For him, she was a promise, a drug—a slow, inescapable venom, poisoning his relationship with his wife. He felt the brush of Soraya's fuchsia scarf as she rushed past, imagined the taste of the rain on her chapped lips. Even before their affair had begun, she became a persistent ghost in his marital bed.

Their friends and family would have gasped had Akash and Jaya divorced. His parents were staunch opponents of divorce and separation. With years of a harmonious arranged marriage behind them, they would never have understood, and Akash would have been incapable of facing them if his marriage failed. A remarriage remained unthinkable unless one partner had been widowed, let alone a love match between Akash and Soraya, a Hindu and Muslim.

*Did I really watch you burn, with only a bruised shoulder to show for it? Did I give my marriage to you a chance? Am I completely rotten to my core, incapable of loving my wife?*

Round and round his thoughts went, like a carousel.

*All you wanted was to hear I love you. I could have stopped you from lighting the match.*

He was responsible for it all, as surely as if he had lit the match himself. He clung to the hope that she might still be okay as he sat, crumpled on the pavement, one thought consuming him as daylight turned to dusk.

*I have to make this right.*

Jaya floated back into a body that did not feel like hers. She groaned as whispers and the hum of machines reached her ears, followed by her mother's voice.

"Oh, Jaya, what did you do?"

"How can one sister burn while the other sleeps?" said her sister, piercing through the haze of nothingness.

Jaya opened her eyes. The faces of her family swam before her as fluorescent hospital lighting buzzed above their heads. Her parents and her sister stood vigil at her bedside in a cramped ward. Ruhi rushed to hug her, features twisted in worry, but Jaya winced at her sister's touch. She shut her eyes and wished for darkness again. Waves of pain crashed over her like none she had experienced before, a throbbing and clenching she could not localise.

"Jaya?" said Ruhi, her voice lined with tears.

Jaya struggled to remember what had happened. She opened her eyes with trepidation and looked down at her body, still detached from the consequences of her actions. Starched hospital sheets entombed her form, and something cool lay on her legs and side. She reached under the sheets and her fingers found thick bandages. The pain of a flurry of knives shot through her. She couldn't move her legs.

Ruhi reached for her hand and said, "No, no, don't touch anything. I'll let the nurse know you're awake." Her sister's hands were wrapped in light bandages.

Jaya remembered the flames and Akash's betrayal with a rush, and cried out. She waved her hands at her family, wanting to be alone, then glanced again at Ruhi's bandages and remembered through the haze that her sister had rescued her, not Akash.

*He is not only a cheat, but a coward.*

Ruhi disappeared into the corridor.

Jaya's fingers traced her face, her heartbeat accelerating, fascination and panic interlacing, as the recent past came flooding back to her. Her face felt normal. She breathed a sigh of relief.

"Where am I?" The words came out as a croak.

"KB Bhabha Hospital. Do you remember what happened?" Her father's voice was heavy with sadness. He rested his hand gingerly on her arm, just above where an IV line pierced her skin.

Jaya reached for the truth but the complexity of the answer eluded her. She remembered lighting the match, but she didn't recognise the woman who would have done that. How could she not know she had been capable of such an act?

It was easier to lie. "I don't remember."

He searched her face for answers. Beside him, her mother sat still. "Was it an accident?"

"I was cooking samosas." She recalled her feeling of hopelessness, which dogged her even now. All because of Akash. She had wanted to press reset but the world had remained the same.

*I should have died.*

"My daughter, what will become of you now?" said her father. "Where is Akash?"

*So he has not come, not even to the hospital.*

Jaya didn't respond. The skin on her legs seemed to sizzle and pulse as if she were still shrouded in flames. She longed to tear off the bandages, to see what had befallen her, to itch her skin until she found some relief. Yet the physical sensations bore no comparison to the emotional ones. She remembered Akash's face at the kitchen window.

*He left me to burn. Instead of punishing him, have I freed him to be with his lover? How can he not be sorry? If he cares at all, he would have tried to save me, and he would be at my bedside now.*

She felt his absence keenly, and the shame wrapped itself around her like a blanket of thorns. In that moment, her emotional core—the part fed by love and promise—transformed into a block of ice. What remained was simply a carcass of the woman who had stepped from her marital home that morning.

She could find no answers to soothe her parents' worries.

Ruhi hurtled into the room, followed by the more sedate entry of a doctor wearing blue scrubs and a serious expression.

The doctor pinned Jaya with a stare that stripped away her pretences. "It is good that you are awake." She turned to the rest of the family. "Can I have a few minutes alone with my patient?"

"Jaya would want us to stay," said her father, squeezing Jaya's hand.

"It really is better this way," said the doctor.

Ruhi glanced from Jaya to the doctor. "We'll be right outside," she said, and ushered her parents into the hallway.

Jaya fixed her eyes on the doctor's hair, a frizzy mop tinged with the orange of fading henna.

"I'm Dr. Tarpana. How are you feeling?"

If she had to answer questions, it relieved her the doctor happened to be female. Who knew how a man would judge her? "Uncomfortable."

Her legs had been elevated under the sheets. Their mass appeared greater than they should, even under the thick bandages, as if they belonged to someone else, someone not as slight as her. She tugged at the sheets with her hand.

Dr. Tarpana stilled her movement with her palm. "You went through a huge ordeal. Being caught in a fire is an attack on the entire body. Can you tell me what happened?"

Jaya snatched her hand back and focused on the soot underneath her nails, uncertain of how far to trust this woman. Blisters dotted the pink skin of her palm. "I was in the kitchen cooking. The oil caught fire."

"I see." Dr. Tarpana paused. "Jaya, your sister's intervention saved your life. The burns on your legs are the ones I am most concerned about. They penetrated deep into the skin. It's going to be a long journey from here."

The words floated over her. How she wished it had been Akash who had saved her. As it stood, Jaya didn't know whether to thank Ruhi or hate her for not letting her die, but in the bright light of the hospital ward, her heart lurched to think she might never have seen her sister again. She tried to sit up, but the doctor held her in place, and her legs refused to obey. The effort caused her to cry out in pain.

"I'll get the nurse to bring you some more morphine. It's best to stay still for now, if you can. We want to inflict as little trauma to the affected areas as possible."

Jaya motioned to her shrouded legs. "They don't feel like mine."

"They're swollen. You received second degree burns to fifteen per cent of your body. We had to cut away the dead tissue and clean your wounds. We had to amputate two of your toes. The ones that survived are splinted. We've applied cooling gel and thick dressings to give your skin as great a chance of recovery as possible."

Jaya heard the words as if through a filter. Each word dipped with weight, until Jaya could no longer understand the sum of its parts. The information was too much.

*Amputation. Dead tissue. Burns.*

She jolted as the flames seared her mind, as real as the bed she lay on.

Across the ward, a man with what looked like acid burns gazed at her, pity on his face.

Dr. Tarpana's face loomed again through the haze, talking about administering electrolytes and antibiotics. She kept on, but Jaya caught only fragments. She nodded periodically, as words swirled around her: the risk of sepsis, compromised immunity, physiotherapy. This alien world was not hers. She had not caused this.

"You'll need skin grafts. We're just waiting for the theatre to be free. Massage from a professional is key. Too much contact, and we risk disturbing the healing process. Too little, and your skin and muscles will become unsupple, risking reduced mobility."

*Too much. Better to live in fantasy than to be confronted with harsh truths.*

She longed to unhear her diagnosis, but there would be no going back. She was nearly at the finish line. Surely it could not get any worse.

Jaya focused on the doctor's face, her solemnity, the steady hands in contrast to her own trembling ones. "I want to see. I want to see what I look like."

Dr. Tarpana considered her for a moment. "It's better to wait. It's too soon."

"I need to see. Please."

*All because of him, and he isn't even here. I wish he could see what he's done to me. Would he worry about me or would he wash his hands of me? Was there ever anything there?*

The doctor called a nurse, and the blood rushed into Jaya's ears. Together the doctor and nurse peeled back the sheets and removed the bandages from her legs with infinite care, first one and then the other.

Now Jaya could correlate her pain with the physical symptom. She gasped and her vision swam. A moment of disassociation: a lifetime of consequences. The smooth skin of her legs had been replaced by raw, open sores. Where her skin had been almond in colour, it was white, as though the pigment had given up in face of the onslaught, melting like a wax figure in an oven. It glistened under the harsh hospital lighting, and there was no place for Jaya to hide. Two of her toes on one foot were no longer there. She flinched from the sight, shutting her eyes, but still the image of her new body played underneath her closed lids. She willed the gods to take mercy upon her, to rewind the tape.

"Jaya," said Dr. Tarpana, bending close, trying to project empathy that failed to reach over Jaya's walls. "It might not seem like it, but you've really been very lucky. The fire has done minimal damage to your muscles. Much depends on how fast your body heals, but I see no reason why you won't be able to continue life as you know it."

Jaya blinked her eyes open. Her wounds remained. Her foot did not magically become whole. She could not imagine a humdrum life like her mother's, one borne of duty rather than passion. She had never wanted a pale imitation of love, and now even that had been axed from her life. She had wanted change. Couldn't fire bring renewal? Instead, she had fuelled the flames. Who would want her now? "Life as I know it? My life is over. What have I done?"

# 3

**Tears of grey** clouds lay scattered across the horizon and daylight slipped away as Akash returned to his in laws' house in Bandra. Market-trading had ended and the streets were emptying. Resistance and hope weighed down each step he took. Perhaps Jaya had just wanted to frighten him. Perhaps she had flung off her clothes and survived. His fear roped around his neck and clung fast, tight and unyielding. He approached the window he had been at hours previously. There, through the glass in the half-light, he saw the blackened floor, and just beyond, Jaya's mother, weeping at Lord Vishnu's shrine, wringing her hands. She collapsed in a heap on the floor as Akash watched, her face scrunched up with sorrow.

*No. It can't be.* Bile filled Akash's mouth.

A man loomed into view, a hair's breadth away, breaking Akash's sightline to the mourning older woman. His father-in-law's usually neat hair lay dishevelled against his forehead. Bloodshot eyes pulsed in anger as they met his own. The old man drew his finger to lips and motioned with a cocked head to the front door.

Akash crossed to the entrance, his head clouded with horror.

The door drew open, and Jaya's father stepped outside into the balmy evening. He stood a head taller than Akash, his body sinewy from age and the Indian heat. A nerve pulsed in the corner of his downturned lips.

"Uncleji—" said Akash.

The older man's voice erupted in hoarse rage. "You!" He rushed at Akash, planted two hands on his chest, and shoved him to the ground.

Akash lay in the gutter.

His father-in-law turned to the house to make sure no one had heard the commotion. He swung back round to Akash. "You are the reason she did this! I trusted you with my daughter and you betrayed us. Was one woman not enough for you?"

The fault was Akash's. There could be no question.

"Please." Akash made no attempt to get to his feet. His body coiled as tight as a spring. He wrung his hands together. "I need to know, is she okay?"

"No. It will never be okay." A shadow passed across his father-in-law's face, washing away the sorrow and anger, leaving only coldness. "Jaya is gone."

"Gone?"

*No, please. Please make it right.*

"Gone." He shuddered. "Jaya is dead. You're no longer welcome here. We want nothing to do with you. You're not wanted at the funeral. Let us grieve our beautiful daughter." His face crumpled. "Don't come back here, Akash. Next time, I won't be so gentle." He spat and a gloopy ball of spit and tobacco landed millimetres away from Akash's leg. His father-in-law swivelled on his heel, crossed to the threshold of his house, and clicked the door shut without a second glance.

Akash went limp. It seemed to him he had entered a parallel universe. The nightmare could not be his own. His mind swam with images of Jaya: tendrils of her hair curling on the pillow as he'd left to meet Soraya that morning; her distress in the rose garden as realisation of his affair dawned; Jaya lighting a match robotically, as if her own life were an after-thought; the swirling flames. Her father's cold voice pronouncing, "*Jaya is dead.*"

It was all so clear now. Awareness of his own selfishness hit him like a boomerang. *I did not cherish her. I did not save her.* There was no escaping who had lit the match that killed Jaya. His shame and guilt extended and twisted until it morphed into a monster he was unable to contain. Ice wrapped itself around his heart, protecting him from pain.

His logic warped. He could not go home. The thought of it made him physically sick. Instead, he wandered through dusty streets, aimless, empty-handed. Somewhere along the route, he lost his bag. He had no papers. No wallet. His teaching certificate, sponsored by parents, disintegrated on the wind. He couldn't face the gossip about Jaya that would inevitably poison every friendship. He had earned those black stains, he had driven her to death, but he was too much of a coward to face them. There would be some, too, who would lay the blame entirely at Jaya's feet. Akash could not stomach that, either. *Why didn't I save you?* He felt more protective of her in death than he had in life. Already he wished, more than anything, that she would rise from the ashes like a phoenix, unharmed and willing to start their marriage anew.

He craved a blank sheet, a new beginning, for his soul to be washed clean. *What have I thrown away?* Maybe they could have loved one other, had he given Jaya a chance. He had rebelled against the marriage as if he were a teenager, not a grown man. Now, she was a charred body waiting to be dust. How could he live with himself?

He approached a disused railway bridge. It provided shelter from the fast-cooling night. The inky night, unlit by stars, bled into the underside of the bridge and seeped into his skin. Akash sought out a pocket of light provided by a lonely street lamp and leant against the curved stone wall. His teeth chattered from the chill or exhaustion. He pushed his hands into the pockets of his trousers. His fingers touched the gold wedding band he had removed that morning en route to meet Soraya in the rose garden. The ring had cooled without skin contact. A sob caught in Akash's throat as he replaced it on his finger. He twirled it round and round, mirroring the motion of the firestorm in his mind.

A man loomed out of the darkness and lurched towards him. An almost empty bottle clanked in his hand. Akash drew back as the man collapsed next to him, but not before a strong smell of gin washed over him.

"You look like your best friend died," said the man.

Akash gave him a blank stare, only half registering the words.

"Oh shit, bad day, man? Here, have some of this." He offered the alcohol to Akash and flashed a comforting smile, showing his stained teeth and a gap where his lateral incisor should have been. "You looking at this?" He pointed to the gap with a grimy fingernail. "You'd think I lost it out here." He threw back his head and laughed. "But, no, I was playing cricket with my brother, must've been about eleven. I took a googly in the mouth. You should've seen the blood. I was lucky it was only the one. My mother cried but I liked the fuss. She let me eat kulfi for weeks while the gum healed."

Akash considered the man. They were of a similar age, although neglect had shrivelled the other man's body. Skin and bones remained, and his back curved like a wave. Akash took the bottle from the man's extended hand, not wanting to offend and needing to drink. He put the bottle to his lips, draining the remnants. The alcohol burned his throat. He lifted his arm to toss the bottle aside, but the man laid a hand on his arm.

"Best not to shit where you sleep, know what I mean?"

Akash found his voice. "Sorry."

"No harm done. I'm Tariq." He swept his hand through the air, indicating the half-moon concrete tunnel. "This is my sometimes home. I say sometimes, because I have to fight to keep it. Sometimes I win; sometimes I lose. If I lose, I make sure I live to fight another day. It's a good place." Gratitude shone from his face. He pointed above them. "Not much rain gets through. Unless it's monsoon, and then that's a bit touch and go." He clambered to his feet as though it cost him great effort. "I like you, man. Not often I have a conversation partner. You can stay awhile if you want."

The emotions of the day weighed on Akash like a rock on an insect. *I killed my wife,* he thought over and over. He needed a brief respite. Besides, he had nowhere else to turn. He looked deeper into the darkness and made out a blanket and a saucepan.

He felt lighter knowing no one would look for him here. "That's kind of you," he said. "I'd like that. You know, just to catch my breath."

Tariq bowed low before him, a solemn expression on his face. "Follow me. I'll show you around."

# 4

**During Jaya's convalescence**, her mother visited for an hour most mornings. She sat and patted her daughter's hand, tutting underneath her breath. Her mother meant her to know Jaya had caused this; she was responsible for her own downfall, and as such the sympathy she received was by the grace of her mother's superior morality, not something she deserved. Those hours trapped in bed, pretending to appreciate her mother's efforts, widened the already existing divide between the women.

On Wednesdays, like clockwork, always at 4 o'clock, after her weekly laughing yoga meeting with the ladies from the temple, her mother stayed for a longer visit. She maintained the club lifted her spirits even in the direst circumstances.

Jaya had accompanied her once, and it struck her as surreal that women who gossiped about one another in everyday life could face each other in a circle and force laughter.

"Hahahahahaha."

She joined in with her hand on her belly. *I feel ridiculous.*

"Hahahahahaha."

*Oh, this eye contact is awkward. What is that one man doing here?*

"Hahahahahaha."

*No, this is not for me. Maa looks like she is really enjoying herself. Will she notice if I leave?*

After the fire, her mother insisted she needed the laughing club more than ever. Jaya had brought shame on the family. She had driven her husband away. The guilt hung in the air between mother and daughter like an executioner's axe. As the weekly laughing yoga session ended and the women stood about nattering, she could just picture her mother holding court like a great lady, careful to keep her worry a secret from her friends lest Jaya's situation colour the family reputation any further.

Despite her disappointment, Jaya's mother did her duty as a woman. She brought fresh *chapatis*, taken from the pile she made for her husband each morning, together with leftovers from the night before. This time when Jaya peeked inside the bowl, she found fried okra and tiny potatoes swimming in ghee.

"Thanks, Maa. It's nice to have a break from the hospital food."

Her mother sniffed. "You know I like feeding you all. Your grandmother taught me well."

Jaya nodded. Her mother and she were rooted in different generations, but she had been brought up to believe that a woman's duty was to care for and nurture others, to be obedient and selfless, to teach those values to future generations.

"You still haven't told me why you did it," said her mother.

"You know why," said Jaya, overwhelmed by weariness.

The questions pained her. Her father may have chosen not to openly challenge Jaya's portrayal of events the day of the fire, but her mother just knew. She knew the way a mother would know if her child was up to no good even if they were not in the same room. She knew because if a mother chose to see the truth, there could be no artifice. Even if the words spelled out one reason, her mother's radar could sense a slight rise of the voice, a hesitation that rendered all lies useless.

"Aah Jaya, I don't know anything," said her mother, exasperated. "Only that Akash hurt you, as men have always hurt women. It is nothing new."

"It was to me." The double standards stung. Why had Akash not been obedient and true if it was expected of her?

She wanted to be alone. Her skin ached and itched as it knitted together. It made her irritable and angry, despite the painkillers. One day she wanted to move, the next she wanted to give up. The nurses tried to keep her comfortable. They changed her pressure bandages daily. Bathing helped to soothe the discomfort for a short while, but always, the itchiness returned, and the indignity remained a constant presence.

She wanted to go home, but she didn't know where home was. Home had been the house she shared with Akash. Her childhood home was not a sanctuary. The fire had happened there. It underlined her new status: that of a deserted wife.

"What was your intention, Jaya? Did you want to die or was it a protest?"

Silence.

"Did you want Akash to feel guilty for his affair? I told you men will be men!" Her eyes narrowed. "Or was it us you wanted to punish? What, you think we chose the wrong man? Oh, the arrogance of youth." She flung up her hands.

Jaya's vision blurred with tears. She couldn't fight herself as well as her mother. She picked out a spot on the pale hospital wall and willed herself to be stronger.

"Why didn't you listen to me? You can't fight tradition. Women like us just don't."

"Then who else, Maa? Wait, you wanted me to roll over, just continue the charade." Bitterness reached out, unchecked and violent, like a physical blow.

"Did you really expect to change anything? All you have done is bring shame on us. Your husband is gone. Has he visited you here? How are we expected to afford the bills, Jaya?"

Though Jaya's treatment had taken place in a government hospital, her burns required expensive specialist treatment. Guilt had become an ever-present companion. Her parents struggled financially. Her studies had been a last parental investment before they had washed their hands of her, and passed the responsibility over to her husband as if she were livestock, not a thinking person with her own hopes and dreams.

Try as she might to shake off the chains of reality, her present was as clear to her as the scars on her body. She could not bear the toxic mix of anger, shame and financial worry that poisoned what love remained in her life. The thought of her parents not having enough money clawed at her, and it was only amplified by her mother's visits.

"I'm sorry," said Jaya. "We can use my university fees." Her world grew smaller still.

"Yes, we may have to. But know this, Jaya. Your Papa and I, we agreed to university for you to improve your life, Jaya. And now look what you have done! And Akash, not even he wants to clean up this mess. You are now our problem to fix." Tears cascaded down her mother's face. "You used to be beautiful. What husband would want a wife such as this?"

Jaya's anger flared. Akash had cheated, not her. She had believed in love, and he taught her the crumbling reality of her idealism. He was free whilst she remained here, trapped. "I am alive, Maa. I am alive. Doesn't that count for anything?"

Her mother glanced up through tears. "Maybe it would have been better if you had died."

Hours turned into days.

Days turned into weeks.

The baths, the dressings, the skin grafts, the pain medication, the physical therapy: it all blurred into a nightmarish cycle. Jaya ignored calls from her friends from university. What good would it do to keep up contact with those who would make her feel worse? Their lives progressed, while hers remained stuck.

Neither did she make friends with the patients that came and went. She cowered at the thought of exposing her vulnerability to strangers, and had no energy to support them through their own suffering. The only person who pierced through her armour was Ruhi. Still, she worried about the burden she placed on her younger sister, and the recriminations Ruhi would receive from their parents for her unflinching support of Jaya.

She longed to be able to care for herself, to save the embarrassment and cost of medical care. Even basic tasks like washing herself eluded her. She had no inclination to dress up and look beautiful. She no longer felt like a woman, just a thing. She had worn hospital gowns since her admission. It made bathing and changing dressing much easier for the nurses. Independence had become a distant goal. A dream.

When the therapist suggested she try walking, fear overwhelmed Jaya despite her irritation of being pushed around in a wheelchair. Ruhi came to the rescue, a cheerleader even on

Jaya's darkest days. Today, she insisted on accompanying Jaya on a short walk through the hospital gardens, and wouldn't take no for an answer.

"You can do this, *yaar*. You just need to start."

So Jaya hobbled along on crutches while Ruhi strode ahead, opening doors, beaming in the sunlight while Jaya grumbled behind her. Her legs were still sore and each movement felt unnatural. The missing toes on her left foot meant that progression was slow and unsteady, as if she were a toddler learning to walk again. A dressing gown covered her body, but her cheeks flushed when she met strangers. Could they see underneath to the monstrosity that was now her body? Her oddly shaped feet poked out from under the gown, sheathed in both socks and slippers to hide them from prying eyes.

Ruhi looked so beautiful fresh from her shower, dressed in a simple *salwar kameez* the colour of ripe limes and smelling of cocoa butter, that Jaya felt grotesque by comparison.

She turned to face her sister. "Why did you save me, Ruhi?"

"Because I love you, even if you don't love yourself."

Jaya's stomach churned.

Akash had watched her burn and not lifted a finger to help her. If only she could forget. She held that knowledge to her as a beggar holds his last copper. She wouldn't betray Akash by telling her family the hideous truth of his cowardice.

"It would have been easier if I had died." She wondered if she would ever know contentment. What was the point of it all if not?

"Who would it be easier for? For you?"

"For us all. Maa wishes I'd died. She said as much. Or perhaps she'd prefer me to wait until I am a widow, and then place myself on the funeral pyre with my husband." Jaya regretted her words as soon as she had said them. Now she had ruined their walk, too.

Ruhi threw up her pretty manicured hands. "Maa doesn't mean it, you know. It's just her way. She loves you."

"She worries about the bills and I don't blame her." Again, the clawing guilt.

"Do you know what I'm interested in? Not Maa, but you. You're clever. You're strong. You were going somewhere. Don't let this stop you."

They stopped by a maple tree, its branches fanning out over them, leaves flame-red and sharp like the fire that haunted her.

Her sister faced Jaya and grasped her arms. "Why did you do it?" she said. Ruhi's breath came in short bursts. She blinked back her tears, molten brown eyes clear over crescent shadows, and it hit Jaya how her act had impacted them all.

Jaya's heart pounded while she searched for the honesty she owed her sister. Her jaw slackened as she released the hold on her control. "Honestly? I don't know why I did it. I was on auto-pilot, not thinking clearly. Or maybe thinking too much. I felt trapped, unloved, and the fire offered me a release. It breathed. It hated. I felt at one with it." Her words were barely audible above the hissing of the breeze. "I wanted to punish Akash, to make myself into the unlovable creature he sees when he looks at me."

"You wanted to punish him? What did Akash do?" The lack of censure in Ruhi's voice almost became Jaya's undoing.

Her voice sounded alien, even to her own ears. "Didn't Maa tell you? Akash is in love with another woman." A bitter laugh, laden with shame, pierced the tranquillity of the gardens. "Because he lay with her instead of with me. Because however different I am from Maa, I too only have a future when a man determines it. I didn't want to be second best. I wanted to come first."

"He betrayed you?" Ruhi cried in great heaving sobs, and Jaya reached for her, wobbling on the crutch that prevented her from enfolding her sister in her arms. "Why fire, Jaya? Of all things, why choose that? It's so violent."

Jaya hesitated. "Fire. I chose fire because it was there, Ruhi. No other reason. It was the weapon that presented itself."

Ruhi reached for her hand, making a conscious effort to slow her breath. "You are stronger than this, Jaya. I know it. I won't let you give up."

Jaya's crutch clattered to the floor.

"You're my big sister. I need you."

"How could you need me? You are the favourite, now more than ever." She made an effort to smooth the deep trench lines digging into her brow, the ones that undoubtedly revealed her bitterness. Maybe her sister would know how to soothe her, how to make this all go away. Ruhi soared above challenges. She always knew the right thing to say. Jaya could never compete with that, though she loved her sister for it.

"No," said Ruhi. "I am the protected one, because you take the steps first. I learn from your triumphs and your mistakes."

Jaya's muscles tensed until her shoulders became rocks. Her throat ached with the effort of holding back tears. Ruhi deserved a better guide.

"What do you expect me to do?" Jaya's voice rose up the octave in challenge to her sister. "In a society like ours, where girls are measured by beauty, what chance do I have? Will anyone respectable even want to hire me now? A married woman, abandoned by her husband, flunked out of university, with hideous scars and a limp?"

Ruhi sighed. "Have you tried talking to Akash?"

"Have you heard anything I've been saying, Ruhi?" Jaya swung towards her sister in exasperation. "Akash is not coming back, and that, at least, is a blessing. I'm not what he wants. Maa would force me to live with him as man and wife, and I couldn't bear that. I can't imagine his parents taking me back either. Why would they, when their son has abandoned me?" She shrugged, a grown woman lost in the maze of her present. "My bride-wealth was not significant enough for it to be worth their while."

"You will come home. You will get a job, and you will start over," said Ruhi. "I believe in you."

That pressure weighed on Jaya. She saw no way through this forest, even with Ruhi by her side to light the way. "Maa won't like it."

"Leave her to me."

Dr. Tarpana picked up the notes at the end of Jaya's bed and leafed through them. "How are your parents? The nurses mentioned they haven't been visiting as much."

Nothing passed by Dr. Tarpana's attention. Over the past weeks, Jaya had come to respect her. She set aside the sketch pad she used to while away the hours in hospital, and answered with honesty. "Busy keeping up appearances."

"They must be worried about you."

"Yes." She had been a terrible daughter.

Dr. Tarpana sat down in a chair at her bedside despite the hustle and bustle of the ward. "Never forget how fortunate you are."

"Fortunate?"

"If you'd been found any later, you'd have risked long-term disability."

Jaya grimaced. "Lucky me, it's just scars, missing toes and a limp..."

"Don't underestimate the psychological impact, Jaya. If you would just agree to counselling—"

"I don't need counselling." What she wanted, more than anything, was to be left alone rather than poked and prodded as if she were a specimen in a petri dish.

"Tell me then, what do you need?" said the doctor.

"Independence," said Jaya.

"Is that what you're going to get at home?

Jaya fidgeted with her pencil. "I don't know where home is anymore."

"Be straight with me, Jaya, and I can help you. Was this really an accident? There's a small community for women not far from here. I can get you a place if you need support."

"How many times do I have to say it?" Jaya examined the tan line on her finger where her wedding ring had once sat. She had discarded it as soon as she had been lucid enough. Ruhi had noticed and fished it out of the fruit bowl when she thought Jaya was asleep. "It was an accident. After all this, you want me to turn my nose up at my parents? How would that look? They are not the bad guys here."

"Then who is?" said the doctor. The calm radiating from her irritated Jaya.

"Please, stay out of it. I'm going back to my family home. It's all arranged."

# 5

**Three months later**, Akash had grown used to sleeping on pavements. He became accustomed to the musty scent of his own body, and the city's grime that coated his skin. The longer he stayed away from home, the less he contemplated returning to his social circles. His love for his family had not diminished, but his self-love, poisoned by guilt, ebbed so low that he could not imagine anyone would forgive him. Living on the streets had become his penance for Jaya's death. At times, he reimagined the chapters of their history, envisaging he'd paid her attention when they had lain in bed together, had lingered to enjoy the taste of her mouth, the touch of her skin, the smell of cocoa butter after her bath. Too often, his rewritten memories morphed into something else entirely, images he didn't understand: Jaya's head on Soraya's body, or soft skin becoming charred by degrees until his fantasy became a nightmare.

He no longer knew the luxury of regular meals. This punishment of his body soothed his spirit, but sooner or later Tariq insisted he eat. Sometimes they frequented Chas Chamak, a nearby restaurant which offered leftovers to homeless people. A queue formed as night fell, and Akash waited silently with Tariq, his embarrassment cloaking him, his eyes downcast, until he realised his torn clothes and unkempt beard rendered him unrecognisable from his old acquaintances. Normal people, those with security and families, averted their eyes from beggars anyway.

More often, he and Tariq scavenged from rubbish bins, targeting the ones near restaurants or grocery shops. Tonight, they were on one of their raids. Tariq, as usual, had buoyed his courage by drinking deeply from the bottle. He leapt from one bush to another, like a schoolboy playing an undercover agent, grinning in mirth. Seconds later, he keeled over on the floor, blue with a hacking cough, a regular ailment from his years on the streets.

"Sshhhh," said Akash. "They'll hear us."

"I feel invincible having you by my side. Let me enjoy it."

"You want another beating?"

"Nothing I haven't had before."

"One day it might kill you. I don't want that on my conscience too."

"Lighten up, man."

They had run into trouble before when searching for food. The best places tended to be in the bins of restaurants, grocery stores and wealthy houses, but they risked retribution if caught. The morality of Bombay had clear definitions. Trespassing was a dangerous game to play, even for unwanted goods. The men of this country did not hesitate to take the law into their own hands. For all his bravado, Tariq was useless in a fight.

Akash lifted the lid on the dumpster and leaned it against the back alley of the restaurant. The last worker had turned off the lights inside the building half an hour ago, but the manager's car lingered outside. Likely, he had walked home, but Akash didn't want to take any chances, especially with Tariq in no fit state to be of any use if they were discovered, other than perhaps shoot at assailants with an imaginary gun.

His friend crept up behind him.

"What will we be having tonight? *Chicken tikka masala* or *karahi gosht*?"

"You know I'm vegetarian, idiot."

"*Aloo gobi* then, or *vegetable pilau* with *raita*?"

Akash reached into the bin and pulled out a black bag. He tore a hole in the bag with his ragged thumbnails and stretched the opening wide. The two men crouched over the spilled contents. Tariq crowed with delight when he opened a plastic container and found some curdled bean curry. Akash held his breath as he plunged his hand through the wet and pungent waste.

"I have naan and some mangoes."

"A veritable feast!" said Tariq, his voice booming in the alley, then disintegrating into a cough.

"Sssh!"

It was a good haul and a few more sacks waited in the dumpster. Akash stacked his finds neatly on the ground and rose to his feet to retrieve another bag. He heard footsteps, their rhythmic purpose out of sync with Tariq's drunken demeanour. He turned.

"Oh shit," said Tariq.

A portly man in his forties held a stricken-looking Tariq by the shirt sleeves. His friend wriggled, but the man's grip remained firm. In his other hand, he held a cricket bat, grey in the moonlight. The man ran a tongue over his teeth, trying in vain to wipe away the tobacco stains there. He addressed Akash. "Are you stealing from me? I know this scum, but you, you're new around here."

Akash looked from the man to Tariq then back again. "I'm sorry, Sir. We weren't doing any harm. It was being thrown away anyway." The contrite tone he adopted hid a steely core. Perhaps he deserved to die, but he needed to make sure Tariq wasn't injured. A man didn't heal well on the streets; empty bellies, the elements and the lack of security put paid to that.

The man inched forward, dragging Tariq with him, until a hair's breadth separated his nose from Akash's. "What's mine is mine. I can do what I want with it. If I want it in the bin, it stays in the bin. You hear me?"

The bulbous veins in the man's nose loomed in the streetlight.

Akash's heart thundered in his chest. He flexed his fingers, then quick as a flash, he thrust the man backwards with one hand while holding Tariq upright with the other. The man's grip on Tariq loosened as he fell, and together, Akash and Tariq ran, scooping up their finds as they fled.

"I should have hit his bald head with a mango. Now that would have been a story worth telling," laughed Tariq.

"You're laughing about this? He could have done serious damage with that bat," said Akash.

"I know, man. Sometimes it's good not to dwell," said Tariq.

Akash's breath eased as they returned to their den, grateful to be safe. They had been away too long, but thankfully their possessions had not been stolen. Blankets, a tarpaulin, two cooking pots lay strewn on the ground, together with a book of poetry he had found abandoned in a park. He missed books. Akash dropped their haul into a pot caked with food from a previous meal. On balance, it was cleaner than the ground.

"Who was that man anyway? Do you have history?" he called over his shoulder to Tariq.

"Zahid Khan. He owns that restaurant. It's a thriving business but there's not a kind bone in him. He's caught me going through his bins four, five times perhaps. He hurt me pretty badly a few times. It's his fault I keep going back, though. The stuff they sell there is good, even second hand." Tariq winked. "Seriously, the *daal* would make your mouth water. Creamy, with just a hint of chilli. It makes me hungry just thinking about it."

Tariq settled onto his blanket, and reached underneath its folds to pull out a blunt blade, which he used to peel back the skin of a mango. He took a bite of the flesh and a line of juice slithered down from the corner of his mouth to his chin where he let it remain, oblivious or unperturbed.

"This is freedom, isn't it? Starry skies above, two brothers out here in a city that's sleeping, no responsibilities. It feels like Bombay belongs to us right now."

Tariq, ever the idealist. One day it would cost him. Tariq had been the driving force behind their friendship. In the initial days after Jaya's death, when Akash had barely eaten or spoken, Tariq had brought him water, gaily nattering away. Over time, his directness and persistence had drawn Akash out of his shell. He had shown generosity in teaching Akash to survive, though Akash had now surpassed his teacher. Tariq had survived more by chance than skill. They bonded over their need to find someone to rely on. Everyone else considered men living on the streets to be untrustworthy and dangerous. It helped to have one another, and for Akash, Tariq's cheerfulness and zest for life, despite their environment and prospects, acted as a counterbalance for his internal battles.

"Man, it's hard getting you to crack a smile sometimes," said Tariq.

Akash shivered. Nights on the streets were tough. At least in the day the hot sun went some way towards banishing the cold that had crept into his bones. He threw a blanket around his shoulders. His wedding ring glinted in the half-light, impotent and sad. "I'll be right back. Don't eat it all, and make sure the rats don't get it."

"Okay." Tariq didn't glance up, too engrossed in his meal, accepting of Akash's nightly wanderings. He knew Akash's story and showed no judgement. It might have been different in the real world, where you came by friends more easily.

It had become Akash's ritual to walk to the shore at night. Tonight, he took comfort from the swirling depths of the Arabian Sea, peace from the breath of the lapping water. The moon peeked from behind a cumulous cloud. The stillness of the air crept into his bones. He was too sullied for organised religion; a lump of fear formed in his throat at the thought of visiting a temple. But he had forgotten neither his God nor Jaya. This ritual had become his nightly remembrance of them both.

First, he removed the blanket from his shoulders and walked into the dark sea of stars, seeking renewal, letting it soak into his skin. He cupped his hands, scooped up some water and poured it over his head, letting the water trickle over him. Taking a rag from his pocket, he dipped it into the ripples encircling him and mopped his bare skin: the creases behind his knees, his arms, his neck, his face. Finally, he retreated to the shore and sank to his knees, drawing his palms together at his heart, holding a picture of Jaya in his mind's eye. Jaya, innocent and a little afraid, wearing a ceremonial red sari on their wedding day.

"I am sorry," he said, propelling his voice across the surface of the water. "I wish that hadn't been our ending. I wish I'd tried. With every part of me, I wish you peace. I pray to Lord Vishnu, who removes our fears, for peace, for Jaya and for me." He stayed a moment, his head bowed, a burning ache in his throat where his tears had caught. The breeze cooled his wet skin.

It did not occur to Akash to stray from his native Bombay, the city he knew so well. Fortune did not owe him a fresh start; and Akash was unable to take it. His grief spilled into the decisions he made for his future, a form of self-flagellation. He cut himself off from the world as he knew it. A lotus floated past him on the waves of the sea. He followed it with his eyes and then stood to return to Tariq. It was easy to fall into a half-existence, to give up responsibilities, expectations. Akash chose the existence least painful to him; he became a ghost, a half-man, a drifter.

# 6

**Jaya woke in** the childhood bedroom she had shared
with her sister before her marriage. The freshness of the year paired
with the bleakness of her situation weighed heavily. Ruhi snored on
a mattress on the floor, arms flung wide, the sheets crumpled across
her calves. Grey light filtered through the curtains, indicating night
had cast off its midnight wings and day would soon dawn. Paint
peeled off walls decorated with posters of Bollywood stars: Rishi
Kapoor, his head cocked to one side; Sridevi, her eyes rimmed with
*kajal*, heavy jewellery adorning her neck; Mithun Chakraborty,
muscular in a vest.

Jaya closed her eyes and tried to sleep. The smoky scent of the
fire and burning flesh filled her nostrils. Her legs throbbed; her skin
stretched and itched with every waking moment. The sensation had
become as familiar to her as breathing. She had forbidden herself to
think of Akash, but even when her conscious mind succeeded in
blocking him, he crept into her subconscious. She took a deep breath
and blew out the air in a deliberate whoosh, seeking calm. Once,
twice, a third time. The blissful release of sleep would not come.

Ruhi lay oblivious to the world.

Jaya envied her sister's peace. A tear traced a path from the
corner of her eye, dampening her pillow. Nearly four months had
passed since the fire. Jaya had returned home with the sense she
should be grateful for a roof over her head, that she should earn her
keep and shield her parents from the gossip of prying neighbours.
She ventured out only at night, when the streets of Bandra were
deserted and the market traders had gone home. The smell of fried
wares and too ripe vegetables lingered in the air, and she took

pleasure in these walks under the cover of night, when she did not have to be concerned about the curious glances of strangers when they saw a young, head-scarfed woman limping. The scarf she now wore provided an extra layer of armour against those judging her, and gave her a tunnel vision of her own, so she did not witness how she measured up in the eyes of the world. Without it, she felt naked.

Each day, she tended to the household chores, relieving her mother of the responsibilities that had kept her tied to the home. A silent pact formed between the two women as duties seesawed from mother to daughter. The washing, cleaning, and even the cooking gradually fell to Jaya. If she was not caring for her husband, she would care instead for her parents.

Flashbacks to the fire overwhelmed Jaya when she worked at the stove. She sweated as they claimed her, and the flames engulfed her again, her beauty peeled back in layers, until all that was left was a rotting corpse and a grinning husband. Still, she would not let him win, nor let her parents witness her weakness, so she continued, stubborn and anguished, cooking their food, standing on the rug which now covered the blackened floor. Her mother bought the groceries, returning laden with okra, green beans and blood-red tomatoes. Both women were relieved that Jaya remained hidden from the world in the small kitchen. Afterwards, Jaya worked slowly, hindered by her unsteady gait and pained limbs, to wipe away all trace of her labours, save for the steaming plates of food she produced.

She was trapped in a nightmare. She had fought for permission to go to university and agreed to the marriage to step away from her mother's sphere of influence. Now it had become all too clear how she fell short of her mother's vision of a good Indian woman. The ropes of ancestors and her own mistakes bound her to a future she no longer controlled. If she voiced her fears, she would seem ungrateful, and likely lose the fragile support of her parents. A good Indian woman did not complain; she was a dutiful daughter, she served her husband, she bore children, she worked herself to the bone not for her own progression, but for the progression of her loved ones.

Anger unfurled within her, pulsing, uncontainable. Jaya could not live her life within a box, but lighting the match had severed her chances of escape. She lowered her feet carefully off the bed. Her legs were still partially bandaged. Her strength was returning and Dr. Tarpana was pleased with her progress. Even her toenails were growing back. The missing digits on her left foot reminded her of what she had lost. Beauty. Love. Hope. A wretched smile lifted the corners of her mouth. *Will I ever be touchable again? Will I ever determine my own fate?* She hobbled over to the mirror, allowing bitterness to pool in her mouth. Her reflection mocked her in the half-light: a young woman burdened by her body. To the right, Sridevi's flawless beauty in a traditional dance pose had been immortalised on the poster. With a spark of rage, Jaya scooped a carved wooden jewellery box off the dresser and hurled it at the mirror, shattering the glass and the peace of the pre-dawn house. Her image fractured into dozens of pieces at her feet.

"You can't hide away forever, Jaya," said Ruhi, kneading feet sore from a Kathak dance class.

They sat on a small patio at the rear of the house, overlooking a triangular piece of yellowed turf. Two steaming cups of *chai* flavoured with cardamom, cinnamon and creamed milk rested on a crescent table before them. At twenty years old, Ruhi had finished her secondary education and had hopes of becoming a Bollywood dancer. It was a dream their parents tolerated, as long as Ruhi contributed to household expenses with wages from her waitressing job at the bazaar. It helped Ruhi had already been promised to an eligible man, one she happened to be besotted with.

Bombay was booming, and many parents encouraged real estate for boys and tourism for girls as safe job options. Jaya had been studying hotel management, though she would have preferred art. Now, the thought of returning to her course repelled her.

"I can't go back to my old circles. How would I face them? Everything has changed. The deal was that I make myself useful. We can't afford both university and medical bills, and I've missed too much anyway," said Jaya. "Besides, I am content."

Ruhi raised her eyebrows. "Rubbish. After smashing the mirror this morning, you can't look me in the eye and say that." She eyeballed her sister, her dewy skin make-up free, her hair scraped back into a bun at her nape.

Jaya stared back then dropped her gaze, her cheeks flushing. "I will find my way."

"Where's your fight? It's been five months. Five months of sorrow, anger and blaming. Only you can rebuild your life, Jaya. No one else but you."

Their mother appeared at the patio door, her hair wrapped in a turban, bringing the stench of henna with her. "Jaya, I thought you were going to cook *roti*. I'm colouring my hair. Your father will be home soon."

"I was just—" said Jaya.

"I can't have a grown child not pulling her weight," said her mother.

"Maa, we just sat down, give us a few minutes," said Ruhi.

"Now, Jaya!"

Jaya hurried inside, followed by Ruhi. Together, they added ghee, water and a large pinch of salt to the flour to make the roti dough. They kneaded the mixture, dusted the work surface and rolled the dough into perfect circles. Jaya breathed through her rising panic as she heated a griddle on the stove. *I can do this.* Too soon to be near the flame, too soon to overcome her need to escape into nothingness. She placed the dough in the pan and watched while bubbles appeared on the topside, remembering the surface of her skin when she had burned, the singed, sizzling pain of it. Akash loomed large in her mind's eye, watching the flames ravage her with a curl to his lip.

Ruhi lay a hand on her arm. "You okay?"

Jaya flinched and held her sister's gaze. Ruhi could see through her lies, she knew, but it didn't deter her. How could she lean on her little sister? "Of course."

Another deep breath. She flipped the rotis with quick fingers, swallowing her panic though it bloomed in her throat, and transferred the bread to a plate. The stack multiplied and Ruhi buttered each one in turn. Both girls worked in silence. Their togetherness soothed Jaya at least: the rhythm of the roti-making brought order to the chaos of her mind, the coolness of the dough contrasted with the heat she still remembered. Finally, Ruhi spoke.

"You are not their maid, you know. You're strong. You just don't know it yet."

Jaya laid her head on Ruhi's shoulder. "Are you ashamed of me?"

Ruhi wrapped her lean arms around Jaya. "Of course not. I wish you could hear my voice in your head. I wish that was all you heard for now. It all feels dark to you, but I have an idea though to help you find joy."

That evening they squeezed into a rickshaw painted the colours of a bumblebee. The streets of Bombay heaved and spluttered, and the driver wore his recklessness like a badge of honour. He weaved in and out of the traffic as the girls held on for dear life.

Ruhi giggled. "We've not been out together for a while. I thought this would be fun," she said. Her dark hair flew out behind her like an arrow.

The rickshaw driver rounded a corner in haste, and Jaya's voice came out like a gasp. "Where are we going?"

"You'll find out soon enough."

"Will I have to speak to anybody?" She didn't need any more judgement.

"Not if you don't want to."

"There won't be much walking?"

"No," said Ruhi.

"We can leave if I want to?"

"Yes," replied her sister.

Jaya's disquiet eased. She had tied a navy-blue headscarf at her chin, and wore a navy-blue salwar kameez hemmed with lace, with loose kurta underneath. The trousers masked the angry red scars that looped around her legs, but the waistband irritated her torso. She covered her head with the matching *dupatta*, trying her best to avoid attention from passers-by. It would have been the norm for sandals to complete the outfit, but Jaya had chosen lace up shoes despite the humidity to conceal her abnormalities.

Soon enough they reached their destination, an apartment block near Mahim Bay. Ruhi gave the driver a handful of crumpled rupees and the two women stepped out onto the road. A sliver of moon lingered behind a bank of clouds.

"So, where are we then?" said Jaya, trepidation colouring her voice.

"This way," said Ruhi, cupping her sister's elbow. "This was meant as a birthday gift for you, but it's perfect for now. A friend told me about this place."

They entered a rickety lift. The cabin swayed and lurched as it ascended to the top floor. The doors ting-ed and opened out into one big space with bright white walls and wood flooring. In the middle of the room a small table was decorated with an aquamarine scarf and a vase of forget-me-nots. Scattered here and there were artist's easels. At some, women stood painting. Silence reached across the room apart from the scratch of paint brushes and the odd murmur.

A slim man crossed the room to greet them, smiling a welcome. "Hi, I'm Firoz." Smudges of colour dotted his hands. "How nice to see new faces here. Are you both here to paint?"

Ruhi laughed. "No, I can barely draw a line. My sister, on the other hand, is an artist. Or should be. It's been a while, I think. I'm just here for moral support."

The man turned to Jaya and in his eyes, she saw kindness. "Is that right?"

Jaya nodded her head, her heart clamouring inside the walls of her chest. It seemed too soon to be stepping out of the comfort of her home environment, but then, often home felt like a prison.

"Follow me and we'll get you set up," said Firoz.

They stayed. Jaya sat on a stool and painted while Ruhi watched and encouraged in gentle whispers. For the first time since the fire, Jaya found a way to direct her attention wholly outwards, towards the cloudy vase filled with the forget-me-nots and the little teak table it was perched upon. In that hour, she found peace.

# 7

**Jaya had spent** hours alone in her room as a girl with a sketchpad and pencil, scratching intricate designs into the paper. Soon she graduated from pencils to paintbrushes. Her father had been artistic in his youth too, though now he ran a video rental shop. To her mother, art represented a down and out's dream. Song and dance, she could stretch to—Bollywood movies, after all, appealed to the masses—but who made money with art? Her mother grew irritated at her pursuit. Any of Jaya's artwork she uncovered inevitably disappeared, most likely slung out with the household rubbish. So, Jaya took care to conceal her portfolio under the bed, wrapped in a scarf so it could be mistaken for crumpled clothing.

Ruhi's gift to her could not have come at a better time. Jaya came to love her art classes at the penthouse. Once a week after sundown she sat at her easel, reminded of the promise of an empty canvas. First, the colours she chose reflected her mood: inky blacks, swirling greys, deep blues. Soon, encouraged by Firoz, they evolved to a more joyful palette. She created fresh perspectives and new worlds, losing herself in colour. Slowly, she realised there remained room in her life for beauty and promise, even when life seemed cheerless, her prospects bleak.

Her subconscious thoughts were a different matter. That morning, Jaya woke slick with sweat from a recurrent nightmare. Fiery knives slashed at her in her dreams. As always, a distracted Akash stood half-watching her plight, reluctant to intervene. Her dream self-willed him to help her. She prayed for him to be her knight in shining armour. Instead, he receded from view, dissipating into a blank space and leaving her alone to pull the knives out one by one, a silent scream on her lips.

Ruhi slept through Jaya's night terrors, but when morning came she tutted at the blue-green circles under her sister's eyes, touched her wan, clammy skin and appeared to know of Jaya's battles.

This morning, stickiness and the heavy musk of sleep pervaded the room. Jaya's legs lay above the sheets. In public, pride led her to shield from prying eyes, but here, in the sanctity of her bedroom, she could not bear to have them covered. Her skin no longer welcomed the cocoon of the covers; the warmth of her bedclothes instead triggered flashbacks to her ordeal and phantom burn pains. The sight of missing toes left an acidic taste in her mouth. The fire had waged war on the once-smooth skin of her legs, now raw and ravaged. A stitch rose in her chest where it stubbornly lodged.

Jaya sat up in the grey morning light and reached for her sketchpad. Underneath her fingers, a man's face took shape. She let her pencil flow, allowed instinct to create the picture. Beside her, Ruhi stretched her lithe limbs and opened her eyes. Jaya pushed aside her pencil.

"What are you working on?" said Ruhi, her voice thick with sleep.

Jaya handed her sister the sketch pad. Black smears marked the tips of her index and middle finger where she'd smudged the lead. Akash's face stood out against a charcoal background, his features unmistakable: dark, long-lashed eyes, prevalent cheekbones, hair cut short, ears slightly too big for him to be classically handsome.

"Oh." Ruhi passed back the pad and sat up, eyes bleary with sleep. She looked her sister full in the face. "You're good, you know."

"Thanks." Jaya held her breath, hoping Ruhi would ignore the subject of her drawing.

"You know why you've drawn him, don't you? Why your subconscious can't let go?" said Ruhi.

"Do tell." She had grown tired of people extracting her emotions for her, as if she did not know herself, as if their opinion mattered more than hers.

"You love him."

Jaya stiffened, anger clawing at her throat. "I hate him."

"Yes, but you love him too. Those feelings you had for him, they don't disappear overnight." Ruhi's clarity infuriated her.

Jaya's cheeks grew hot, her head throbbed. "Next you're going to tell me everyone makes mistakes." She didn't want conflict with Ruhi; her sister had stood by her without flinching. It riled her that Akash was the root of their discord.

"I'm on your side," said Ruhi. "I get it, that's all. I know you, you fall deeply. Like that time when we were kids and you played *Carrom* with Saif while the rest of us were tearing around. It took you months to forget him. When you give your heart, you don't just take it back. That's not how you work." Ruhi flung back the covers and swung her legs over the side of the bed, effortlessly graceful. "Look, if it were me, I'd need some answers. I wouldn't let him off so easily. Go find Akash, Jaya. Show him what happened, give him a chance to explain. It might be he disgusts you, or you discover your story is not finished. Without that, you won't be able to move on."

The monotony of doing the laundry depressed Jaya. Her mother was meticulous about standards in the house, like any good Indian woman. Those standards translated into tasks for Jaya. Washing machines were the preserve of Europeans and the wealthy. Three times a week, Jaya separated the dirty clothes into lights, colours and darks, and washed them by hand in a bucket. She sat on a stool, as her mother had always done, grateful for the support for her legs. Even so, the labours pained her back and her neck, leaving the pads of her fingers wrinkled but her nails sparkling. Above all, she loathed washing saris. The endless yards of material, with running colours, were impossible to turn out to her mother's satisfaction. She had already ruined two beyond repair.

She heard muffled voices downstairs as she toiled, rhythmically kneading her father's shirts, lifting them in and out of the water. Her mother called up the stairs.

"Jaya, there's someone here for you."

Jaya's heart lurched. She let the shirt slide back into the water and wiped her hands on her thighs. From her mother's neutral tone, the visitor was unlikely to be Akash. She looked down at her clothing: her long, shapeless dress; her misshapen, socked feet. A cursory glance in the mirror revealed a halo of frizzy hair. She smoothed it down and sighed, then made her way unsteadily down the stairs. Her breath caught in her chest at the sight that greeted her.

The woman wore a slim-fitting salwar kameez with tapered sleeves and elegant silver sandals with a slight heel. Her hair hung loosely just above chin level. Jaya had only seen her once, but she would remember that face forever. Her blood rushed to her face and her heart leapt to an irregular drumbeat in her chest for all to hear.

"Isn't it nice to have a visitor?" said her mother.

Jaya resisted the urge to run and hide. "Maa, could we have a moment please? To be alone?" Her voice croaked and she struggled to form the words.

"I've tried, I have really tried to teach her manners," her mother called out over her shoulder as she departed.

"We haven't met. Not properly. I'm Soraya Mansoor." The woman's hands rested on a slight bulge at her midsection. Not perfect after all.

Jaya clung to the bottom of the bannister, fury and embarrassment unfurling in her belly. She resented how unclean and unfashionable she happened to be in comparison to the other woman. She lifted her eyes to meet Soraya's, anger and resentment coursing through her veins. "I might not have known your name, but I know who you are."

"I am sorry."

"Are you? Then why did you do it?" The words came tumbling out, an affront against the laws of Indian hospitality.

"Because I could, I guess. His attention was a balm to my ego." Her callous disregard for another woman's happiness fuelled Jaya's anger.

"Do you love him?" Jaya spat the words out.

"No." A tiny word, a world of meaning.

Jaya drew herself up to her full height, but still came up only to the woman's chin. "You ruined another woman's marriage and it wasn't even for love." Her voice crescendoed. "Get out—now!—Before I do something I regret."

A shadow hovered behind the glass door leading to the kitchen. Her mother emerged.

"Jaya, what is wrong with you? Is that any way to treat your guest?" She turned to Soraya, all cheap perfume and backcombed hair. "Do come in, have some chai or water at least. We do not treat guests that way in this house."

"No!" Jaya's voice bellowed, clawing any attempt at congeniality away from her mother's face. She jostled past Soraya to throw the door open, gripped the other woman's arm and manhandled her onto the street. Her throat was raw with unshed tears. "You're leaving."

Soraya nodded, not a line between her fine eyebrows, her expression wiped of passion. She cast her eyes over Jaya. "As you wish." She turned on her heel, hips swaying as she negotiated the littered pavement.

Jaya flushed. "Stop!"

She ran out onto the dusty street in her house dress and socks, gesturing wildly, restraint abandoned. Without doubt, she looked mad to passers-by: one crazed, unkempt woman; one sane, elegant one.

Soraya pivoted, glossy hair spinning in an arc, almond eyes questioning.

"Why come here now?" said Jaya.

"At first I didn't know what happened. I haven't seen him—"

"I'm supposed to believe that?" Jaya's insides clenched.

"I can only tell you the facts. It's for you to decide what you believe." Soraya paused. "I heard the rumours at university. I asked around. Eventually someone told me your address. A clerk at the university. She figured it would do no harm since you weren't coming back. I guessed you'd be here. What woman would take back a man who cheats on her?"

The salt burned in the wound of Jaya's broken heart. "Why are you here? It's not for me, I know that much."

"I need a fresh start," said Soraya. "And the past, it has a trick of sneaking up on you."

"And Akash?" Jaya formed no intention with the question, but his name rolled off her tongue and hung in the air, a question mark.

"He's yours if you want him."

Her nonchalance stung. Jaya reached for a scathing retort but found herself unable to deliver one in time.

"For what it's worth, I'm glad you're ok." Soraya's hand rested on the curve of her stomach.

"I don't care what you think." Jaya threw her one last venomous look, pushed back her shoulders, and walked home, one foot after the other, putting all her effort into a steady gait.

The smallness of Jaya's life over the past months made her claustrophobic.

Ruhi's words rang in her ears. *You need answers. Your story might not be finished.*

Try as she might to forget them, Soraya's words haunted her too: *his attention was a balm to my ego.*

Her husband had betrayed her for a woman who did not even love him. More than anything, the knowledge that Akash had been there when she lit the match and had not returned to check her fate lay like a rock on her soul, obliterating the light, skewing her sense of self-worth. How could he have left her to burn? Still, she could not reconcile callous behaviour to that degree with the man she knew.

She bent over to put on a clean pair of socks, the old ones sodden with sweat, covered her head with a chequered cotton scarf and shut the door behind her. The night breeze chased her fractured thoughts around her head. She drove her chin to her chest, and walked first to Bandra Fort, where moss-covered stone walls loomed high over the Arabian Sea. A little further took her along Bandstand Promenade to Lover's Point, where she and Akash had stopped once to eat spicy *puris* as the water thrashed against the rocks. For a moment, Jaya thought she saw him there amongst the crowds. She rushed to keep up, not trusting her eyes, such was her yearning for him. Her unsteady balance slowed her down, and by the time she had fought her way through the throng, the man had slipped out of sight.

She traversed the streets, hate mingling with love, second guessing even the harmonious times they had spent together. She wanted to believe in the good in him. If Akash was the villain, it would mean her own judgement was flawed, that she had loved foolishly. Had he always been thinking of Soraya? Plotting his escape? Could she wrestle back control from the other woman, despite it all? How satisfying it would be to have the last laugh, to resurrect her marriage, to create something out of the ashes, or to tempt Akash back only to spurn him, as he had done her. Either way, she steeled herself for the truth. Ruhi was right: she needed closure. Highly likely, Soraya had spun her a web of lies, and Akash had started a life with his lover. Jaya needed to know. More than anything, she yearned to know if Akash thought of her at all. He had not been her protector, but he was still her husband.

The hour grew late and the stars hid behind a laburnum tree as she approached the entrance to the house which had been her marital home. She still possessed a key, but instead of using it, she turned it over in her palm, rang the doorbell, and waited, gnawing on her bottom lip. A light shone at the back of the house. Eventually slow footfalls approached and the door opened, releasing a waft of incense.

Her mother-in-law appeared in the crack, a tea towel on her shoulder. She grasped Jaya, shaking her, no words of greeting, only anguish. "Where is he? Where is my son? Is it true you haven't seen him?"

"I haven't seen him. That's why I'm here," said Jaya, stepping back out of the older woman's reach. How could she believe that Akash was not hiding behind these walls, that he had not contacted his family?

Her mother-in-law clutched her again and sobbed, her made-up face crumpling in the half-light. She had never shown such vulnerability when they lived under the same roof. Maybe she was telling the truth, Akash had disappeared from their lives too. Jaya's heart clamoured in her chest like the hooves of galloping horses. If Akash was not here, was he with Soraya?

"The police won't look for him. A family dispute they say. But we were happy, weren't we? They say he'll come home when he is ready. Four months. Four months with no word. Will he come home, Jaya?"

Jaya didn't know the steps to this dance. She didn't know what to reveal or how to respond, so instead she said nothing at all.

Her father-in-law loomed up behind his wife, shaking his head. His voice was robotic, devoid of emotion, but something else prickled underneath. "You've said enough, Sheetal." He put his arm around his wife. "Go inside. I'll talk to Jaya."

"But what has happened to our son?" said Sheetal, already scuttling away, wiping her streaming tears with the tea towel.

Her father-in-law turned to face her. "What are you doing here, Jaya?"

"I came to speak to Akash."

"You see he is not here. We have given up hope that he'll come back. Sheetal... she isn't coping very well." Her father-in-law's demeanour hardened. He puffed out his chest. "Your father asked us not to contact you. I keep my word. Go. Go home where you belong."

Jaya stared at him, reading the grief and pride on her father-in-law's face. Akash was gone, but if Soraya hadn't lied, then where was he? She would find no answers here.

"Papa called you?" Why wouldn't her father have told her if the two men had spoken?

"Yes. He said it was easier this way. There is no marriage with one of you gone. Your place is back with your parents. Akash has disappeared. Your father suggested a clean break, that we keep the dowry."

"I see." Jaya drew in a steadying breath, determined not to fall apart here, or show how her spirit had found hope only to be crushed again. She pressed her house key into his plump hand. "Well, I won't be needing this."

Her father-in-law lingered on the doorstep. "You don't look like yourself, Jaya. I am sorry it turned out this way. You were a good daughter-in-law." He began to close the door, blocking her view of the inside of the house, and part of her longed to use her foot as a stopper, demand acknowledgement of her pain and loss. "Take care of yourself." He threw the comment at her like a scrap, as if she had been discarded as easily as a piece of rubbish.

She turned into the night, where she no longer had to pretend.

The door clicked shut behind her.

# 8

**Akash teetered at** the top of the ladder above J.R. Merchants, a hardware store in Andheri East. The sign swung next to him in air leaden with heat. Beads of perspiration clung to his forehead. Not an ounce of fat encumbered his body. Without the luxury of regular meals, he had grown lean with physical labour.

He stood five or six metres from ground level. Tariq steadied the ladder with one hand and reached up to hand him a paintbrush. It made sense for Akash, the more athletic of the two, to be the one at the top of the ladder. Tariq's fear of heights had, in the past, proven to be debilitating, and he could not be relied upon to stay sober for a job. With Akash as the more responsible one, they contributed to the twilight economy as a pair.

It suited businessmen to give them a few rupees in hand for odd jobs such as hanging up signs, clearing away rubbish and carrying bags of shopping for customers. Men like them did not make a fuss about conditions or the level of payment. The jobs came with unreliable regularity, but amounted to enough to cover basic items they could not scavenge for, like toothpaste and alcohol. Both men had grown used to alcohol as a nightly sedative, especially to ward off the cold when the nights cooled.

Akash brightened up the sign with careful strokes of white, and then climbed down rung by rung to the ground. Tariq had been in an effervescent mood since morning, giddy at the thought of the spending money they would receive.

"So, tell me, if money was no object, what would you do with our earnings?" said Tariq.

"We're hardly going to be millionaires."

"Play along, go on." He grinned. "A movie maybe? The new Sri Devi one."

"A romance? No thank you." Even in theory Akash balked at the thought of having to watch love songs and big joyful dance sequences.

"Ok then, an action one with Amitabh Bachchan."

"We play action heroes all the time. How it is that I've gotten into so many sticky situations since meeting you?" said Akash, a twinkle in his eyes. "I hardly need to watch action on the big screen. Besides, if we're millionaires you should aim higher."

"A bungalow then, on Juhu Beach where we'd hear the sound of the water. You'd love that."

"I don't know, Tariq. With money comes responsibility. I'm not sure I could live like that again."

"You mean with money comes options," said Tariq. "We could start afresh, have families even. We'd have something to offer."

"Other than our bare wits," said Akash, a wry smile playing on his lips.

"Yeah, and our bodies." A goofy grin transformed Tariq's face, instantly making him appear younger than his maltreated body indicated.

Akash's spirit lifted in response to Tariq's playfulness, and then immediately plummeted when his friend spun in a circle with the tray of paint, almost splattering its contents onto the pavement.

Akash's hand snapped out to steady him. "Watch it!"

"Relax, yaar. Always so uptight. You know, the old shamans used to have a way of finding out if members of their tribe were fully healthy. Do you know what they asked?"

"Surprise me," said Akash.

"They used to ask: when was the last time you danced, when was the last time you sang?"

"I sing sometimes."

"No, you don't."

Akash smiled. "No, I don't."

Together they folded up the ladder and walked towards the back alley. Akash rapped his knuckles on a flimsy door. A moment later the owner of the hardware store appeared. Akash allowed his gaze to rest somewhere around the elderly man's shirt collar. The old man treated him kindly, but Akash understood that adopting a subservient manner was expected of him as a homeless man. It fed the ego of his transaction partner and led to easier interactions.

"Janghir *Saheb*," he said, careful to use the deferential mark of respect, reserved for elders or better men. Handing over the remaining materials, he continued, "We've finished. Would you like to have a look?"

"Lead the way."

They walked towards the front of the shop, the old man using a cane to support himself. Once there, he surveyed the paintwork and nodded with satisfaction.

"You missed something there, but overall you're a good worker, Ash. I like you," said Janghir Saheb.

It wouldn't have done to use his own name. In many ways that man had died with his wife.

"This can be messy work, but you clean up after yourself. You show initiative beyond other men of your sort I've employed." He pushed a small stack of rupees into Akash's hand. "Next time, you work quicker, I pay you more."

Akash crumpled the notes in his hand, enjoying the feel of the currency.

Janghir Saheb glanced at Tariq. "Tariq here tells me you studied to be a teacher. It's strange, living the way you do when you could earn a decent living. And that," he gestured to the wedding band on Akash's finger, "tells me you have family."

Akash experienced a spark of fury and abandoned his calm exterior. His eyes flashed a warning. "With all due respect, it's none of your business, Janghir Saheb. Thank you for your payment." He turned on his heel, leaving Tariq to make excuses and scamper after him.

They bought spicy potatoes from a street vendor with their earnings. Back under the railway bridge, they ate in silence with their fingers and licked them clean. Turmeric turned their fingers yellow.

When they were finished, Akash left for his nightly ritual at the shore and Tariq pocketed the remaining money so he could go in search of some alcohol.

Akash's feet knew the route by now. This time, he took a detour, drawn towards a block of flats. He hurried along, glancing furtively behind him, clutching a plastic bag with a t-shirt and pair of shorts he had stolen from a market. Rickshaws hurtled past, jostling for space on the road. Yards ahead he caught sight of a woman's silhouette. It could have been Jaya, apart from a limp. He blinked back his tears and bumped into a couple walking by hand in hand.

They tutted and crossed the street when they noticed him watching them, jealousy wrapping itself around his blackened heart. He didn't blame them. He looked unkempt, dangerous.

Sometimes, looking through the windows of apartments at family life brought him solace. He imagined he was not alone, that he could be part of a family, worthy of the intimacy they shared. He drew close to a window facing the street, and as he watched, a young woman in a high-waisted polka dot salwar kameez wrapped her arms around her young son. Her hair fell into her face as she spoke to him. The boy giggled and buried his head in the fullness of her skirt, then darted underneath its folds as she scolded him.

Akash held his breath, trying not to rustle the carrier bag in his hand. He almost believed he could be them, and for a moment, a flicker of happiness touched him. A clatter behind him alerted him to the fact he had company. Akash turned, his face flushing.

Moon-like eyes sat in a child's grubby face. She must have been about seven or eight. She clambered onto a nearby crate and looked back at him, unblinking, parents nowhere to be seen. Her wordless scrutiny made him feel dirty. Did she need his help? He couldn't rescue himself, let alone her. Akash rushed past her, yearning for the cleansing power of the sea and prayer.

At the seashore, he checked he was alone then dropped his plastic bag on the sand. The starless night offered him some privacy. He stripped down to his briefs, all haste, his fingers fumbling with the buttons on his speckled shirt, and kicked off his sandals. Then he walked into the cool black water, shivering as it caressed his body.

"I'm not sure I can survive without love, Jaya," he whispered into the night. The finality of her death pained him. It left no room for his redemption. He talked to her to retain some kind of connection, but at times he struggled to imagine what her answer would be. Sometimes she appeared to him as a loving friend; at others, she transformed into someone vindictive and vengeful; most often, she remained silent, her judgement of him all too clear.

Tonight, he heard nothing, just the spray of the water and the echo of his own thoughts. He turned onto his back and floated, holding his breath until his lungs cried out for air. He inhaled, angry at himself for giving in, for having a life, however small that life was. Still on his back, the waves rocked him. He pressed his head back, immersing the crown of his head, his ears, until just the oval of his face showed above the water. He tried to talk to Jaya again, listening for her response above the churn of the water in his ears. *Would it be a release to let the water swallow me, as the fire did you?* he thought. *Would anyone look for me?*

Nothing.

*Am I too cowardly to even take my own life?* Akash shook his head, banishing his dark thoughts like orphaned planets across an endless universe. He dropped his feet to the seabed, his toes mingling with silt. Collecting his dirty clothes from the sand, he bent over, bare back and briefs to the beach, to give them a cursory wash in the surf. Once he'd wrung them out and packed them into the carrier bag, he slipped on his clean set of clothes and turned in the direction of home, of Tariq.

Tariq sat with his legs splayed wide, a bottle of whisky between them. The bridge had felt claustrophobic, so they had come to a park.

Akash laid out his newly washed clothes, now stiff with saltwater, to dry on a park bench.

"Want a swig?" said Tariq. He swung a bottle of malt in a wide arc towards Akash.

Akash grimaced. "Not tonight."

"You know," Tariq slurred, "after what happened with my job, and losing my money, my girlfriend, I lost my humanity for a while."

"Your humanity?"

"Yes, my joy, my empathy, what makes me, me."

"Why do you think you lost it?"

"There was this older guy, on the streets you know. He looked out for me. Not a lot, but you know, would give me a heads up when trouble was coming. Then, one night, we set up camp next to this abandoned bus stop. And in the morning, Rohit was really still, and I knew, I knew he was gone. Taken by the cold, or an infection, or heartbreak, who knows? And I waited. I did nothing, man. I carried on cooking and sleeping next to this dead man for days. I didn't report his death to the authorities, I just carried on until the stench overwhelmed me and someone realised. And then I left, before they came to take him, and I didn't look back." He shook his head and tipped the whisky into his mouth. "I've never told anyone that. He was my friend."

Akash reached across to rest a hand on Tariq's shoulder. "I'm sorry. It's tough out here. What could you have done?"

"Acted like he mattered. That's what I could have done. We may be out here, but we matter." Despite the alcohol he had consumed, the hopelessness of their situation, and the guilt he bore for abandoning his friend's body, a gentle wistfulness played on Tariq's features.

"Do we matter? Do we really?"

"Do you doubt it?"

"Sometimes," said Akash.

Tariq grimaced. "'Sometimes.' I hate that word."

# 9

**Jaya's life with** Akash, culminating in the fire, became a central point around which everything revolved. While she recovered, her parents' house became her prison; she, a caged bird, restricted from her natural purpose of living, singing solely for the benefit of others. Only the painting class, her means of escape, kept her sane. In time, the need to breathe away from her familiar circles overwhelmed Jaya, and not even her nightly walks soothed her. Only then, with Ruhi cheering her on, did she step out freely during the day, and make slow steps towards wider integration.

She continued to live with her parents, bound by daughterly responsibility. She was the eldest child, after all, and her focus on them freed Ruhi from similar bonds. Jaya serviced their needs first thing in the morning and last thing at night: cooking, laundry, cleaning. They demanded it, and she gave it, but not without restraint.

"The food has finished, Jaya," said her mother with a frown.

"I cooked first thing." She woke each day at the crack of dawn.

"We ate it for lunch." She offered no apology for devouring all the contents of the saucepan without leaving any for her.

A swell of anger, quick, like lightening in a storm, at the servitude and selflessness expected from her. "You can cook, Maa."

"We've run out of flour and potatoes. I had nothing left to make." Had her mother always been this helpless or had encroaching old age taken away her last remnants of independence?

Jaya's patience snapped, an elastic band pulled too tight. "You could have gone to the market." She had been job-hunting all day, and her art class took place tonight. That she would not compromise.

"The kitchen is your domain now, I've served my time." Keen eyes glowered over pursed lips.

"Maa, I give gladly when I choose to give, but you and Papa are able to look after yourselves. Don't pretend otherwise."

They locked horns, time and again, two women in a too small space, one vying for independence, the other for authority. Through it all, not once did her mother acknowledge the resilience it took for Jaya to face the room where the fire had consumed her.

Only Ruhi knew the strength it took, the techniques she used to calm her racing heart, to quell the avalanche of memories that returned without warning.

"I am loved." Again and again, alone in the bathroom, she chanted the affirmation aloud, moon eyes reflected back in an ageing mirror.

"I can do this."

"I am enough, just as I am."

She spoke the words until they came involuntarily, an echo in her mind, a reaction and a balm in moments of panic and despair, the rhythm and syntax imprinted on the shreds of her pride.

To her surprise, she won. Not overnight, but gradually, as a basin fills with river water. The flames of the stove ceased to echo in her mind, and only in the nightmares of her sleep did they resurface. And still, she kept the secret that Akash had been there when she had burned, a morbid spectator in her hour of reckoning. She protected him, though he had failed her, and her sacrifice gave her strength.

Despite it all, she refused to accept her life was over, not even when pitying stares from fellow women pierced her thin armour.

"Where is your husband, Jaya? Was it your poor cooking he ran away from?"

"It'll be too late for you to have children if you wait too long."

"Women aren't made to be alone."

They gossiped, in their tired old circles, neither elevating the other, each satisfied with the frisson of excitement other people's bad fortune brings. She should have thanked them. Over time, she grew stronger, and noticed only on the periphery of her consciousness when thoughtless or spiteful old ladies at temple threw verbal missiles her way.

"There she is," came the whispers. "Her sister is so beautiful, she has done so well, a fine man for a husband. This one was married once. Who knows where her husband is now."

"She grows old, like us. And she is her father's burden."

"It's not right when a woman puts herself before family."

In some ways, she was grateful. Exposure to the toxicity of small communities drove her out of her shell when she had wanted to cut herself off from the world. It made her artful, able to manipulate when before she might have bowed to the pressure of belonging.

She played her role, as best she could, but in between, she lived. She found a job at a small community theatre, which fed into small television productions. First as a secretary, then as a costume and set designer. She enjoyed being in the shadows of the performances rather than centre stage, took comfort from the lights going out and all eyes being on someone else, and from the interactions with the cast. The theatre became not only her livelihood, but her lifeline. Still, she looked for Akash in the faces of strangers who filled the auditorium and walked the streets. One day, perhaps, her own life would play out like a perfectly scripted play.

# 10

**The years sped** past and in the blink of an eye, the buoyancy of youth settled into heavy-footed middle age. In many ways, Jaya was a pariah. An Indian woman in her mid-forties, deserted by her husband, childless, scarred.

That morning, her chores complete, Jaya stood in front of a long mirror in the bedroom she had once shared with Ruhi, who now was mistress of her own home and family. Despite the hand fate had dealt, or perhaps because of it, Jaya had shed the remnants of a submissive younger self. In its place emerged a woman borne of complexity and trauma. Gone was the meek woman, gone the drab salwar kameez she had chosen after the fire, gone the headscarf she had used as a curtain to avoid the glare of strangers.

In their place was the costume she had adopted, the one her ageing mother, ever the bringer of harmony, rolled her eyes at. The folds and dimples in her discoloured skin were hidden from view beneath a long, full skirt in turquoise. She dressed in bright colours, a deliberate attempt to obscure the dark wounds of her past. Heavy kohl lined her eyes, complementing the straight line of her mouth and giving her the look of a warrior. Her hair had always been her crowning glory, thick strands of curly jet black, now peppered with grey. She didn't dye it; she didn't see the need. Her naked mirror image pained her, but she had learned to distract from the scars on her lower body with elaborate clothes that lifted her spirit and made her feel stronger. Showing her true self was anathema to her. She needed neither pity nor judgement; in fact, they enraged her. Only her feet looked odd, perpetually clad in closed shoes, even when her socked feet grew damp in the Bombay heat. She liked to joke with Ruhi that it took her half the time to paint her toe nails.

Jaya took equal joy and pain from how life had turned out for Ruhi. Her sister had a loving husband, a ten-year-old son and her own home. Casting agents still chose her to dance in Bollywood blockbusters, such as *Rangeela* and *Kuch Kuch Hota Hai*. She had Shah Rukh Khan on speed dial. Jaya, for her part, preferred a quieter life, the shadows to the sunlight. She took pleasure from her role as an aunt to her nephew, and showered him with kisses and gifts. Spending time with him never failed to remind her how different her life could have been.

Jaya threw a shawl around her shoulders, and closed the bedroom door behind her. Downstairs, she peeked into the living room where her mother and father watched a talent show on the television. The curtains hadn't been opened. She hurried over to open them, not wanting to be late.

"See you after work. The okra curry and puri are on the stove ready for your lunch. I'll make some fresh rotis later."

"Thank you," said her father.

Her mother appeared to be too engrossed in the programme to look up. She often sulked when Jaya left the house. Hers was, as her mother would say, a non-job. *Well,* thought Jaya. *It's a non-job that makes me happy.*

Away from home, Jaya breathed deeply, drinking in the scent of the city, spices mingling with exhaust fumes. She boarded a bus towards Juhu and reached her destination a half-hour later. She walked the short distance to the Tara Theatre, her head high, gentle curves wrapped up in her colourful ensemble, her step light, balance slightly off centre due to her disability. A single storey building, which extended back like a wormhole, housed the theatre. Outside, faded lettering stretched across the facade, and a small window showcased flyers from past productions. Inside, a long corridor led from the front desk to dressing rooms, washrooms and a large practice area. At the end sat an intimate performance space containing seats in worn green velvet for 150 people and a half-moon stage.

Jaya made her way to a small workspace containing two small desks. She collapsed into a swivel chair, discarded her shawl and grabbed a pen. Swatches of fabric, a pot of pencils, a small set of water colours, and a stack of newspapers from the past week lay scattered across the desk. Jaya picked up a script buried under the fabric and annotated it, immersing herself immediately in the drama of the piece.

She was chewing the biro, working out a design concept for their forthcoming play, when a touch on her shoulder startled her.

"Ravi, you scared me."

"Always straight to your desk, Jaya. You know I miss you when you don't come and say hello."

In his late-thirties with slicked back hair and terrible taste in fashion—too high trousers, gaudy, printed shirts—Ravi had been showing her a lot of attention over the past few weeks, and Jaya didn't understand why. Any hint of romantic attention sent her into a frenzy of self-doubt. Besides, Akash might not be here, but she was still his wife. She belonged to him.

"Can I borrow yesterday's newspaper? I didn't manage to watch the cricket and I want a wicket by wicket account." He grinned and reached over her for the paper.

"No, I'm not done with that yet," said Jaya.

Her sharpness wiped the smile off his face. "Sorry, I didn't mean to be a nuisance."

She struggled to keep her voice level. "Don't worry."

"Listen, I was thinking, why don't we go for food together after work tonight? There's a restaurant I've been meaning to try. It's supposed to be really good."

It was the second time he had suggested going out together. It sounded oddly like a date. Jaya grimaced, and a look of upset flashed across Ravi's face. Now she had wounded him twice. She tried to extricate herself from the situation.

"I have elderly parents, they'll be waiting for me."

"I know how good you are to them, Jaya. I admire that, but surely they can look after themselves for one night? They can always call you if they need you."

She had an old Nokia phone precisely for that reason.

"You must have someone else you can go with," she said, fumbling for any reason to stay within her trusted environments.

"Not really." Ravi shrugged.

It bothered her to fall foul of the rules of female decorum, schooled as she had been by her conservative parents. Male and female friendship existing outside of the security of chaperones or groups constituted a dangerous game to play, especially without concrete intentions. She paid little heed to gossip but it seemed silly to needlessly fuel it. She threw a glance at Ravi. He had not accepted her excuses and standing her ground would make her seem churlish. It's not as if anyone would believe Ravi happened to be romantically interested in her anyway.

"Okay. Just this once."

"Great. Come find me when you're ready," he said, his smile lighting up the dark interior of the room.

When he had gone, she scooped up the pile of newspapers and pulled them to the middle of the desk. Then, painstakingly, as if her life depended on it, she waded through the papers as she had done for twenty years, lingering in particular at the death notices, looking for any sign of the husband who had been lost to her.

Ravi chose a restaurant called Arjun, situated a stone's throw away from Juhu Beach. Above the door awning to the restaurant hung a golden statue of an archer. He held the door open as they entered. Jaya flushed at his attentiveness. He happened to be the same height as her in his suit shoes with a block heel. She herself wore simple, flat, lace-up shoes. In bare feet, Akash had been at least a head taller. Not that Ravi was a suitor; they were nothing more than friends.

The restaurant overflowed with people, unusual for a Tuesday evening. The room, rectangle in shape, with a large window facing the street, was packed full of tables. The lighting was dimmed, deviating from the slapdash Bombay eateries she was accustomed to. This was a restaurant for special occasions, for special someones. Diners—many of them couples—leant forward in animated conversation, voices booming, making Jaya even more conscious of her reticence, her unease. She sat opposite Ravi, willing him to speak first.

"It's lovely, isn't it?" said Ravi, looking at the menu with satisfaction. "Aren't you glad you came?"

"Of course."

During the work day, she had concocted a multitude of graceful excuses not to attend, but anything she came up with seemed tinged with untruth, obviously so. In the end, she had decided to get this evening over and done with, but worried that Ravi might see more into tonight than she wanted. She found comfort in her work, art, long walks, and in Ruhi and her nephew. Spending time with Ravi took her away from her carefully curated existence, unnerving her. Her weakness, her lack of cool, irked her. A strong woman, whose Achilles heel happened to be men. She laughed at the irony. Every second person walking on the streets had the ability to throw her off kilter. She resolved to do better, whether Ravi wanted friendship or more.

"I've been wanting to spend time with you away from work for a long time, Jaya."

For a brief moment, Jaya considered fleeing the restaurant. Ravi reached out across the table and she balked, snatching back her hand from where it had lain next to the gold-embossed menu.

"I've done it again, haven't I?" he said. "I didn't mean to make you uncomfortable." The corners of his mouth folded downwards. With his slicked back hair, he resembled an unhappy seal.

Jaya strove to reassure him. "No, no, I'm not..." Her voice trailed off.

"I won't do it again."

She hid her embarrassment behind the menu. "Why don't we order? It looks nice."

They ordered a dish each—*aloo gobi* for her, *mutter paneer* for him—and a naan bread and plain rice to share. She turned down his offer of wine and they settled on water. She didn't want to get too friendly, and she drank so infrequently she couldn't trust herself to remain sober. When the food arrived, they ate with their fingers in stilted silence. She scooped the curried cauliflower and potatoes up with her naan, wondering how quickly she could leave, while Ravi devoured his cheese and peas with astonishing speed. They each took a breath and started speaking at once.

"Listen—" he said.

"So—" she said.

Ravi smiled, revealing shiny, even teeth. "No, you first."

She nodded, eyes downcast. Twisting her finger in a wayward curl, she tucked it behind her ear, playing for time. "I don't want to mislead you, Ravi." *He did say he liked me, didn't he? He's younger than me. Why would he be interested in a washed-up woman like me?* She needed to nip this in the bud. "The truth is, I'm not looking, you know, for anything romantic." She hesitated. "I'd like to be your friend, though."

Ravi folded his napkin in silence, his brow furrowed, then looked up to pin her with his eyes. Jaya squirmed in her seat.

"Yes, let's be friends, but can you keep everything else open, Jaya? Don't decide yet. Give it a chance."

She shook her head, the faintest of movements. *I'm married!* The words filled her mind, a silent assault she hid from him. How could she be truthful when it would only open the gates to gossip and ridicule? Her status as a deserted wife was nobody's business but her own. She drew in a shaky breath. "I have to get back. My parents will be waiting."

Ravi averted his gaze, looking around the room at anything but her. "I'll order the bill." He beckoned a waiter. The man, dressed in a simple black uniform with high-collared shirt, balancing four plates, nodded to indicate he would be over soon.

Jaya fidgeted in her seat.

A second man approached, this one in a dinner jacket. He couldn't have been more than twenty. His manner was self-assured; he was clearly not a waiter. "Did you enjoy the evening, Sir, Madam?" he said.

Something about him struck Jaya as familiar, something in the curve of his lip, the look in his eyes.

"I'm Arjun. My mother and I own this restaurant. This is your first time here, I think? I make it my business to know my customers." He smiled, and something stirred in the deepest recesses of Jaya's memory.

Ravi stretched out his hand to shake Arjun's, his strained demeanour thawing. "I've wanted to come here for quite some time. We enjoyed the food."

*But not the company,* Jaya thought. She mumbled her agreement.

"That's my mother Soraya over there," said Arjun. "We'd be happy to see you back anytime. I'll arrange for your bill."

Ravi thanked him while Jaya's eyes drifted over to Arjun's mother. Her hands became clammy as she stared at the woman.

The woman stood tall, talking to a customer as she handed over a jacket. Her sari showed off her svelte body, a bit on the skinny side. She held her chin high, and her hair had been cropped shorter than the last time Jaya had seen her twenty years before. Slowly, she shifted her gaze to Arjun, and she understood now why he had seemed familiar.

There was no question in her mind; the physical resemblance of this man to his parents could not be mistaken. He was the son of Akash and Soraya. Jaya reeled, the food in her stomach threatening to make its way back into the world.

Ravi was paying the bill. "Jaya?" He pierced through the litany of thoughts racing through her head, yanking her out of her ever-present past.

"Get me out of here. Please."

He took one look at her, stood up and took her arm, nodding his thanks to Soraya.

"Thank you for coming," she said, as they passed. "Wait." She grasped Jaya's arm. "Do I know you?"

"No," said Jaya, without stopping, manoeuvring through the door, under the archer, to the street where the air filled her lungs and her breath caught in her throat in the shape of a sob.

It angered her. It angered her that Soraya had taken Akash from her. That she had a son and a successful business. That she was beautiful. It did not seem fair. Nothing was fair. Soraya had thrived, while she had struggled. She doubted whether a single scar marred that perfect body.

Ravi had followed her out onto the street. "Are you okay?" he said, concern etched on his face.

"No, I'm not okay! I'm not okay!" Akash had a son. He and Soraya had created something she had always wanted. A loving relationship, a family of their own. How could this be fair after all she had been through? She wanted to be by herself. She began walking. She didn't want to stay there outside the restaurant.

"What's the matter, Jaya?" His fingers grazed her shoulder. "It's okay. You don't have to see me again."

"You think this is about you?" she spat. How could he be so self-involved when her whole world had taken on a new shape? Jaya spun to face him. She lost her footing and tumbled to the floor. Her skirt crumpled around her thighs revealing her scars, pitted white skin amongst smooth brown patches. Horrified, Jaya checked to see if she had been seen.

Ravi rushed over to help. A group of teenagers passing by sniggered.

"Look at her. She looks like a cow."

"Nothing holy about that."

Ravi turned on them. "Leave her alone!"

To Jaya, he said. "Let me help you up." He reached over to readjust her skirt, his eyes focused slightly to the left of where she lay sprawled.

She smarted. He didn't even want to look at her. "Take a good look, go on! See if you still like me."

He averted his eyes.

"No? I thought so. I don't need romance, okay? I told you already. I open myself up to someone new, I get hurt. That's just life. I give my love and I get punctured. And I don't recover. Why does everyone always think people recover?" Her voice trembled and she hated herself for it.

"Jaya..."

"Go! Just go!" She picked herself up, anger coursing through her veins, vengeance even.

Ravi walked away, shaking his head.

*I am enough, just as I am. I am enough* chanted her internal voice, over and over. But she didn't feel enough. They would all be sorry. She would not open herself to new suitors. She would never divulge the secrets of her past to a stranger, never let anyone see the marks on her skin, the curdled milky white of her legs, the jagged lines on her torso that reminded her of a shark bite when she dared to look at her naked body in the mirror. She would not open herself up to pain.

# 11

**Akash pressed his** face hard against the window. He stood there for over an hour, his breath misting over the pane as he devoured the picture of family bliss in front of him. The objects of his interest immersed themselves in the hustle and bustle of family life, so much so they did not notice him. Soon they would chase him away, shouting obscenities, the mother fearful and the father full of rage. Little did they know Akash was no monster. He was a weary, broken man. He breathed in the everyday happiness of strangers because his had been lost to him the day he ran.

He was perhaps forty-six years old, but he and Tariq rarely marked their birthdays, and with no wife or children to spoil him, his certainty waned. His memories fragmented and the years fell away like a snake shedding its skin. The seasons came and went. His friendship with Tariq buoyed him, and he no longer needed wider social interaction, but love, he missed love. Long ago he had decided he could not live without love. It had taken painful years to accept his wife's death. Now, with Jaya an ever-present ghost in his mind, he looked for Soraya, hoping to salvage something of the man he had been. He searched for her for so long he lost track of time, until even Tariq did not understand his driving need.

Akash walked the streets of the city, a haggard, foul-smelling man with yellowed, crumbling teeth, wearing his shame like a comfortable old coat. Self-important businessmen strode past him in dark, tailored suits, an army of men with tiny mobile phones pressed to their ears, moving fast and rendering him invisible. He revelled in his invisibility, grateful for it. He disappeared into the cracks and crevices of the bustling city, mingling with the dust from the stinking streets, merging with the spicy vapours that rose from Bombay's kitchens and restaurants and street corners.

He wished at these moments of invisibility to disappear altogether, but his bond with Tariq kept him from the precipice of suicide, as well as the hope that he could one day have what he had given up: a family. Not even the oblivion of sleep soothed him. His only joy arose from his nightly escapades to the families of Bombay, witnessing them love and argue and comfort each other. Sometimes he pretended he was their grandfather, out on an errand to bring sweets home for the children, *jelabi* perhaps, or some *mango lassi*. These moments of make-believe became a balm for his soul. Akash dove deep into their worlds for as long as possible each night, sustained by their lives, rooting and hurting for them. His alienation was complete.

Tonight had come to pass like every other night since he lost it all. As darkness fell, he made his way through the city's streets in the sticky air, drawn to a white-washed bungalow in Juhu he hadn't visited before.

"I know you don't like me doing this, Jaya. I'll be careful, I promise," he said out loud. It had become his habit to speak to Jaya. Somehow, their separation did not seem so final that way. Apart from Tariq, she was his sounding board. He didn't need or expect an answer from her.

Glittering white lights framed the house as if from a fairy-tale and, as Akash approached, the pungent smell of pink rose bushes overwhelmed him. He crept across the courtyard, camouflaged by the grime and dust that had become his natural attire. It was the best and worst decision he had ever made.

As he peered through the glass, a maid with flour in her hair kneaded dough for roti. A baby slept in a basket, wrapped in a deep orange swaddling blanket despite the heat. Nearby, a young woman in an embroidered salwar kameez, perhaps twenty years of age, sat in a rocking chair. At the table, a man read a newspaper, his dirty bare feet in contrast to the sterile extravagance of the floor tiles. From time to time, he looked up to speak to the woman by the baby. Then an older woman entered the kitchen and Akash's stomach lurched as if he was riding a ramshackle fairground ride.

"Forgive me, Jaya," he whispered.

He recognised Soraya before she turned. His mouth fell open in shock and his heart thundered. The hair on the back of his neck rose in anticipation. His chest constricted as he caught her in profile.

She stood taller than the average Indian woman. She pushed her shoulders back with pride and her sari pulled tautly across her body in haughty dismissal of accepted styles for older women.

As she turned towards him, Akash's head emptied for a moment before an explosion of unwarranted thoughts filled its cavity. *Is this my chance at happiness, Jaya? I wish I could be someone else. Someone without my history. Someone cleaner, fitter, richer, more deserving. The old me.* His legs shook, and he flailed as his feet became tangled in the fairy-lights, falling against the pane of glass with a dull thud. For a moment he held his breath, considering himself lucky.

Then all hell broke loose.

"*Yeh kya hai?* Maa, call the guards! Muna, stay inside with the baby!" shouted the man as he grabbed a flour-covered rolling pin from the kitchen worktop and dashed out of the room.

Akash staggered up, held captive by the almond-shaped eyes of his former lover for a long moment before stumbling back into the shadows on feet that didn't want to do his bidding. She couldn't have recognised him. Relief replaced his shame at his sad state. He ran, his legs weighted as though submerged in tar, passing landscaped gardens and a swimming pool. He headed for the street, still reeling from the sight of her, and made it onto the gravel drive before the man even reached outside. His pursuer fought against the humidity, slow and heavy, cursing as the gravel slowed his bare-footed progress. Glee bubbled up inside Akash as if from a dormant volcano, uncontrollable and unwelcome. He imagined the story he would tell Tariq. Joy at finding a link to his past threatened to send every other emotion into the stratosphere.

He had to get away. Experience taught him the rich were the most vengeful if they caught him. Like gods in their palaces, with iron-wrought fences, sleeping guards and noisy dogs to keep them safe, they rose up in squawking outrage at their pillaged sanctity. Fat, manicured men, with great wealth and photo-ready families, belonging to the ranks of the privileged few in a city where the streets teemed with the god-forsaken. This one continued his cries of outrage as he chased after Akash, driven on by his anger and hatred.

The guards, woken by their master's shouts, unleashed their snarling hounds. Akash screamed when a large dog, its fur ravaged, sank decaying teeth into his bare leg. Fear filled his belly at last, like a serpent unfurling and stretching deep within him. The young man from the kitchen caught up to him and the men surrounded him, their eyes filled with self-righteous anger. Vice-like they gripped his forearms, paying no heed to the dogs still snapping at his legs. An outbuilding with dimmed lights nestled in bushes a few hundred yards away. There they made their way as Akash's leg bled and bruises sprang up beneath his skin as if he were an ageing piece of fruit.

He had grown accustomed to this dance. There would be no police: sweet relief. The beating he'd receive would render him unrecognisable, even from his Soraya's eyes. This amounted to a small mercy. Having looked for her, Akash no longer knew what he wanted, whether he could betray Jaya's memory in this way. He knew what would happen now. He would become the outlet for his tormentors' collective rage. They'd guard him selfishly, unleashing their fury until they decided to free him. When it was over, they would nurse their bloodied knuckles with satisfaction and retell the story of this night a thousand times, earning praise from their listeners for the justice they delivered. When the surge of power and pride left their slackening bodies, it would be replaced by seeds of shame, but only in the best of them. Either way, Akash would return to the pink-rose bungalow as soon as his body healed. His self-destructive nature knew no other way.

So it began. Like countless times before, Akash gave himself over to reverie as the men did their worst, but this time his ageing memories of his Soraya intertwined with the ones he had just made. He let himself see her soft body through the vibrant blue of her sari. He breathed a sigh of relief. Jaya might be dead, but Soraya was alive and well. He consoled himself with this as the blows rained down on him.

The men found their rhythm.

It did no good to fight back and Akash took the punishment gladly, not for the crime he had committed by trespassing, but as penance for that ill-fated day long ago when the fire had engulfed Jaya. His blood tasted salty on his lips as they took it in turns to pummel him.

The men grunted from exertion. One struck him with a slipper, and the slap of the leather made Akash groan. The young man from the kitchen lashed out silently, his expression grim. A rib cracked with the ease of glass.

Akash curled up into a ball on the cool stone floor, screwing his eyes shut while he waited for the flurry of punches to stop. He heard a belt-clasp being unfastened and braced himself for the impact.

Stillness filled the room.

A rustle of silk reached his ears.

Akash kept his eyes clenched shut, too afraid to open them.

# 12

**Firoz paced the** room, taking care to avoid creaky floorboards, stopping to provide encouragement to one student and advice to another. He paused by Jaya's easel.

"You're quiet today," he said, interrupting her train of thought.

She had been conjuring up images of Akash, Soraya and their son. The interruption blew one such image out of her mind in which Akash sat with his family around a dinner table while Soraya fed her toddler squares of torn chapati.

"I'm always quiet," said Jaya. Blue paint had tinged the pads of her fingers.

"We've known each other long enough. Your spirit is compressed today. Your energy still."

"Any other revelations you have for me?" said Jaya. Her attempt to sweep up her tumbling thoughts with the strokes of her paintbrush had obviously not worked.

Firoz was a yogi, in his sixties, very new age. The type of man who rose at dawn for his sun salutations and stopped painting to contort his body into different shapes. Pupils here learnt not to bat an eyelid when he did downward dogs, tree poses and cat cows in the middle of class. With his long ponytail, harem trousers and loose shirt, he was always yoga-ready.

After all these years, she still found peace in this art studio. Her skill had progressed, and she no longer needed guidance. She continued to come for the sense of community she found here, the freedom. She could have painted at home, but it felt good to cocoon her art away from her mother's lip curls, to have a home away from home. Being here healed her. Some weeks, Firoz didn't even take payment from her. They had become friends. The payment he did accept subsidised materials: paints, canvases, the steaming chai he prepared for students at the end of the class. She found ease in their shared passion and her friendship with him.

"I love this game. You tell me my quirks, I tell you yours. Where would you like me to start?" Firoz teased. When she did not respond as playfully as she might have done, he squeezed her shoulder, moving to her side to consider her canvas. "Who is this fine man?" he asked.

She had discarded a landscape she had started, of the outlook from Bandstand across the Arabian Sea, a recurrent theme of hers. Instead, a face emerged from beneath the swirls of her paintbrush, made up of monochrome blues.

Firoz knew her work. He had noticed her talent for life drawings in particular. At the beginning, she had often painted self-portraits. Initially, they had been dark, painted in blacks and greys, her face either in profile or distorted. Over time, her catalogue had grown, and as the years progressed she had realised her colour palette had evolved, becoming brighter. This latest painting presented a regression of sorts.

She had drawn Akash, too, hundreds of times.

The face before them was new for Firoz, just as it was for Jaya. She transcribed it from the picture she saw when she shut her eyes, the image that floated under the nebulous pink of her half-closed eyelids. This likeness proved tough for her to do justice to. She had seen Soraya and Akash's son only once, after all.

"He has your eyes."

Jaya resisted the urge to swipe her paintbrush across her work. It wouldn't do to bring drama into this calm space. She took a deep breath and examined her work. Had she really inserted herself into the picture?

She kept her voice steady and light, baiting him, taking the opposite view to the lectures he gave his students, the ones she had heard a thousand times over. "Oh, to be a computer scientist rather than an artist; to find wonders in binary code rather than the convolutions of life."

"That's why we are artists, Jaya, to see the world in all its colours," said Firoz, his voice gaining volume as he turned their private conversation into fodder for the class. "And to choose which shade represents us. Painting is about perspective, after all."

He addressed the class, his eyes shining. "How lucky for us that we are Indians!" The class tittered, looking towards the white girl in the corner of the room, the one from Spain with basic Hindi. The Spaniard watched Firoz, riveted, a bright tie-dye scarf wrapped around her neck. He smiled at her apologetically, his hands waving in a flourish as he continued. "Do you ever wonder why there are so many artists, singers, and dancers in our culture? Why every Indian is a poet? It is because our culture, our traditions, suffocate us. Our duties confine us. And so, creativity becomes a conduit. It frees us, allowing us to understand ourselves and others better."

The class, many long-time attendees, listened respectfully. They had heard variations of this theme before, and Firoz's energy captivated them more than his observations.

His reflection swam in the window behind him.

"This need to understand led to the invention of language, of alphabets, of arranging sound into music, of putting colour on a canvas. What we paint here does not have one meaning. Art is complexity, ambiguity. It has unstable and multiple meanings. It is unmaking and remaking. It is creating anew." Firoz clapped his hands together, two staccato beats. "Okay. That's all for this week. Finish what you're doing, clean up and join me for chai."

After the pupils had gone, Jaya helped Firoz tidy away the bronzed tea urn and chipped cups.

"That was quite some speech," she said. She loved him for his ability to divert her from the darkness she contained.

"I meant every word." Firoz chuckled. "Besides, you know me. I love being the centre of attention."

"I hadn't guessed." A wry smile twisted Jaya's lips.

"I'm not blind you know. Are you going to tell me what's bothering you?"

She wiped her hands on a dish cloth and impulsively hugged him. They were over fifteen years apart in age and he had become a father figure to her. Even so, she didn't want to vocalise what had been bothering her. Saying it out loud would make it real. She didn't want to believe that Akash was playing happy families with another woman, that he had stolen a future that should have been hers. That he stayed with Soraya when he walked away from her.

She drew away from him, rebuilding the wall that only Firoz and Ruhi could scale, if only briefly. "Ghosts from my pasts, that's all."

"You can overcome anything."

Jaya tilted her head to tip the curtain of her hair forward. "Can we really overcome our pasts?"

"I'm certain of it. We can't change the past, Jaya, but we can move beyond it. Just as flowers overcome by weeds sometimes need to find another route to sunlight." His eyes pierced hers and in the bright studio light, it was almost too much. "One thing I do know. There is no escape from our demons without self-love."

"I love myself, Firoz." She met his eyes bravely, though inside she shook.

His smooth baritone was infinitely gentle. "I'm glad. Without self-love, all else disintegrates."

The opening of the new play at Tara Theatre had been scheduled for a week's time. Jaya fought the temptation to call in sick to avoid Ravi. The costumes would not be ready in time if she did and Jaya couldn't deny her sense of duty. The first day, she snuck into work, remained at her desk and felt eyes boring into her back even when she was alone. She wondered if her outburst had ruined the sanctuary she had created for herself at the theatre. Perhaps here, too, people would gossip about her. She realised that, for the most part, Ravi had been a victim of her heightened emotions; Soraya and her son were the cause of her upset. Her embarrassment peaked when she remembered Ravi had seen beneath the folds of her skirt. Still, this was work, after all, and the theatre was too small to harbour overt animosity.

The second day, she went into warrior mode: a vibrant, emerald green salwar kameez with a tulip skirt over silk trousers, a slash of orange lipstick, and thick kajal swooping upwards from defiant eyes.

She entered the theatre, bringing a sound wave of spluttering vehicles with her. She stood up straight and pushed back her shoulders, determined to lance the boil and get on with her day. In the practice room, Ravi, a sound and lighting technician, conversed with a group of actors.

"Hi everyone," said Jaya.

He turned, a flash of mustard yellow on top teamed with green trousers. "Oh, hi."

"Can I speak to you for a second?"

"Sure," he said. To everyone else, "I'll be right back."

They moved to the side of the stage.

A cursory apology fell from Jaya's lips. "I'm sorry about the other night."

"That's okay." He nodded and made to move away, then changed his mind. "For what it's worth, what happened the other night—when you fell—it didn't change my mind about you. I didn't want you to be embarrassed. I was trying to be a gentleman. That's why I didn't look. Don't blame me for what happened."

Jaya sucked in her breath.

"Are you going to tell me what it was really about?" His eyes were flecked with green. "Is it something to do with those boys, the ones who said those ugly things? They were kids." He leant closer. The stench of coffee swirled up from his breath, making the air stale between them. "I'd like to know your story, Jaya, if you'd like to tell me."

Jaya listened to the faint voice inside herself, the one almost drowned out by shame and dispassionateness for this man she had almost written off. The voice she paid little regard to, the one that made her weak instead of strong. Ravi had surprised her with his understanding, with his tenacity in the face of her hostility. For the first time since Akash left, Jaya found her body reacting to another man. She flushed, her reluctance to engage wavering.

She smiled at him. "Thank you for your graciousness," she said.

He caught her eyes and smiled back, and a small part of Jaya healed.

For the second time, Jaya disobeyed the rules of female propriety and agreed to go for a lunchtime walk with Ravi. Strangers, had they known their circumstances—that she and Ravi weren't bound by family ties—would look upon them with suspicion for spending time together alone. Jaya pushed the thought aside. Indians were a conservative group, their behaviour dictated by traditions, quick to police the morals of others. She knew she should be wary, but she felt an invisible tug towards Ravi. He had not rejected her although she had given him every reason to. When he asked for her story, a part of her had opened. She felt *seen* rather than pushed aside; she had even forgotten about Akash for a moment. Akash had been her silent partner for so long, she hadn't known that was possible. She wanted to chase that freedom.

A walk suited her. The theatre quickly became airless. Pounding the streets would clear the cobwebs in her mind. Besides, she preferred it to sitting face to face from Ravi across a table. She didn't want to feel exposed. Jaya had suddenly become more aware of how her appearance might come across to the opposite sex. For years, she had dressed for herself, and this sudden desire to impress Ravi reminded her strongly of her youth, when she and Ruhi had tittered together over the boys they saw but barely spoke to. The change to her emotional status quo flustered her. Her thoughts ping-ponged around her head. She didn't even trust her instincts that this could be more than a friendship.

She was older, married, washed up.

He had youth to offer and was unburdened.

The road wound past bistros and street vendors, newsagents, electronic and entertainment shops plastered with posters of India's stars. Ravi waited while she pressed a handful of rupees into a beggar's hand. The woman beamed through a face slicked with sweat and grime. They continued, an unresolved cloud of questions hanging in the air as they meandered, a gap of two feet between them.

Jaya filled the pregnant pauses with chatter.

"Things change so fast. My parents still have a huge record and video collection. New-fangled technology is not for them."

"I like the scratch of the needle against old records. It reminds me of my childhood. It's what first interested me in sound. It's why I do my job," said Ravi.

His shoes clipped the pavement, his gelled hair static despite the breeze. Jaya wondered what he would look like if she styled him. A breeze whipped her curls up and over her face. She held them back, turning to him as he addressed her.

"Don't we live in the best city in the world?"

"I wouldn't know," she said. "I've only left India once. We went to Nepal by train and bus. I liked seeing my parents outside of their familiar surroundings but the journey was so long even my sister was ratty. My parents missed their home comforts."

Her honeymoon with Akash had been in Goa. She shook her head to expel the memories of herself sitting primly on the beach in her sundress, burrowing her toes into the white sands, whilst Akash plunged into the surf. If she had known her future, she might have felt differently about showing off her body.

"You've never been on a plane?"

"No," she said. She only had one stamp in her passport. "How about you?"

"I've travelled. London, Bangkok. Last year, America."

"Did you like it?"

"Honestly? I liked the idea of New York. The Statue of Liberty was great, Central Park, these amazing stores." His brows furrowed as he dug into his memories. "Macy's, where a wave of perfume hits you. Ground Zero, this empty expanse of sorrow. Coney Island with its amusement parks. Manhattan, this hub of capitalism—the stock exchange is there. I went with my brother. We took a lot of pictures. But something was missing for me."

"What was?" Jaya liked seeing the world through his eyes. Usually she travelled only through the plays and novels she read.

They stopped at a traffic light to cross a road back to the theatre. The ghost of a hand print hovered against the small of her back, barely touching her. She was tempted to mould herself into it, but in the end, she arched away, startled by her instinctive reaction, the beat of her heart irregular as her pulse sped up. She knew relief at her resistance. Had she submitted, Ravi might have taken her for a hussy.

"Oh, I don't know. I missed India," he said as they started across the street. "In America, there were world-class restaurants, but people didn't even hold the doors open for each other. It was more than that, though. I missed the sense of being connected to my environment, of family values. We were anonymous there. Alien."

"You want to belong," said Jaya, struggling to make herself heard over the honking of cars.

"Doesn't everyone want to find their place?" said Ravi.

"I'm not sure. I like being alone."

They had reached the theatre. Their half an hour together had raced past. Ravi pushed his body against the heavy glass door to the theatre and held it open for her. She brushed past him and they lingered in the empty lobby.

"You know, it took you a while coming out of your shell with me."

Jaya glanced at her feet. The lobby had suddenly become a too intimate space. "You must have other friends. Why did you persevere?"

"Isn't it obvious?"

She recognised this dance that suitors did. It echoed back at her from her past, from romance novels and films. She mulled over the words and a frisson of pleasure rippled up her spine. Even so, she didn't trust herself. She had accepted, a long time ago, that romance didn't lie in her cards. Not anymore. She needed to hear Ravi spell out what was happening, if this was more for him than a passing dalliance. She didn't want scraps of love; she wanted the real thing.

"It's not obvious to me," said Jaya.

"I like puzzles," he said.

His response insulted her. Jaya drew back, creating a stranger's distance between his body and hers.

Ravi noticed. He held out his hands to her, but she left them there, hovering in the air.

"That came out wrong," said Ravi. "I didn't mean it the way it sounded. You want to know my intentions, is that it?"

That word sounded like a gong in Jaya's head, a warning symbol, a starting shot in the age-old contract of man and wife. Intention, betrothal, marriage. She see-sawed. She couldn't go through all that again. *Akash, where are you?* Her stomach heaved. There was one thing that had been her protection all these years, the final defence if her heart started to open.

"There's something you should know," she blurted out. "I'm married."

# 13

"**Arjun, take the** men and go inside. You are finished here," said Soraya. "We will speak of this later. Now leave us be."

Her voice left him awash with memories, but still Akash did not glance up.

"I won't leave you with him," said the man called Arjun.

"Go."

"We'll wait outside. Call if there is anything. I'll hear." Leaden footfalls scuffed the floor as they moved away from him. A slamming door told him they were alone.

"It's been twenty years since we have seen each other, Akash."

A tremor marred her voice. Akash crouched with his head bowed, a swollen mess of jutting bones and thick, oozing blood. He flushed hot with humiliation as he opened his eyes and his vision adjusted to the gloomy light. She had disarmed him by using his name. This moment, on his knees, bloodied and trapped, caught between desire and fear—named by the woman who'd been the catalyst for his shame—became the pinnacle of his powerlessness.

"Have you nothing to say to me?" Soraya grasped his chin with clumsy fingers, forcing Akash to hold her gaze.

His pulse quickened, drowning out the sound of her voice.

Her breath warmed his face, transporting him back to another time and place when they were lovers.

"How is it that you suddenly reappear, like a common Peeping Tom at my window? You, who left that day from the rose garden, convinced of your love for me, and never came back." Her sari brushed against his knees and she let go of his chin in disgust. "You look as if you have come back from death itself."

"Soraya." Her name tripped off Akash's tongue more easily than his own.

Rusty lipstick stained her lips, and he watched, entranced, as her frown lines deepened. His fingers twitched with the need to trace the emotions playing out on her face. He almost tasted their reconciliation, but underneath, guilt churned in his gut. "I had to leave. There was no going back. Not after what happened."

"You didn't even say goodbye. You gave no thought to me when you left."

Soraya's vulnerability took him by surprise. Years had dissolved like salt as he came to terms with Jaya's death. Eventually, fantasies of Soraya had threatened to seep through the wall of loneliness he had built around himself, but he could not have conceived of the messy humanness of their reunion. He remembered her as strong, ambitious and contrary. She embodied everything his wife did not. He took his courage in both hands and looked at her closely as he considered his answer, moved by the paper-thin translucency of her skin and the wrinkles threading their way around her face.

"You were strong. I didn't worry about you, but I did yearn for you. You were never truly mine, Soraya. I did not deserve happiness, and when I decided I wanted more for myself, it was too late. I had made the streets my home. I couldn't find you. I had begun to wonder if you were a figment of my imagination, made up of mists and magic rather than flesh." The words slithered off his tongue, the truth diluted. He hid that even now, doubled over before his ex-lover, it was Jaya he remembered.

"What is it you want from me, Akash?" Soraya stood unmoved.

He no longer knew what he wanted. His thoughts turned like a piece of driftwood on the choppy ocean. What had he been chasing all these years? "I want to know that you are happy."

"Liar," she said, her voice a whisper.

His cheeks flushed with heat.

The door to the outbuilding swung open. Soraya pushed herself up and away from him, leaving him to shrink back into the corner of the room. Akash's pursuer, the man she called Arjun, entered from the darkness outside. It occurred to him with a start how physically similar they were: willowy bodies, fine hair, pronounced cheekbones. This was Soraya's son.

"Maa, enough of this foolishness. Go and rest. Let me deal with our intruder," he said, looking at Akash with disgust.

"You will apologise, Arjun. I know this man," Soraya said, her face colouring with displeasure. "Take Akash Saheb to the Red Room to get cleaned up."

Akash glanced up in surprise, startled at the term of respect, the courtesy Soraya had chosen to show him in the face of her son's anger.

She continued her scolding of Arjun. "Shame on you! You're lucky he hasn't asked for the police. How would we explain that you took it into your hands to play God tonight?" To Akash she said, distant and formal, "My son has hurt you and for that I am sorry. If it's acceptable to you I will ask my neighbour — a doctor — to examine you, and tend to your abrasions myself."

Akash nodded his agreement. He craved human touch. He searched her features to see if he could find any of the love she once felt for him there, but her face had hardened into a blank canvas.

Soraya turned and walked into the moonless night. He could see now how frail her shoulders had become beneath her sari blouse. The need to protect her overcame him, but he followed her son.

Arjun led Akash through the house. The young man's suppressed anger radiated from beneath his skin. They passed a myriad of rooms and Akash lost his bearings as the central corridor of the house twisted this way and that. Heavy chandeliers and sumptuous sofas lurked behind half-closed doors. Eventually, the cool marble hallway ended at an oak door unlike the rest, with ornate markings on the wood and a thick-set lock. Arjun showed him into a room of the deepest red filled with the sickly scent of incense sticks, and took his leave without a word.

After living under the open sky, the opulence of his surroundings oppressed Akash. He had entered the underbelly of a serpent. He did not belong in this room with its draped silk curtains and mountainous bed. He caught sight of his bruised and bloodied appearance in a gilded mirror, touched a gash on his cheek and winced. Nausea rose like a wave through his stomach until he retched.

He took off his dirty shirt and mopped the blood from his face. Fragments of furious whispers reached him through the walls. Part of him wished to escape even now, back to Tariq and what he knew. After some time, Soraya entered the room. Akash sucked in his breath, dazzled by her, this phantom of his past. *Have I really found my way back to love?* An older man followed Soraya, their interaction easy with familiarity.

"This is my neighbour, Akash, Dr. Mittal," she said. "Subash Saheb, this is Akash."

Soraya left while the doctor checked him over, peeling back his bloodied, worn clothes, tutting at his crumbling teeth and emaciated frame. He checked Akash's blood pressure, held a cool stethoscope to his hot chest, noting the protruding rib cage. He examined the bruises and cuts on Akash's skin, shaking his head in silent censure. Eventually, he touched Akash's leg, where the bone had healed badly from an old injury. Akash sat, embarrassed by and unused to the scrutiny.

"You have two broken ribs, but you will live. Take plenty of rest, eat well, try not to get into any more trouble." He gave Akash a stern look, picked up his medical kit and left the room.

When the doctor had gone, Soraya returned with a saucepan of warm water, a rag and a small bottle of ointment. Akash sat on the bed while she cleaned him with hot, salty suds that stung.

"Thank you for asking the doctor to come," said Akash.

"I remember when we first met. There was nothing you would not do for me," said Soraya.

She swabbed his cheek with the cloth. The pain was bittersweet. He did not complain. Instead, he examined her as she worked, taking pleasure in the attention he received. Dirt and blood mingled in the saucepan at his feet. At last, she finished.

"Do you think of Jaya often?" said Soraya.

"She is always there."

She. Even unspoken, her name hung around his neck like a millstone. He could hear the part of his consciousness that had become Jaya's voice scolding him for being here with Soraya, but hadn't he punished himself enough? The thought of another chance at love intoxicated him.

"I am sorry, Akash, about what happened to her. She lit the match, not you."

He didn't want Soraya's sympathy for him to come at the expense of compassion for Jaya. He had not protected her in life. His displeasure reared up, scalding her. "I drove her to it! She lit that match because she blamed herself for my faults. She gave everything of herself to me. And I did nothing, nothing except give my love to you. I walked away while she still burned. What kind of man does that?"

Soraya stood up. She'd paled compared to the woman in his memories, her skin a sickly sherbet colour in the dim light.

He wished he had kept his composure.

"Did you ever see her again?" said Soraya.

"Her father sent me away. It was too late."

Soraya looked deep into his eyes, as if she were trying to capture his soul. "I never wanted your marriage to fail," she said.

"Maybe it was you I should have married," said Akash. Giving voice to the words were a betrayal of his wife. Even in death he abandoned Jaya. The gash on his cheek throbbed.

Soraya hesitated and he sensed she was holding something back, but she said, "We can't change the past."

He persevered, anxious to find out the information that mattered most to him. "Are you happy, Soraya? Is there a man in your life?"

"I have no need for a man, Akash. I have riches more than I need. I have a son and a granddaughter. I am content."

"But are you happy?" He wondered if there was room for him in her life.

"Yes, I'm happy but there are always battles. Isn't that the thrust of life? Rest now. We can speak in the morning."

"I can stay here?" He thought of Tariq alone on the streets, but his body needed the rest. One night couldn't hurt, especially after so long. In the morning, he could return to Tariq, accompanied by the ghost of his wife and the loves he had squandered. "I don't deserve your kindness."

"Perhaps my prayers have been answered," she said. She held his gaze and for a delicious moment, Akash believed maybe he could be hers and she could be his again. "I will see you in the morning."

She turned and closed the door behind her, a sad smile nestling in the corners of her mouth.

He listened to the sound of her retreating footsteps, then stretched out gingerly on top of the bedcovers. He had longed for a reconciliation with Soraya, but unease crept forward from the edge of his consciousness. He drifted into a heavy sleep and encountered the familiar dream of Jaya with flames dancing above her head like lovers in a deathly embrace. When she turned around, he saw mournful eyes and flesh dripping from a charred face and realised it was not she, but Soraya who stood aflame before him.

# 14

**Akash woke aching** and disoriented. His body appeared colourful in the warm light of the morning, with deep greens, inky blues and red splotches joining to form new horizons on his skin, a brand-new country. The door to the bedroom stood ajar, and he wondered who had checked on him while he slept.

Someone, perhaps Soraya, had left a pile of clean clothes in the bathroom. He showered, savouring the privacy that appeared miles away from washing in the sea or in a public bathroom. The hot water rushed over his body, stinging his open cuts, sweeping away dirt and dust. Once he finished, he wiped himself with a towel, eager not to leave stains on the plump white cloth. He dressed in clean clothes that hung on his frame, and bent over the sink to gargle and rub the sleep from his teeth with his index finger. The scent of coconut shampoo clung to hair thinner than it had been in his youth. The strands hung limp and long, swept across his forehead and curled over the collar of his borrowed shirt.

A rustle outside the bathroom indicated he was no longer alone. For a moment, he fought an impulse to stay quiet and hidden in the sanctity of the bathroom.

"Akash?"

Soraya's voice jolted him into action. He fretted over what he should do with his soiled clothes and pushed them into a cupboard under the sink before opening the door.

She stood at the bedroom door, dressed in a salwar kameez the colour of over-ripe tangerines. The march of time had not stolen her beauty. A sweet smell of incense wafted around her as if she had just finished her morning prayers, but she had never been pious. She held a tray of steaming chai, papaya cut into small squares and fresh puri with mango chutney. He usually fended for himself. It humbled him that a woman would bring him food. She owed him nothing. The meal, laid out on elegant crockery, overwhelmed him.

"You look better. You found the clothes then?" she said.

"Yes, thank you."

"Did you sleep well? I'll apply more ointment to your wounds once you have eaten."

"It wasn't my injuries that disturbed my sleep," he said.

He wanted to pull back the layers of their subterfuge, but she ignored him and pressed on. "You must be hungry."

"Thank you for preparing this."

"It was our maid, Geeta."

He took the tray from her and sat on the bed, noticing the rumpled sheets and her nearness. He swallowed with difficulty, convinced she could hear every gulp. Salt from the puri found its way into the crease in the corner of his mouth and stung a cut nestled there.

The bed and food made him think of Tariq, alone on the streets. He turned to Soraya. "I appreciate all this." He gestured to the food, the room. "There is nothing I'd like better than to speak to you, but first, I need to check on my friend. Just a few hours. He'll be worried about me not being back." He picked up the cup and hurriedly drank his tea.

"My driver can take you to your friend later, don't worry," Soraya assured him.

His voice grew firm. "No, it has to be now. I'm sorry. We've only had each other. Tariq will think the worst. It's not far. I'll go on foot." He put the cup down and the chai sloshed over the edge, staining the bedclothes. He mumbled an apology, worried he seemed ill-mannered or, worse, ungrateful. He didn't want her to think any less of him, or for her welcome to shrink to nothing. He hesitated. "Can I come back to see you?"

"Of course. I'll tell the guards to let you come and go as you wish. I have one request, though." She pushed her hand through her hair. "Stay out of Arjun's way. He's still upset about yesterday. I'll talk to him."

Jaya tucked her nephew into bed, pulling the sheets up to his neck, and left a soft kiss on his forehead. At ten years old, he grumbled at the fussing from his aunt, but she treasured these moments of borrowed motherhood. Downstairs, Ruhi had placed some chai and sweet treats on the table.

"I heard him beg you for another story. Is he asleep now?"

"He will be soon. Love him. You don't know how lucky you are," said Jaya.

"Yes, I do. I think maybe when you have two, or three or four, you take it for granted. But with one, every moment is something to be treasured, because you don't get to do it again," said Ruhi.

"You could do it again you know."

Ruhi laughed. "Nah. All those sleepless nights? I need my beauty sleep. Besides, it was hard enough trying to get into my dance costumes after one pregnancy. You know what Maa says—you gain a fist on your waist with every child."

Jaya sank into a chair and swept up some imaginary crumbs from the smooth surface of the table. She enjoyed being in Ruhi's apartment; it was more modern than the house she shared with her parents. "She always tells me I turned her into a whale. Of course, she was a ballerina when she was expecting you."

"Ah Jaya, you're in each other's pockets all the time. You know she tries to wind you up. Papa's getting weaker by the day. I really see his age now. Were they offended you came here?" Ruhi broke a corner of a caramelised almond square and placed it in her mouth. It crunched as she chewed.

"Oh, they're re-watching an old classic. They'll be fine tonight." Jaya recognised how easy it would have been for their sisterly bond to fall victim to their mother's petty attempts to play them off against each other. She didn't want to waste their evening talking about their mother. Just as she didn't want to fill in her sister about Soraya and the man she suspected to be Akash's son. The knowledge sat uncomfortably on the cusp of her tongue, like a paper cut on the fleshy part of a thumb.

Ruhi chattered on, oblivious to Jaya's train of thought. "They'll sulk later, though," she said. She brightened up. "Still, it's not often we get to do this. I like having you to myself."

Spending time with Ruhi always lifted Jaya's spirits. However much she loved her nephew and her brother-in-law, she treasured these rare moments of Ruhi's undivided attention. She didn't have to pretend in their relationship. There was immediate intimacy; it was liberating to disengage from the polite dances of social need. Here, there were no storms to weather, just acceptance, and she loved Ruhi fiercely for it.

She liked to think that even if she and Akash had survived, their heterosexual marriage would have come secondary to this sisterly bond, that somehow, her relationship with Ruhi would remain pure, beyond corruption. It struck her as infinitely sad when women erased their common history over a perceived slight or out of sync expectations. It gladdened Jaya that she and Ruhi had been strong enough to withstand petty jealousies, that they had created room in their relationship for differing points of view and personalities. Over the years, she had determined that she and Ruhi shared a profound love story of their own, one that orbited above the drama and betrayal of romantic relationships.

That was why she blurted the words out without meaning to, an ejection of truth when she had intended to keep her paranoia secret. "I had a shock the other day. I've been meaning to tell you. I saw Soraya."

Ruhi put her tea down with a clank. "*The* Soraya?"

"I'm sure of it. She owns a restaurant in Juhu. I recognised her straight away. And her son."

"She's married?"

"I don't know. But, Ruhi, the son. He looked like Akash."

Ruhi froze, and then she picked herself back up. "You can't think that—"

"What else am I supposed to think?" Too often Jaya felt like the younger sister in this relationship, the clueless one, when she longed to be the guide, the lioness.

Ruhi pooh-poohed the suggestion with a wave of her hand. "You've been through a lot. It's just your imagination working overtime, putting two and two together, making five. Just put it out of your mind, okay?"

She was right, of course. What good did it do to dwell? Akash had made his choice. However great the temptation to return to the restaurant, to follow the threads back to Akash, how could she force a man to stay with her if he didn't want to be there?

A moment passed in silence.

Jaya watched her sister struggle to inject light-heartedness back into their conversation. Ruhi pushed stray bits of hair into her topknot. They escaped again immediately so she blew them off her face and picked up her tea. The mystery of Soraya and her son sat between them like an elephant in the room.

"So, tell me then? Who's this Ravi I've heard you mention a few times?" said Ruhi, waggling her eyebrows up and down.

Jaya laughed. She couldn't help herself. "You look ridiculous doing that."

"Ha! You avoided the question. Now I know you've got something to hide!"

Jaya's cheeks coloured. "He's just someone from work. What are you talking about anyway? I'm forty-five years old. I'm hardly going to start looking for a Romeo now, am I?"

"Well you know how I feel about it. It'd be good for you to live a little, to have someone look after you for a change. Have some fun, yaar!"

"I'm not going to be throwing my knickers about, if that's what you mean!"

"So he *is* more than a friend." Ruhi's face lit up with glee.

Jaya relented. "Maybe. But I ruined it."

Ruhi waved her hands impatiently. "That can wait. What's he like? Is he Hindu?"

"Yes. But young. And not that handsome. But kind."

"Young? Go, sis! A little bit handsome then?" Ruhi beamed. "And kind, kind is good. Kind you can work with."

"Aren't you forgetting something?" said Jaya. "I'm still married."

She watched Ruhi's crinkled laughter lines disappear and solemnity steal into her eyes. "You deserve this. Forget about Akash. It does not have to be forever, but you deserve this. Take it, Jaya."

Akash made his way through the twisting corridors out into the open. Being under an open sky again relieved him. He had found the luxury of Soraya's house oppressive after years of living on the streets. How surreal to walk away from her just after they had found each other again. He wanted to sit down with her and unravel the years. That would have to wait. Tariq needed him. Their shared experiences made their bond stronger than biological ties or romantic love.

He resisted the urge to run past Soraya's guards in their sheltered outpost. Yesterday he'd been an intruder; today, an invited guest. Still, his adrenalin surged as the men trained their eyes on him, disgruntled. The dogs growled. True to her word, Soraya had relayed her message. Akash passed them without incident, his heart hammering in his throat.

Once on the roadside, he glanced down at his too-big clothes, ran a finger through his freshly washed hair. Tariq wasn't going to believe his luck. He skipped along feeling foolish, his step light, eager to spill his story to his friend. He stopped at the railway bridge first, where he had left Tariq the night before. He heard the raucous sound of men laughing before he turned the corner. Akash's anxiety spiked. He recognised one man's voice.

He sprinted toward them. Under the bridge, in between their scattered belongings, lay Tariq. Above him, with his foot poised to kick, stood Zahid Khan, his bald head gleaming. Behind him, making up a triangular formation, were workers from Zahid's restaurant, who doubled as his henchmen when he was up to no good.

"Stop!" said Akash, pushing his feet hard off the pavement in his efforts to reach Tariq quicker.

It was not enough. Zahid's kick exploded in Tariq's face, hitting his cheekbone. Tariq groaned, and wrapped his arms around his head in an effort to protect himself. The henchmen pulled him to his feet, pinning his hands behind his back, leaving Tariq's cheek to bleed freely.

"Leave him alone!" called Akash, almost there.

"Your friend comes to your rescue again," said Zahid. He tittered. "Or are you more than friends? I wouldn't be surprised, dogs like you." He raised his foot and took aim at Tariq's crotch. Tariq doubled over in pain and the henchmen allowed him to crumple to the ground.

Akash ran to his friend's aid, shoving the men away, using his own body as a barrier between Tariq and their aggressors.

"I was worried about you," said Tariq faintly.

Akash felt for a weapon on the ground behind him. His fingers found the handle of a saucepan. He focused his attention on Zahid and let the other men fade into the periphery. He could not take them all on. The saucepan was a back-up plan, not a trump card.

"What are you punishing Tariq for?" said Akash. He turned to his guardian angel. *Jaya, if you can hear me, help us.*

Recently, the run ins with Zahid had escalated. They no longer happened after chance encounters. Zahid was above action and reaction. He no longer needed an excuse to seek out a human punch bag. He took pleasure from it. The beatings he dealt out came in the form of surprise attacks, always with his henchman in tow, armed with steel-capped shoes or an iron bar. Zahid did it for fun, for stress relief, to make himself feel stronger. Vagrants just happened to be an easy target.

Akash knew Zahid well enough by now. The other man had no sense of perspective; there would be no bargaining with him. He hoped to buy time for Tariq to get to his feet. Usually Akash placed more value on Tariq's life than his own. Today, he noticed a change in himself, an extra alertness, a clenching in his own body that indicated he feared for his own safety, too. He could not jeopardise his life when he had just found Soraya. What would she think if he never went back to her?

"Do I have to have a reason to hit him?" said Zahid. "Don't think you're safe either. If the government won't clean up the streets and remove filth like you, I'll have to do it." He crowed at his men. "In service of the community, you know." They nodded, eager to please him. Zahid considered Akash, eyes narrowed. "What is it about you being a knight in shining armour anyway?" He swung back his leg, and pretended to kick, then rooted both feet back to the ground, his portly frame wobbling. "You have a death wish?" He looked closer. He laughed. "I see you've already had someone else's shoe in your face."

Behind Akash, Tariq tried to get up. Akash signalled for him to stay where he was. The henchmen had lost interest in the protracted conversation. One in particular kept glancing away, keen to move on. Zahid must have sensed the stage was so longer entirely his.

He shrugged. "I've done my exercise for the day. Stay out of my way." He drew his face close to Akash's, his breath hot. "You know, you smell different. You look different. Don't get above yourself, will you? Small men should know their place. Like women."

Akash's hand closed around the saucepan behind him, but this time it was Tariq who slowly unpeeled his friend's fingers from the makeshift weapon.

Zahid sauntered out into the light without a second glance.

Tariq lifted himself up. "That was close. You weren't going to attack him, were you? We would never have escaped. It's better to just take it. They always let us go eventually." He patted Akash's shoulder then pulled him closer, leaning against him before pulling back to touch his bleeding cheek. "Thank Allah you showed up, or thank the stars, I don't know."

Tariq's belief in Allah wavered, but was never entirely gone. It circled him. It ebbed and flowed in line with his despair and joys. Faith remained entwined with his upbringing. Tariq always mouthed a silent *shukar* before a morsel of food passed his lips.

Akash searched for a cloth in the disarray around him. He doused it with cooled, boiled water from a container they used. "What an arsehole," he said, handing Tariq the cloth to hold to his face. "And those brutes of his, following him around like strays."

"I'm just glad they left," said Tariq. He flinched as he dabbed at his cheek.

Whatever beauty Tariq had once possessed had fled long ago. The streets brutalised a man; they were lucky to be alive. He and Tariq had survived by looking after each other. It pained Akash that he had very nearly failed to uphold his side of the bargain. He had failed Jaya because of Soraya. He had almost failed Tariq for the very same reason. *How easily I forget, Jaya.* What if he hadn't come back in time? He resolved to do better.

"Where've you been anyway? I was worried," said Tariq. "Those aren't your clothes. And you've been hurt. Unless I passed out, Zahid didn't attack you. Who did? What happened?"

The wound on his face looked better now he had washed it, but it still concerned Akash. He sat down next to Tariq and stretched out his legs in front of him. He recognised every bump and crack in the uneven ground beneath him. Its characteristics had become as familiar to him as the lines on his palm, and comforted more than the plush environment of Soraya's home.

"I've been with Soraya."

Tariq's mouth gaped. "*The* Soraya? What? How?"

"I was walking—"

"Looking through windows again, you mean."

"Yes." Akash's brow clouded. Was it his search for Soraya that had driven his compulsion to look through stranger's windows? Had that demon been purged?

"You know how dangerous that is." Tariq motioned towards Akash. "Is that why you have those bruises and cuts?"

"It was her house, Tariq. Soraya's. She stopped them beating me, invited me inside. I didn't even trust my senses. She's hardly changed."

A whirlwind of emotions played on Tariq's face. "Is that what you came here to tell me? That you have found your long-lost lover, the one you cheated on your wife with, and that you're going back to her?"

Akash recoiled as if he had been slapped. Tariq rarely struck out. "I don't know if Soraya feels the same way." Neither did he know if he could ever forget Jaya. He didn't want to.

"You're so stupid." Tariq spat the words. They hung in the air, irretrievable, a spike in their friendship.

"I wasn't planning on abandoning you, if that's what you mean." Tariq's lack of support stung. Akash had grown tired of the emotional rollercoaster of the past few days. He could not understand why Tariq would be so argumentative unless his concerns centred on himself. "Can you only be happy for me when the chips are down? I've been looking for this woman for years."

"You think this is about me? All these years trying to understand what happened to you, Akash, and you're still so blind. The Soraya you have found, she was always the unattainable woman, the mistress, the goddess. Your love for her was nothing more than a sham. A get out clause for a little boy who was not ready to love fully."

Akash sprung to his feet, hovering above Tariq. "How dare you? Do brothers judge each other? I'm here for you whenever you need me." His fury ricocheted across the confines of their makeshift home.

"I'm your brother, Akash. I can only tell you what I see to be the truth."

"Nobody can know a man's heart, his intentions," said Akash. "The rest of the world may laugh and judge. They may gossip and theorise, but you can't know who I loved and who I did not."

"Tell me then. Who have you spoken to at the shore each night during your ablutions? Who do you pray to, Akash? Tell me that? Who has driven you to live on the streets all these years?" Tariq flung his hands up in exasperation. "You still can't see it, can you? Real as she is, Soraya is a mirage. It was Jaya you loved."

"She is *gone!*" The word reverberated around them, then plummeted, a stone in the language of men. Reborn grief stirred to life in Akash's stomach.

"Yes, she is," said Tariq, shaking his head. "And still you chase your own tail like a hoodwinked dog, as if you've learned nothing at all."

# 15

**Akash returned to** the bungalow. The guards let him pass as he entered. This time it seemed the pink roses clinging to the outside of the house were wilting, though only a day had passed. His argument with Tariq suppressed his joy, and he grew resentful that his reunion with Soraya could not be more joyous.

She welcomed him at the door with a half-smile and ushered him into the bowels of the house, back into the deep red room where he had spent the previous night.

"You were quicker than I thought you'd be. I thought you'd spend some more time with your friend," she said.

Her beauty took his breath away, and he made sure not to open his mouth too widely when he spoke, lest she caught sight of his yellowed teeth.

"He knows where I am. He's no longer worried."

"Good." She paused. "You weren't exaggerating when you said you'd made the streets your home. Your body is broken and not just from Arjun's beating. How did you survive?"

He hesitated, unsure of what to reveal. His hair fell into his eyes and he made no attempt to brush it aside. "Tariq and I met just after it happened. I'm not sure I would have survived alone." His sadness at their quarrel lay like a knot at his core. He needed to make things right. He continued, haltingly. "We have our routines. Our safe places. It turns out I'm quite a good handyman. We work odd jobs. Rubbish disposal. The smell lingers in my nostrils long after I finish. Loading or unloading for grocery shops or hotels. Hanging up signs for businesses. The sort of jobs you don't need papers for. Afterwards they press a few rupees into your hand. Show enough gratitude and they are pleased to see you another day."

"What happened to the teaching degree?"

"I never went back."

"And your life is enough for you?" Here, in the luxury of her home, the differences between them couldn't be greater.

"I fantasise sometimes about what could have been. I talk to Jaya in my head. I have Tariq." He had lost count of the number of drifters he had made friends or enemies with, lone men and women passing through. Sometimes, they found their feet in some kind of real life; more often, the streets sucked away their health and hopes. "Memories of you, of my younger self kept me going."

"Nonsense. Yes, you loved me, or perhaps the idea of me. But no one lives on air and memories. Twenty years you drifted. What did you eat? Where do you sleep?"

"Sometimes a man's history is better left hidden. You insist on knowing details that diminish me."

"A man is a man, despite the clothes he wears or the trophies on his shelves."

"If only that was true. You really believe that, Soraya?" He thought of Tariq and how he had been targeted by Zahid that morning. He thought of Arjun taking a free hand to beat him only yesterday. "There is no humanity left for a man, woman or child on the streets."

"I've witnessed the suffering. Even behind tall walls, I am not immune to it," said Soraya.

Akash wanted to please her, but he was unable to hold his tongue. He needed to pierce the bubble of her illusions, to make her understand how it had really been. "Most are. Beggars and the homeless, addicts and the mentally unsound, all lumped together, all distasteful or, worse, invisible."

The homeless were a familiar sight in Bombay. When the working day ended, and the revellers retreated, the street people became more visible. Whole families slept on roadside pavements, covered by light blankets. The better-equipped used rags or tarpaulin as meagre tents. They slept on handcarts and railway platforms, on the beach and in parks. They existed in the periphery of conscience. Luckier men preferred not to dwell on this seedy side of the city.

They suppressed their empathy or learned to unsee because it was easier that way.

"You slept in the open?" Her interest in him lanced a boil; he felt validated by it, as if he could displace his own demons by talking about them. Was this not love, this openness? Was this not what he had been looking for?

"We sleep under a railway bridge. Or on the sand. Not during monsoon. We find somewhere raised. The steps of a church or temple. We go back to the same places. For a time, we sheltered in the shell of an old rickshaw until a younger, stronger man took it for himself. Not even two of us were enough to win against him. Sometimes fire drives a man to succeed, even if he is all alone. You learn who to trust. One woman I knew used to be terrified she would be crushed by a tree unearthed by heavy rains, but that never worried me."

"How casual you have been with your life!"

Akash laughed. Bitterness cut through his voice. "Perhaps with myself. But never with others, not again. Not after Jaya. I still mourn Sonal, a three-year old on the streets, who got jaundice. She died from hepatitis—deteriorated before our eyes—because her mother could not afford the medicine she needed. I think about whole families who risk cholera by drinking dirty water. I've witnessed it so often. Or the men and women who do unspeakable things to obtain drugs. All because they are unable to face reality."

"And you? What is it you do, Akash? Do you poison your body with drugs?"

"No, but I don't blame those who do. You become an animal, defecating in a corner because basic sanitation is unavailable. In the early days, I drank. I slept days away because the oblivion of sleep erased my past. It erased my sense of self."

They had been talking to one another on the bed, chastely, metres between them. The intensity of the conversation drove Soraya up onto her feet, where she leaned against the window frame. She avoided his eyes as she asked, "Where did you wash?"

"Why worry about washing when I can't wash away the dirt from my soul?" The words spilled from his mouth before he could call them back. His stomach churned from the argument with Tariq, and now even this conversation with Soraya had been spoiled by the dirty secrets of his past. *Why am I here, Jaya? For love? For acceptance, or for redemption?* He made an effort to tame his harsh tone. "I washed in the sea. Sometimes I used a bucket, filled with dirty water. Who feels clean using dirty water for their ablutions, a mix of cholera, sweat and dust from the city?"

Soraya came to sit next to him on the bed. She placed her hand on his arm and warmth seeped into it, providing a balm for his sadness.

"You think it is another world I inhabit here," said Soraya.

"I don't resent your good fortune," he said, welcoming the opportunity to talk about her rather than himself. "I'm glad. You were always ambitious. Did you marry? You said there was no man in your life but your son—are you widowed?"

"There is no man in my life. None other than my son, at least. I had no wish to marry. The fortune I amassed is mine. My parents allowed me to invest the dowry they would have given me. I made a few good business decisions. I was patient. We now own a restaurant in Juhu and one in Bandra. We have loyal clientele, influential ones. If you have money, people are more willing to tolerate your uniqueness."

The nature of her success sank into his consciousness and left a bittersweet imprint. He admired her but on some level, it belittled him too. A businesswoman in India was not to be scoffed at; Akash had no doubt Soraya had fought tooth and nail to establish her name. Even if Tariq had been wrong, this love he wanted to resurrect had no chance. *Forgive me, Jaya.* Soraya had grown even more unattainable. He swallowed his feelings of inadequacy.

"I always admired your strength. I thought I could absorb it just by being near you. You brought up your son alone?" said Akash. Soraya retracted her hand, and the rough skin of his arm felt lonely without her touch.

"Yes. His father left a long time ago. Geeta, our maid, helped. Another girl in my position would have suffered. Money gave me freedom," she said. "And you, you've been alone all this time?"

"Yes, apart from Tariq. We've become like brothers," said Akash.

"You know, if you'd come to me, I could have helped you."

"I didn't go back. I couldn't face anyone, not even my parents." His face crumpled. "The shame paralysed me. I don't remember much from those first months. Eventually, I turned up on your doorstep, but you were gone."

"We moved," said Soraya, her voice trailing off. She ran her hand through her short, greying hair. "Why didn't you try harder to find me? Neighbours knew where we moved, friends, too."

"A man has his pride. And besides, it was my punishment."

She returned to the window, lengthening the distance between them before she opened her heart to him. Soraya, who always held on to her control. The early evening light shone through her sari, changing its colour to a burnished bronze. "Maybe I needed you."

Her focused on her words. They drove away the doubts Tariq had inserted into his mind. "Maybe our time is now," he said.

A weighted silence hung in the air between them. Soraya turned and her silhouette blotted out the sun behind her. "I've noticed you aren't wearing your wedding ring. Do you remember, you used to slip it into your pocket all those years ago?"

She had sidestepped his unspoken question. He needed to know what this amounted to. Time passed through the hourglass relentlessly and he had none to waste. He kneaded the base of his finger, where his wedding ring had once sat, confused as to why Soraya would ask about the ring. "I kept it on my finger after Jaya died. Is it a widowed man's duty to continue to wear his wedding ring? I don't know."

She looked at him aghast, like not wearing his wedding ring was a further betrayal of Jaya.

He took in the lines that furrowed her brow, and her censure smarted.

"In any case, it was stolen," he rushed to tell her. He had hated them for it, the brawling, thieving men who took it. He had fought to keep that link to Jaya, that emblem of fidelity and love he had not earned.

Soraya came towards him, searching his eyes for a truth she could not find. "You really don't know, do you?"

Akash recoiled, his heart pounded in the cavity of his chest. "Know what?" Even as he uttered the words, he sensed their terrible weight. The hazy light hid her expression, leaving him without anchor.

"You're not a widower, Akash. Jaya is not dead. She is very much alive."

# 16

**The performance at** Tara Theatre began at eight
pm. The audience piled into the cramped theatre, and, as usual, the
operational team doubled up as ticket assistants, welcoming guests and
showing them to their seats while the actors readied themselves. A
Jagjit Singh album played softly in the background, the unhurried
nature of his *ghazals* the perfect prelude to tonight's play, a gentle story
of sisterly love in rural India. It was Jaya's favourite script to date.

When the curtains opened, she sat at the back of the theatre on a
foldaway plastic seat. She had seen the play countless times during
rehearsal, but the first night in front of an audience made for a special
experience. The actors came alive on the stage, feeding off the audience's
attention. Everything progressed like a well-oiled machine, the seams of
reality hidden from view. Jaya revelled in the distilled truths of these
make-believe worlds, of complexities unravelled and laid bare.

Whereas once she would have remained still and focused on the
proceedings, tonight she could not help but fidget. Time and again she
peered into the sound and lighting booth, where Ravi worked
shrouded in shadow. She had not forgotten Ruhi's encouragement to
pursue a relationship with him, and try as she might to push thoughts
of Ravi into the recesses of her mind, they bubbled up to the surface.

Ravi would have to be both absurd and a glutton for punishment
if he still wanted anything to do with her. Jaya had told Ruhi as much,
as she sought to hide pangs of disappointment she did not quite
understand. She preferred hiding behind walls to the vulnerability of
romantic relationships. Inviting a man into her life would cause
nothing but trouble, so she resolved to redraw her boundaries, to take
joy from the familiar, and to banish anything alien.

Tonight's play reinforced her point of view; the themes found an unusual synergy with her life. Ordinarily, the plays performed at Tara centred on big loves, or on the most prized relationship in Indian culture, that of father and son. Traditionally in Indian story-telling the love between sisters came last, deemed less important than brotherly bonds, or the love between a mother and son. This play elevated the relationship between sisters and Jaya welcomed the parallels to her own life. She prized her relationship to Ruhi above all else. Though she could not deny she had some residual feelings for Ravi, murkily clouding her heart like silt on a riverbed, it pleased her to think the universe had aligned and sent her a message.

By the time the intermission came around, she had convinced herself that her dalliance with Ravi had been a blip, a close call, a reminder to maintain the distance that protected her from a broken heart. She decided to ensure he had no illusions that they could be anything more than friends when she next saw him.

As the audience filed out of their seats, she pushed her way to the front of the room and took up position by the stage to serve ice cream from a small cart: mango, caramel, pistachio and vanilla. Engrossed in serving her customers, she was startled by a hand at her elbow.

"You've been hiding from me," said Ravi.

Jaya's heartbeat raced.

Her own hateful body betrayed her by responding to him. She could not refute the physical impact he had on her. He only had to be near for her skin to prickle in response. What a foolish response, as if she were a teenager and not middle-aged.

"Just busy," said Jaya, struggling to keep her voice level. She returned change to an older woman wearing large yellow gold earrings and nodded her thanks.

Today he wore all black, as she did; their uniform for performances. A badge pinned to his shirt pocket, black etchings on silver, spelled out his name. Ravi Johar. Johar, a nice name: Sanskrit for 'jewel'. She shook her head to discipline her wandering mind.

"*Memsaheb*, a little quicker maybe?" said a man waiting for his ice-cream. Jaya scowled at Ravi and passed the man two tubs.

"I'll get out of your hair," said Ravi. He withdrew to the shadows while she completed her duties. Jaya's fingers became clumsy knowing he watched. After she'd served the last person in line, he approached again, standing closer to her than a stranger might have.

"You should have told me, you know." His eyes gleamed in the dim light.

She imagined green flecks dancing in their depths even though she could not see them.

*We couldn't be anything anyway.* The words hung on her lips, but instead of saying them, she said, "I'm sorry." She caught herself looking at his lips, the way his mouth curved slightly higher on one side than the other.

Around them, the audience returned to their seats, a quiet spreading as the shuffling and chatting eased.

Ravi whispered in her ear, a secret just for them. "I've tried to stop thinking about you."

Was he teasing her? She couldn't be sure. She could feel his breath on her ear, and, for a moment, she wondered what it would be like to turn her body into his, and let his strength envelop her. She heard Ruhi's voice in her head. *Give him a chance.*

"Can I... Can I walk you home tonight? We should talk," he said.

If only he had acted out of turn, shown himself to be mean-spirited or aloof or uninteresting, she could have withstood him. She teetered between her mental walls and her emotional needs.

"Okay." The word escaped her before she could apply the brakes. A tiny word of agreement that opened a door she tried so hard to keep shut.

"Great." The gelled black helmet of his hair receded from view as he made his way back into the sound booth.

She longed to feel the vibration of his voice in her ear again.

The moon was a luminescent orb above the city skyline when they left the theatre at midnight. Dust swirls reached up to greet Jaya and Ravi as they stepped onto the street in the city that never sleeps.

"I usually take the bus," said Jaya.

"We can share a rickshaw if you're tired," said Ravi.

"Let's walk the first part. I can't sleep straight after a show anyway. You'll have to go before we get to my door, though. My parents wouldn't like it and I wouldn't like the questions."

Ravi grasped her arm and pulled her to face him. The cars passing them blended into the periphery of her consciousness, periodic purrs with luminescent headlights that slid over Ravi's face as he talked.

"Why didn't you tell me you were married?" he said. "I was tempted to leave you alone, to retreat into friendship, but anyone I asked, there's been no mention of a husband, only your parents."

His intensity moved her. He had spoken to their colleagues about her. She mattered to him.

Jaya's confidence bloomed. She met his eyes, and let the scales of subterfuge fall away.

"I am married, Ravi, but he left me twenty years ago. He was unfaithful and I couldn't accept it. He never came back."

"Your scars?" She found no judgement in his eyes. The dark in her was drawn to the light in him.

"I set myself on fire the day I found out... I wasn't myself."

He drew in his breath. A nerve pulsed in his cheek. Then he folded her into his arms, there on the arterial road leading from Juhu to Bandra. "I knew you had a history. The marks on your body tell a story," said Ravi, speaking into the halo of her hair. She rested her head flat against his collarbone and felt the words rumble through his chest, a lullaby to soothe her. "He is gone then, and you are free."

Jaya melted into him, sinking into her knees so she could fit her head under his chin.

"I don't even know what we are," said Jaya.

"A promise. Nothing more. Nothing scary, or untoward. Just a promise."

# 17

**Soraya repeated her** words. "You're not a widower, Akash. Jaya is alive."

Akash sucked in his breath, retreating from his body, as if he were a spectator of his life rather than a participant. He retracted from the Red Room in Soraya's house, saw her at the window, noticed himself stock still, unspeaking, and then with a whoosh, his mind caught up with his present, and confusion swept all else into insignificance: Tariq; Soraya; Zahid; his lost family; his enemies and friends on the streets; the people who pretended not to notice him, day in, day out. All else became nothing. *Jaya, can this be real?*

"What do you mean, she's alive?" His voice came out as a stutter. "What do you mean? I saw her. I saw the flames. Her father told me she had gone. Those were his words. He meant she had died, I'm sure of it. I saw her mother weeping at Vishnu's statue, the burns on the floor. What are you telling me?" He shook his head, but still the familiar image of Jaya burning, the sound of her screams as the flames tore at her, tormented him, the violence of that act seared for perpetuity on his brain, like the imprint of a photo on polaroid.

"I spoke to her after it happened," said Soraya.

A sob ripped from Akash's throat. "She recovered?"

Soraya approached him from the window and crouched in front of him. Her tangerine scarf dropped from her shoulders and fell to the floor in a silken heap. He focused on it, counting the folds where it lay. Anything to pause the thoughts racing through his head, to bury the idea that the years of punishment he had imposed upon himself had been for nothing.

"She recovered." Hooded eyelids over exquisite eyes. "I hadn't thought of her in years. But I think she might have visited our restaurant the other night, right here in Juhu. Do you see now? Guilt has robbed you of all this time. Guilt far greater than anything you did."

He heard her words as if through a tunnel. He no longer processed them. *All this time, I've talked to you in my head, and you've been here in Bombay, Jaya.* He'd believed Jaya had died, her body now ashes, scattered in the holy river, in a ceremony he'd not been invited to, was not welcome at. He recalled her father's anger the night he had returned. *Jaya is gone. Jaya is no more. You are no longer welcome here.* Soraya couldn't be right. If she was, it would mean he and Jaya had never been more than a few miles apart. He had to find out the truth. *Are you alive?* The question echoed through his head. He needed to see her. He needed to replace his last image of Jaya with a truer one. He needed to check if she had really lived, what she had done with her life, whether she was happy. If she could come through her pain then maybe he could, too.

"What would you have done if you had known?" said Soraya.

Akash didn't respond, so she repeated herself, and it irked him that she couldn't see he needed space to process news of this magnitude.

He focused on her words, his answer slow and deliberate, bobbing up, crystal clear from the rattling depths of his mind, the result of decades of self-reflection that had not pierced the fog of his mind until now. He didn't care if he offended her. The words felt so true on his tongue he could almost touch them. "I would have stayed. I would have nursed her back to health. I would have loved her, and never have thought of you again." *I am coming, Jaya.*

"Why is that?" Soraya's words were cold, her expression tight.

"Because I didn't know love until Jaya showed me what it was."

Akash entered a topsy-turvy world where nothing was real and everything masked in clay that formed to make new shapes, shattering his certainties. He made no excuses to Soraya about the reason he needed to leave. There could be no course of action for him except to find out the truth.

Soraya asked only that he return.

Akash set out, his confusion a palpable ball of knots and electrical impulses at his core. He knew instinctively where his search for Jaya should start. Long ago he had mastered the geography of Bombay. He'd learned through trial and observation where he and Tariq could live in relative safety, where they could find protection from the elements, a level of privacy and sources of food. He possessed an intimate knowledge of the city's roads, its parks and waterfronts, its high-rises, mansions and slums, its hidden corners and secret passages.

There had been one pocket he avoided: the street in Bandra where he had been knocked into the gutter by Jaya's father, where her childhood home stood, where she had lit the match that changed the course of their lives. It could be that she no longer lived there, but as he made the pilgrimage to her house, he prayed with the faith of his childhood that the tortuous uncertainty would be short-lived and he would find a clue to determine the veracity of Soraya's revelation.

The sun had dipped from its highest point by the time he arrived in Bandra, signalling mid-afternoon. Tariq's words rang in Akash's head as he threaded his way through the city. *You still can't see it, can you? It was always Jaya.* He weaved through the throngs of shoppers already hunting for bargains on Hill Road, amongst dazzling displays of colourful bangles, ornate dresses, scarves and disco dresses. Waves of nausea rolled through Akash's stomach as he neared the side street where Jaya's parents' house stood.

Each step he took brought him closer to his reckoning. The nausea surge found a new high when he finally stood before the house. From the outside, there had been no change. It lay squeezed between two other dwellings, greying paint crumbling from its exterior walls. Dilapidated shutters framed the windows, just as they always had. It would have been sensible to wait until the cover of darkness to approach the house, when the streets had emptied somewhat, but Akash could not restrain himself. Every cell in his body needed to find out what happened to Jaya.

He looked around furtively to ensure he wasn't being watched, then took a step towards the kitchen window, his heart leaping ferociously against his ribcage. He had to be quick. His eyes adjusted, filtering out the bright daylight and slowly focusing on the dark interior of the house. The floor had been repaired, the charred markings of the fire erased. Akash recognised the kitchen table, decked out with a new table cloth. Beyond the tiny kitchen, in the living room nook where it had always been, sat the garlanded statue of Lord Vishnu. Blue light from a television set illuminated the god's face periodically. Akash's anxiety peaked. Somebody was home, though he couldn't see who.

There could be no doubt. Jaya's family still resided here, but nothing Akash had seen confirmed whether she herself had survived. He glanced down at himself, at his wiry fingers and borrowed clothes. He traced the bruises on his face. He had changed physically from the man he'd been twenty years previously. If Jaya's father still lived, he would be in his seventies. Would he still recognise Akash, or harbour the same passion from the night of the fire? Akash couldn't be sure. Jaya's father had warned him to stay away, and he didn't want to risk discovery, to add insult to injury for a grieving father, to uncover wounds from the past unless it was necessary. *But what if you are still alive, Jaya?*

The chatter of a group of passers-by prompted him to retreat to an adjacent alleyway bordering on a small supermarket. Akash resolved to wait, out of sight, and watch the house. The hours passed and thoughts spun like a fractured compass in his mind. He thought only of Jaya: the life of growth they could have had together, a secure home, the promise of children, all of which he'd discarded like a schoolboy on a whim. The city moved around him. He recalled the earnest and artistic wife who had made every effort to love him. The wife, who had not questioned him when he snuck away to be alone like a sulky child in the days after their marriage. The wife, who upon discovering his affair, had asked only if he still loved her. *Are you in that house right now, Jaya?* He trained his eyes on the house for any sign she might be alive. He feared it as much as he desired it; the chance of redemption versus a return to purgatory.

A man tapped him on the shoulder, all bristling energy and false politeness. "Are you going to move from here, brother, or are you going to buy something? This loitering—it's not good for business." The man's moustache expertly masked the thin line of his lips. Beady eyes sat beneath square eyebrows.

Akash gaze returned to the house.

"Eh! I'm talking to you."

Akash turned to face him, his body language stiff—back rigid, fists clenched—a warning. "This pavement isn't yours, just as it isn't mine."

"You'll be sorry you said that," said the man, heading back into his shop.

Akash ignored him. A magnetic pull tugged him towards Jaya's parents' house. He pivoted, slowly, his mouth dry with fear. It took him a moment to recognise her. There, with a stack of newspapers under her arm, dressed in a flowing skirt and embroidered tunic, strolled Jaya. In his mind's eye, she had never grown older. This woman wasn't the girl he knew. Her curves had grown heavier with middle age, her hair hid flecks of grey. Chaos engulfed him. In that moment, the universe disintegrated and reformed again. He stood frozen to the spot in the alley, tears of joy and relief threading down his face that she had aged, that life had not been stolen from her. It was such a commonplace activity: a woman coming home. Except for the fact Akash had always imagined that she had been robbed of the everyday.

Akash shuddered and heaved. He felt a powerful urge to run towards her, to call out, to kiss her and hold her and apologise, over and over for what he had done, and what he had not. *You are alive*, his head called out, stretching across the distance between them. Jaya reached the house, and turned in his direction, her foot poised over the threshold. Akash flattened himself against the wall of the alley. Could it be that she felt his presence, that a bond still existed after all these years?

When he looked again, she had gone. There, in the alleyway, with market-goers ambling past, he cast his head back against the peddle-dashed wall and sobbed like a priest who had regained his faith. Pent-up emotion travelled up and out of his body; he had been freed from his guilt for Jaya's death. Questions fired through his head. *Are you happy? Do you have a family of your own? If your father told me you had died, what must he have told you about me? Is this our second chance?*

A scuffle to his right roused him from his introspection.

"There he is! Making noises like an animal, upsetting our customers." The supermarket owner with the square eyebrows, together with another man and a couple of teenagers.

They stepped towards him, a heavy first footfall to scare him into submission. Akash blinked, pushed away from the wall, and set his balance. Then, with a glance at a newly lit window upstairs at Jaya's house, he tore down the alley way and slipped into the shadows, the laughter of the men ringing in his ears.

Slow to anger, but even slower to forgive when his temper was tested, Tariq barely offered a grunt in greeting when Akash returned to the railway bridge that evening.

"Look at you, standing there like you're a guest, like this isn't your home anymore," said Tariq.

"I'm sorry, Tariq," said Akash. "I know now you were trying to help, that you weren't judging."

"Oh? What made you come to that conclusion, genius?" The sharpness of his words contrasted with the gentleness of his eyes. A gracious apology thawed his anger, but he could not resist the satisfaction of a last jibe. "I don't need a part-time family you know."

"I'm sorry I've been absent."

"It's not you physically being here. We're not Siamese twins. I wouldn't expect that from you." He sighed. "It's just, I'm so used to us being on the same page, Akash. This morning came from nowhere. You won't let a woman come between us, will you? Even if we disagree."

The fight had gone out of Tariq. A cloak of weariness had wrapped itself around him. He stank as though he had been lying in his own bodily fluids all day. The last thing Tariq needed was for Akash to burden him with the twists and turns of the past few days. But the secret burned in Akash's throat.

"You were right," said Akash. Only if he spoke it out loud would it be true.

"What do you mean?" Confusion splashed across Tariq's face.

"It was always about her. All my angst, my heartbreak. It was all Jaya." A tremor marred his smooth baritone. "She's alive."

"Jaya is alive? Your wife is alive?" Tariq's incredulity reverberated across the hovel they called home. "Are you sure?"

"I saw her. Well, Soraya saw her, and I didn't believe her." The words flew out, a broken dam. "That's where I've been today. I went to find out, and I saw her. I really saw her! She's alive, she's really alive." He broke down and tears clouded his vision, so that he did not see his friend approach, but felt his hand on his shoulder, the slight touch an inadequate comfort for his confusion.

Tariq shook his head. "I can't believe it. Akash—this is wonderful! Did she see you?" He drew away when his cough surfaced, sputtering and wet.

"No. I can't process it." Akash drew in a haggard breath. His thoughts jumbled together like the bottles of coloured sand that could be bought on the beach. "She's in that very house, where it happened, where her father told me she had died. And I believed him."

"He must have had his reasons. I'm not excusing it, but maybe he was trying to protect her."

"Was I such a monster? She is my wife. She must think I abandoned her." A gust of wind blew into the tunnel, scattering the pots and cutlery they had hoarded over the years.

"What are you going to do?" said Tariq.

How could Akash tumble into her life now, after all this time? "Is it fair to disrupt her life after all these years?"

"Could you live with yourself if you didn't make contact?" He could always rely on Tariq's directness to cut through the meandering mess he made of everything.

Akash hesitated, nerves pulsing in his belly. "No."

"Then you need to find a way, for both your sakes."

# 18

Jaya grimaced and tugged at her clothes. It had taken her an age to decide what to wear. She owned a number of tried and tested outfits for her daily life, but her wardrobe did not contain appropriate clothing for a party. She pulled at the scarf around her neck and smoothed the new sequinned tunic over her hips. She wore silky black trousers underneath. Opaque pop socks covered her feet. She applied powder and her usual warrior eyeliner and smudged the kohl a little with her fingers to make her eyes appear bigger. Finally, she coated her lips in fuchsia pink and ran her tongue over her teeth to make sure none had found its way there. Grainy toothpaste residue lingered in her mouth. She gave her reflection a cursory check and turned off her light, ignoring the stack of newspapers piled up behind her bedroom door. It had been days since she had scoured the death notices.

"Why is Ruhi having friends over on a Sunday night? Don't they have work the next day?" muttered her mother, waiting for her at the bottom of the stairs. Her expression morphed into something approaching disgust. "What are you wearing?" she said, her voice rising with her eyebrows. She scanned her daughter from head to toe, lingering on Jaya's asymmetrical feet.

Jaya kept her voice level. "I bought it from the market. Do you like it?"

"A bit tight, isn't it? Pull your scarf over your breasts. Honestly, any one would think..." She fussed over the scarf, rearranging it in the style she herself wore. Jaya stiffened. Her mother tutted. "Girls these days, going out at this time of night."

Jaya gritted her teeth. "It's Ruhi's house, Maa." *I'm forty-five years old*, she thought.

"Lucky for you your father has fallen asleep in his chair." In the living room, the television blared. Her mother continued, enjoying her flow. "Otherwise he would have something to say about this. Take your keys. I won't wait up for you." She never did.

Outside on the street, Jaya slipped her keys into her clutch and lifted her head up to the sky where charcoal clouds hung on the horizon, blotting out a sea of stars. She breathed in the city fumes, feeling alive and unconstrained away from her parents, before remembering what she had agreed to do.

It had been Ruhi's idea. She had visited their parents, and afterwards, while their parents immersed themselves in the latest episode of their favourite soap opera, Jaya and Ruhi retreated into the garden to drink chai and exchange news beyond the sphere of their mother's eavesdropping.

"Come on, yaar. It will be so fun. Step out of Maa and Papa's shadow for once. Sometimes I think you live in this closed triangle." Ruhi gestured abruptly with her hands, a geometric shape carved into the air. "Home, the theatre and the art studio. Be spontaneous. It's just some of my dance troupe. Six or seven people max. We're going to play *Antakshari* after Devan is in bed."

"I guess I can come and look after Devan if he wakes up." She loved her nephew, and this way she could give in to Ruhi's pleading but still have a crutch to lean on if the party was awkward. It wouldn't have been the first time she had fallen asleep next to her nephew to escape the company of adults.

"I want you there to enjoy the evening, Jaya. Not to be a babysitter." Ruhi smiled coyly and sipped her tea. "Besides, it's the perfect occasion for Vinod and me to meet Ravi. I've been dying to meet him, and this way, there's no pressure. He'll be one amongst many."

Jaya balked. "I can't bring Ravi."

"Why not? What are you going to do? Invite him home for dinner with Maa and Papa? This is perfect. He gets to meet your family. Well, the coolest member of your family." Ruhi winked. "I can make sure he is right for you."

"I'm tired, Ruhi. What with the current run of shows at Tara, I need an early night."

Her sister saw through her lie. "Please, Jaya. Remember how we used to play *Antakshari* as children? How carefree we were. You'll have such a blast. Ravi will, too."

It had been years since Jaya had played *Antakshari*. True, they had spent happy hours in their childhood entertaining themselves with it, competing over the most unusual song choices and who had the best singing voice. Ruhi had always insisted she was the winner, of course, and Jaya had let her. She had last played *Antakshari* at university, raucous games filled with banter and cheering. It seemed like a lifetime ago.

Jaya tidied up her cup and sweet treats on the table to indicate the conversation topic was over. "What would all your friends think? I can't do that. An old maid like me turning up with a man. No, it's not for me."

"My friends will be too busy having fun to focus on you. And even if they did, none of them will think anything of it. This is the 2000s. We're not in Rajesh Khana territory where women hide behind their dupatta and pretend to be all shy. We're emancipated, yaar."

"Are we?" Jaya raised an eyebrow. She had finished her chai but the scent of cinnamon and clove wafted in the confines of the walled garden.

"No, maybe not, but it's heading in that direction. We don't want to be like the Americans, but a middle ground would be good, wouldn't it? Besides, if it really worries you, think of it this way: I'm married and I can chaperone you. And Ravi, after all the chasing he has done of you, wouldn't it be nice to include him? I remember, after the fire – " Ruhi whispered the word, as if it were a demon rather than an event Jaya had overcome. " – you used to ask why no one ever approached you, not even the ones who didn't know you were married. I know now. Very few people are sure enough of themselves to ask someone out. Especially in our culture."

"What do you mean?"

"Indians have so much bravado. We are natural flirts. Look at me and Vinod. We flirted, danced together, but it took his aunty to bring us together. No one likes to lose face. Whatever you look like, however old you are—"

"Thanks!"

"Oh shut up, Jaya. You're Madhuri Dixit to me, the bee's knees. Toes or no toes."

"I was teasing," said Jaya, chuckling. "I know *you* love me."

Ruhi ignored the interruption. "It takes courage to pursue someone, that's all, knowing you might be rejected. No wonder we flounder when we are left to our own devices without aunties and uncles to match us up."

Ruhi had a point. Jaya hated disappointing her sister. Besides, it would be nice to be with Ruhi and Vinod without feeling like a spare wheel. Jaya accepted the invitation, and shyly invited Ravi along, who beamed and pocketed the piece of paper on which she had scrawled her sister's address. That's how she found herself en route to Ruhi's house, on a Sunday night, dressed up to the nines, feeling nervous and foolish, praying that her social awkwardness wouldn't trip her up in front of Ravi, and that her sister wouldn't embarrass her.

She arrived at Ruhi's apartment just before the other guests. Her sister looked beautiful in trousers and a sleeveless kitty party top, baring her delicate dancer's arms. She opened the door to Jaya but didn't stop to talk, instead dashing to lay the dining table with vegetable samosas, *bhajiya*, rice and *daal*, an array of chutneys, juice and a small selection of alcohol. Vinod, Ruhi's husband, looked bemused as his wife whizzed past, a whirlwind of activity compared to his sedate air of calm.

The guests arrived in ones and twos, full of smiles and chatter, taking off their shoes in the entrance hall, scooping up food onto paper plates, eating with their fingers and licking them clean. Ravi entered last, the only man in a suit jacket, shaking everyone's hand, eager to please, devouring the food, oblivious to a speck of pastry lodged in his tooth until Jaya pointed it out. Ruhi didn't introduce them to her friends as a pair and relief flooded Jaya, though she made sure she remained close to Ravi's side, and found his exuberance took the pressure off the need for her to speak. She nodded and smiled, and spoke only when directly spoken to.

"So, you're Ruhi's sister?" said a tall girl called Yasmina.

"Yes," said Jaya.

"You don't look alike."

"I suppose we don't."

Her sister crossed the room, deer-like in her grace, and came to a standstill in front of a tapestry embroidered with a scene from *Ramayana*. She clapped her hands to command her guests' attention, and Jaya was pleased about the interruption.

Ravi stood beside her.

Her body became hyper alert at his presence a hair's breadth away as her sister spoke.

"Listen up, everyone. You know the rules. Two teams, one on either side of the room. Jaya, Ravi, Simran, Anil, Rehman; you are one team." Ruhi smiled at her husband and pulled him towards her. "Vinod, me, Khalid, Hana and Yasmina are team two. One team sings two lines of a Bollywood hit. The next team sings a song starting with the letter the previous song ended on. We have food. We have drink. We have *tablas*." Her friends cheered. Ruhi pointed to a few drums in the corner, their exteriors made of intricate carved wood in an elephant design. "Extra points for dancing. Let's play!" Ruhi flung herself to one side of the room, and her team followed, laughing.

The green velvet sofas sat snug against the walls. The teams positioned themselves, some cross-legged on the carpet, with a table resting between their thighs, others a level higher on the couch. The game began, a to and fro between the teams of ghazals and dance floor hits, of laughter and applause, so much so that Jaya's nephew woke, and she excused herself to take him back to bed. She wondered whether Akash would have sung as raucously as those here. The temptation to stay with her nephew was strong, but in the end, Ravi came to find her and insisted she sit next to him on the sofa.

So she nestled there, in a small space, between Ravi and a girl called Simran, awkward at her closeness to him. She tucked her deformed foot behind her leg so no one would see it, and let the front row do most of the work. The smell of alcohol rolled off Ravi in thick waves, but she found him to be an amicable drunk. Eventually, as the night wore on, she joined in the singing, first reluctantly, then with increasing gusto, especially when the tune suited her soprano voice. Ravi, too, did his fair share of singing, and she witnessed how he was freer than she, and wondered if his confidence stemmed from the fact he was a man, or the younger sibling to his brother, or because he had been born that way.

When all the guests had left, Jaya kissed her sister goodbye, an empty exhaustion settling like a blanket over her. Ravi teetered at her side.

"It was hard to speak to him in the chaos, but I like him," whispered Ruhi into her ear, as Ravi said his thank yous to Vinod. Out loud, once Ravi had finished slapping her husband on the back, she said, "I'm glad you came, Ravi. Maybe we'll meet again, if Jaya decides to keep you." She giggled, high on the success of the evening. "You'll walk Jaya home?"

"Of course," said Ravi, "and thank you. The food, the company, the game. I enjoyed every minute. We'd better go, otherwise you won't get rid of me. I'll be singing in your living room until dawn." He grinned, and her sister beamed back, but to Jaya they were a motley foursome. She couldn't imagine Ravi ever really being a part of her family.

They waved Ruhi and Vinod goodbye and began the walk home. A crescent moon cast a sliver of light onto the dimly lit street. The roads had cleared but pollution hung in the air like fog.

"I'm only ten minutes on foot from my sister's house. You're not tired?" said Jaya.

"No, I'm glad to get some time alone with you," said Ravi. His hair was no longer held captive by gel. It rose up like a lion's mane, full and shaggy.

"I wasn't sure about tonight, but I'm glad we went," said Jaya.

"You weren't sure about the singing or the people?"

"About taking you, more than anything."

He turned his gaze on her, shrewd and kind at once, his breath sour. "What were you worried about?"

Jaya shrugged. "What everyone might think, what you might think."

"And now?"

"I had fun. And I think I've tried so hard to be good, that maybe I've missed out on fun before." She felt light-headed after the stuffy heat of the sardine-packed apartment, and it must have been witching hour, because words spilled out of her mouth before she could summon them back. "All the love I have missed out on, staying alone. What if I had been more selfish over the years? Thought more about me? Is it wrong to sacrifice virtue for a little love?"

Ravi's eyes darkened. He grasped her forearms, and then, before she could refuse, his lips swooped down on hers, dry and hard. His lips drove into Jaya's with bruising pressure, his tongue prising the cave of her mouth open. For a brief moment, she gave herself to him, wondering if that was expected. She wanted nothing more than for the world to melt away and to feel bonded to him, but only Akash's face swam before her. She became unresponsive, a porcelain doll.

Ravi continued, his whisky breath suffocating, oblivious to her lack of participation, her unease. His hand descended to her waist, pulled her closer and inched up towards her breast.

Jaya lashed out, furious at both his plundering of her and her own uncertainty. She pushed him away with all her might, her balance tipped forward, so that when the bulk of his body retreated, she stumbled.

Ravi lurched away from her, dumb-founded. "I don't understand. I thought this is what you wanted."

She used self-righteousness as a shield for her momentary lapse, her confusion, and the more she thought about it, the angrier she grew. "What made you think I was inviting you to touch me? I'm not that kind of girl," said Jaya. Heat rushed to her face. He was willing to risk her honour. She surveyed him with a sinking feeling of an evening ruined. Whatever magic had encompassed them had been dispelled. If only she could save face, their evening could be salvaged.

"Relax, Jaya," said Ravi, stepping towards her. "I felt you kiss back." Street lighting illuminated his bloodshot eyes. The evening's exertions had taken their toll. He trailed a finger down her bare arm. "Let yourself enjoy it."

She shuddered and her mind flash backed to a very different experience long ago, her and Akash underneath sweaty bedclothes.

"No!" She hated her own confusion. Ravi's unwillingness to accept her stand unnerved her, and for a second she grew fearful. Though cars and rickshaws sped past, the streets had emptied of pedestrians. The moon above seemed less romantic than eerie to her. "I mean it, Ravi. This is too much. Even if I had said yes, have you no respect, that you touch me here in the open street?"

She assembled her argument as he watched her in disbelief. Perhaps she had returned his kiss for a moment, but it had been a mistake. Younger generations risked public intimacy in nightclubs or in the ghost-light of a cinema, but this would horrify their parents. Soraya may have been able to succeed without sexual inhibitions, but then she represented a hothouse bloom, that rare breed of Indian woman who had created her own family and fortune outside of the confines of traditions. Jaya had been cut from a different cloth. Her DNA spelled out conformity and caution, a result of her upbringing and experiences, or perhaps character.

Surprise registered on Ravi's face. "But all that talk of sacrificing your virtue for love... I thought this is what you meant." Could the drink have really distorted his judgement so soundly?

Jaya kneaded her temple to ease the cloud of tension that had gathered there. "I meant it felt good to let down my barriers and step outside my comfort zone."

"Well that's not what you said." His eyebrows knitted together in reproof.

Justifications did not appeal to Jaya at this late hour. She wanted to go home and close her door. She raised an arm to hail a passing rickshaw.

"What are you doing?"

"Going home."

A rickshaw pulled up beside them. She could have easily walked, but she needed an escape route. She needed to think about her reactions to Ravi's advances. She climbed into the cab, and called out her street name to the driver, withholding her house number lest Ravi overhear.

Ravi clasped her shoulder, his voice a low hum barely audible above the stream of nightly traffic. "I don't enjoy arguments and drama, Jaya."

"Let's go," she said to the driver, shrugging Ravi's hand off.

"What's the use!" said Ravi, flinging up his hands up.

Jaya stared straight ahead as the rickshaw sped away, bumping over potholes. The taste of disappointment pooled on her tongue. Kissing was not a great matter, she supposed, except it was to her. It spoke to her longing to be loved from depth of emotion, rather than biology. She longed to lock her past away. Even without the flashback that had visited her while she was with Ravi, she knew one thing with certainty: she had not enjoyed the kiss.

Of course, this may have been because she hadn't opened herself up to accept Ravi. He had felt alien to her, no surprise as it had been twenty years since she had kissed a man. Even so, something in her gut felt sour. It had been less of a kiss and more of a groping. She had been the lesser partner, the unwilling recipient, hadn't she? Ravi hadn't waited for a signal she was truly ready. Her feelings about him had seesawed from the very beginning. Perhaps her instincts had been right.

# 19

**Akash slept under** the bridge, listening to Tariq
snoring in his sleep and the sound of the tarpaulin they kept for
monsoon thrashing in the gusts. He slept fitfully, tossing on the hard
ground, his body refusing to find ease because of the spinning cogs
in his mind. *You are alive, Jaya.* He was at once overjoyed and
dejected, daunted by the thought of wrong-stepping again, of
making a bad situation worse. His old nightmares punctured his rest,
the fire more ferocious than usual, although logically he knew now
that Jaya had survived.

He woke in the chill morning air, drenched in sweat, his throat
parched. Akash gulped down some water, envious of the peacefulness
of Tariq's sleep. The sun rose higher, filling the crevices of their
hideaway with yellow. Akash closed his eyelids and let the sun warm
them, meditating on Jaya and Soraya and the years he had spent
running. He would run no more. In that moment of calm resolution,
an idea crystallised. He kicked himself for not thinking of it sooner.
Only one person could help him: the person Jaya loved most of all.

He rearranged Tariq's wayward blanket, tucking it under his
friend's shoulders, and crouched to use a small piece of flint on the wall
of the bridge to scratch out a message for when his friend woke up. He
had promised to be more considerate and he didn't want Tariq to worry
that he had disappeared again. Then, he plucked his towel from
amongst the small pile of his belongings and headed down to the beach
to wash in the sea. He wanted to be presentable for what followed.

At the shore, Akash undressed quickly down to his briefs and
waded into the surf. The sea sloshed against his thighs, curling the
hair there in different directions. He cupped his hands to scoop up

some water and let it run from the crown of his head, over his chest in rivulets. He clasped his hands together and prayed.

"Lord Brahma, Vishnu, Shiva. Goddesses Lakshmi, Saraswati, Durga. I pray not to one of you, but to all of you. Have you answered my prayers for peace? Were you listening all along? I beg of you, help me do what's right. What should I do?"

He listened, and no one answered, so he closed his eyes and floated in the sea, the cool waves lapping at his body, encompassing him. It did him good to remember his insignificance. It made him braver. He was only one man. Could one man make a mess of his whole life? He hoped not.

"She is alive!" he shouted out across the sea face. Passers-by shook their heads at the madman in their midst. Akash didn't care. He pushed out of the water, determination written in the lines of his body. He wiped himself off and got changed into the clothes he had borrowed from Soraya. He folded his towel and tucked it behind a tree, and then he set off for Bandra, to put his plan into action.

If Soraya's wishes were to come to fruition, she needed to convince Arjun to accept Akash. Her son had been at loggerheads with her since Akash's arrival. He simply could not understand why Soraya had allowed a vagrant into their house.

"Maa, why on earth have you allowed this man, who was spying on us through our window, to come and go as he pleases? I can't believe you'd put Muna and the baby in danger," said Arjun. "Is Akash really worth the risk to you?"

Soraya sighed. She and Arjun had argued with a previously unfelt passion over Akash. At twenty-two years old with a young wife and child, her son's natural instincts were to protect his family. They had circled around the same argument since last night and Arjun was growing frustrated.

"He's not a risk, Arjun. He's my friend and he needs help," said Soraya.

"Since when do we bend over backwards to help virtual strangers? If he was really your friend, I would have known about it."

Soraya raised an elegant eyebrow. "Don't you forget — this is my house."

She had raised Arjun to speak his mind and not fear confrontation. In that, he was very much her son. In truth, they scarcely argued. Even as a child his maturity had been evident. As a single mother, she fostered independence in him. She had brought him into her business from the time he could walk. They ate together, lived together, worked together. Their natures were in tune to the exclusion of everyone else. It had been a surprise when her son had found a wife so early. Not that she minded. It was just not a path she would have chosen. For Soraya, marriage was not an enabler. She cherished freedom above all else.

"I mean it, Maa. This is out of character for you. Muna is worried too."

"I'll speak to her."

"That's not the point. How do you know him?"

"He was important to me once," she said.

"So you've said. What I don't get is why."

They stood in the hallway of the house, a generous space propped up by marble columns with pink veins threading through them. Soraya walked over to a sofa, her sandals slapping a beat on the cool stone beneath her. She sank into its depth and tucked her feet behind a curved leg, playing for time while she stilled her ragged breathing. She took in the curl of her son's hair, wet from his shower, and the shape of his lips, full like his father's. Soraya motioned for him to come and sit next to her. He hesitated and then joined her, sitting awkwardly a few feet away.

"A long time ago, we were lovers."

Her son looked at her with a gaping mouth. "What? How did you..." Arjun flushed.

For the first time, Soraya experienced chagrin. She swallowed it down. She would not be cowed by standards set for other people. Her choices, to remain unmarried, to raise a son alone, might have been unusual, but she would not apologise for her past. She owned her choices.

"We met at the university at the end of our third year. I studied Business. He had his heart set on teaching. He was already married. We... had an affair. I'm not proud of myself. Initially, I didn't know. When I found out about his wife, I didn't much care. It felt real, somehow right. We talked. I thought I was in love." She was not convinced it had been love, but it was easier to explain to her son this way.

"What happened?" said Arjun.

"Akash's wife found out. She saw us in the park. I heard later she had doused herself in cooking oil and lit a match."

Arjun stared at her, horror clouding his face. "Did she die?"

"No. She lived." Soraya hesitated. "I think I might have seen her in the restaurant the other night."

"She was there?" He was aghast. "And Akash? What did he do after that? Why is he here when he should be with her?"

"Akash ran, and he did not come back. Not to me, and not to her. The whole university was talking about it. I didn't see him again until you did," said Soraya. She stood up, anxiousness creeping into her, despite her determination to inject calm into this conversation, to make Arjun understand. "He didn't know, Arjun."

"That she had set herself on fire?" Disbelief darted across his features.

"That she was alive. I told him last night."

"The man is either a monster, or a fool."

"He did not light the match." Soraya implored her son with her eyes to understand, but he turned away.

"He cheated on his wife. You were complicit. He abandoned her." Arjun shuddered. "All these years, you've hidden this from me. I thought I knew everything about you. I want him out of our lives."

She recognised that voice. He had used it as a child, as a teenager, as an adult. The voice of obstinacy he had inherited from her. She had to make him understand and she knew only one way to achieve that, but she risked losing him with the truth. She thought she had all the time in the world, but in the end the sands of time were finite.

"Arjun, I can't do that." Soraya steeled herself. She searched his face, her legs shaky beneath her. Finally, she spoke again. "The reason he is here, Arjun..." The words spilled out of her mouth. "It is because when he left, I was pregnant."

Arjun watched her lips, still and unmoving, an apparent disconnect between her words and his understanding. Time slowed, and the colour drained from his face.

# 20

**On the way** to Bandra, Akash spent the last remaining rupees clinking in his pocket on slices of mango sold by a street merchant. The gloopy fruit sated him and would provide enough sustenance until his next meal. His body no longer protested against meagre offerings. His stomach had shrivelled in time, or perhaps he'd become desensitised to its hunger pangs.

He waited for Ruhi, doing his best to be invisible. It posed no difficulties for him, unless he paused for too long in one place. He had neither age nor beauty nor power to hook the gaze of passers-by. The presence of a vagrant amounted to a blip in the minds of most, warranting a curled lip at worst, a pitying stare at best. It didn't matter if Akash had washed and changed his clothes, or if he had combed his hair. Something about his slumped posture and lack of purpose marked him as a down and out, someone who would never belong. As if he would never be the architect of his own story.

Regardless of fate and fortune, a window of change had opened for him. He didn't want any trouble. Not even the fear of encountering the supermarket owner, who had chased him away from Jaya's house, convinced him to alter his planned course of action. He traversed the streets, slinking in the shadows, taking care not to step too close to the wares being sold in case he made the shopkeepers nervous.

Akash surveyed the house, disappointed to find an absence of comings and goings. He longed to see Jaya but for his idea to work, he needed to find Ruhi. *I won't disrupt your life, Jaya. Only your sister can judge if I should walk back into your life or disappear.* His instinct told him sooner or later, Ruhi would turn up at her parents' house, as dictated by the norms of Indian culture. A daughter would not be forgiven for lack of care towards her elderly parents, unless something had happened to Ruhi in the intervening years? Akash waited, fraught with worry about whether he would stumble across her, and the inevitable cold reception if he did.

Time passed slowly, and he found himself visualising Jaya's reaction when she saw him. In his mind's eye, she went from a demon, all jutting angles and fiery anger, to an angel, charitable and tender. There was no middle ground. He groaned. Ridiculous to assume he could waltz back into Jaya's life, however much he desired a second chance. How he longed, this time, to find out her innermost secrets, to give her the security and the love she deserved.

But what did he have to offer? It wouldn't do to dwell. He focused on the task at hand, studying the faces of passing women, hoping to stumble across his sister-in-law, worried that the passing years would have made her unrecognisable to him.

He needn't have worried. A few hours later, just when the temptation to give up overwhelmed him, he caught sight of a familiar face meandering through the market, a little boy in tow. A lump formed in Akash's throat at the realisation that Ruhi now had a child.

The years had been kind to her. The child was lean like his mother. Ruhi was slender as the day Akash had met her, though she must have been nearing forty. Both mother and child had the same dark eyes that resembled Jaya's, round like vinyls Akash had collected before he left his old life behind.

Akash approached the pair, his heart hammering in his throat, causing him to jumble up the words he had practised in his head.

"Ruhi."

She didn't hear him. Her head was bent over her son's, her entire focus centred on his animated chatter.

Akash repeated himself, this time with more urgency. "Ruhi."

He touched her shoulder and she jerked, her face registering surprise.

Her eyes searched his face like sweeping flashlights. He watched the emotions dance across her face with growing trepidation. The shock came first, then the fury.

She rounded on him, her elegant visage swallowed up by a banshee's menace. "Akash! You!" She dropped her son's hand, let her shoulder bag fall to the ground, and pummelled his chest there in the midst of the shoppers and tradesmen, not caring who witnessed her outburst and what they might think.

Akash stood unspeaking, rocked by Ruhi's onslaught, soaking up her rage.

"Mama, what are you doing?" said her startled son.

Ruhi looked from Akash to the boy. She turned to her son. "Nanima will be waiting for us. I can see you from here. Go on ahead, Devan. I'll be right there." She grasped his shoulders and turned him to face her. He couldn't have been more than ten. "Don't say a word about this to anyone, especially to Nanima. Promise me?"

The boy nodded, unsure but obedient.

She handed him the discarded shopping bag and pushed him towards his grandmother's house.

Ruhi swung towards Akash. She wrenched him towards a quiet enclave that smelt of piss. "What are you doing here after all these years?" she said through gritted teeth, all the while assessing him from head to toe, as if she could read his secrets just by looking at him.

"I didn't know she was alive, Ruhi. I promise you. I just found out. I saw her the other day just by chance." Mentioning Soraya would be stupidity; it would only turn her more against him. The white lie burned hot within him. "I thought she had died in the fire."

"You mean you wished she had died." Her voice dripped with ice.

"No! It changed my life."

Ruhi shoved him.

He did not defend himself.

"It changed *your* life? You stupid, stupid man. You did this to her." Ruhi stood up tall. "But do you know what? She's happy. It took her a long time, but Jaya is finally happy again. No thanks to you."

She had changed from the sweet girl he remembered. The Ruhi he had known had treated him like a brother, teased him, sought his advice. His behaviour had cost him more than his wife.

"Look at the state of you, Akash." She eyed him with disgust. "Even if you thought Jaya had died, why disappear? Why not stick around and pay your respects at her funeral? Why not say goodbye?

All these years without closure... It wasn't just the cheating. It was the walking away. You made her the subject of gossip. You humiliated her twice."

He hung his head, and when he looked up he saw a genuine willingness to understand that, for a moment, diluted her anger. Everything rode on convincing her to allow him see Jaya. He wouldn't do it without her agreement. He and Jaya were now strangers and he would not jeopardise her emotional equilibrium for his own sake. He relied on Ruhi's judgement but wished more than anything that she would say yes.

He revealed one of the secrets of that night, knowing it was his ace of cards but reluctant to cause trouble. "I disappeared because your father told me it was for the best. He told me that Jaya had died and that I should never come back."

A stillness girdled Ruhi, as if a lasso had been drawn around her accusations and pulled tight. "What did you say?"

"Your father told me Jaya had died. I believed him. I should have come back, but I couldn't escape my grief and I didn't want to add to yours." He splayed out his hands as if in prayer, begging her to understand.

"I don't believe it," she said, but her anger fizzled out, towards him at least. She released a long breath. "What do you want, Akash?"

"I want your permission to see her." *Please*, his internal voice called out, *please give me this chance.*

Ruhi's brow furrowed. "Why?"

"She's my wife."

"A lot has changed."

"I won't make her do anything she doesn't want to, Ruhi. I can be the husband she always wanted, or a friend." He paused, and swallowed the pain. "Or even a stranger, but I need to talk to her."

"Tell me the truth. Are you with Soraya?"

He met her eyes and held them, spoke the truth. "No."

"Do you have children?"

"No." A single syllable that pained him. He wished it were different.

Ruhi breathed out, ostensibly relieved. "I won't let you hurt her, Akash." A storm of thoughts wrote themselves on her face. "But banishing you was not my father's decision. Neither is it mine. You are still Jaya's husband."

"I'll do anything you ask."

"She has a fuller life than ever before. She is happy." She held his gaze, searching for his intent, and seemed to come away satisfied. "But maybe you will help her crystallise what she really wants, who she really wants."

"Thank you." He wanted to hug her, but he held his distance, not wanting to cross the line Ruhi had clearly marked in the sand. She no longer viewed him as family.

"Not so fast, Akash. If you hurt her, you will never see her again."

"I understand." His heart raced at the thought of seeing Jaya again after all these years. Not a fleeting glimpse, but a prolonged meeting, where he could drink in the sight of her, listen to her voice for real this time, not just an echo in his head.

"These are my conditions." The tension reemerged in a flash, leaving him a tightly coiled spring as he listened. Ruhi counted out her points on her fingers, her movements slow and deliberate, leaving no room for manoeuvre. "Number one: you will not see her face to face until I say you can. Number two: you will not reveal who you are until I say. Number three: you will woo her with anonymous letters delivered to Tara Theatre in Juhu. She works there. That way you can get to know each other again without the burden of the past. See it as a trial. If you pass, I won't stop you from walking into Jaya's life again for real."

Dismay filled Akash. How could he write to Jaya without revealing his identity? Still, he had no choice but to agree.

"Do we have an agreement?" She held out her hand, and he folded it into his calloused grip.

"Yes." His mind whirred.

"How do I find you?"

He was too ashamed to reveal his home just yet. "I'll find you," he said.

Ruhi nodded and stepped into the main road to continue on her way. At the last moment, she pivoted. "Akash?"

"Yes?"

"It's good to see you."

She did not stop for an answer. A group of shoppers swept her forward, and when Akash emerged into the street, the crowd had swept Ruhi away. Salty tears of gratitude sprung from his eyes. He hugged the promise about meeting Jaya to himself like a thief with stolen jewels.

# 21

**Akash returned to** Soraya's bungalow as he had promised he would, although his head was filled with thoughts of Jaya. Though it had only been a few days since he had pressed his nose up to the glass of the kitchen and recognised Soraya standing there, he had become a different person, as if the scales had been lifted from his eyes with the knowledge that Jaya lived.

Still, he had given Soraya his word that he wouldn't disappear, and so, he waited at the outhouse while the guard called the mistress of the house to let her know he had arrived. The guard listened carefully and hung up the telephone.

"Madam is at the restaurant. She'll be back before the sun sets. She has asked me to escort you to the Red Room. You're not to leave. Follow me."

They trod the now familiar path through the gardens towards the house, along the winding corridors to the room where Akash had spent his first night after Arjun's beating. The door clicked behind Akash, and he waited patiently at first, then with increasing dissatisfaction. He searched in vain in drawers for a pen and paper, so he could at least begin writing to Jaya. *Will you wait for me a bit longer, Jaya?* He could not override the feeling that something might befall one of them, and put an end to his dreams of reconciliation. He needed Jaya's forgiveness to live. Perhaps he even needed her love to be happy. His head spun with the ripples of his new-found knowledge.

It bewildered him to think how often he had spent his nights under the same stretch of sky as both Jaya and Soraya without knowing how close they happened to be. Soraya's Juhu bungalow was located just east of St. Joseph's Church. Its courtyard was one of a handful of places where Akash and Tariq felt safe to sleep at night. It struck Akash as surreal to return to this grand house. He had lived long and shabbily enough to know that pain formed a part of life. Still, it thrilled him to have a second chance. This time he was determined to make the right choices.

Akash waited at the window. He may have whiled away the past twenty years, but now he found an urgency to put things right and counted each minute that passed, felt every wasteful second. At last, Soraya approached through the gardens of the house, just as he himself had hours before. He noted her beauty this time with detached appreciation. Her elegant procession on tiny heels, the swishing of her sari.

Yards away, she buckled and glanced around furtively. Then she vomited into the earth and wiped her mouth with the train of her sari.

Akash looked on, dismayed, worried but reluctant to embarrass her by intruding on this private moment. In the end, he stayed behind the net curtains while she passed by, unwilling to catch her unawares. A few minutes later her heels sounded in the hallway outside his room. Akash swivelled towards the door. There stood Soraya, pale in the evening light.

"Sorry to have kept you, Akash," she said, coming to embrace him. "I wasn't sure you'd be back after what I told you."

"A promise is a promise."

Teeth the colour of moonstones contrasted with blood red lipstick.

"I saw you out there, Soraya. Are you unwell?"

"It's nothing to call the doctor about." Bitterness tinged her voice. "First, tell me, did you find her? Did you find your wife?"

He wasn't sure what the right answer was and so he opted for honesty. "Yes, I found her." Exhilaration swept through him.

"And what do you intend to do?"

The open-ended question threw him.

"You have a home here if you want it, Akash, for as long as I am alive."

Warning bells sounded in Akash's head. What did she mean, *for as long as I am alive*? Besides, he had no desire to leave Tariq. How could he attempt a reconciliation with Jaya when he lived under the same roof as his former lover? No, he could not accept Soraya's generous offer. There was too much at stake.

He said simply, "I should leave."

"No, your place is here," responded Soraya, sitting on the bed. *With me.* She left the words unsaid, but they still found him.

Once he would have given anything to hear her say *your place is here with me*, but she never had, and now the time had passed. Besides, he found happiness underneath an open sky, he was accustomed to it. The bungalow didn't feel like home. This was her world, not his. A man had his pride.

"I am so grateful to have found you, Soraya, I really am, but my place is not here. It never was."

She turned her eyes on him, and he found a humility in them he had never seen before. It pained him to see her pride shrivelled, the characteristic that defined her more than anything.

"I won't keep you here against your will, Akash. But if you could spare me just a few weeks—what are a few more weeks in the grand scheme of things?—I would be eternally grateful."

His feet were poised to leave. Already the Red Room felt like a prison, but he had loved this woman once. What could he say in the face of her plea? "Of course. But I don't understand."

Relief flooded her face. "You will."

Akash stayed, though the urgency to restore his relationship with Jaya and find out the secrets of their years apart permeated every fibre of his being. Over the next few days, he and Soraya adopted a routine. He followed her lead when meals were served to him in his bedroom, away from the family. Sometimes, he accompanied her on strolls around the garden. The white expanse of the house and its pillared entrance loomed beside them as they wove their way through the landscaping, stooping at intervals to marvel at tiny blossoms the colour of candy sugar.

He still didn't understand her need to keep him here. Soraya told him of the springtime tulips she had planted, which would soon be on their way. Her eyes betrayed a sadness he didn't question, and he dispelled the notion that she had a rivalry with Jaya. His instinct told him it was something more. Still, he had promised Soraya two weeks, and come what may, he'd take his leave then. *Wait for me just a bit longer, Jaya, and I will give you my all.*

They swapped stories, hot stepping around uncomfortable topics. Soraya spoke of her son and her business, and the friendships that had paid the price for her success. She confessed she'd stumbled into the restaurant business. By the time her passions crystallised, the restaurant had surpassed her initial expectations and it seemed ill-fated to pursue a career as a fashion designer, particularly with a young son to provide for.

For his part, Akash confided in Soraya the reason he limped. Cornered and beaten by a group of drunk men on the eve of his fortieth birthday, his shin bone had broken. With only slight attention from a back-street doctor, it hadn't healed correctly. He saw that day as a gift: he understood, finally, that drink diluted men's morals and stole their best selves. In the worst of men, it extinguished their humanity.

Fearful of upsetting Arjun, he did not stray from his room often, better to avoid the prying eyes of Soraya's brooding son. The Red Room frightened him. It became his prison rather than a sanctuary. On the streets of Bombay, Akash had spent endless nights picturing himself sinking into a mattress, having a bed to call his own, a door to close and someone to hold. His blessings had multiplied a thousand-fold over the course of a few days. Though his fortune had changed, he slept poorly. His surroundings oppressed him.

The Tuesday of the first week, he slipped out to see Tariq.

"I brought you something." He handed Tariq some bread and paneer packaged in silver tin foil Soraya's maid had found for him. "Have you had any trouble?"

"No, it's all fine, big brother. Always quiet without you, though." He punched Akash's shoulder lightly.

Tariq munched while Akash filled him in on his pact with Ruhi and Soraya's strange request.

"What I don't understand," said Tariq, "is why Soraya insists on you staying with her for two weeks without telling you why. Does she want a chance to lure you away from Jaya again? Is her ego behind this?"

Akash shook his head. "I don't think so. She seems uneasy, always on the cusp of some revelation that she draws back from. I promised her two weeks, but it seems like an eternity. I feel trapped. The bed is too fine."

Tariq laughed, spitting out tiny fragments of cheese in his mirth. "You're complaining about a good bed, you lucky sod? You're in a palace and you long for a stable. Not many men are so discerning!" He guffawed.

Akash threw a spoon at him. The murky utensil missed its mark and bounced at Tariq's feet. A hearty laugh met Akash's chagrin. Playful moments like these eased his loneliness and brought their bond into sharp focus.

His sleep at Soraya's house was never peaceful. The bed's mountainous cushions loomed large even when they had been tossed aside. Nightmares haunted him, and he drifted into a dreamless slumber only once he slept on the floor. He missed the blanket of sky above him in spring, and the clarity the wind brought him in autumn. He pined for the city landmarks, which had come to be his living room. He craved the moist feel of the air and the silence in the dead of the night that was interrupted only by the footfalls of roaming dogs. At Soraya's house the continuous hum of the air-conditioning irked him, as did the golden ornaments and the freshly pressed clothes the maid brought him each morning. He missed the simplicity of owning two pairs of worn clothes, which he himself washed by hand. More than anything, he missed his nightly ablutions in the holy river, the time of day he guarded jealously, when he stood under moonlight to offer prayers of repentance to his wife; the rituals he had lived by as a homeless man, when he fought to purify his soul and peel away his layers of shame.

Despite Soraya's kindness and his concern about the secret she harboured, Akash's resentment prickled. Soraya once more stood between him and Jaya, and he was left in no man's land, his longing for Jaya a pitiful mix of love and anguish. But not for long.

"I must go. Will you do me a favour?"

"Anything," said Tariq.

"I need you to deliver this to Tara Theatre for me. Just leave it on the front desk." He fished a letter out of his pocket and smoothed it out. Spelled out in careful script on the envelope was one word: *Jaya.* He could not presume she still used his surname. For once he was grateful his handwriting had deteriorated over the years through lack of practice. Jaya would not recognise the script as his. It had been painstaking work to thread the sentences together to reflect what he wanted to say without giving away his identity. He handed Tariq the letter with infinite care. "I'll be back soon."

Tariq swatted him, tenderness beneath bravado. "I know you will. I'll take care of this for you. Be well, brother."

# 22

**Arjun had shown** little interest in the colour scheme of the nursery, so it remained for his mother and wife to put their mark on the child's room. Soraya insisted on swirls of yellow paint: a clear favourite in her mind as it did not set gender bias at an early age. Muna had convinced her mother-in-law to include a border of tiny pink blooms in the scheme.

It flattered Muna to be sought out by the older woman. With her own parents long deceased and a sister who lived overseas, she longed for the love of family. She moved in with Soraya and Arjun the day of her marriage and soon discovered her mother-in-law was forthright and intelligent, but not maternal.

Soraya was not a typical grandmother, or at least not the type of grandmother Muna had grown to expect from the experiences of her friends. At forty-five, Soraya was too young and too successful to be selfless. Though there were nights when the baby did not settle, and her cries echoed across the house, not once did Soraya offer to soothe her or give Muna's frayed nerves a respite. She preferred to watch from afar, a proud grandmother, who bought Leela pretty dresses and left chaste kisses on her forehead.

Not that Muna minded. Before Leela's birth she sensed she had been a poor companion, unable to compete with the memory-laden conversation that dominated the dinner table in her marital home and centred around Soraya's shared experiences with her son. Discussions about the restaurant business floated over Muna's head, and she took a back seat while her husband and his mother delved into the intricacies of resources, clientele and marketing. Cooking had no place in Muna's repertoire—her recipes had no place in the kitchens of one of Bombay's top restaurants—so she could not even impress with that most feminine of skills.

With Leela's arrival, the three had become a four, and balance was restored. By surviving a traumatic birth and fully claiming a role for herself, she earned a newfound respect. Motherhood came naturally to her, when she suspected it had not to Soraya. Occasionally, her mother-in-law revealed something about her own life and Muna learned to wait patiently for these moments. After all, her husband shared many characteristics with his mother; the apple did not fall far from the tree.

They stood at the chest of drawers in the far corner of the nursery, Muna changing the baby's nappy and Soraya wrinkling her nose in distaste.

"I almost forgot how bad it smells when they do that. I admire you, Muna. You're more patient than me," said Soraya. "I was relieved when Arjun was out of the baby years."

Leela gurgled and stretched to touch the flowers adorning the wallpaper.

"Really? I don't mind the nappy changing. Leela smells of milk and is always warm and pleased to see me. I think I'll miss this bit."

"You're lucky to have disposables," said Soraya. Her smile did not stretch to her eyes.

"Arjun will come around, you know," said Muna.

"I know my son. It will take time. I'm not sure how much time I have."

Alarmed, Muna glanced at her mother-in-law. Leela whimpered, chubby fists grasping at her mother. "Is something wrong?"

"No, of course not." She held Muna's gaze, and sheer willpower sparked in the depths of her irises. "It's nothing to worry Arjun with."

Muna moved towards her mother-in-law, concern spooling across her face. "Tell me what's wrong, Maa."

"There's nothing to tell. As you get older you realise it doesn't make sense to wait to undo the mistakes of the past."

Leela fussed. Muna used deft movements to replace the soiled nappy with a fresh one. Then she grabbed a small sheet from a nearby chair and swaddled the child. She cupped Leela's head and carefully placed the child in the nook of her arm before turning to Soraya. "What can I do to help?" she said.

"I don't want to bother Arjun with my petty health troubles. What you can do is encourage him not to see Akash as a monster. Will you help me, Muna?"

It niggled Muna that her mother-in-law, capable, proud as she was, had asked for help. She pushed aside the seeds of disquiet. "Of course. If you think this is the best way."

"It is."

"You don't think it would be better for them to get to know each other at their own pace? I know Arjun isn't comfortable with him being here." Muna kissed Leela's head, placed her in her cot and drew the curtains shut, motioning for her mother-in-law to follow her out of the room. They hovered in the hallway.

"Akash is here because Arjun needs to know his father and because I need him. Maybe it would help for me to tell you more of my story. Walk with me, Muna, while Leela is sleeping. I could do with some air and Geeta will call us if the baby wakes."

Muna nodded and Soraya stopped to ask the maid to listen out for the baby. The two women walked down the winding staircase, leaving the cool air-conditioned house for the sticky heat outside. A light breeze played with the hem of their salwar kameez as they meandered through the landscaped gardens towards the vibrant blue swimming pool. Soraya sat on deck chair and Muna followed suit, kicking off her sandals and pulling her legs up onto the freshly-washed cushion.

Soraya's face clouded with thought. "My father sent me away to an aunt when he discovered I was pregnant. He was angry at first, my mother too. She came from a more traditional family, you see, and it wasn't the future she envisaged for me. But when you have only two daughters, you fight harder for them than if there is a son to take all the glory. And my father...Indira Gandhi had swept into government again on a wave of popularity...it gave him hope. She was strong and determined and unafraid, and he wanted that for me."

"I can see that. A woman in the top job. India dominated South Asia under Indiraji. It's impressive," said Muna.

"Oh, she had a dark side, Muna, but don't we all? The tragic glamour of that family means their flaws come under less scrutiny. But, who said women have to be good? Who said we have to be full of light and laughter? We are only human."

"The pregnancy was why you didn't complete your degree?"

"I was doing Business. I was good at it, but I had no choice but to leave. I left university. A few months later we moved to Juhu. My father persuaded my mother to give my dowry to me to invest in a business. There would be no marriage for someone who had given birth to another man's child," she laughed drily. "Papa believed in my business acumen even though he was furious."

Muna dropped her voice to a whisper. "Did you not think about...getting rid of the baby?"

"Abortion? How many children are killed today in unsafe back street procedures because they are the wrong gender? No, it's not for me. I was stubborn. I had made the choice. I decided to live with it. Besides, I was 23. I had not been raped. My health was not in danger. The child was not malformed. I grew with Arjun. I wasn't a bad mother."

Muna remained quiet. Arjun's recollections of his childhood told the story of a mother who was generous with her time but unyielding with her discipline. Soraya had taken pride in imparting knowledge to her son, but he feared her fury at mistakes and misadventures. She had laughed easily though he seldom experienced her hand on his brow during illness or the warmth of her embrace. Muna imagined the struggle of a young unmarried mother attempting to be both father and mother to her newborn child and her sympathy for her mother-in-law flared.

"I can't imagine how difficult it must have been for you."

"My parents had money. I've never wanted for anything. I had the help of a maid. My sister resented having to give up our home, and how suddenly we internalised. The parties stopped. We focused on Arjun. My mother resented it too, I think. I could feel it in her silences. But Arjun soon won them over. They were doting grandparents. I wish you could have met them," said Soraya. "And then the restaurant bloomed, and within a few years I had a staff of ten."

"You were successful, despite the setbacks," said Muna.

Soraya looked up sharply. "I never viewed Arjun as a setback."

"Sorry, I didn't mean that. I meant leaving university."

Soraya waved away the apology. "Yes, I was successful. I realised that though it was hard work, I had more freedom being self-employed. I could work flexibly. I didn't need to worry about bosses second-guessing my commitment or firing me just because I was pregnant. Five years later I was able to buy a second site. All that time Arjun was growing, and I saw how, even though he was young, I depended on him and I didn't need a man."

"You didn't miss Akash Saheb? Or resent him for leaving you in your situation?"

"He wasn't mine to start with. What right did I have to be angry? I took him from another woman. Initially, I didn't know he was married. When I found out, it didn't cause me any sleepless nights. I know now how foolish that was. Our deceptions, they never quite stay hidden." She shrugged. "We were just weak. And though I tried to find him, to tell him about Arjun, soon it didn't hurt to think of him or what could have been. My life was moving forward."

"Arjun told me about Akash Saheb's wife and the fire." Muna dipped her head forward and allowed her hair to partially shield her face. "You didn't consider tracking Akash Saheb down, marrying him?"

"I am Muslim by birth, Muna, just as you are a Hindu. I may not practice the religion of my ancestors, but Akash came from a traditional family, and there was no prospect of us marrying. There were two reasons for his parents not to accept me. I am Muslim and he was already married. His wife was alive. No. It was best for me to forget about him, to concentrate on Arjun and our future."

"I am sorry, Maa. I wish it could have been different."

"How can I explain it? You're so young. You don't know your own strength yet. It took me a long time to give voice to what I think I knew all along. It's why I was scared but I wasn't crushed when I realised I would be an unmarried mother. It's what Papa tried to teach me all those years. That I am enough. Even without a man, I am enough."

"He sounds like a good father."

"He was," said Soraya.

"Did you love him? Akash Saheb?"

"In my way. But you understand, the personal is political. There is nothing more personal than the bargaining that goes on within marriage. I'll do your laundry; you bring home the bread. I will look beautiful on your arm; you give me children. I will cook for you and keep the house clean; you be successful at work. I was glad to be free of that."

Muna blinked and stared at the horizon, uncomfortable with Soraya's directness.

Soraya rose and walked to the pool, where she trailed a toe in the cool water. "I admire you, Muna. I knew you were different from me when you married my son."

"I love him. We're not perfect, but I love him."

"I know." She paused. "Help me make Arjun understand. I don't want this anger to consume him."

"I'll try but he needs time. And it doesn't help to have Akash Saheb under this roof, when all those years he was absent."

"Akash doesn't know yet he is Arjun's father. I owed it to Arjun to tell him first. They can't be together until Arjun can think clearly, until his anger has subsided."

"Just give him some space. He will come 'round. And I will try to soften him."

Soraya nodded. Then she turned towards the house, her orange scarf making waves in the air as she went. At the pool, Muna listened to the quiet.

# 23

**Designs and fabrics** covered Jaya's desk like a quilt and she found it impossible to narrow them down. She hated how men could disrupt her focus with such ease, a careless word, unwanted touch, a casual affair. Today she channelled her warrior self with a corseted top and stern pencil skirt in raw silk. Her eye make-up was winged, large slashes extended far past the corner of her eyes. She wore this armour with ease, her shadow self, the one she adopted to make her way in the world. Her real self came to life mostly in Firoz's studio. She counted the hours down to nightfall, after she had cooked for her parents, when she could head to her art class and paint her frustrations onto a canvas.

At lunchtime Ravi came to find her. He took in her elaborate attire and wolf-whistled, low and clear. A friend of his nearby tittered. Ravi shooed the woman away, jocular, roguish.

Jaya's hackles rose.

His demeanour changed when he turned back to her. What did he remember from their date? She surveyed him unkindly, her nose lifted into the air a notch. He was dressed in muted colours, as if he had decided to blend in for once rather than stand out. *Or maybe because he has a hangover and it would make his headache worse*, thought Jaya, cattily. It made her feel better to witness him looking worse for wear. She still felt a keen disappointment at his behaviour.

"I can't remember how I got home last night," he said, sheepishly. "One minute we were at your sister's place, I was singing at the top of my lungs. The next I was waking up in bed feeling nauseous."

"You didn't drink that much, but it hit you like a wave," said Jaya, her voice tart, keeping him at arm's length.

"Sorry about that," he said, colouring, red cheeks against slick hair making him look effeminate. He propped himself up against her desk, a barrel on stout legs. Whatever she had seen in him had faded fast. "When can we pick up where we left off?" he whispered in her ear, an attempt to be sexy that made her skin crawl. His pores reeked of alcohol.

Jaya stood, pushing back her swivel chair. Granted, she was unpracticed in delivering romantic signals, but it appeared Ravi had short-circuited, that he had ignored her bristles and interpreted them as attraction. Where once his persistence had impressed her, now it grew tiresome.

She cut through his dance. "I've decided, Ravi."

"Decided?" he said, puzzled.

"At the restaurant in Juhu you asked me to hold off before I made a choice." She ploughed on, determined to have her say, put up her walls. "I want to be friends," she said, not caring if he took offence at the limp olive branch she offered. Her hands instinctively reached for the stack of newspapers, her ritual of scanning for Akash's name as instinctive to her as breathing.

"You want to be *friends*?" Her rejection of him clearly stung. He did not move from his perch on her desk, but stayed there, obstinate and still.

"Do you even remember what happened last night?"

Their colleague still lurked in the background. Ravi noticed and grew bolshy.

"I'm a drunk, not an amnesiac." He held her eyes, pinning her like a butterfly against a board. "Come now, Jaya, you did ask for it. A thing cannot come into existence without a cause that produces it."

Jaya's hackles rose. "What's that supposed to mean?"

"Just that a girl like you can't invite a man to an intimate evening, spout words about freedom, and be surprised."

"Cause and effect. That's your excuse?" said Jaya, ice lining her voice.

"It's as good as any other."

Fury filled her, transporting her back to her parents' kitchen, another man, flames that rippled through the oxygen-less air. "And the fire. That was my fault too, was it?"

"Well, he left for a reason, didn't he, Jaya? And you lit the match."

She ignored the gasps behind her. Their audience had grown. Ravi couldn't hurt her. She had told herself the same things a thousand times before.

"And what did I do to deserve an arsehole like you?" She sank into her chair, holding up her hand to wave him out of her vicinity, brushing him away as if he were a mosquito. She burned with anger, and this time it made her strong, not weak. She knew now that Ravi was a pretender, just as Akash had been, and she would not let a man fool her. Not anymore. She was no longer a mosaic built entirely of duty, sacrifice and submission. Power surged through her "Leave, Ravi!" The starched nature of her clothing produced a stiffness in her movements. Together with her makeup, it imbued her with the look of a geisha. Out of the corner of her eye, she noticed Ravi flounder, his mouth open like a goldfish's. She sensed his eyes on her back before he scurried away.

That would teach her to be more discerning about who she invited into her life.

Ruhi stopped by the house while Jaya was making roti for dinner. Jaya had been surprised to see her. Usually family gatherings happened at the weekend and not mid-week. Still, it was a welcome balm to have Ruhi visit. It took the edge off the atmosphere. Naturally warm and intuitive, Ruhi sidestepped their mother's prickles with ease.

This evening they didn't have that problem. Mondays were a favourite of Jaya's. Their mother attended laughing club. As soon as she returned, her face sour despite the hour long laughing therapy, Jaya would leave for the art studio. Sometimes the best way for her mother and her to coexist was to be passing ships in the night.

Usually, Ruhi welcomed the chance to spend time alone with their father. Tonight, she insisted on helping Jaya in the kitchen. More than that, Jaya noted the sting in Ruhi's voice when she had greeted him. She had neither teased nor embraced him. Their father had noticed it too, especially with Ruhi, his favourite, the one who had a sunny disposition, who had provided him with a grandson and socialised with the film industry's superstars. Papa was fragile these days, more alert to slights, less able to shake them off or counter them as he had done as a young man.

Jaya pitied him.

"What was that about?" she asked her sister, dipping into a whisper to prevent their father from overhearing.

Ruhi shrugged. "I don't know."

"You were harsh with Papa. Has he annoyed you?"

"I'm just having an off day, that's all, Jaya." She avoided Jaya's eyes.

"Go make it up to him before Maa comes home." She could have worded it better. Ruhi was bound to take aversion to her bossy tone.

"No," said Ruhi, a jagged edge to her voice.

Jaya let it go. "Fine, help me with these then." She handed Ruhi a spoon to butter the roti.

Ruhi accepted the spoon absent-mindedly, weighing the silver up in her hand. Jaya passed her the margarine and resumed shaping the dough in the palm of her hands, rolling it out, then transferring it to the iron griddle. The bread sizzled, black discs appearing to dot the finished form. Next door, their father unmuted the television, comforted by the sound of women at work in the kitchen.

"It was fun the other night, wasn't it?" began Ruhi. She swirled a gloop of margarine on a hot roti with the underside of the spoon. The margarine became a pool of shimmering yellow on its surface.

"Yes. Until we left. Ravi drank more than I thought. He tried to kiss me."

That caught her attention. She glanced up. "Did you kiss him back?"

If Ruhi had been herself, she would have been more excited. She understood how Jaya enjoyed being alone, but simultaneously craved the validation of a partner.

Jaya hesitated, reluctant to admit her momentary lapse with Ravi. She was thankful now that he had pushed hard, that he had revealed his true character. She was even grateful that Akash had invaded her thoughts. "No. He misread my signals. I didn't want that at all."

"I know you like to be in control but take the kiss as a compliment. He likes you," said Ruhi, sweeping the flour off the work surface into her palm.

"He was pushy, Ruhi, aggressive even. I saw him today at work, and again he was brazen, unapologetic for misreading me. As if I had led him on. To be honest, he's a first-class jerk."

"Oh." Shocked, Ruhi hugged her sister, suddenly an open book once more. "I'm so sorry. How dare he? Are you okay? I wish I'd asked Vinod to walk you home."

"I'm okay. It's not your fault," said Jaya. She meant it. "I sent him packing today with his tail between his legs. It felt good."

"Maybe we both got him wrong, maybe Ravi wasn't the man we thought he was." She paused and stared at Jaya with an intensity only shared by sisters.

"Spit it out, little sister."

"Well, he woke you up to the possibility of a relationship. I know some people can be happy alone Jaya, I just don't think you can."

"I'll take that under consideration."

"I knew a woman once, a long time ago, who was brave enough to love someone when she didn't know if he loved her back."

"Ruhi..." A low voice, a warning not to go any further.

"I like who the woman is today. But I miss the other girl, the one who believed in love."

"That's enough, Ruhi." Jaya frowned.

"None of us are static. We change from one day to another until we don't recognise the person we were a few months before."

"You sound like one of those things from China with the little shreds of paper in them." Jaya fumbled for the word. She grasped it from the floating baubles in the tree of her mind. "A fortune cookie."

"Vinod, Maa, Papa, Ravi, Akash, you, me... we show different faces to different people. We all have secrets buried under our skin. We can never know how a chance encounter, a lie, an accident, a misunderstanding can change us."

Jaya shook her head, nonplussed. Even now, she hugged the secret to herself about how Akash had watched her burn through their kitchen window, compelled to protect him in absentia. Would her sister be so understanding if she knew? "What has gotten into you today, Ruhi? Go home, get some sleep."

Ruhi smoothed down her t-shirt. "Maybe you're right. I keep putting my foot in it." She sighed. "I better go and make amends with Papa."

Jaya watched her sister's disappearing back, noting how she had mentioned Akash when she had avoided saying his name for decades. How odd. She shrugged and, chores accomplished, made her way upstairs to prepare for art class.

A lamp sat on the desk, casting shadows across the Red Room. Deep in concentration, Akash was writing his second letter to Jaya. He had spent most of the day sweating over the words, using sheet after sheet of paper. He had no inkling whether Jaya had received the first letter yet, but writing to her the first time had broken a dam. Pouring himself into a letter to her became a tenet of his day, replacing his prayers at the river. Now he knew she lived, he fretted over every word that could not express the fullness in his heart, every choice of phrase that might give away his identity and void his contract with Ruhi to remain anonymous. He composed a sentence or two then, unsatisfied, scrunched up his words into a ball and tossed them away. The wastepaper basket overflowed.

He needed a break from the page, from the hopelessness of expressing his love for a woman who was his wife but couldn't know. Above him on the wall, hanging on a small bronze nail, was a calendar. The picture depicted the Gateway of India. He took it down, and leafed through it as he had done countless times while he had been Soraya's guest. On the streets, he lost his orientation: days blended into weeks, into months, into years. Now, in the womb of his room, evading the emotional strain of writing to Jaya, he resorted to calculations, painstakingly working out how long it had been since the day she had burned: 21 years, 7 months...

A rush of noise in the hallway outside his bedroom jolted him from his focus. Seconds later a fist banged against the door.

"Open up, Akash! Open this door, right now! It's Arjun. I want to talk to you!"

The moon shone through the window signalling the late hour. Akash's heart thumped in his ribcage. The atmosphere between him and Soraya's son remained fraught. "What do you want?"

"Are you going to talk to me through the door? I'm not here for a fight, if that's what you're worried about. We need talk man to man."

Akash opened the door and shrank back towards the bed. Arjun threw him a disgusted glance and sat on the floor in his dress trousers, opened the buttons at the neck of his shirt and motioned for Akash to sit next to him. Silence stretched between the two men until Arjun turned to look Akash squarely in the face, his mouth set in a grim line.

"I'm sorry," said Akash, unsure of what he was apologising for.

"That's a little rich after all these years."

Akash crumpled his face in confusion. "I'm sorry, I don't understand."

"You're really going to play the fool?"

"Your mother asked me to stay for two weeks. After that, I'll be gone. You won't have to see me again," said Akash.

"You expect me to believe that you will give all this up in two weeks?" Arjun waved his hand to indicate the sumptuous surroundings.

"I'm not here for your money." His voice was shrill, showing his fear. He wanted more than anything to be with Tariq in their hovel right now. Even Zahid Khan would be preferable to this. At least he knew what he was dealing with.

"No, just food and a free bed. Those clothes you're wearing are mine, by the way."

Akash cowered from the intensity of Arjun's gaze. "You want me to leave, that's fine. I'll say goodbye to your mother, and I'll go. I understand."

"She wants you to stay." Arjun's brow furrowed and he let out a low whistle. "You really don't know, do you? I didn't believe her but she hasn't told you, has she?"

"Told me what?" The air crackled with tension.

Arjun got to his feet, and looked down at the older man. "Akash, I'm not just Soraya's son. I'm yours."

"What?" Akash paled as recognition crept up on him. "No, that's not right. Soraya, she wouldn't have hidden that from me..."

"I'm twenty-two. You do the maths. We're not so dissimilar, you and me. Look closely."

Akash's heart swelled and exploded, shattering into tiny fragments. *Jaya, you and I never had a child, but...* All that he had missed, all that he had gained, raced through his head until his synapses overloaded. He had a son. He had a grandchild. "But she...she never said." He wrung his hands together, his eyes imploring.

"No, she didn't say a word to me either. Until you arrived. And we can't turn the clock back, can we?"

Arjun placed a hand on his father's shoulder, where it sat awkwardly. Then he pivoted and left the room, leaving Akash reeling in his wake.

# 24

**There could be** no doubt of the truth of Arjun's announcement. The veracity of it hit Akash like an epiphany. Wave after wave of horror crushed him as he absorbed how many experiences he had missed, the irony of being a man who yearned for love and had thrown all his chances away.

The next morning, he went to find Soraya. Wary of overstepping boundaries and of upsetting Arjun, it was the first time he had ventured upstairs in the house. He followed a sound of rustling to a door left ajar and then called out.

"Soraya?"

She emerged, holding a glittery burgundy *lengha choli* she had been folding. "There was a party at the restaurant last night. I'm just putting everything away," she said, by way of explanation. "Is everything okay?"

She disappeared back into her bedroom and he followed, and noticed how the decor here contrasted with the heavy opulence of his own room. Soraya's room consisted of sleek lines and furniture in white and pale blue, all elegance and minimalism, no fuss or fawning. She slid back the glossy door of a sliding wardrobe and placed her clothes on a hanger.

"Arjun came to see me last night."

He had her full concentration now.

"Oh." Her face fell. "I guess it was only a matter of time."

"You didn't tell me."

"I owed it to him. He needed time to process it."

She had not told him she was pregnant and neglected to tell him even when he reappeared in their lives. The time he had lost burned his throat.

"Is that why I am here?"

"It's one of the reasons."

"You were strong to raise him alone." He understood at last that while he had been unpacking his own burdens, Jaya and Soraya had faced their own trials with more grace than he had possessed.

"I had someone to hold close to me. What did you have? Aren't you angry, Akash? I stole your chance to be a father." She didn't look apologetic and he realised she wouldn't have changed her past. This was a woman who was completely at ease with herself and her choices.

He envied her surety.

Arjun was a grown man and had little need or desire to know his father. Akash could not turn back the clock, so instead he buried the pain of that lost opportunity deep within him. "I lost my claim to you when I walked away. What right do I have to question you?"

Soraya nodded, accepting his words. "Ask me anything you want," she said, beckoning him to follow her to a chaise lounge, a striped affair in silver and sky blue.

He sat beside her, awkwardly, two parents discussing their child without the bond of intimacy that parenting should bring. He might never have an emotional bond with Arjun, but he had a deep need to hear his son's story, to understand the child he never knew.

"Why 'Arjun'? Why did you choose that name? Your parents can't have approved."

"They chose a Muslim name for him. He was Samir. It means air. To me, he has always been Arjun, after the legend you loved."

"The archer." The hair on his arm rose as he remembered telling her of his love for the story of Arjun, once, long ago, when they were both young. "What a fool I've been not to see that he was mine." He took Soraya's hand. Without colour her nails were brittle and weak.

"Will you walk with me in the gardens, Soraya? Pour your memories into me. There is nothing I don't want to know about our son."

Soraya was holding something back, Akash was certain. The maid tried to tempt Akash with his body weight in samosas and spicy bhajiya, and Akash grew stronger, but more impatient, too. He ate sparsely, his stomach used to a meagre diet. Staying at the bungalow stalled his possible reconciliation with Jaya and it also poisoned any rebuilding of a relationship with Arjun, who remained convinced that Akash was taking advantage of his mother. Despite his burdened psyche, his body healed faster than it had done before. He drank enough mango lassi to colour the Ganga while he waited for his freedom.

Soraya, for her part, showered attention on her family. She conversed with their son, cooked with Muna and played with Leela, bouncing the baby on her knee until she gurgled with delight.

But still, a piece of the puzzle was missing. Soraya evaded his gentle pressure to understand the truth that escaped his fingers like a ghost. On Thursday, she spent an idyllic day visiting the markets with her daughter-in-law, and returned beaming with excitement. She beckoned Akash from his room, ignoring the sullen stares of their son.

"I have bought trinkets for you all," she said.

"Maa, we have everything we need," said Arjun, quickly quieted by his wife.

Soraya smiled at her son. "This is for you. A book of Gibran poetry. I know how much you like him." She handed him a smooth, leather-bound book with yellowed pages.

Arjun reached for the book and kissed her chastely on the cheek. "Thank you."

The baby crawled into her mother's lap, and Akash wondered at her innocence. He could think of no place safer than a mother's lap.

"And this, this is for you, Muna. I know you caught me buying them, but thank you for humouring me and not saying anything." She smiled and passed her daughter-in-law a plastic bag, which held a beautiful hand-embroidered scarf and a jar of saffron.

"You, *beta*," she said, touching Leela's cheek, "get this. A silver teething spoon. Arjun used to have one as a baby. But first, we must wash it." She handed it to Muna, who hugged her.

"And finally, Akash, we'll have to go shopping for some properly fitting clothes for you, of course, but for now, this is what I bought." She walked to where he stood bare-footed at the edge of the room in a pair of oversized shorts and a vest. "It's a locket. I've put a picture of Arjun and Leela in it."

Arjun frowned.

"I don't know what to say," said Akash, taking the locket awkwardly, feeling the ridges of the letter *A* engraved on it.

"Thank you is enough," said Soraya.

He noticed her laboured breathing, and finally the scales fell from his eyes: her insistence he stayed, her need to tell her son the truth, the translucency of her skin, how she had vomited in the garden.

"Thank you," he said quietly.

He returned to his bedroom, where the enormity of her secret overwhelmed him. That evening, Soraya visited him in his bedroom with a cup of chai and some slices of melon on a tray for him. He took the tray from her and turned to her with a heightened, accusing voice.

"This afternoon, those gifts... they were a goodbye, weren't they?"

Soraya glanced at him in surprise and then visibly relaxed. The tension drained from her body until she was no longer the erect and proud woman he knew. She leant against the doorframe, her expression, for once, an open book, relief spilling from her pores. "I've been waiting for the right moment to tell you."

"How sick are you?"

"It won't be long."

"Your doctors? You must have the best doctors."

She smiled wryly and he saw no pity. "All my options are exhausted. I've made my peace."

Her words pierced him like a shard of glass. The walls closed in on him like a shrinking womb. He started to panic. "Outside, I need to go outside."

Soraya took him by the hand, speaking to him gently as if he was a child and she was his mother, leading him through the winding corridors until Akash could no longer breathe. Then suddenly they were sitting on a sofa swing in the garden. Soraya held Akash's hand, the pad of her thumb tracing circles over his calloused skin.

"But—"

"It is my time, Akash." She laid a hand on his arm. How wrong it was that she comforted him rather than the other way around.

He opened up his arms to her, and she came. Sadness, raw and uncontainable, pulsed within him. "I'm so sorry," he whispered into her hair, stroking the grey strands of her hair away from her face.

She lifted her head. "I need to ask something of you."

"Anything."

She whispered in his ear, as if the words were unfit to be heard out loud.

"Arjun will not accept this," said Akash, shaken.

"That's why I cannot ask him." She shuddered. "Will you help me?"

Akash nodded, his promise a headstone in the cemetery of his soul.

Arjun watched his wife praying from the door. A scarf covered her head and she was holding a tray laden with water, fruit and incense. He wrinkled his nose against the sickly scent as Muna made her offering to the shrine of Ganesha, which sat in the corner of the room, the idol garlanded by flowers. Leela lay on a mat on the floor, her babbling accompanying her mother's mantras. Arjun had not been brought up as a man of faith, but the scene brought him a moment's peace.

He scooped up Leela from the floor and sat on the bed, cradling her while Muna completed her ritual. He flattened the folds of the dress the baby wore, made for her by hand by her mother, suddenly noticing how much pregnancy weight Muna had lost. There remained only a slight paunch. He looked down at his own belly and grimaced ruefully.

*High time I cut down on the curry.*

His wife turned, blue shadows underneath clouded eyes, and caught his expression. "What? Now it's not okay for me to pray?"

"Course not, Muna, you know I don't mind you praying. I like it, even. It brings me solace to know you have that covered."

"Oh, sorry," she said, looking unabashed. "Ganesha is the remover of obstacles. We could do with his help right now."

"What's that supposed to mean?" said Arjun.

"Well, for starters, you have a newborn, but the amount you're around here, I've started to question what your priorities really are. You said you were ready for a baby."

"That's not fair, Muna. I've had stuff to deal with..."

"Then talk to me!"

"There's nothing to talk about."

"Yes, there is! I would do anything to have my parents back, Arjun, and here you are, with both yours here, ready to be one big, bustling family, and you put your barriers up. Enough sulking, already. Deal with it."

"My mother lied. My father's a homeless man, and worse, a cheat. Not everyone forgives as easily as you, Muna."

"Not everyone knows how quickly loss comes, Arjun." She lowered her voice and sat next to her husband on the bed. "So Maa lied. So Akash Saheb isn't what you expected. She fell in love. She did the best she could. Is that a crime?"

"Stay out of this!" Arjun bristled, his voice a warning shot across the room that startled the baby.

Leela cried.

"You used to have ambition. Now it's all about family. My family. Stick your nose out, I mean it. This is my business." He glared at her and handed her the bawling baby.

"Just brilliant. Thanks Arjun, well done," said Muna as she rocked the child wearily.

# 25

**Bushra, who worked** on the front desk at Tara
Theatre, found Jaya snipping away at a blue bandini fabric. Usually
Bushra was all fluster and bluster, not the right sort to be the first
point of contact with customers. Still, as the director's aunt, not even
complaints subdued her. Her immunity made her insufferable.
Today, she happened to be Jekyll rather than Hyde, and approached
with a smile that split the heavy layer of make up on her face.

It took Jaya a moment to realise what all the excitement was about.

"Look, look, my dear. It came for you," said Bushra, waving a small
rectangle of pale yellow in the air. "Hand-delivered, no postmarks, with
just one word on the top—your name." She giggled, aiming for a girly
tittering no doubt, but sounding instead like a donkey.

Jaya reached out her hand for the letter.

The older woman came close enough for the scattering of hair on
her upper lip to look menacing and for the scent of her body odour to
be suffocating. "There's a little flower drawn at the back. Tell me, have
you a suitor? Is this from Ravi? A little birdie told me—" she said.

Jaya sighed. "Thanks for bringing it to me. Let's keep this to
ourselves, okay?" It remained an unfortunate consequence of not
having a visible man at her side, that she either was lumped
together with the maiden aunt brigade or any hint of romantic
attention resulted in shrieks of utter childishness. The rumour of
a great romance would be all around the theatre by lunchtime,
no doubt.

Bushra held her finger to her caked nose. "I'd never dream of
telling anyone." She rocketed down the corridor, fizzing with the
exaggerations about to spill from her mouth.

Jaya shook her head and laid down her scissors. She turned over the letter in her hand, pausing to examine the flower drawn on the flip side of the envelope, and carefully coloured in with a green colour pencil. The letter was a romantic gesture, she supposed. Had Ravi still not understood that she wanted to be left alone?

She inserted a finger into the envelope and slid it across to break the seal. Out fell a single sheet covered with evenly spaced blue ink. Jaya frowned. The lettering was oddly familiar to her in its mixture of loops and jagged lines. A memory dislodged in the recesses of her mind that she couldn't quite decipher. She read and the world fell away.

> *Dear Jaya,*
> *You might ask how I come to write to you. I hope you'll take this letter in good faith. We knew each other once, a long time ago, and I am too shy to see you face to face. It seems to me that I have known you forever, but it could be that I have reassembled the pieces of you and you are someone else entirely.*
> *The world has become so alien that there have been times I've been afraid that there is no space for me in it. I am a romantic man, but the irony is I've lived most of my life without love. It was my own fault. I chased false gods and pushed away everything that was good.*
> *They say everything happens for a reason, but I've found that to be a deceit we are told as a comfort. How can such trite words be comforting after great suffering? I'd rather face cold truths. Sometimes we are to blame for our troubles: we are hoodwinked or stupid, or we tumble into our mistakes with our eyes open. At other times suffering visits us out of the blue, and it is neither fair nor a lesson to be learned. It is just something we dig through, until we feel nearly whole again.*
> *I wonder if we hold the reins to our destiny, whether we can undo the patterns of old. I'd like to think so. Hope is a powerful thing. Maybe more powerful than love.*
> *I can't tell you who I am, but I hope that one day, I will. Until then, if it's acceptable for me to write to*

*you again, please leave a piece of red cloth in the*
*window at Tara Theatre. I'll be waiting.*
*Your friend.*

Jaya put down the letter. A chill ran down her spine. She knew with certainty the scribe was not Ravi. She touched the pad of her index finger to the ink and ran it across the page, lost in thought. She had an aversion to strangers, but this man said he knew her. She could not explain it, but she wanted nothing more than to receive another letter from him. The views he articulated reflected her own. Just like her, he had lost his way. His curious mix of hope and hopelessness mirrored hers. Perhaps a kindred spirit had stumbled across her path. She didn't understand why, but his thoughts, his lettering stirred buried memories in her. She needed to find out his identity. She tucked the letter into her handbag, submerging it underneath the books and make up pouch. Then she went to fetch a piece of red cotton from the store room.

That afternoon Akash slipped away from the house and found Tariq at one of their old haunts, laying his clothes out to dry on a park bench, having washed them in a public bathroom.

"I have something for you," he said in greeting.

He clapped his friend on the shoulder and handed him a parcel of food he had taken from Soraya's fridge. He hadn't thought to ask. Such were the excesses in the rose bungalow that a few morsels of curry and shreds of bread would never be missed. He could already feel his survival instincts had been numbed by the cool walls of Soraya's home, creeping indifference at the surplus of food, when once he had been forced to scavenge.

Tariq knew no such luxury. He smiled his thanks and unwrapped the brown paper bag, uncovering a foil dish. The smell of masala potatoes seeped out. He sat on the bench next to his wet, worn clothes and devoured the food. Akash waited as his friend ate, enjoying a comfortable silence borne of years of friendship, of two men who had seen each other at their lowest ebb and remained true without judgement.

Tariq had aged more quickly since he had been alone. The curve of his back had grown more pronounced, his ever-present cough more violent.

"Have you been okay? I wish I could be here with you."

"You don't need to worry about me," said Tariq.

Akash would have liked Soraya and Tariq to meet, but he could think of a dozen reasons why it was not a good idea. He would have gladly shared his room and food at the bungalow with Tariq, but that would infringe on Soraya's hospitality and sour relations further with their son. Now Akash knew Jaya to be alive, it represented a betrayal to invite his best friend to meet Soraya. Besides, Tariq reminded Akash of his own poor health and lack of sophistication. Even now, a smear of sauce sat on his upper lip where an uneven moustache had begun to sprout.

"What is that slug on your lip?" said Akash, falling into the teasing patterns of their relationship though he did not feel light-hearted.

"Your smile does not reach your eyes today, *bhai*. Tell me, what is wrong? I delivered your letter. Do you already have a response?" His concern whistled through the gap in his stained teeth.

"I have not been back to check."

"The two weeks you promised Soraya must almost be up."

"I know her secrets now."

Tariq pushed the remaining food away from him and swung to face Akash, his eyes solemn. "Tell me."

"She has an aggressive tumour. Brain cancer. Her prognosis is bad, she has weeks rather than months. Maybe days. I can see her getting weaker. She hasn't told her family."

"I'm sorry, Akash. It seems unfair after you have just found her again."

"She wants me there so she is not alone. Her strength puts me to shame. She's not scared of death, only of losing her dignity." Akash paused, his head in his hands.

"There's something else." Tariq knew him too well, as if he were a concerto with one wrong note sounding out.

"The boy. Arjun. He's mine."

Tariq's mouth gaped. Silence stretched out between the men while Tariq digested the news. He stuttered. "That's wonderful...

isn't it? You've always wanted a family. Soraya was pregnant when you ran? She hid it from you?"

"She found out afterwards. She tried to find me. How many people have I abandoned?"

"It's not your fault."

"Yes, it is. He hates me. His mother wants us to repair our relationship, but I don't know where to start." Akash slumped on the bench, and shredded a leaf from a bush next to him. Movement helped him think. "I have everything I ever wanted. A roof over my head, food, a family. My wife is alive. It all seemed so unattainable. Still, all I feel is a deep sense of foreboding about the future, Tariq. I don't know what to do."

"You prove you can be the rock, Akash, when your family needs you." Tariq's earnest words cut through the muggy city air. He coughed. "You might have abandoned them once, but this is your chance to make good. You may not get your happy ending, but maybe you'll win your self-respect back." Tariq rose to clear away the remnants of his meal. "What about Jaya? What will she think when she finds out about the boy? Are you going to tell her?"

"I don't know."

"You can't keep this a secret, Akash. Secrets destroy."

"Sometimes they save us. If she knew I was writing to her, do you think she would want to speak with me?" *Do you want me in your life again, Jaya? Do you need me like I need you?*

"Not if you are going to go behind her back again. You have to tell her," said Tariq.

"What if she can't forgive me for not coming back?"

"You're back now, aren't you? It takes courage to correct mistakes."

Akash could not allow hope to bloom only to have it crushed. He kept the fantasy of a life with Jaya locked up tight in a box. No fingers of light would thread their way into the box until he could be sure he was worthy of her. He turned to Tariq, replacing emotion with brusque practicality, feeling stronger for it.

"For now, Soraya and Arjun have to come first." He hesitated. "After that, it will be Jaya's turn." *Wait for me.*

Akash had passed Soraya's Juhu restaurant on many occasions and never once imagined she owned it. The sign on the restaurant door read *Closed* when he arrived there. Akash ignored it and pushed open the newly washed glass, smoothing down his too large trousers as he crossed the threshold, setting back his shoulders with determination. He could understand Arjun's wrath, but with Soraya so ill, they could not continue this dance of bull and matador. He needed to find a way to pierce through Arjun's anger, to find a way to reconcile. Perhaps he and Arjun could talk more openly away from Soraya, away from the confinement of the bungalow.

The tables had been arranged for the evening meal, but with service an hour away, the chefs were in the kitchen preparing over hot stoves. Spices drifted into Akash's nose. He heard Arjun before he saw him.

"What on earth are you doing here?" A hand grabbed his arm, clawing into the skin beneath his shirt, man-handling him to the door before Akash had uttered a word. "You ambush me at my place of work? I have to put up with you at home, but not here."

"Wait! Arjun. Listen." Akash spun to look at his son. It had been a mistake to come. Fury had carved grim lines into the younger man's face. His jaw was locked, his body driving Akash forward so his sandals slipped on the velvet carpet. A glass crashed to the floor from a table adjacent to them.

Arjun swore.

"Don't you dare command me to do anything. You lost that right twenty-two years ago." The whites of his eyes widened in rage.

"That's why I'm here, Arjun. I don't want to lose any more time." Even to his own ears the words sounded pathetic, not enough after the years without a father. A grown man did not need a stranger to father him, especially when the father had failed at life.

"What do you have to offer me?"

"I don't have a lot, Arjun, only what you see. But I will stand by you. Now I know I have a son, I will stand by you. Whatever I can give, I will."

Arjun laughed scathingly. "You are a man who always runs. It's only a matter of time."

"There may come a time when you do need me."

"I have my mother. I have Muna and Leela. I have the business. I don't need you hanging onto our coat-tails, leeching off our success."

"I promise you this is not about me," said Akash. Soraya's secret tingled on the edge of his tongue. The boy deserved to know how unwell she was, how little time he had.

Arjun looked past him onto the street. "Go."

Akash considered betraying Soraya's confidence for a fleeting moment, but he could not thwart a dying woman's wishes. "Okay. As you wish." He placed a hand on his son's face, a moment of tenderness amongst chaos. Arjun's mask relaxed, and beneath it Akash glimpsed the hurt before the mask fortified once more. Akash freed himself from his son's grip and shook himself off.

"See you at home, Papa," said Arjun, his face contorted, his voice dripping with sarcasm as Akash retreated.

The bungalow stood a mile from the restaurant. Akash set off, engulfed by sadness at the broken relationships around him. He realised that Soraya had but one regret, and that was to leave her son without a parent. If only he could mend that bond before she died, it would bring her peace. Akash trod the streets, listening to the rhythmic beat of his sandals against the concrete. He walked on autopilot, as was his habit, a way to bring stillness to his churning thoughts. Only when he stood directly before it did he realise where his subconscious had brought him. There, as the sun fell in the sky, in the gleaming window of Tara Theatre, tucked behind a glossy film advertisement, was a red cotton rag.

# 26

Soraya sat in the corner of the kitchen tracing a finger from her elbow to the translucent skin of her fingers. How thin her skin had become. She grimaced and shook her head to dispel morbid thoughts. Silence filled the house and echoed in her ears. Muna and the child slept after a fretful day during which the baby had either clamoured for her mother's milk or been attached to her breast. Soraya wished she could talk to her own mother about her illness; a mother's love always helped. Instead, she had polished the kitchen worktops to a shine, as if cleaning were a tonic for anxiety, though the maid had only just left for the night. Then she had turned off the lights and pulled up a chair to wait for her son.

The decision to wait in the dark was deliberate, driven by Arjun's wilful avoidance of her. They had lived together for so long that his habits had become as familiar as her own. The kitchen remained his first stop when he came in from the restaurant. He often brought food home for the family. Even if he returned empty-handed, he stopped by the fridge for a cool drink to recover after the bustle of the restaurant. Not so since their conversation. Yesterday, for the second day running, with the kitchen occupied, he deposited the take-away in the hallway.

She accosted him there, determined to have her say. "Arjun? Long day?"

"Not now, Maa. I'm tired. I need to see Leela, and then bed."

"Can we talk? It's important."

He paused to look at the long winding corridor ahead, which led to Akash's bedroom, displeasure marring his face. Their eyes met: a cool stare and a penitent one. "Tomorrow, maybe," he had said, before walking heavily upstairs.

Arjun's recent spate of late nights at the restaurant were tied to her revelation rather than work, Soraya had no doubt. With a manager installed at each, the restaurants ran themselves. She did not blame him for his anger. She and her now dead parents had been complicit in a lie about Arjun's paternity, and now he had uncovered the ugly truth.

Initially her parents had not mentioned Akash, as if hers was a phantom pregnancy without male input. As Soraya's stomach expanded, her parents urged her to find Akash and marry him. They did not know he had a wife, or that he was Hindu. It seemed easier that way. They knew only Akash had fled. It did not occur to them she was as much to blame as he. Once Arjun arrived, her parents loved him with such abandon that his parentage became irrelevant, especially when paired with Soraya's success. Eventually, they claimed Arjun as their own with the same passion as they ignored Akash's existence.

She could almost see it now: six-year-old Arjun, long eyelashes, with ears too big for his head, burying himself in the folds of her sari and asking with muffled voice about his father. His school education had been mostly uneventful, but on that particular day, a father and son cricket match had taken place. Soraya's father attended in lieu of his own, but a seventy-year-old man had not provided enough protection against the curiosity of the other children about the absence of Arjun's father. When awareness dawned, the tears had come.

Soraya had expected the question eventually, of course, but it still winded her. She had bent down to take her son's hands in her own, looked him in the eye, and told him "Beta, your father died before you were born, but don't be sad. We have each other, and you'll never lack for anything. I'll be both Maa and Papa to you."

"But you can't play cricket."

"You can teach me."

That afternoon Soraya bought a large cricket bat and a small one, and a ball that gleamed like an apple. She and Arjun played in the garden until the light dimmed, even though she was wrapped in seven yards of sari and the dinner menu for the following day required approval. *This is what it means to be a mother*, she thought. Arjun did not speak of his father again until the eve of his ninth birthday.

"Maa?"

"Yes, beta?" said Soraya, breathless from blowing up balloons.

"You said Papa died."

"Yes." She looped the rubber end of the balloon around her finger and tied it before pushing it away.

"How? How did he die?"

She gulped. "He was caught under the wheels of a car." The lie tumbled out before she could call it back.

"Oh. Did it hurt?"

"I don't think so."

"Good." A moment of quiet followed. "Can we have ice cream at the party?"

"Would you like that?"

"Yes!"

"Then of course we can." Soraya pulled him into her lap and breathed in the smell of his hair as she held him, her regret at odds with the bright party decorations littering the floor around them.

The years passed and Arjun's childhood fled. As her son grew into adulthood, Soraya's lie grew more truthful, fortified by the passage of time and lack of scrutiny, until she almost believed it herself. The lie suited Soraya. That was, until Akash lurched into her life once more.

Soraya could have been angry at the intrusion, her forced hand. She feared the repercussions for her relationship with Arjun, but she couldn't help but consider the timing to be serendipitous. With her parents no longer alive and her own impending needs, luck had presented her with an opportunity to make amends to both father and son for keeping them from one another.

She wouldn't give Arjun the chance to escape her a third time. She waited in the dark for him, raking over the past, eager to begin the process of renewal. The minutes became an hour, and suddenly headlights swept across the facade of the house. Soraya steeled herself as a car door slammed, the front door clicked open and footfalls sounded her way. Moments later her son traipsed into the kitchen, set a brown paper bag onto the worktop and opened the fridge door. He poured some mango juice into a tall glass and tipped it into his mouth. A moment later he spluttered to see his mother, still and serene in the half-light of the still open refrigerator. He slammed it shut.

"Maa, what are you doing here?" He flicked on the spotlights above Soraya's head and she blinked. "It's nearly half eleven. I thought you'd be in bed."

"Who did you think was going to eat that then?" She nodded towards the food on the counter. Oil seeped out of the paper bag and smeared the newly-washed surface. The smell of curry dispersed in the air around them.

"Oh, it'll keep 'til tomorrow."

"It's time to talk."

"You've been waiting here to ambush me?" Arjun raised a bushy eyebrow that reminded Soraya of his father. "I've had my fair share of surprises today."

"What's that's supposed to mean?" She couldn't bear to fight again. Not when the cancer stole from her energy reserves, when all she wanted to do was lie down.

"Akash came to the restaurant."

"I didn't know. What did he say?"

"I threw him out."

"Your anger isn't helping anyone. Let's talk. Please."

"Fine. Let's do this." He emptied the rest of the glass and drew up a chair into the shadows.

The spotlights above Soraya exposed her and left white spots swimming in the periphery of her eyes.

"You told me he was dead," said Arjun.

"I lied. I'm sorry."

"Why? Why did you lie for so long, Maa? Why did you lie at all?"

"I didn't have a better truth. I didn't know where he was. I thought you didn't need him."

"You were wrong." Bitterness rang out, giving an odd note to the usual timbre of his voice. "I dreamt of a father as a boy. I built him up in my head."

"You never told me."

"Why would I? You were doing your best. I was happy, but I lacked something everyone else had. And now, after all these years, you reveal your dirty secret. I missed out on a father. I missed out on siblings, cousins, grandparents. You kept that all from me. It's your fault. And what's more, he's a disappointment. Not the hero I dreamt about as a child. He's ghost of a man. Someone who peers through the windows of unsuspecting families." He shuddered. "To think, I beat my own father with these hands."

Soraya felt her powerlessness keenly, the arguments spiralling out of her grasp. "There is nothing I can do to make this better, Arjun. But believe me, even grown men need their parents."

"I think I'll take my chances."

"Arjun." Her voice delivered a low warning.

"The only way we're going to fix this, Maa, is if he goes."

"He stays."

"Then I won't be held responsible for my actions."

Soraya gripped her armrests and leaned forward, struggling to keep her composure.

"You might be the heir to my fortune, but while I am still here, this is my house, not yours."

"So I'm supposed to accept all of this?" Sadness filled his eyes.

"You know I didn't mean that," said Soraya.

"I know exactly what you meant."

The chair clattered to the floor as he left. Soraya's face crumpled, then she rose to put the food away.

# 27

**A breeze blew** stale air into the small room. Jaya sat on her bed, rereading the letter. She had read it so often that it had frayed along its folds. Twice, she had replaced the red cotton in the window at Tara when the cleaners had removed it. Despite her signal that she was willing to accept a second letter, one had not come. Perhaps the correspondent had missed the signal or was playing a cruel joke. Perhaps he had lost interest, had somehow seen her up close—her limp, the hips that had widened with age, the wrinkles that lined her skin—and decided otherwise.

Even as a young girl, long before marriage, she had found her beauty to be lacking. She had thought of herself as a wallflower rather than a rose. She was neither siren nor virginal, but somewhere unhappily in between, with thick ankles, a too big nose, unruly hair. After the fire, she had longed for the body she once had. The irony was that with each passing day her beauty faded even further. Her wallflower days were the apex. If only she had appreciated herself more then.

Unfortunate that her self-loathing had chosen tonight to resurface. She hadn't slept well either. Her old nightmares had returned, where Akash stood, unmoving while she burned. She had woken with the taste of smoke in her mouth, her tongue like sandpaper. Her exhaustion had followed her to work. After the day was over, she would have liked nothing better than to complete her chores at home and then undress and crawl underneath her bedsheets and escape into the oblivion of sleep.

Instead, she was expected at a wrap party for the latest production at Tara, a play about a broken family that had been filmed for television. The director brimmed with excitement and a black mark would appear against the name of any staff members who didn't show up. She would have to attend and mingle with the guests, regardless of how tired she felt and how little she wanted to play cat and mouse with Ravi. She consoled herself that showing her face would be enough. An hour at the party, a quick change of clothes, and she could unwind at Firoz's art class. She could check for another letter while she was there.

She stood wearily and crossed from the bedroom to the only bathroom in the house—a shoebox tiled in olive green ceramic squares that contained a small basin, toilet and wet-room style shower enclosed by a flimsy curtain dotted with mauve shells. The bathroom's saving grace was the lack of a full-length mirror. Jaya slid the lock into place and unpeeled her clothes. She tied her hair on top of her head with a scarf and stood under the shower head, ignoring the voice inside her head, which crowed about how ugly she was. The pipes squeaked as they released scalding water onto her skin. She watched as the streams of water took different routes down her body, around her breasts, over her pubic hair and then dispersed over her scarred legs. The water provided a barrier, and if she semi-closed her eyes, the effect of her scarring blurred and she appeared almost normal again. She reached for a bar of soap and scrubbed her body, taking extra time underneath her armpits and in between her legs, just as her mother had taught her.

When she finished, she turned off the faucet and reached for the largest towel. She bent to rub the water droplets from every inch of her body. The fire had irreparably damaged hair follicles where she had been disfigured. Still, she maintained a brisk towelling technique. Everyone knew that Indian women who didn't rub between their eyebrows were prone to monobrows, and an Indian who did not take pre-emptive measures against hair could quickly leap into ape territory. Jaya had seen it in some of her classmates who had to decide between merciless mockery by their peers or paying a small fortune for frequent and arduous hair removal.

Once dry, she slipped on a floor-length nightdress solely for the purpose of darting across the corridor to her room whilst preserving her modesty. She had always been a prude, more so since her accident.

A shuffle outside the door alerted her to her mother's presence. Nowadays her father avoided taking the stairs more than once a day.

Age had wreaked havoc with his knees. Jaya sighed. She didn't have time to lurk in the bathroom. The party started in less than an hour. She unlocked the door and came face to face with her mother.

"Food was good today, Jaya. Your father enjoyed it. Next time boil the potatoes a little longer and it will be perfect." There was always an adjustment to be made to please her mother. Sometimes Jaya felt the criticisms stemmed merely from a lack of conversation, a way to fill awkward silences. "You are off gallivanting today, also?"

Jaya nodded, squeezing around the older woman in the cramped corridor. "An after-party. I must get dressed, otherwise I'll be late." She made her escape, disappearing into her bedroom. Over her shoulder came her mother's parting shot.

"Ruhi's parties are always so wonderful. Will there be any real stars at your party?"

Exasperation overcame Jaya. She had been too generous. However she might try to pretend to herself, her mother's wounding of her occurred so often, it could not be accidental. She twisted to face the older woman, pinning her with her gaze, intent on unveiling her true colours. "Do you always have to be so cutting? What did I ever do to you?"

Her mother lifted a painted eyebrow in surprise. "You took my youth," she said simply. "And you never left."

Tears clogged Jaya's throat. She refused to allow them to surface. "You think you gave the best years of your life to me?"

"Yes." Her mother drew herself up to her full height, seeking to intimidate. This time she would not succeed.

"Funny, that, because I feel the same."

"How dare you! A daughter respects her elders."

"Because elders are usually kind and wise. I don't see any of that in you." Jaya spat the words, determined that they found their target. She wanted her mother to understand that anything she had given, she gave because she wanted to, not because it had been demanded of her. "I'm a good daughter. Not because of you, but because of me. Because of who I am. I stay here not for you, Maa, but for Papa, and what it would do to this family if I left."

Her mother unleashed a bitter laugh that reverberated between the walls. Downstairs, her father had turned off the television. She imagined him in the stairwell, straining to listen. "Oh, you think he's a saint? Well, you don't know him very well then, do you?"

This was why she didn't battle her mother. No good ever came of it, no wins to buoy her. It remained a joyless struggle. "Whatever you say, Maa. Like I said, I'm late. Don't wait up for me."

"I won't."

Jaya turned on her heel and shut her bedroom door, quietly, with infinite control despite the raging sea of her emotions. She leant against it, coaxing her breath to return to a normal pace. Eventually, she dressed for the party.

Firoz greeted her with a warm hug. Jaya sank into his arms and breathed deeply of the incense burning behind him.

"I wasn't sure you were going to come. We're halfway through already," he said, helping her with her bag. She had changed out of the lime salwar kameez she had worn to the party at Tara, but her make-up was heavier than she usually would have worn to paint.

"I left as soon as I could," said Jaya. She had left as soon as possible without offending, keen to avoid a brooding Ravi drinking in the corner as if on a mission to blot out his evening. She couldn't be sure, but from across the room his expression had seemed jeering when it was directed at her.

Jaya shook her head to dispel the memory. It soothed her to be in the bright light of the studio after the dark confines of the theatre, where the smell of wine and spirits filled the room. Here, the incense cleansed the air. She was not compelled to speak to strangers and silence was welcome. Firoz had already set up a workstation for her.

She kissed his cheek. "Thank you."

"Don't mention it." He floated over to a student, stretching out his arms in front and cracking his knuckles as he went.

Already Jaya felt better. She settled herself on a stool and ran her hand over the blank canvas. Then she picked up her palette and squeezed out some colours from the tubes stacked neatly at her easel. The brush felt at home in her grip and soon she was lost in her creation, light strokes of her brush already creating something new. Art as therapy. She wanted to paint her own future. Purples and greens and yellows found a home together on the page, and Jaya discovered her evolving spirit there. She didn't want to suffocate under the burden of familial duty and male whims. There, in that moment of clarity, she remembered Ruhi's words about love, and decided that love didn't have to be sacrificial. It could be strong and demanding. She could take. Forty-five minutes later, when Jaya studied her canvas, and the creation that had intuitively emerged under the guidance of her hand, she recognised a self-portrait, beautiful in its hard edges and strong bright colours. To hell with duty. It was her turn.

When class was over and she did not hurry home, Firoz questioned why. He sat cross-legged on the floor, his bare feet dirty, and patted the space next to him. Jaya joined him, not minding when her skirt rode up to reveal a flash of her patchy skin. She would find no judgement here.

"Your parents won't be waiting for you, Jaya?" Firoz stretched to one side until his upper body made a crescent, mirroring the moon outside.

"They can wait. It's been a long day I am too tired to move anyway," said Jaya, leaning into her friend.

"Let me hail you a rickshaw," said Firoz. "You look exhausted."

"I'm enjoying your haven. Just a few more minutes."

"I like having you here, you know that. There's no rush." Once, Firoz owned a small apartment. Now, he lived in his curtainless studio, sleeping on a tuck away mattress, the stars twinkling through the vast windows. The smell of the paints comforted him, she knew. His nights here were dreamless, wholesome. His studio felt more like home to him than his apartment ever had.

Jaya glanced at her friend, pensive. "I get now why Ravi showered me with attention. He could see me coming. I think he saw me as someone vulnerable. Someone left on the shelf, who might sleep with him. I mean—" Sarcasm coloured her voice. "I'm lucky to be thrown scraps, right? Ravi is younger, handsome..."

Firoz harrumphed, his brow creased in disagreement. "Didn't sound handsome to me. Especially that dress sense. A mustard shirt? Not that I can talk." He indicated to his luminous yoga pants.

Jaya laughed.

"Besides, you can't know what his intentions were. Sounds to me like drink might turn the prince into a frog."

"You don't need to spare my feelings, but I love you for it." Jaya stood to fetch them a cushion each from the cupboard where Firoz kept his overnight belongings. Exhaustion was less a creeping problem than a crashing wave. She threw Firoz a cushion and collapsed onto one herself. "Do you ever wonder if you'd be happier in a relationship? I was reading the other day about how unmarried men and women have shorter lives. They have worse mental and physical health." She shrugged. "It makes me sad. It seems so unfair."

Firoz settled himself on the cushion, a square of emerald and crocus yellow. "You know me, I've never had time for generalisations. We all need interaction but I enjoy my solitude. I take care, eat healthily, nourish my spirit with art and yoga. I have dear friendships." His eyes twinkled at her. "What more does a person need?"

"Unconditional love?"

"Is there any such thing?

"I don't know." Jaya paused. "I fought with my mother tonight."

"It's always fireworks with you two."

"It's going to be awkward going home."

"She'll be asleep, I expect. You can stay if you like. I can make us some fresh *puri* in the morning." He gestured towards his electric stove.

Jaya smiled. "No thanks. I'd never leave." Firoz's world view refreshed her in its simplicity. He wore his identity like a flag for all to see. He made no excuses for who he was. Neither did he demand or offer respect based on age, status or gender. "It's always like tiptoeing around a bed of nails with her. She's not like that with everyone. Only with me."

"I love you, Jaya," said Firoz, "but you know, it's almost impossible to live up to parental or romantic ideals."

"So it's my fault, then? I disappointed her?"

"No. Maybe she disappointed herself, and simply tried to transfer her expectations to you. It's your choice whether to accept them. It's almost certainly too late for your mother to change, but you, you can change everything. You just have to want to."

# 28

**Soraya told him**, "Tomorrow is the day. The day I am free, and you are also."

Akash had longed for his freedom, but now it had arrived, he wished instead to rewind time. It was so final. This woman didn't belong to him. She was majestic, still in flight. How brightly she lived. He could not bear to see her wings clipped, but she did not flinch from the plans she had laid out, the ones she had been considering even before he reappeared in her life. Soraya embodied glory in her surrender. Her courage and her determination to protect Arjun shamed him. She wanted nothing from Akash, except perhaps comfort. She understood the loneliness that arrived like an unwelcome guest in the final throes before death, and she had chosen Akash as her buffer. Bulbous sorrow grew at his core at the unfairness. It looped around him, lending heaviness to his limbs. He fought to keep his sorrow prisoner, unwilling to burden her with its weight.

Sometimes he caught her fleeting glances underneath thinning eyelashes, assessing him, wondering if he would carry out his side of the bargain, stay at her side until she was gone. It pained him that she didn't have full trust in him, although she was right. His mind never strayed more than a step from Jaya despite the final journey of the mother of his child. How eager humans were to project themselves into the future without perceiving the gifts of the present. His sojourn with Soraya had been a blessing not only for her, but for him: to collect his thoughts, plan his way back into Jaya's life, a place of safety where his body and mind could grow stronger, a chance to get to know his son and say goodbye to a woman he had loved.

She knocked on his door at eight in the evening, having spent the day with her family. He recognised the gentle rap of her knuckles, muffled by the heavy wood. She entered, her face a pale moon against the indigo of her sari.

"I've said my goodbyes. Leela is asleep, and Muna is tired." Her voice caught in her throat, a stumble that she sought to hide. "Arjun is at the restaurant. He won't be back until the early hours." Her distress played out in gentle waves across her face that she tried to control.

He alone knew the secret she carried with her and as a result, he felt even more bonded to her. Akash held out his arms. "Tell me what I can do."

"Hold me."

He folded her into his arms and it was more than an embrace between friends. He could tell, could feel in the chemistry between them, the stillness of the air, the slow sensual movements she was making against him that she wanted more. He responded, first hesitantly, catching her lip between his, sucking gently, wondering all the while if this was a betrayal of Jaya. He wasn't sure. It felt like a goodbye. Like gratitude for the dying woman's belief in him, for the gift of their son.

He moved to the window to draw the heavy curtains. They blocked out the fading light and a new world opened up inside the Red Room. He returned to Soraya and they melted into each other. He poured all his gratitude and love for her into his touches. *Farewell, brave woman*, his mind called out.

After countless years without touch, his movements felt unpractised. He eased her onto the bed, folded back the bedding and drew it over her with infinite care. Her bones were fragile birds underneath his calloused fingers. They tangled in each other's limbs, but Soraya grew frustrated with her sari. The material stretched out, a barrier to the human contact she needed.

She caught his face in her clammy hands. "You don't have to do this for me."

They both needed to say goodbye. "I want to."

She sat up, a gradual lift to ninety degrees, his hand in the crook of her back to aid her. She stood and walked to the door, smoothing her hair, and for a moment he thought she was going to leave.

*Perhaps that would be for the best.* He thought of Jaya. He thought of Soraya's physical weakness. *Are you even strong enough for this?*

She locked the door and turned to face him. The red tones of the room brought a pinkness to her cheeks that relieved his worry. Her expression was solemn. Her eyes pierced him, candid and unrelenting. She flicked the light switch off.

Off came her sandals. Light spooled through a gap in the drapes and found her silhouette. Her movements jerked. She was not without pain. He opened his mouth to stop this madness then heard her take a deep breath, sensed rather than saw her smile in the shadows. He froze, entranced, while she unpinned her sari at the shoulder. His memory of Soraya's naked form was confined to twenty years ago.

"Hold this," she said, handing him the corner of the fabric.

Akash held the silken threads between his trembling thumb and forefinger. Soraya spun in a circle, her arms aloft like a dancer. The garment unravelled, and fell in deep folds at her feet. She stood without fear in her blouse and petticoat, her skin gleaming in the half-light. The air-conditioning left a trail of goosebumps along her skin. He took her into his arms and covered them both with a sheet.

"You're beautiful." He meant it, though her fragility and pale skin struck him again.

"One last show of strength." A hint of bitterness tinged her words.

The words of comfort which came to him in that moment rang untrue, and he knew how she loathed pretence. Instead of responding, he pulled her towards him, banished thoughts of Jaya and comforted her with his body. He took all the dreams of Soraya, which had sustained him on the streets, and poured them into loving her. No one existed apart from the two of them. It had been so long since he'd made love to a woman that his gratitude overwhelmed him. Slowly, his nerves dissipated and he immersed himself in what Soraya offered. Not youthful Soraya, but this broken one.

She returned the pressure of his lips, and waited patiently as he fumbled with the hooks of her front-fastening blouse.

Akash didn't need to know what this was anymore, whether it was distraction from what lay ahead, a goodbye, or an honouring of a memory. He exiled logic and embraced instinct and intuition. He dipped his head to trace his lips across the mounds of Soraya's breasts, still encased in a nude lace bra.

Emboldened, he discarded his borrowed clothes and pushed them onto the floor. He pulled her closer and she wrapped her arms around his neck. Akash returned her touch, his fingers straying to the waistband of her petticoat. With a start, he recognised his own arousal. It had been so long since he had felt this way. Their act resurrected an ancient part of Akash, needs he had buried long ago.

He drank in Soraya's smell, the texture of her hair, coarser than he remembered. Her mouth parted and he tasted her, taking care not to crush her with the weight of his body. He took it slowly, and it felt like an act of worship rather than a carnal desire. She gave herself to him freely. When her hands ventured between his legs to cup him, he could not hold back. He entered her, concentration on his face. The rhythm they found was not flawless but it did not matter. She threw her head back as he moved, her skin like paper, pushing against him, urging him to go deeper. Hot, salty tears rolled down his face.

They came to each other as different people this time, no longer as lovers but as if this represented a parting between lifelong friends. Youthful passion had been replaced by the hurts and uncertainties of life, and a complex cocktail of emotions coloured their joining: anguish, regret, love and acceptance.

When it was over, the room grew large again and he honed in once more to the hum of the air-conditioning and dusk approaching. He ran a hand over his face to wipe away the trace of his tears and passed her a towel. They lay side by side, fingers entwined. Her feet were cold on his calves and he bent to take them in his hands one by one and enclose them in the heat of his palms.

After a few minutes they slept, skin against skin. Soraya fell asleep first, peacefully, without struggle. Eventually, Akash relinquished himself to shadowy nightmares, haunted by the knowledge of the knife hidden beneath her pillow, her gift to herself from the market: a gift of release.

When she woke, her hair dishevelled, and found him watching her, Soraya smiled, then addressed him, her almond eyes pools of darkness beside him. "It is time."

Soraya changed into a simple salwar kameez in yellow, the colour of hope. Then she returned to him. Dawn came, basking the room in a golden glow, bringing with it the sound of springtime birds at the window. Akash didn't know how long he had stayed there with Soraya, watching the first blush of light and listening to the birds as she faded away.

After some time, the mother of his son, one of the only people he had truly loved, was still. He passed a hand over her eyes to close them. He had seen her death as she'd willed it: a release, a means for her to retain her dignity and escape her suffering, heroic even. But in the cold light of day, it didn't feel that way. There was a savagery to it he couldn't escape.

A curtain of grief descended over him and he cried out in his selfishness, beaten by the knowledge that she was gone. He tightened his grip on her body, thinking back to a few hours previously when she had arched in his arms, willing himself not to forget the texture of her skin, the sound of her voice, the way she felt in his arms. *I will never be able to share this grief with you, Jaya.*

The chill permeated his bones despite the heat of the rising sun, but he stayed holding her, until the sounds of the waking house broke his spell. Then he sprang into action, taking the locket she'd given him from the dresser, placing it in a pocket just above wear his heart lay. He found his last letter to Jaya and pushed it into his sock. Even in his desolation he understood how angry Arjun would be, how he'd no longer be welcome in this house, despite Soraya's last words.

*Be a father to my boy.*

He needed air. He kissed Soraya's forehead and eased himself off the bed. Her head lolled. A painful ball of tears formed in his throat as pulled back the curtains and opened the window. Fresh and stale air mingled together. She would never see this sight again. Her gardens would exist in their splendour long after she had left this world. Her tulips drooped in homage to her, orange petals bending low to brush the earth below as if it were a prayer mat.

He returned to her, desperate to read peace into her vacant expression. Instead, she looked pained, just as she had these past few weeks. How could he think of Jaya now? It seemed callous to seek happiness after this loss, lacking in respect somehow.

Soraya's body was cold by the time their son found them. Akash had pulled the knife from her abdomen, arranged her in a position of repose and smoothed the covers. The red of the room masked the blood. He sat by her head, committing her face to memory. The door flew open and Akash's heart drummed against his ribcage, despite his innocence.

"Akash, I've been looking for my mother. She's not with you—" said Arjun.

A long moment passed as Arjun took in his mother, her pale face and closed eyes. Akash sat at her head, solemn and still. Only a fluttering of his eyelids betrayed his emotion.

"Maa?"

No answer.

"What's going on here?" Arjun walked to the bed and drew back the covers. His mother was fully dressed. He saw the wound in her stomach, and the blood that had pooled beneath the covers, and spread in blotches across the lemon hue of her salwar kameez. Then he saw the knife. A huge roar erupted from him, filled with anguish and sorrow, and he buried himself in his mother's body.

"Help, somebody, help!" said Arjun. "Please, call an ambulance. It's Maa!" He lifted her into his arms, shaking her, calling her name. "Maa, Maa, look at me, please. Open your eyes." A sob escaped from his throat.

"Arjun, I am so sorry." Akash's words rung with inadequacy, but what son wants to hear that his mother took her own life? Arjun was strong in anger. *Blame me, son. Let me be a pariah, if that's what you need.*

The ivory handle of the bloodied knife gleamed against the sheets. Arjun looked from his father to the knife, taking in the crimson smears on the older man's t-shirt. His face morphed into someone unrecognisable and Akash was turned to stone, not prepared for the venom though he had willed it.

"Get away from her!" said Arjun, disgust and anger pulsing across his face. "Please, somebody come!"

He set his mother down on the bed with infinite care, before turning to his father and shoving him hard against the wall.

Akash crumpled on the floor in a heap, the back of his head sore, his mind a whiteout of anxiety and grief. *Are you proud of me now, Soraya?*

Arjun bent down to his father, his face ashen, and held him by the collar. "You will pay for this."

Footsteps hurtled towards them.

"I know."

# 29

**Jaya considered her** warrior self in her reflection. Was it true that presenting a strong external self healed the internal one? She could not be sure, but surely the two halves of her personality would knit together if she willed it. The wounded woman and her lion counterpart, the one who could determine her future, who was neither victimised nor pitied, who took no prisoners.

She closed her bedroom door, not quietly as she usually would have done, but loudly, announcing her imminent arrival to her parents downstairs, eager to disrupt their stone slumber in front of the flickering box.

"There you are, Jaya." Always the hidden censure in her mother's voice. "We need milk. Can you bring it on your way in?"

"I'll be late, Maa." A warning in the sharpness of her voice. She no longer accepted her role as maid. It brought her neither gratitude nor affection. It certainly did not bring her fulfilment. What did bring her happiness was her work at the theatre, spending time with Ruhi and her nephew, art, long walks. That was what she would be doing more of, no apologies. "I am going to the beach after work."

"What do you want on the beach? You'll get dusky."

Jaya's patience wore thin. "What is wrong with that? If you need milk, you and Papa can go over the road yourselves. It's not far. There are some rupees in the kitty in the kitchen."

Her father piped up. "But we are tired."

Jaya snapped. "I am tired after a long day."

"It is your responsibility as a daughter..."

Jaya refused to rise to the bait. "I do my duties well."

Her mother's legacy to her had been unwelcome. Centuries of female schooling handed down by matriarchs: to endure, to suffer in silence, to assimilate. Jaya didn't want to be the good girl anymore, conditioned by society to fulfil everyone else's needs before her own. She wanted the freedom to be flawed, to be ugly, to be piercingly honest if she chose. No more excuses. No more apologies.

She slung her bag over her shoulder, heavy with books to choose from after her walk, and closed the door behind her.

A female inspector handcuffed him. "Akash Choudry, of no fixed abode, you are being arrested for the murder of Soraya Mansoor of Juhu Beach."

Akash did not protest. His mind spun like a compass, thoughts loosened from the magnetism of north. He had been unable to provide Arjun with a father's protection growing up, but he could do it now. He could hide the fact Soraya took her own life.

Soraya had died on a Friday, the holiest day of the week for Muslims. Akash was certain she would have smiled at the irony of it for a non-religious woman. They hadn't spoken of the timing of her death with regard to the calendar, only for its impact on Arjun. Would it be more distressing for Arjun to witness his mother's deterioration, or would a cleaner break be better in the long run? Soraya had been adamant that the truth be shrouded from Arjun. She didn't want to risk her son convincing her to change her mind. What were a few more weeks, when she knew Death would be waiting all the same?

Akash focused on Arjun, sitting on the porch, head in hands. He willed him to look up so Arjun could witness the love in his father's face, know that he was not alone. Behind him stood Muna, helplessly trying to console the crying baby. Akash flushed in shame as his head was pushed into the car by the policewoman, though he'd done nothing wrong.

A crowd had gathered at the roadside. Rumours had already spread of Soraya's death. She was well known in Juhu, not only for her restaurants, but as a long-time inhabitant of the area, a single mother who stood out, successful in her own right. The onlookers jostled, peering into the car as the police drove Akash away. The inspector sat next to him. A colleague of hers occupied the driver's seat, focused and still, carefully manoeuvring past the small crowd as he pulled away from the house. Akash fixed his gaze rigidly ahead, squirming under the glare of those gathered, taking solace from the cold metal of Soraya's pendant in the pocket at his heart. His second letter to Jaya remained hidden in his sock, though both items would be found soon enough.

It had been a long time since he had ridden in a car, or even a rickshaw, but Akash took no joy from it. The city sped past, a different one to the place he had discovered inch by inch on foot. He saw a pale reflection of Soraya in the sheen of the glass and swallowed hard before looking for her again. She had gone.

"Where are you taking me?" he said.

"To the station," said the inspector. Her voice was low, a calm beacon in the midst of his wretchedness. She turned to face him and he noticed how easily she could be mistaken for a man with the angular lines of her face, the hair cropped short. "It's not far. You'll be questioned there."

Handcuffs chaffed Akash's wrists and he fidgeted on the cool leather seats more from nerves than discomfort. Their journey took them past Bombay High Court dominating the early morning horizon with an imposing array of triangular stonework, gothic arches and spired towers. Above him, the tricolour saffron, white and green of India's flag fluttered in the wind. Akash gulped, overwhelmed by the symbol of the justice system. Not long afterwards, they pulled up outside a square block with slits for windows. A flurry of journalists waited. Somebody had already alerted them to the death. Akash shrank back as the vehicle drew to a halt. The wiry officer in the driver's seat climbed out of the car.

The prospect of living without freedom hit Akash. "There's been a mistake!" he said, a quiet urgency in is voice.

"We'll find out soon enough. A couple of weeks here will give both you and us the chance to think." The inspector had a glint in her eye. "Let's get you inside." She opened her door.

Akash wasn't stupid. He had known this could happen after Soraya's death, that it was likely. It had seemed callous to question Soraya about himself in the final hours of her life, to make it about him when she faced her final journey. Now, it struck him how his allies had all but disappeared. Tariq was holed up on the other side of the city, powerless to help, wondering where Akash was. Soraya was dead. Their son thought the worst of him. The Indian courts were no friend to the poor. He had no fancy lawyer at his disposal. Could he live in a cell for the rest of his life? Would he survive without the sky above him and the dust between his toes? Could he give up the chance of seeing Jaya once more?

"I didn't do it!"

"All in good time, Mr. Choudry. You were found at the scene of the crime. We will need the autopsy and crime scene results. There is plenty of time for explanations."

Her colleague opened Akash's door before pulling him out into the sunlight. Eager faces thrust dictaphones towards him, but Akash captured only fragments of the onslaught.

"We have seen a rise of violence against women in India, Akash. Our readers want to know... did you do it?"

"Were you jealous of her success?"

"Is it true you were living at her house at the time? How could you accept her hospitality and then take her life?"

The voices rose above his head as his police escorts, their expressions grim, guided him through the throng. The inspector held his elbow and guided him into a building deprived of light. Inside, grey plaster bulged on the walls and wooden benches gave the impression of gloom, like they had been pilfered from an abandoned church. There he sat, in a hallway devoid of oxygen waiting to be processed. His stomach rolled, thinking of Soraya's lifeless body, how the fingers of her hand curled like a dancer's even in death.

A police officer beckoned him, pulling him aside with brisk movements, searching him with hands that resembled meat cleavers and functioned with the certainty of experience. The man located his locket and Jaya's letter within seconds, confiscating them. Akash cried out, stripped of his dearest possessions.

"These are mine, for now," said the policeman, sneering. "What secrets are you hiding, huh? We'll soon find out." He yanked the locket open, smirking at the pictures it held, then reached for the letter. Akash jerked forward to retrieve it, only to be pushed back.

"That's my prisoner, Gulam. Hands off," said the female inspector.

"Ever the killjoy, Inspector Fortes. He's all yours." He shoved Akash towards her. "I'd keep his cuffs on, though. Animal like that."

"Come with me, Mr. Choudry. It's time for your explanations," she said, ignoring her colleague.

Akash followed Inspector Fortes into a sparsely furnished room. His Adam's apple throbbed. For all their time on the streets, and the petty crimes Akash and Tariq had committed, they'd not once been arrested. If Akash were away for too long, Tariq would worry. Akash craved nothing more than the company of someone who knew him to be innocent, no questions asked. The inspector indicated for him to sit opposite her. He shuddered, feeling like an animal in captivity, doomed to wait for small mercies beyond his control. She removed his restraints, and he eased into the chair, massaging his wrists first, then kneading his temples.

"What's going to happen to me?"

"It depends what you have done. You have the right to a state-appointed lawyer."

Tariq used to joke that there was no crime in Bombay unless a rich person was the victim. A lawyer wouldn't help. It was best to get this over with.

She pressed the record button on a tape deck. "Interview at 11.42 in the morning of 12 March 2003, with Akash Choudry, 46 years old, of no fixed abode, regarding the death of Soraya Mansoor, 45 years of age, of Juhu Beach. Let us begin."

Air-conditioning chased goosebumps up Akash's bare forearms.

"Where were you in the early hours of this morning?" said Inspector Fortes. Her posture was exemplary, as if a rod had been attached to her back.

"At Soraya Mansoor's house in Juhu."

"Where specifically?"

"In the Red Room, the bedroom she allocated me for my stay there."

She leaned forward. "Where she was found dead?"

"Yes," said Akash, resignation creeping into his voice.

"Why were you staying with Ms. Mansoor?"

"I was staying at her request." Would he be failing Soraya to tell the truth of her death, although it would hurt Arjun? When Soraya asked him to be a parent to Arjun, what did she mean?

"And before that?"

"On the streets of Bombay, under bridges, on pavements, in church courtyards, wherever I could find shelter."

"What relationship did you have with Ms. Mansoor?"

"We were lovers over twenty years ago. I am the father of her child."

"Of Arjun Choudry?" said Inspector Fortes, raising an eyebrow in surprise.

"Yes."

"When did you become aware of this paternity?"

"Less than two weeks ago."

She found this of interest, and scrawled illegible words onto a ring-bound notepad in front of her, underlining the words in a heavy hand.

"I see. And did you harbour any resentment towards Ms. Mansoor? Because of her wealth, the late knowledge that you had a son?"

"No. I was grateful. She gave me a family, she invited me into her home."

"Where you killed her." Inspector Fortes's voice lashed out like a whip, filling every corner of the room. "With this." She placed a clear bag on the table. It held Soraya's knife with its serrated blade, about six inches in length. Dark smears of blood dulled the blade in contrast to the ivory white of the handle.

Akash shrank back, horrified. Could he tell the truth, though suicide was forbidden in Islam? Arjun would think his mother had chosen to leave him, though she would have given anything to have stayed. He remained quiet, the truth captured by the straight line of his lips, poisoning him.

"You like the idea of prison, Akash? The thought of a full belly, a roof over your head?" The inspector chose her words carefully, speaking with slow deliberate annunciation, striking fear into him. "Let me get one thing straight. A man such as you would not survive long in prison. The guards, they will not protect you. The filth in there, they have no conscience. They would smell your weakness, and you would pay. Is that what you want?"

"No!" said Akash. "I can't sleep in a lightless box. Maybe this is the punishment for all I have done."

Inspector Fortes placed her hands on the table before her. A stillness came over her. "And what have you done, Akash?"

"My wife. She...I...ran. I didn't come back." He clenched his fists.

"Your wife?" A look of puzzlement crossed her face.

"My wife. Jaya. I left her when she needed me."

"Leaving someone is not a crime punishable by law, Akash. We are talking here about Ms. Mansoor. Have you committed a crime before? Something you would go to prison for?"

He shuddered. "No."

Inspector Fortes leant across the table, smoothing her hands over the glossed wood. "All these years you have lived on the streets of this city. You fear prison, don't you? It's the sky you crave, the stars, and the sands?"

He met her gaze for the first time. "Yes."

"There is no freedom for a man who has committed murder." She paused. "But I think you are your own worst enemy. The only thing that can help you is the truth. I'll get to the bottom of what happened this morning. I'll need the autopsy and crime scene results before deciding how to proceed. Until then, you'll be put in a cell here at the police station. You understand, I can't release a man such as you, unemployed, no fixed abode, arrested for such a serious crime."

He nodded.

"For the tape."

"Yes, I understand."

She turned off the tape and stood to cuff him again. They walked the length of a corridor, to the back of the building, where he could see men piled behind bars like animals in a cage, with no room to sleep and barely any to stand. She handed him over to the officer in charge, and nodded to him solemnly. As she turned away, she said to a colleague, "I know criminals. That man isn't a criminal. He didn't do it. I can feel it in my bones."

# 30

**Jaya didn't expect** to find her family waiting up for her when she reached home, not after the way she had spoken to her parents. Neither had she expected a call from Ruhi on the emergency phone buried at the bottom of her handbag. The ringtone, an old Lata Mangeshkar track from the 1980s turned up to the highest volume setting, pierced the quiet of the beach. Jaya was so engrossed in her novel, by Jhumpa Lahiri, that it took her a few seconds to recognise the sound as her own phone.

Ruhi's terse voice filtered through the earpiece. "Come home, Jaya. We need to speak to you."

"We?" said Jaya.

"Maa, Papa, me."

"What's going on?"

"Just come home."

She hailed a rickshaw, wondering if one of her parents had taken a fall or if they lay dying. Then she shook her head, willing only good thoughts to enter it.

The evening had cooled when she unlocked the door and entered the living room. Her family rose from their seats, stacked in height order: her father the tallest, then Ruhi, followed by her mother, her eyes glinting with — what was it — glee?

Jaya addressed her sister. "What is it? What's so urgent?"

"Have you seen the news?" said her father.

Ruhi held a hand to her father's concave chest, quelling him. "Let me, Papa." She turned to Jaya, and her sister had morphed into a little girl once more, eyes wide pools of darkness, protected where she stood, nestled between their parents. "Akash is alive."

A vice-like grip on Jaya's chest, pressure like none she had felt before. "You found him? Is he well?" She had expected as much, after her suspicions about Soraya and her son, but this blow hit her anew, confirmation that Akash had chosen to stay away all these years.

Her mother's voice, sharp as glass shards, cut through her thoughts. "He was arrested for the murder of Soraya Mansoor, a businesswoman."

Jaya swayed, a ball of grief knotting in her stomach. All this time searching for news of him, and then this. This wasn't how she wanted their story to end. Maybe it wasn't Akash's fault. Soraya had it coming, didn't she? Her pride, her vanity, taking what didn't belong to her, violating the unspoken rules of sisterhood. It had all propelled her to this fate. Ironic, that her lover had been her executioner. But no, however she considered it, Jaya could not reconcile this version of Akash with the man she had known. If the boy in the restaurant happened to be Akash's son, surely that was sacred, and would have prevented Akash from laying a finger on the mother of his child?

Her mother continued, oblivious to Jaya's turmoil. "The woman was well known, I hear. Poor thing. Who knew we would have a killer in the family?" she tittered. "I always knew Akash was trouble."

"No, you didn't Maa, or else you would never have agreed to the match. We know how exacting your standards are," said Ruhi, taking an uncharacteristic swipe at her elder.

Their bickering grew hazy. Jaya needed to know only one thing. "Are you sure it's him?" she said, fighting to retain logic.

Now, when she had begun to feel free again, the shackles of her past had come to haunt her. To know Akash's whereabouts at last, in these circumstances, it was almost cruel. All the time she had spent looking for clues about his fate, and for him to now come tumbling into the frame, not a valiant knight, but with blood on his hands. It couldn't be true.

"They said his name, clear as day on the news, beta," said her father, leaning on his cane. "There was some footage too, taken with a telephone. It was grainy but I know it was him. He looks old, uncared for. He deserves it after what he did to us."

"He didn't do it to *us*, Papa. He did it to *me*," said Jaya. Her legs did not feel like hers.

Ruhi looked at her with concern. "Are you okay? I don't believe it, Jaya. There has to be some mistake, but we wanted you to hear it from us."

Somewhere in the recesses of her mind, a light switch flicked off. Jaya spiralled into darkness where melancholy waited. Voices filtered through to her from far away.

When she woke, Ruhi was applying a damp cloth to her forehead.

"Let's get you upstairs. You need to rest. That was hard news." Her sister took her weight as they climbed the stairs. "Would you like me to stay?"

"I need to be alone." She pushed everyone away because they were not Akash, but he had shown himself time and again to be the villain of the piece. A sob caught in her throat.

"Okay. I'll call you in the morning."

That night, her old dreams returned to haunt her. Licking flames, burning skin, rising, scalding heat she could not endure, and at the window, not a frozen, distraught husband, but a gleeful one, enjoying the spectacle he had created, feeding on her anguished screams.

Arjun's hands shook as he lifted a glass of water to his lips. He swallowed slowly.

"Thank you for coming to see me," said Inspector Fortes.

His mother would have been pleased to see a woman in charge of the investigation. "Of course. Has Akash been charged yet?" He spoke the name with disgust. Admitting their biological relationship was anathema to him.

"No. I thought it best to speak to you in person. We have the autopsy and crime scene results." She shuffled her papers, placed them on the table in front of her, and looked him in the eyes. "Akash Choudry did not murder your mother, Mr. Mansoor."

Arjun stood, sending his chair clattering to the floor. Above him the blades of the fan revolved in slow motion, filling his ears with a sudden din. "Of course he did! He's insane. He killed my mother out of jealousy and lust. I'm sure of it."

"Sit down, Mr. Mansoor. Let me explain." Her tone held no room for dissent. "We have the lab reports. We've conducted a psychological evaluation of Mr. Choudry. No evidence of psychosis has been found. He was simply too scared to tell you the truth—"

"Bullshit." Arjun sat rigidly, teeth clenched. "Decades of living on the streets with no income, no family ties, no home? I'd call that the definition of madness. He is hardly an upstanding citizen. My mother was a clever woman, but even she was duped by him. I thought he was at best a disappointment, at worst a danger. I didn't want to be proved right."

"It's bad luck that brings Mr. Choudry to where he is today, not madness," said the inspector.

"Okay, maybe he's not insane, maybe he lashed out in a moment of confusion." Arjun's anger flared. "But he's a monster, I have no doubt. He's got previous form. He had an affair with my mother when he was already married. When his wife found out, she set herself alight. And how about how he first found us? Spying through our windows, he was."

Inspector Fortes cut through his passion with ease. "Did you report that crime at the time?"

"No."

"Mr. Mansoor, it's my job to investigate the crime at hand. There is nothing I can do about a crime you failed to report," she said sternly.

Fury rose and bubbled within Arjun's lungs, stealing his breath. "You have the knife. You saw him that day. How can you say it wasn't him?"

"Tell me what you saw, Mr. Mansoor. If it helps, tell me again what you saw," she said, raking a hand through her short hair.

"My mother wasn't in her bedroom or the kitchen. I looked all over the house, by the pool. Then I went to his room, the Red Room. Maa was lying on the bed. At first I didn't realise something was wrong. I thought she was perhaps sleeping. But she was so still, and my father was there. It was eerie. Just the way he was, so close to her." His voice broke. "I shook her. But she was gone. There was this wound in her stomach, a knife on the bedclothes."

"What, exactly, was Mr. Choudry doing?"

Arjun grimaced. "I think he was stroking her hair. He was crying."

"Do you think it is normal for a murderer to express kindness to the victim after the fact? Is this the normal behaviour of a psychopath, someone who has deliberately set out to kill a woman in her own home? Let me tell you what I saw. I saw a scared man, a distraught man who kept looking for you, not with anger but with concern. I see a man weakened by poverty and malnutrition, who finally had everything he wanted. A family. A home. Why would he jeopardise that?"

"But—"

"No. It's my turn. Let me finish," said Inspector Fortes, raising a hand, a stop sign. "More importantly, the clues about his person, the evidence we have uncovered, it all tells a story. Akash Choudry lied, but he is no danger, neither to you nor to anyone else. I'd stake my career on it."

"Pah!" Disgust crawled like insects over Arjun's skin.

"The hidden paternity can't have been easy, Mr. Mansoor, but here is the truth, if you are willing to hear it, and what I will announce at the press conference later today. The toxicology report was clear. The autopsy showed your mother had terminal cancer. Her doctor's records confirmed it. She had weeks to live, if that."

Arjun paled. "Nonsense. She would have told me." Even as he spoke, he knew it was true. He recalled how pale his mother had become, how thin she had grown even for her. Guilt settled in his stomach like a stone. His mother had always been there for him, and he had failed her.

"Is there any reason why she might not have told you?" Round eyes, sad eyes, sought to make this easier for him.

He sought for the truth. "To protect me, perhaps, but I don't believe it. My mother was honest to her core. She embraced the hard reality of life."

"Even if she thought she was leaving you alone in the world?" The inspector fiddled with her pen. "Did you have any inkling?"

"She was frailer perhaps, but I put it down to working too hard. I even bought her tickets to Goa to make her rest, but I was angry and never got 'round to surprising her." A hand clenched around his heart and twisted. How could he not have comforted her? And now his chance was gone. How scared she must have been. If his father had known, why hadn't he told him? His anger swelled.

"The angle of the knife, the pattern of the finger prints and blood spatters, all points to Akash Choudry's innocence. Mr. Mansoor, your mother committed suicide."

An anguished whisper escaped him. "No. My mother is the strongest person I know. She wouldn't have given up. She was happy. The business was going well, she was enjoying the baby. She was pleased to see my father." He buried his head in his hands. It had always been the two of them. How could she be gone? He wanted to crawl into a corner and turn off his thoughts. "The last few weeks haven't been harmonious. We argued. I couldn't believe she had hidden my parentage from me. But she would have told me, I know it."

"Do you want my advice? What has happened will be difficult for you to bear. But in the end, your mother decided her fate. Don't take that from her. She was a remarkable woman."

Arjun nodded, the words floating over him, not really finding a target.

"As for your father, is there anything to hate about a man simply because he is down on his luck? Why do we assume that it was only he that benefited from your mother's generosity in her final weeks? I've found nothing to suggest your mother was coerced. I met her once or twice at your restaurant. She wasn't a woman to be cowed or bullied. Perhaps your mother needed him."

Arjun looked up, assessing the woman before him, her too short hair, her stern gaze. "And what if I ask for a second opinion?"

"This is a cut and dry case, why else do you think my superior gave it to a woman?" said Inspector Fortes drily. "It's within your power to have the case reassessed, rightly or wrongly. My experience has taught me that evidence is subjective. We are but building a story. Mr. Choudry's fingerprints were on the knife. Find the right lawyer, and you might get the result you want. Someone who paints your mother as a woman without the protection of a husband." She shrugged. "The justice system serves the rich better. Akash Choudry is not a man who will come off well in a court of law. Who knows?

Your efforts could portray him as someone who preys on others. He could be subjected to many long years of incarceration. I can't stop you from applying for a new autopsy, or pushing for a case against your father. But my advice to you is don't punish him or paint your mother as a victim. That's not who she was."

"Are we finished here?" asked Arjun.

"Yes."

"My mother's funeral can take place now?"

"Yes."

He walked slowly to the door, his mouth set in a grim line. "Thank you for your time."

# 31

It took a week for Inspector Fortes to conclude the investigation and ensuing paperwork. A week for her to sanction Akash's release. In that time, he experienced new lows of dignity. He pissed in a pot in view of other prisoners, was unable to wash himself when he stank and was unsure if the odour came from himself or the other men in his proximity. He had his legs spread while sleeping, an object thrust into his backside until tears came into his eyes and by chance the sleeping guard happened to wake. He knew better than to complain out loud. That would have earned an even greater punishment.

When Inspector Fortes came to find him, he bowed his head in gratitude.

"You are free to go," she said.

"The investigation?" His voice cracked. He had barely spoken in the cell. Not that he had missed it. Years of limited social contact had weaned him off the necessity of speech.

"Is concluded. The coroner has ruled Ms. Mansoor's death a suicide."

She accompanied him to the front desk and passed him his belongings: the locket, intact, and the torn envelope for Jaya. It seemed a lifetime ago that he had written it. He tucked it into his sock. He no longer felt the urge to woo her, even to see her. He felt depleted, as if only hibernation would help. Only disappearing altogether would calm the uncomfortable tide of his thoughts.

He grasped the inspector's arm. "Have you spoken to my son?"

"At length. Give him time. He isn't a bad man. Neither are you."

She bade him goodbye at the exit to the building, a hushed space without the press vultures. They had lost interest, Akash supposed, now he had been acquitted. It would be somebody else's turn soon. As he crept out into the sunlight, his eyes blurred and he shielded them. He filled Arjun's shirt and trousers better now, despite his ordeal. Lack of movement and regular food, however meagre, had added weight to his frame. It seemed unfair to have increased in size when Soraya's body wasted away.

He wondered if she had been buried promptly in accordance with Islamic scripture. Perhaps there was a fresh mound of earth where she lay that he could visit to pay his respects. He looked up at the sky, at the wisps of clouds linking together like gunmetal chains in the blue. He paused on the steps of the police station. A sparrow landed there and cocked its head. Akash crouched and held out his hand, his gnarled bones twig-like as they neared the bird. It took flight, the beat of its wings in time with the pump of his heart.

He no longer knew where he belonged, his psyche not whole but divided into thirds, a magnetic pull towards the son who hated him, the wife he had abandoned and the loyal friend who waited. He planted a careful foot on the ground ahead, willing himself forward into a future that dissolved as he watched.

Akash and Tariq lay on the beach, looking up at the stars. It had taken Akash most of the day to make his way to his friend. The thought of unwrapping his problems for Tariq repelled him. He didn't want to drudge over the pain. It turned out the hardest thing had been to show up. His spirits had lifted when he found Tariq, not stratospherically, but enough to keep at bay the dark cloud that pressed him.

"She was so lucky not to have any regrets," said Akash. It suited him to look away from Tariq while he explained. A hint of sympathy would break him. "She had it all worked out. I'm so lucky to have found her. I would never have known Jaya and Arjun lived had it not been for her."

"You could say that she hid it from you," Tariq's voice trailed. "But it helps to be positive." They knew each other long enough to know when the black lurked underneath bravado. "And that's why she wanted you to stay? To sit with her as she died? To be her partner in death?"

Akash nodded.

"Shit, that's seriously messed up, yaar. What a burden she asked you to carry," said Tariq, shaking his head.

"It was an honour. But this sadness, it's crushing me." Akash gripped a handful of sand in his fist and let it crumble away.

"You did as she asked."

"I guess. She didn't once change her mind." Still, doubt plagued him about whether he had done the right thing.

"Then what is the problem? The police have let you go," said Tariq, confused.

"I destroyed a family in the process."

"Not you. Life. Life happened. That's all."

And so Tariq listened, without recriminations, to Akash's abridged story of Soraya's final hours, never doubting the veracity of his friend's innocence, never prying for the details that were too painful to give.

"I know I keep saying it, but I'm sorry, yaar. I can't imagine what you've been through. I'm glad, too, that you're back here with me. I missed you," said Tariq.

Was it selfish for Tariq to make this about himself, his loneliness? As if he preferred them to be together to deal with the trials of the streets, that deep down he hadn't wanted a happy ending for Akash. Akash shook his head. He couldn't let these thoughts take hold of him. Tariq was an ally. Perhaps his only true friend. He stood, a deathly weariness hanging over him, and spread out a threadbare blanket next to Tariq while his friend nattered on.

Truth be told, his time in the rose bungalow with Soraya, Arjun and his family had felt like being caught up in a beautiful dream that was not his own; an attempt at love and belonging after all these years he didn't deserve, an interlude, a trick of vengeful gods, seeking to punish him. Although he had been cast out, Soraya's house, a stone's throw away, still called to him like a lighthouse. It was a fool's errand to vex Arjun any further, however much he needed to witness for himself how his son was coping.

"Is there no chance of reconciling with your son?" said Tariq, his bald head glinting under the streetlights.

Akash closed his eyes. Tiny balls of light danced before him. Tiredness had found a permanent home in the crevices of his bones. He couldn't escape it. He yearned for an end to it all.

"Look, if you need to talk about more than the bare bones, I'm here." Tariq paused. His cough reared up and filled the silence between them.

Akash didn't want to talk. "I need a piss." The public lavatories provided not only a place to relieve himself, but privacy that was in scarce supply on the streets.

"I'll come with you."

Tariq followed him inside the ramshackle building, which housed a row of cubicles, each with little more than a hole in the floor wedged in between partitions the colour of cooked egg-whites. Akash entered a stall and squatted to empty himself. The floor breadth measured little over half a metre. Claustrophobia closed in on him, equalled by his relief to be hidden away from prying eyes.

The unwelcome familiarity of this place hung like a lead balloon in his belly. He had used these toilets, time and again. Over the years it had become a habit to use public toilets where they were available, though many of the homeless people he knew defecated openly on the streets of the city. What did hygiene matter for men who had nothing? Still, it had become habit for Akash not to relieve himself near where they slept. The streets of Bombay were already full of dangers and irritants. Adding the stench of bodily fluids to their hard-won sanctuary for the night would be idiotic.

Outside, Tariq waited, supportive, demanding. Akash longed to be alone with his thoughts for longer than the few minutes the lavatory afforded him, but Tariq had been ever present since his return, sensing Akash's vulnerability. Tariq's feet drummed impatiently, his socked ankles visible underneath the cubicle door, together with the worn laced-up shoes he had scavenged from a dumpster.

Akash sighed and hoisted up his trousers over dirty underpants which made a mockery of him. He smelt Soraya's perfume behind him and spun around, ridiculing himself as he did it. He sucked in his breath to see a shadow there. He didn't know if it represented a figment of his imagination. If he looked closer, he could make out a withered womanly shape that he felt sure was Soraya, nothing like the vibrant woman she had been, but her all the same. He blinked, but the shadow remained there, not uttering a word. Its presence both comforted and terrified him. He sensed rather than witnessed a smile that did not reach its eyes, a midriff unblemished by the pools of blood he kept expecting to bloom, yellowed skin. He reached out to touch it, trembling, but his fingers slid through, with just the tiniest hint of resistance.

Knuckles rapped on the door and Soraya faded into nothing. "Hurry up, yaar. We can't leave our stuff out there unattended for too long."

A clamp squeezed around Akash's lungs. He considered taking off Arjun's shirt, wrapping a sleeve around his neck like a tourniquet, and pulling. Would he have the strength to complete the act before Tariq entered? How forlorn he would look, a man partially unclothed, found dead on the filthy floor of the public lavatories. With his bladder now empty, at least he would not wet himself. Or he could find a piece of glass on the beach and take his life under the canvas of the open sky. *Am I even brave enough to take my life? Jaya, help me.* It surprised him how his subconscious had injected Jaya in his thoughts. As if her name were a prayer forever engraved on his soul.

This time a fist thumped the door. Akash jumped.

"Coming."

He stepped out of the cubicle, easing past Tariq, and looked behind him. His heartbeat heightened. He half expected Soraya to still be there but the cubicle stood empty. Akash needed time away from Tariq's searching questions. He did not have any answers. Answers had been escaping through the porous net of his brain all his life.

He gave his hands a cursory wash at the greying ceramic basins and surveyed his blood-shot eyes in the cracked mirror. His mind boomeranged between three axes. Soraya was gone; Arjun hated him; Jaya lived. The most important question remained: did he want to die or did he want to fight for his family? He swept wet fingers through his thinning hair and wiped the remainder of the moisture on his trouser legs. Tariq caught his eyes in the mirror.

"Ready?"

"Ready."

# 32

**Arjun sat slumped** in the corner of the *ghusl* room adjoining the mosque. A funeral attendant waited silently by the door, affording the grieving son some privacy. Sweat ran down Arjun's back despite the air conditioning keeping the room cool to minimise the disintegration of the corpses laid out here. He touched his forehead to a marble counter, enjoying the cold against his skin. Outside the sanctuary, rickshaw engines whirred and horns beeped as Bombay heaved to life. With his eyes shut, the temptation to expel the last few weeks from his memory overwhelmed him. In sleep, his mother's face haunted him, calling out words he could not understand. Arjun had considered drinking alcohol to reach oblivion, but there would be time for that later. He would not miss this chance to say goodbye.

A relentless ticking reminded him of the passage of time. Arjun opened his eyes and straightened his back. He shuddered as he took in the sight of his mother lying lifeless on the cold steel table. His vision focussed slowly on the clock above the doorway and the solemn attendant standing beneath it. The clock's hands hovered at just before eight in the morning. Panic gripped him and he edged closer to his mother, anxious about the imminent arrival of a group of women to wash her body and prepare it for her last rites. Four days had passed since her death, the need for an autopsy superseding her right to burial.

The slight delay both distressed and comforted Arjun. Since his mother's death, the grains of time had alternately frozen and poured relentlessly through the hourglass. While their faith demanded she be buried immediately, he wanted longer with her.

Too soon they would take away her body. He had so much to tell her, so much to ask. He was not prepared to commit her body to the earth just yet.

"I'm sorry I couldn't protect you, Maa." He motioned to the room with its marble and steel cladding, and the large wash basins lining the walls. "I hope this is what you wanted."

He smiled wryly, recognising the irony of being beholden to Muslim traditions when his mother scarcely practiced the faith. He knew she had found the social norms at the masjid alienating for single, unmarried mothers. A two-by-two culture pervaded. More than this, Arjun suspected the fierce independence of his mother clashed with the patriarchal society she found there. As a boy, he had rarely set foot inside a mosque; even less as an adult. Still, there had been times when he'd been taken ill in his childhood, that he remembered his mother muttering a prayer under her breath, an instinctive reversion to God whilst under stress. He'd thought hard about what form her final passage should take. In the absence of instructions to the contrary, he decided to proceed in the same mould as the funerals for his grandparents.

It had only ever been the two of them since he was a young boy. Though they had lived under the same roof as her parents until he was five, there had been no question that Arjun belonged to her alone. Even when he married Muna, his mother's hold on him persisted, fortified by their shared experiences and confidences. No one competed with that.

"What will I do without you?" His voice cracked. The attendant moved into an annex just out of sight, trying hard to be invisible. "How can I stem this anger towards him? Is it true what the inspector said? Why didn't you tell me?" A serene smile lifted the corners of her mouth where she lay. He searched her face for answers, but her closed eyes rendered it impossible for him to know what she had been thinking. All her wisdom was lost to him. He raised his hands to the heavens feeling clumsy, the movement alien to him. Above him, a fan whirred around a light fitting. "Ya Allah, help my mother wherever she is."

The previous week, Arjun had attended prayers and asked the Imam about what awaited his mother.

The older man stroked his wiry beard and peered through his glasses at Arjun with kindly eyes. His hair underneath the skull cap looked oily. "She said her Shahada when she passed?"

Arjun frowned.

"Verily we belong to Allah and truly to Him shall we return?" said the Imam.

"I don't know."

"No matter. Don't worry. Your mother will await Judgement, and then surely go to Heaven with the righteous."

"I meant what will happen during her burial rites?"

"Oh, of course. Sit down, son." They sat, the Imam cross-legged, with his shirt dress stretched across his knees, and Arjun next to him, keenly aware of the dirt he had missed on his feet when washing before coming into the prayer hall.

"There are no women in your family to assist with the washing of the body?"

"My wife is Hindu. Our daughter is not yet six months old."

"I see." The Imam fidgeted. "Well, we have three ladies, well-practiced, who will tend to your mother gently. She will be brought from the mortuary to the ghusl room here at the masjid on the morning of the funeral. When the ladies arrive, they will wash her three times and wrap her in fresh sheets. The shrouding will be secured with rope. The ladies will pray as they work. There is no gossip." He paused. "There are no injuries on her face?"

Arjun flinched. "No."

The Imam leant forward and touched his leg. "I am sorry to ask. At the end of the ceremony, the outer sheet will be moved aside for the mourners to see the deceased one last time. The ladies will place the body —"

" — my mother."

"Yes, they will place your mother on a woven board."

"I remember from my grandparents' funerals."

"Good. When the ladies are finished, you and the men will bring her into the courtyard for the ceremony. I will lead the prayers."

The fan overhead caused ripples in the stagnant air and played with the edges of the sheet covering his mother. The movement caught Arjun's eye and jolted him back into the present.

"They'll be here any moment, Maa." He placed his hand on hers. Even through the sheet that separated them, her fingers felt stiff, the skin leathery. How often had she massaged cream into her fingers in life? She'd been vain, and though she kept her nails short, he hadn't known a day when they had not been adorned by colour. Underneath the white cotton sheet, his mother's toenails were coral pink. Soon, she would be bare apart from the three large sheets which would be used to cocoon her. There would be no wax in her short, grey hair. The ghusl ladies would wash it with a shampoo that was not her own. They would try to manoeuvre her hands into prayer pose.

A sad smile drifted across Arjun's lips. His mother would be amused by that, he was sure.

The attendant coughed suddenly at his shoulder, uncomfortable. Arjun had convinced him to allow him some time alone with the body, but now he must go. "Sir, it's time."

Arjun took a long look at his mother and kissed her forehead. His feet moved of their own accord away from her, though he pivoted before he reached the exit for one last look at her. Three women, large in stature, filed wordlessly past him. It was improper for him to sit with his mother before she had been washed, but the women showed no judgement. The last one turned to him with a look of sympathy, before ushering him out of the room and quietly shutting the door behind him. Arjun passed through a long corridor until he found himself on the noisy street, worlds apart from the still of the ghusl room inside.

Soon, it would be time for the final goodbye.

The sun shone high above their heads, its beams shrouding the funeral in a haze, obscuring the blue veins on the smooth marble of the mosque's facade. Two minarets stretched skywards and disappeared behind a bank of clouds. Arjun's eyes smarted against the light. Before him, on a woven board atop a beige and green rug, rested his mother, shrouded in white sheets. A lump settled in his throat. His eyes lingered on her stomach area, where the knife had torn her flesh, and then moved to her face. The ghusl ladies had wrapped her head in cloth, covering her ears but leaving the rest of her features visible. Her face had sunk, despite the efforts to preserve her body during the wait for the autopsy.

They stood facing Mecca in the courtyard of the masjid.

"I will now recite Salat Al-Janazah," said the Imam, raising his hands in supplication.

Arjun did not understand the funeral prayer, though the rhythms of the Arabic soothed him. As the Imam prayed, sweat pooled in the small of his back underneath the white tunic that hung to his knees. The high collar constricted his throat and his legs felt sticky underneath the cotton drawstring trousers. Though many of the men at his side and behind him were strangers, Arjun felt the strength of the communal prayer. At first he emulated their gestures, but as the prayer wore on, he rocked where he stood, his eyes trained on his mother's face.

Finally, the Imam finished and gestured to two men nearby. They drew the sheet over her head, an action that anonymised her, though he still recognised the lines of her slight frame beneath the sheets. *Is that the last touch you will feel, Maa?* his mind called out to her. A hand settled on Arjun's shoulder and squeezed. He turned to nod at a stocky man he recollected as a customer from the restaurant. The Imam chanted, and the men joined in, a chorus of voices praying for his mother.

"There is no God but Allah, and Muhammed is His messenger. Verily to Him we return."

The congregation surged forward as the chanting grew louder, carrying Arjun with them. Dozens of strangers surrounded his mother where she lay, and bent as one to pick up the board. He stood at her head, at the place reserved for the chief mourner. As his hands touched the wooden handles, his sadness crashed like a wave on a forlorn beach. *I'm not ready.* They lifted the body effortlessly. Arjun trembled. He placed his arm underneath the slat and linked to another mourner's shoulder, then trained his eyes on the ground ahead.

They carried his mother through the gates, led by the Imam, making their way to the burial ground a few hundred metres away, a queue of mourners following behind. Behind them loomed the bronze dome of the masjid. He caught sight of Muna weeping towards the edge of the crowd, scarcely visible under her headscarf, one of only a few women in attendance. The strength of Muna's mourning for his mother had surprised him. *I love you,* he thought, unsure about whether he meant Muna or his mother. He feared he might drop his hold on the body and fought to still the sobs that tore at him.

"She loved you too, Maa." She couldn't hear him even though his head was only a hair's breadth from her ear.

They traversed the streets, kicking up dust as they went. Nearby Hindu revellers partook in Holi, oblivious to the small funeral procession. Street vendors manned stalls selling packets of colour on the sidewalks. Strangers and neighbours alike, dressed in white, launched colour bombs at each other, leaving puffs of rainbow-coloured powder dispersed in the air. Just ahead, the Imam raised his hands in a vain attempt to ease the excitement of the merry-makers and retain the solemnity of the burial ceremony. Children with stained faces ran by with water pistols, ignoring him, shrieking with glee.

Loneliness wrapped itself around Arjun. He saw his mother's face everywhere. An unassuming tourist in a Nirvana t-shirt and cut-off shorts crossed the street in front of them, taking pictures of the festival all the while. A packet of colour hit the man in the ear. Azure dust hung in the air and rained down on them as they passed.

"Life stops for nobody," said the mourner behind him.

# 33

**After the initial** rush to inform Jaya of Akash, her family clammed up. Her father even turned off the television set, his constant companion, presumably to spare Jaya from any more hurt. Outwardly, Jaya pretended to be unruffled. She fought to confine her emotions under her scarred skin. Only Ruhi guessed what churned beneath the surface.

After her decades-long search for her missing husband, her need for closure, and the kernel of love for him that still existed after all this time, Jaya burned to uncover every microscopic detail about his life over the period they'd been separated, and the crime he was said to have committed. It wouldn't do to search for information at home. She wouldn't give her mother the satisfaction. Instead, she bought newspapers to carry with her to work, used the old television box kept in the make-up room at Tara to scour the channels for a mention of her lost husband, or better yet, a glimpse of him. How could it be, after all this time, she was still invested in what happened to Akash? Each moment of her search sent her pulse racing.

The initial arrest over, the news channels did not rerun the footage of Akash. Quietly buried in the mid-section of *The Hindu*, she found a report declaring the investigation completed and Soraya's death a suicide. Jaya closed her eyes and offered up a silent prayer of thanks to Krishna. Akash lived, and he was innocent—of that crime at least.

Akash loved the city during Holi. The Holika bonfire, the drums, the dancing, the joy, they lifted him above the mundane, connecting him to the community around him. Then came the explosion of colour in parks and in front of temples, when rainbow powder fell all around, and balloons and pistols brimmed with coloured water. Social barriers disappeared for that day as the gods conspired to lasso friend and foe, young and old together, irrespective of faith. Even the homeless were offered Holi sweets, saccharine flavours bursting in mouths accustomed to less vibrant morsels.

Traditionally, Holi was the festival of spring, a chance to frolic and mend broken relationships. As if Akash needed a greater reason to dwell on his mistakes with Jaya and Arjun. The last thing he wanted was to hit the streets as he and Tariq usually would, mingling amongst the merrymakers, showing off their best dance moves.

"You've not washed in days, yaar. It's time to stop moping. Come on. Get down to the beach," said Tariq, throwing Akash a towel, disregarding how the sodden mess would rub on as much dirt as the water washed away. "I'll go and get us some food. I helped out Janghir Saheb the other day." He pulled some scrunched rupees from his pocket. "This will come in handy. We'll have a feast to celebrate Holi." He shook his clothes off and twisted to address Akash, sprawled on the floor on a blanket. "He was asking about you, you know."

"Who was?"

"Janghir Saheb. He has a couple of jobs, but he needs the both of us. He always trusted you more than me anyway."

Akash raised his head, weary. "I'll go and see him tomorrow."

"Go and wash. I'll be back soon."

Drums in the distance. Dust the colour of joy. Ashes. Akash closed his eyes and blocked it all out.

Bushra found Jaya at her desk drawing designs for the new show, her fingers stained with the green ink she liked to use for her first ideas.

"Your sister is here to see you," said the older woman, all bustle.

"Oh, I wasn't expecting her." Jaya put down her pen. Her flawed concentration meant that she hadn't yet come up with anything original.

"She's here all the same."

"It's nearly home-time," said Jaya, pushing back her chair. "Give me a minute and I'll meet her out front." She dumped the pile of newspapers in the wastepaper basket just in case Ruhi ventured down the corridor. An obsession with her cheating husband wasn't something Ruhi would tolerate, however much she urged Jaya to believe in love.

A wall of heat hit Jaya as she walked out into the evening air, where Ruhi waited for her, her training bag on her shoulder. She crossed to where her sister stood.

"Hi, what are you doing here?" Jaya gave her an impulsive hug. Usually Ruhi was the affectionate one.

"You didn't seem okay on the phone," said Ruhi. "I thought I'd come and see how you are. Besides, I was kind of hoping I'd bump into Ravi so I could give him a piece of my mind."

"He's keeping his distance," said Jaya.

"Good."

"Okay day?"

Ruhi hoisted her bag strap higher onto her shoulder. "Yeah, I've been at dance practice for a film.

"Who's directing?"

"Rishi Kapoor."

"Wow. Have you met him yet?" said Jaya. They used to watch Rishi Kapoor's films as children, when he still played a leading man.

"No, not yet. It was just the choreographer and an assistant. Sweaty work and I need a shower before Vinod gets home, but I wanted to check on you without Maa and Papa breathing down our necks. You okay?" She searched Jaya's face, then linked her arm through Jaya's. They started the walk home. "I heard on the radio this morning that it was suicide. Akash was not involved."

A flicker in Ruhi's voice jarred with Jaya. She stopped short on the pavement, not caring about the sea of pedestrians. She knew when her sister was hiding something. Jaya listened carefully, alert to any inconsistencies in her sister's behaviour. "You were always so full of anger towards him. And yet you seem relieved he's off the hook. Why is that?"

Ruhi drained of colour. "I don't know what you mean."

"What has changed, Roo? Have you forgiven him for abandoning me? Why now?"

"Let's go to my house. Let's not talk about it here," said Ruhi. "Please."

"No. I need to know now." The subterfuge angered Jaya. Why would Ruhi, of all people, hide the truth?

Ruhi hesitated. "Okay." She pulled Jaya aside. They nestled between the bright displays of a clothing store selling pashminas. Even here, impatient shoppers jostled them. Ruhi's words rushed out. "He didn't leave you. Papa told him to go."

Jaya turned cold and still. "What did you say?"

"He was trying to protect you, I think."

"I don't understand."

Ruhi blew out a shaky breath. "Akash tried to see you after the fire. Papa told him you died."

A wail took shape inside of Jaya, gathering force, right there amongst the shoppers. "Akash came back? Maa and Papa decided he should go? *They* did this to me?" Her body swayed with emotion. "I didn't need protecting. I just needed the truth. All this time, I thought Akash had abandoned me when I needed him most." A thought catapulted into her mind, barbed, with teeth that tore at her fragile mind. "How do you know?"

Ruhi blanched, held her tongue.

"Oh, I see. You've seen him? You've actually seen him?" said Jaya, failing to keep the ice from her voice. "How long have you known where he is?"

Tears filled her sister's eyes. "I don't know exactly where he is, Jaya. But he is close."

Arguments between them were rare and painful, leaving blemishes on their relationship neither would forget in a hurry, like scar tissue underneath freshly healed skin. Yet by keeping Akash a secret, hadn't Ruhi betrayed her too?

"How long, Roo?" Jaya stumbled over her words. "I told you I 'd seen the boy, Akash's son. I told you and you pooh-poohed me. When did you realise? When?"

"Later, after you mentioned the boy, Akash came to me at the house. He'd found out you're alive after all this time." Kind eyes brimmed with tears. "He wants you back, I think."

"He wants me back? How can he want me back? He has a family of his own, doesn't he?" But Soraya was dead. Akash's lover was dead, and she would become the dead woman's poor replacement. It made no sense, or perhaps it did, because no one ever wanted her just for her.

"I don't know," said Ruhi. "I don't know anything at all. But when I looked into his eyes, I was sure he still loves you. I could see it through his desperation. It was why I told him to write anonymously. To earn your trust." Ruhi's hands splayed, pleading. "I didn't know what else to do. I didn't want him to just turn up. I wasn't sure how you'd react, whether you'd cope, but he couldn't stay hidden."

Jaya's memory dredged up a glimpse from the near past, a flash of anonymous letter tucked into her knicker drawer at home, dog-eared from repeated reading. "The letter. The one I received at work. No post stamps, no signature, just a stranger reaching out. That was him?" She shook her sister. "Ruhi?"

"I didn't want you to be hurt. Was I wrong?"

"I'm not sure. Is it better to close the door on that part of my life or revisit it?" Hot tears trailed down Jaya's face. She could taste the salt on her lips. "I always wanted children. If he'd come back, years ago, it might not have been perfect, but it would have been something. Now, now there is a whole world of history between us I'm not sure we can overcome. My dreams were so bright once. Now, they are pale imitations of themselves. The real ones have escaped like ghosts through my fingers."

Ruhi watched her, wordless, helpless.

Jaya shuddered. "Painting Akash as a monster has been part of what makes me strong. I'm not sure I want him to be a victim. I liked being the one in our marriage who had right on my side. Finding out otherwise is like rewriting my identity. I'm not sure I can go back. Can anyone leave behind a long road of sadness and pain without regret?"

A caress of her sister's hand on her cheek, tender, seeking forgiveness. "What are you going to do?"

"Make my own decisions."

# 34

Rows of graves perpendicular to Mecca lined the burial ground. Arjun's back ached, but he continued the slow trudge to the fresh pit that the gravediggers had prepared for his mother. The Imam stood at the head of the grave as they lowered his mother directly onto the soil on her side, with her face turned towards the holy city.

Arjun bowed his head as men placed a thin slat of wood on top of her. Then, he took soil from the heaped mound beside the grave and threw three handfuls in. His sweaty palms moistened the earth and it fell into the pit with a dull thump. Beside him, each mourner took three handfuls of soil and followed suit until the initial beat of the soil on the slat became a muted sprinkle that stilled to nothing.

The Imam uttered a final prayer, and then he and the final mourners turned their back on Soraya Mansoor, leaving just her son kneeling where she lay. Arjun took out the book of Gibran poetry she had given him and read out loud.

"I am dotted silver threads dropped from heaven

By the gods. Nature then takes me, to adorn

Her fields and valleys."

He dropped the book into the earth and stared blankly across the mounds before him.

After the burial, the men arrived in groups of twos and threes for the wake at Arjun's house. Muna and the women served simple food, and the mourners ate in honour of the departed soul and talked in muted voices. The gathering could have taken place at the restaurant, but this way, Arjun claimed back the house from the shadows cast by his mother's suicide. Once they had finished their meal and disposed of their plastic plates, the mourners came one by one to shake Arjun's hand or pinch Leela's cheeks, and exchanged a few cursory words with him about his mother and how she now journeyed to a better place. Not one of them seemed to know his mother well. He was relieved when the last visitor had gone home. The maid cleared up, and Arjun and Muna trudged upstairs. He felt older than his years.

"Let me help you with that." Muna reached up to unfasten Arjun's collar. There had scarcely been a moment to converse in private with the guests present. "Are you okay?" she whispered, reluctant to wake the baby, who now slept in the adjacent room. "Did it go smoothly?"

He smiled weakly. "We didn't drop her if that's what you mean."

"Of course not. I meant, the burial. Was it peaceful?"

Women were unwelcome at the burial site at the moment the body was committed to the earth, a patriarchal norm that had irked his mother and had prevented Muna from burying her own parents.

"I suppose so." Arjun drew her to him and buried his face in her hair. She smelt familiar, of orange blossom from the body cream she liked to lather on. "It was hard. I wish you could have been there."

"Me too."

"Afterwards, just a mound remained. It seemed odd that people were having such fun on the streets when I'd left a vital part of me behind."

"It seems wrong to play Holi this year with Maa gone," said Muna. She wore the same punjabi suit she had dressed in for the funeral, white with a simple needlework border in pale green thread. "Will we go back tomorrow? I'd like to pay my respects, bring incense and water. Leela could come."

Arjun sat on the bed to peel off his socks. "Yes, we'll do that."

"How about your father?"

Arjun's paused and lowered his foot slowly to the floor. "You want to take my father to the cemetery? I don't even know where he is now he's been released. Probably in the ditch he came from."

Muna's voice was a low hum in his ear. "Akash Saheb loved Maa. She trusted him. It is what she'd want."

Arjun's knuckles turned white. "I don't want to talk about it, Muna." His stomach churned at the thought of seeing his father. He took a deep breath and retrieved a t-shirt and some jeans from the closet. He padded into the ensuite bathroom in bare feet and splashed his face with cold water, then changed briskly. A brief look in the mirror revealed a drawn face and dark shadows under his eyes.

Muna was waiting for him on the bed when he returned. She rested her hand on his arm. "He's innocent. The autopsy proves it. Your father might not have stopped Maa, but he was not to blame."

Arjun set his jaw.

"Speaking to him might give you some closure."

Arjun spun to face her. "Maybe. Maybe, Muna. But my mother was buried today. I can't think about this right now." He stooped to grab some sandals from the foot of the bed. "I need some air."

Two minutes later Arjun drove his car out of the driveway. He instinctively prayed as he drove. He didn't pray to ease his mother's passage into the next life. Instead, every atom of his fibre concentrated on praying that he would never see his father again.

Janghir Merchant, owner of J.R. Merchants in Andheri East, held out his hand to shake Akash's, a swift pumping action. He nodded at Tariq. "It's been a few months, Mr. Choudry. I was hoping to see you sooner. I've had some work waiting for you," he said. "I'm pleased with how the new sign is holding up. A good man takes pride in his work."

"I appreciate that," said Akash, bleary-eyed. He had only come here at Tariq's behest. The more laid-back of the two men, it surprised Akash how Tariq could nag like a fish-wife if he thought it important.

Janghir Saheb's voice dipped into a whisper, mindful of the customers who traversed the aisles of his store. "I was shocked to see the news, but as I told my wife, I'm a good judge of character. I couldn't believe you had committed such a violent act. I was pleased it all got cleared up, and though others might hold it against you, I don't see it as a stain on your character."

A pause, during which Tariq nudged him.

"Thank you," said Akash. He appreciated the sentiment, but he hated that a relative stranger had discussed the details of his life.

"I have a proposal for you. I've been thinking about it for some time." A customer arrived at the till and Janghir waved them aside while he completed the transaction. The man left the shop and Janghir leant forward conspiratorially. "India is booming. My tills are full of rupees. Not that I'm boasting, but, you know, when times are good, isn't it my job to help those less fortunate than me, to create opportunities?"

Tariq and Akash looked at him, nonplussed.

"I'm expanding. There will be two more stores across Bombay. Can you imagine it? My name— J.R. Merchant—in three corners of this city. My father would be so proud." He sighed.

"We're happy for you," piped up Tariq. "A big achievement indeed."

"I want you two to help me get the stores up and running. I'll need someone to take charge of the minor side of the renovations: shelving, signage, heavy-lifting, rubbish removal. While we're getting the stores ready, you can sleep there to ward off squatters. I'll pay you a decent wage, cash in hand. Do your work well, and afterwards there'll be a security job in it for you. What do you say?"

"We'll do it!" said Tariq, beaming.

"But—" Akash didn't want charity.

"I like you both. My idea is good business sense. You've earned this. It would do you well to remember that. You're honest, hard workers. This isn't a handout. I need you as much as you need me." Janghir stroked his beard. "Too often we think in binaries." He tapped his cane on the floor, an incessant beat. "Black and white. Old and young. Punishment and compassion. Masters of their fate and the helpless. But I've found that there is a blurred line between those who are the authors of their fate and the ones who are blown about by events. A small choice, a sprinkling of luck, a helping hand, that's all that it takes. I hope you'll accept."

It seemed a dream to enter the regular workforce, not to scavenge, to earn an honest wage. A door opened in Akash's mind, leading him away from the dark. His eyes filled with tears. He blinked them away and nodded slowly. "Thank you, Janghir Saheb. We won't forget this."

He meant it. Soraya, too had offered him help, but her charity had not allowed him to keep his dignity. Janghir Saheb had given him the chance to piece together his fractured self-esteem.

Janghir reached out across to tap each of them in turn with his cane, a core of seriousness hidden beneath his playfulness. "Don't let me down."

"We won't," said Tariq, earnest excitement bubbling up inside him as he sought to keep a professional facade.

They said their goodbyes, spilling out onto the street.

"Can you believe it?!" Tariq pinched himself. "Who would have thought that old man had such plans for us?" His face fell. "Wait, what if he dies before we start?" He shook off his morbid thoughts. A smile creased the corners of his eyes. "Can this be real?" He sprang into the air, his joy infectious. "This is going to be fantastic, yaar. No more milling around just to timepass."

Maybe Tariq was right. Maybe Janghir Saheb had offered him a beacon of light in the gloom. Maybe, just maybe, he would finally have something to offer Jaya, and even Arjun. *Is this your parting gift, Soraya?* How fortunes could change in an instant.

"Let's go down to the water," said Tariq, irrepressibly jubilant, his joy lending him a glow that took the edge off his ugliness, the worn carcass of his body, awarding him a youthful buoyancy, a glint in his eye. "We might not have time to do this in the daytime soon. Janghir Saheb opens his stores six times a week, you know," he said, excitedly. "We'll be too tired on a Sunday to do anything but sleep and eat. We'll go to the masjid, of course, to give thanks."

Akash laughed for the first time since Soraya's passing. "Never lose your child-like joy, Tariq. It keeps you young."

"Wait 'til Zahid Khan finds out, the brute. He won't be able to push us around anymore," said Tariq. He stopped. "Our star is on the way up, yaar." He hesitated. "You know what you should do?"

"What?"

"You should send the second letter to Jaya. We're on a roll. Maybe the stars will align."

Akash considered for a moment. He had written the letter already. What did he have to lose? He turned to his friend. "Okay."

"Okay?" A slow smile broke out across Tariq's face.

"Okay, I'll do it."

# 35

Home could no longer be a sanctuary for Jaya, not when the people supposedly closest to her had lied. Ruhi's revelation about her parents' dishonesty—she could not imagine her mother had been anything other than complicit—turned her home into a stop gap, somewhere she went to sleep, change and refuel, nothing more. She considered looking for her own apartment. She had her own money. Her salary paid for most of the upkeep anyway. Her father had grown miserly with his dwindling savings. She would have liked nothing better than to release her ire on her parents and demand answers from her father about manipulating her, taking it upon himself to send Akash away.

Still, she knew better than most what it was like to start again with nothing. Living alone was not for the faint-hearted, especially as a woman in India. Her mother's voice rang in her head. *What will the world say?* Jaya grimaced. Leaving her elderly parents alone was unforgivable, and she knew that it took a particular kind of strength to live alone, an acceptance of one's self she was not sure she had. She shook her head, scattering her self-pity in different directions, giving space for anger to rise against Akash, who had set the wheel in motion despite her father's unwanted intervention.

It took all of her strength to act normally when all she wanted was to hold her parents to account. Now was not the time. She needed to map out all the pieces on the board before waging war. The chants she had used to maintain her sanity resurfaced.

*I can do this. I am enough. I am loved.*

Who really loved her? She could not live under the same roof as her parents if she unleashed her anger, so instead, she corked it. Their secret became hers, a sleeping lion in an unhappy home that any one of them could, at any moment, prod into a roaring menace. However, she had grown wise to their tricks; the strings of the puppet had been severed. She waited impatiently, daydreaming about what precise words she would use to shame them into apologising and realising the extent of her hurt.

At the same time, she found herself looking for Akash in the corners of the city, on her way to work, in the queues at the market, in the faces of strangers. She didn't know what she would say to him if she saw him. She willed it. She feared it. She reread his letter until she had etched each word onto her soul, until the words branded her skin.

*We knew each other once, a long time ago. I chased false gods and pushed away everything that was good.*

She kneaded her finger where her wedding ring had once sat. How could she not have realised it was him?

*They say everything happens for a reason, but I have found that to be a deceit. Suffering is something we dig through until we feel whole again.*

His words had comforted her like none other. Could it be true, what Ruhi had said, that Akash wanted to try to resurrect their marriage, that he hadn't wilfully abandoned her?

Jaya had joy in her life. She enjoyed her own company. She had a small circle of people she cared about, but despite it all, she wanted more. She wanted love. A selfish love, made just for her. Could two broken people fit perfectly together? One thing Jaya knew for certain: she wanted to find out. She hurried to the lobby of the theatre, and checked that the scrap of cloth remained in the window. There, tucked behind the poster, was the flag, blood-red, a symbol of rebirth or destruction.

Akash caught sight of the red rag in the theatre window: Jaya's message to him. His heart pumped a jagged rhythm as he approached the front desk, although his anonymity shielded him. He deposited the letter in the hands of a plump woman who worked at the theatre, her makeup like a geisha gone wrong. Soraya's locket sagged around his neck, skimming the light fuzz of hair at the top of his chest. He stroked it like a talisman, left the letter with the over-painted woman and hid in plain sight amongst jostling pedestrians at the busy junction, hoping for another glimpse of his wife.

His wife. How strange for it to be true, though he no longer knew her at all.

Now, he watched, transfixed, as Jaya emerged onto the street. She pressed her weight against the glass door, crossing the threshold he himself had stepped over not an hour previously. Curled within her fingers was a letter: his letter.

A man—perhaps no more than thirty-five—approached from behind Jaya, startling her. Only a few metres separated Akash from her. He strained his ears to hear.

"Can we talk?" said the man. "It's been really awkward between us." He rested a hand on her shoulder, too familiar, as if they had history.

"Oh, go away, Ravi," said Jaya.

"You still hanker after him, don't you? Your husband. There's unfinished history for you. That's why you're not giving me a chance. But likely he's with another woman. There's not one soul mate. You—" he simpered.

Akash hated him. He recognised the flames of jealousy licking at him, the need to dart forward, intervene, push the man away.

His wife rounded on the man, a cool indifference emanating from every pore. "No is no."

The man shrugged and walked away, stiff as a board, a man crushed in the mating ritual.

Akash felt a flicker of hope. Did Jaya really still think about him? She was so close, he could almost touch her. He drank in the sight of her: hair piled high in a bun, strands escaping to frame her face, earthy lipstick and kohl under her eyes. She considered the letter in her hand, studying the lettering, then stuffed it into her shoulder bag without ceremony. A second later, she retrieved it, and re-entered the lobby of her workplace to sit down.

He couldn't help himself. He drew nearer, nearer, until his nose almost pressed against the glass. He needed to scrutinise the emotions sweeping across her face. Did Jaya realise the words were his? Did he stand a chance with her? Could she redeem him?

She was engrossed, her bag discarded on the floor at her feet, her hands clutching the letter. He surely had a few minutes to stay here, staring at her.

What a mistake.

Perhaps she sensed the intensity of his gaze. Maybe he made a sound in his eagerness, audible to all and sundry, just not to him, so captivated he was. Regardless of the reason, Jaya glanced up and, for the first time in two decades, through smeared glass and marketing posters, a husband met his wife's eyes.

Jaya looked up from the letter, drawn by an invisible thread. A man at the window gawked at her with such fervent attention, she felt like a moth pinned against velvet. Partially obscured, he stood curved and sallow, dressed in dull colours. It couldn't be Ravi. The man moved into the small space between advertisements, and suddenly the world blurred and realigned, as if someone had fiddled with the aperture setting on a camera.

Her breathing came in short machine gun bursts as their tired eyes met. The letter fell from her hands, drifting through the air like a disoriented seagull. She stood, electrified and depleted all at once, her balance off-centre.

The man entered the lobby and edged towards her with jittery steps, his path hesitant.

For a moment, Jaya considered running and hiding. She was not ready for this. Maybe, she had been ready since the day he left. Her gut burned with anxiety while her eyes drank in the sight of her husband: a thinning head of hair, bedraggled, poorly fitting clothes, a general air of uncleanliness, arms hanging limply by his side. This man looked beaten and instead of schadenfreude, Jaya felt only sadness.

He reached her. So close that she could hear the sound of his breath, see the lift of his chest. He opened his mouth to speak then shut it again, as if his words had been stolen, as if they did not live up to this moment of their meeting.

Jaya was tempted to close her eyes, to forget the sight of her aged husband and drown in the promise of their younger days. Then she remembered she was no ordinary woman; she was a warrior. Whatever lies her father had told, Akash had still betrayed her.

"It's been 21 years, Akash." She willed her body not to reveal any weakness. She compelled it to be rigid rather than soft, a steel frame he wouldn't dare to touch. She couldn't bear that.

His voice came out as a rasp. "21 years, 7 months, 3 weeks, 2 days."

Jaya's core softened. How much she wanted to believe he had counted the time, that he had cared.

"Can you forgive me?" He reached out to cup her cheek, rubbing the calloused pad of his thumb across her skin.

Somewhere on the periphery, Bushra knocked things over in her rush to disappear into the theatre, recognising their need to be alone.

Jaya's eyes filled with tears and she hated herself for it. She noticed the swirls of hair on Akash's cheeks. "No," she said, pushing his hand away. Her skin burned where he had caressed it. "Where have you *been*? I searched for you for years."

"I am sorry. I mourned you. Not a day passed that I didn't think of you. I didn't know you had survived."

She needed to break their eye contact. Her eyes swept frantically from one side to another. She felt compelled to stay, to lance the boil of their separation, but the air was thinner here, her mind saturated.

Akash stood still, a robot man, waiting for her next move.

Jaya went on the offensive, infinitely preferable to her than vulnerability. "All this time, you were in cahoots with Ruhi. More lies, Akash?"

"It was a trial. To see if I am worthy of you." His irises had yellowed over the years. His hands rose, zombie-like towards her, as if he couldn't resist touching her.

Jaya stepped back so the crease behind her knees pressed into the couch. "You're not," she spat.

Was he assessing her every mark? Did she come up short after all these years? For a moment, she suffered embarrassment at how passage of time meddles with the mortal frame. She shrugged off her shame. She had nothing to apologise for. She searched his person, letting her eyes wander over every inch of him, curling her lips into a sneer to show him how little he meant to her. He wore a cloak of melancholy, but she was certain it was not for her. The mother of his child had died, after all. A flare of jealousy ignited within her. It metamorphosed, a green changeling, imbuing her with strength she sorely needed.

"There you were playing happy families with your lover and son."

He jerked back, a swell of first distress, then pain registering on his face. She didn't regret using words meant to hurt, but even as she did it, she knew she was hurting herself.

"I was her friend, that's all. This time," said Akash. His voice caught, travelling up the octave. "You know about Arjun?"

"It wasn't hard to guess he was yours. I'm glad at least one of us had a child," she said.

Still he did not rise to the bait.

Jaya was no longer certain she wanted explanations. She wanted war. Violence. Something monumental to fill the gap of his missing years. This was too much, too little. Jaya's flight instinct kicked in. She crouched to pick up her bag, instinctively pushing the letter into it, wishing she had the mettle to tear it to shreds as he watched, but she couldn't let those words evaporate. Every fibre of her being called out to read his letter, to have something to hold of his, despite it all. She pushed past him, deliberately aggressive, her moments jerky, unfeminine. *Watch me rage,* she thought. *I am no doormat. You made that mistake once.*

He grabbed her arm as she thrust past him.

Jaya screamed in fury, not caring who might hear, not caring this was her workplace. "Let go of me. Nothing can destroy me anymore. Not even you," she said through gritted teeth.

"I'll never do anything to hurt you, Jaya, but you need to hear this." He trembled. "I am sorry. You asked once if I loved you, and I didn't answer. I love you. I don't know why I didn't know it or say it, but it's true. I love you. Failing you is the biggest regret of my life. Let me in. Let me prove it to you."

How easy it would be to fall into his arms, to wish away the years of hurt. But that would be an illusion. In reality, this broken man could not be hers, and she could not be his. They had gone too far in separate directions.

Jaya shook herself free, a growl taking shape in her throat. It erupted, dripping in venom. "You left me to *burn*. It's over, Akash. It was over a long time ago." The words made her powerful, but they rang hollow. Inside, in a moment of clarity, she admitted it had been her decision to light the match, not his. She couldn't hold him responsible.

The pain of the realisation rocked her, and she turned away from Akash. She sped away, as fast as she could, through the glass door and onto the street, clumsy and blinded by tears that smudged her kohl. She brushed her hand impatiently across her face and it came away marred by black smudges. *An overweight, panda-eyed woman running down the road. How dignified,* she thought bitterly.

She pressed on, demons at her back, hoping that Akash wouldn't follow. Familiar buildings jutted out of the ground like decaying teeth. In one crowded patch, child beggars with pleading eyes and quick fingers clutched at her. The unfairness of life weighed on her like a knife at her throat. The same thoughts snaked through her head — cries against abandonment and betrayal — like a record on loop, and she stumbled across the only truth she knew. She loved him. Despite it all, despite her mistakes and his, all these years she hadn't been able to let him go.

Still, she didn't require male attention to be happy. All those ghazals romanticising heartbreak. She knew better than that. Heartbreak was not to be coveted; heartbreak felt like death. Experience taught her that loving someone was not always enough. She slowed to a walk and lost herself in the crowd. There, in the midst of couples, families, and friends, Jaya's ring finger felt the heavy weight of nothingness.

# 36

**Akash woke as** the sun's rays threaded crimson ribbons across the sky. He groaned as he opened his eyes to the blanket of bricks above him. His night's sleep had been fretful, woven with glimpses of a retreating woman. He chased after her, trying in vain to catch the train of her sari, but she evaded him. He stumbled after her, through a concrete landscape that morphed into a graveyard, a man impeded by his physicality, his legs buckled and bent from years on the streets, his back bowed. When he caught her in profile he recoiled to see a patchwork woman, the nose and chin Soraya's, the lips irrevocably Jaya's.

Flashes of the previous day's encounter with Jaya rushed him as soon as his consciousness returned. He didn't know how to regain Jaya's trust, but it gave him hope that she'd at least retrieved the letter.

He cracked his neck, elevating it slightly off the shirt he had bundled underneath his head as a makeshift pillow. His body ached. Each day, when sunrise came, he was as stiff as a corpse. He didn't crave luxury, but he felt the cold more as he aged. The stiffness eased only with a dip in the lapping salt water of the sea.

Tariq lay a few yards further on a blanket of his own. In colder, wetter weather, they sometimes slept side by side, each benefitting from the other's body heat. Sometimes, they were taunted about homosexuality by unfeeling men who took their own home comforts for granted. They reminded Akash of the schoolyard bullies from his childhood, who belittled others to bolster their own tarnished egos. Their insults didn't bother him. He knew who he was, and he knew what he had to do to survive. As a man who longed for love, he could not imagine that love in any of its forms should be frowned at.

He reached out his foot to kick Tariq, gently first, then with more urgency. "Rise and shine."

Irritated, Tariq shoved him away. He stretched so that his limbs popped out from beneath his blanket in a star shape, muttering all the while. This ritual occurred daily, as familiar to Akash as if they were a married couple.

He was more naturally suited to early wake ups than Tariq. Years on the streets had schooled him to be an early riser. He understood instinctively that it was far better to rise before the city woke, rather than be caught defenceless in the folds of sleep should anything happen. Safety and privacy were commodities appreciated mostly by their absence.

"Seriously, wake up. Janghir Saheb is expecting us. Time to pack up our things, make ourselves presentable," said Akash, already rolling up his blanket and setting aside his wash things, a shrivelled loofah, his towel, a small blade they kept both to shave and as defence. He tossed his loofah at Tariq. It landed between his eyebrows and ricocheted to the side.

"Okay, okay, I'm getting up." His cough erupted and he sat up, rocking forwards and backwards, clawing at his throat, as if plagued by bees. "Man, you really know how to spoil a man's sleep," he spluttered. "I'm not sure what I was dreaming but I'm pretty sure it was delicious." He peeped underneath the blanket and motioned between his legs. "See, standing tall, just like a soldier."

Akash pulled a face. "Keep that to yourself, yaar." He had woken in the night often to Tariq pleasuring himself, and had always pretended to be asleep. Who was he to take away a few moments release? Still, a man needed to do some things in private. The episodes niggled at him, left him with a sense of the animal needs not met on the streets, and how sometimes, baser instincts escaped society's polite grip and emerged, defiant and unapologetic. He locked away his thoughts in a box. They couldn't afford to be distracted this morning. They had a purpose. "Come on, man. Hop to it."

Tariq stood and they worked in tandem, packing their meagre belongings into carrier bags, both men carrying a lesser amount than a normal person might bring home from a grocery store: cooking ware, a couple of worn books, blankets, a tarpaulin and a spare set of clothes. Then they slung their towels around their necks and headed to the sea to wash. Once dry and changed, each took turns using the small blade against their cheeks until they were presentable.

Janghir Saheb and his new store in Bandra West awaited them.

Arjun returned home from the restaurant early the next day, physically and mentally weary. At least he hadn't floundered at the restaurant. He knew the business as well as his mother had. His shoulders ached and he longed to crawl into bed and close his eyes. The sun's blood-orange rays kissed the rooftop of the house. He dragged his feet towards the elaborate arch that covered the front door. Violet geraniums edged with a white trim spilled out over the edge of the plant pots on either side of the pillared entrance. Sadness stung him. Hardly a month had passed since his mother had laboured over these pots, soil smudges across her cheek and crusted under her fingernails.

He spied Muna stretched out on a deckchair by the pool. Leela played on a blanket nearby. Arjun fought the impulse to disappear inside the cool darkness of the house and trudged over to greet them. Leela's downy head expelled the heavy sweet-sour scent of breastmilk. Arjun closed his eyes and lingered there, drinking in the smell of his daughter as he squatted. Then, he trailed a hand over his wife's leg as he claimed the lounger next to her.

"How was your day?" said Muna.

He shrugged, kicked off his shoes and socks, and undid the buttons at his cuff and nape. "That's better," he said, breathing out.

Muna took his hand in hers and traced the pad of her thumb in slow circles on his palm. He tensed his hand, as if to pull it away. Muna held firm, coaxing him with the pressure of her fingers.

"I've been thinking," he said. "Maa wasn't ill. She was full of life."

Muna's gentle voice cut through his denial. "She was ill, Arjun. The autopsy showed how progressed the cancer was. I know that doesn't make her death easier." Her voice trailed.

"It's my father's fault. If he had come to me, or Maa had, I could've helped."

Muna held her tongue. The air stilled between them. Nearby Leela rolled onto her stomach and cooed as cool stems of grass tickled her nose. Arjun watched his daughter absent-mindedly.

"I keep expecting to see Maa's silhouette appear on the veranda," he said.

Muna resumed kneading his fingers. "She'd be telling us to come inside right now. What was that she used to say about the Jinn?"

"The evil spirits sit in the trees after sunset. She didn't really believe in it herself. She was just repeating what my grandmother used to say, that Jinn visit trees, graveyards, forests. Highways, even. My nanima wasn't one for long journeys. They frightened her."

"Maa didn't seem the type to believe that." Muna pushed herself off the lounger. She threaded her way barefoot along the ceramic tiles to where Leela lay.

"She wasn't convinced, just cautious, I think. There were parts of the culture that still had a hold on her." He hesitated. "Our upbringing marks us, I guess, however much we try to escape it."

Muna caught his eye. "Don't forget, you have us." She glanced down at Leela, and squeezed her daughter's bare leg.

Arjun crossed over to where his family sat. Muna smiled up at him, and his heart ached for his mother, who he had never been without. The weight of his sadness hung in his core, and he had no idea how to banish it.

"Shall we go in?"

He picked up his discarded shoes, clothing and blanket, tossed the deckchair cushions in a storage box and followed his wife and daughter inside.

The commotion of the wake that had filled the house after the funeral now seemed a lifetime ago, and the quiet irked him. *I miss your strength, Maa.*

Instead of sitting downstairs, Muna tucked Leela into her cot in the nursery and they retreated to the cocoon of their bedroom, where Arjun drew the curtains, undressed where he stood and sank onto the silk of the bedsheets. Muna changed into a simple cotton nightdress, her heavy plait sitting on the creamy skin of her shoulder.

Arjun beckoned her over to the bed, and that night, they made love for the first time since Leela's birth. The fading light pierced the curtains, throwing shadows into the room that danced across the walls. Arjun's exhaustion momentarily fled as he gave himself to his wife, gentle and rough by turns. Her nightdress slipped off her shoulders as his mouth closed over her nipple, and as he worked his tongue in circles around it, he thought of himself as a suckling baby and then forced the image out of his head. His movements were initially robotic, as if on auto-pilot, but as Muna responded, arching her back and burying her fingers in his hair, he lost himself in her. Her slender thighs contrasted with the bulk of his as their legs tangled, and he trailed butterfly kisses from her jaw to her stomach, still rounded from the birth.

Urgency drove him up onto his knees, and he bent to press his lips against hers, sucking her lower lip, dipping his tongue into the caverns of her mouth. He pulled away to search her eyes, asking silently for agreement to enter her, unsure of whether she'd healed enough from the birth. She smiled, shyly and opened her legs to welcome him. She tensed as he entered her, and he eased in, fearful of hurting her. Arjun worked, his head close to his wife's, whispering his love in her ear as the rhythm of their pairing rocked the bed against the wall. He reached his pinnacle, and as he came down from it, images from the funeral flooded him.

His mother's shrouded body underneath a bank of soil. His father in the Red Room, a womb-like coffin, holding his mother's hand. He shook his head, intent on remaining in this moment, with his naked wife in his arms. This is life, he thought. Not pain. Joy, comfort. A man and his wife.

He propped himself onto his elbows to look down at Muna. Her eyes brimmed with tears in the half-light. Arjun gathered her to him, and reached for the bed sheet, pulling it up and over them. They slept entwined, her face buried in his chest, haunted by ghosts of the past.

# 37

**However much she** tried, Jaya could not erase Akash from her mind, much less her history. What would have happened had her parents settled on another match for her? Would she have lived in wedded bliss? Perhaps she and Akash still would have crossed paths. Would he have stood out for a moment, and then been forgotten as she continued her humdrum existence? It would have comforted her to see other roads mapped out, and to be able to measure her relative happiness.

Her fingers trembled when she read his letters, even with her fourth and fifth reading. She couldn't pretend that she wanted anything other than a happy ending with this man, even years later. It had been an involuntarily reaction to pick up his letter from the floor at Tara before she had fled. Losing the chance to read what Akash had composed would have haunted her. She didn't need another albatross, another millstone around her neck. When she opened it, she scoured the page, turned it to see the flip-side, and tasted a bitter tang of disappointment that the second letter was all too brief. She took it from her purse as she walked the streets, gripping it tightly lest it float away, and began.

> *Dear Jaya,*
> *I never knew I would be such a big keeper of secrets.*
> *When I was a boy, my mother scolded me for telling*
> *tales, but I could never keep anything hidden. I'd burn*
> *to tell her even the most insignificant facts, things she*
> *didn't need or want to know. As a grown man, I have*
> *realised that secrets are comfortable with me. They find*
> *a home in me whether they're welcome or not.*

*It's not in my nature to hurt anyone, yet that seems to be what happens. I had thought once I could protect myself and others by living without love, but without it, everything is bleaker. You see, whether we like it or not, our lives are about love. We dream about it. We are in love, or heartbroken from it. And afterwards, when all is finished and the embers have settled, the circle starts again.*

*I hope you never have to live without love, because I want the stars for you.*

*Your friend,*

*A.*

The rhythm of her steps drilled his words into her psyche, each word perfectly pitched to fill the emptiness she hid from the rest of the world. *I love you*, she thought, then immediately silenced her treacherous thoughts. The final letter was written with a flourish. She understood he'd risked her uncovering his identity although Ruhi had forbidden it. Jaya touched where Akash's pen had scratched the paper and felt a link to the man who was still her husband. Could she trust him? Could she know that even now she wouldn't play second fiddle to the dead woman? That could never be enough for her.

She approached the bistro where she'd asked Firoz and Ruhi to meet her. Outside, a blind boy and his mother begged with their hands thrust towards her. She pressed coins into their palms, then paused on the threshold of the restaurant to carefully tuck Akash's letter away in her bag. Inside, Firoz and Ruhi nestled at a corner table. She kissed each in turn, first her sister, then her friend, one man who had never asked anything of her, who sought only to give.

"Been waiting long?" she asked, gesturing towards dirty napkins strewn on the table beside a plate of sizzling cassava chips and gooey brown chutney.

"Indian time. We were late, too, though not as late as you," said Firoz, mirth creasing the corner of his eyes.

They rarely met as a trio. Sometimes it happened to celebrate Jaya's birthday, but mostly, her relationships with Ruhi and Firoz were one-on-one affairs only. They came together only at her request. In another life, had each not been fiercely loyal to her, they would have perhaps been good friends, both unfettered creatives, prone to speaking their minds.

"Why did you call us here?" said Ruhi.

A fan hummed above their heads, its blades rusted with age, looping, churning. Just like Jaya's stomach. She pushed the food away from her. Even the smell of it made her retch.

Firoz studied her face. "We can do this another time if you want," he said, concern planting furrows on his brow.

"No, I need to say this. It's weighing on me." Still, she hesitated. Akash's name hung on her tongue. He had been a ghost for so long, it felt normal to avoid his name.

"Ruhi and I, we've been talking," said Firoz. "Don't let a man mould you. You're too wonderful to be driven by his agenda. Don't get sucked into this again."

Jaya focused on the peeling paint on the walls. "And what if my agenda is the same as his? What then?" She turned to look at the two people who meant the most in the world to her, but who could not fill the emptiness.

"I thought you might say that," said Ruhi, her hands cupping a cool bottle of Coke.

Jaya watched beads of evaporation thread their way down the bottle. Every nerve in her body cried out for her to take control. To step out of her victimhood. She smiled, her lips curving, hiding the anxiety that was building to a crescendo within her. She needed only to close her eyes to see the flames, to see monstrous, grinning Akash there, delighting in her pain. She could no longer distinguish truth from reality. It would not do. She could not continue without finding out what kind of man he was.

Jaya turned to her friends. "I have a plan. Will you help me?"

Akash's body ached with the pain of the day's labour at Janghir Saheb's store. The monotonous work—hauling planks of wood up and down stairs, hammering crude shelving together, shifting stock from vans into the new premises—helped to keep his mind off Jaya and her rejection. He and Tariq worked with a harmony borne of their friendship, his friend chattering all the while. Only in the pauses, when the exertions eased and the conversation stalled, did Akash allow his thoughts to drift to Jaya. In those moments, he found a glimmer of light. She had picked up his letter when she had fled. And more than this, she hadn't asked for a divorce. *Can it be that you still care about me despite everything?* He banished the idea as soon as it found him. False hope would only hurt him later down the line.

So he worked. When the day was over, Janghir Saheb kept his promise, pushing a bundle of rupees into their hands and telling them to stay in the store and guard it from looters or squatters. He also gave them some ready samosas from the newly installed fridges for their dinner.

"I expect you not to steal," said Janghir Saheb, handing over a small set of keys on a brass ring and pinning the men with a solemn stare, "but if you act honourably, so will I. I am generous to my friends." He tapped his cane as he left, his chest swollen with pride as he surveyed the beginnings of his empire.

After he had gone, leaving just one halogen light buzzing above their heads in the twilight, Akash and Tariq rolled out their blankets side by side on the concrete floor and listened to the hum of the refrigerators and the quiet of the store.

"I'm tired but it's been a long time since I felt such peace," said Tariq, unwrapping his samosa. He gulped down the first one, then the second, smacking his lips together when he finished and revealing turmeric-stained teeth when he spoke again. "We've been indoors all day. Fancy a walk? I need to smell the sky. Maybe we can have a drink with our earnings, a little celebration?"

Akash also missed the thick air of Bombay nights. The store felt strange. "Maybe a *falooda* to celebrate or some mango juice, but leave off the whiskey tonight," he said. He wanted to make a good impression on Janghir Saheb in the morning. He didn't want to risk the older man's disapproval at the inevitable stench of alcohol reeking out of their pores. Tariq didn't always know when to stop.

They switched the lights off, locked the door and pulled down the shutters with a trill and a thud. Akash pocketed the keys they had been entrusted with. Outside, they breathed in the familiar smell of sweat and urine and spices under a cerulean sky dotted with emergent stars. Akash's body found an ease outside that eluded him indoors.

"How about a pilgrimage to Juhu?" said Tariq, nodding his head towards their old neck of the woods.

"Sure. The beach?"

"Yeah, we can get some *paan*. You know, that stall by Malhotra's video shop."

The thought of paan appealed, betel leaf with areca nut and *mukhwas* seeds. Together Akash and Tariq strolled, past palm trees and tooting, spluttering traffic, stopping at a street vendor's makeshift stall to buy mango juice thick with pulp. They sucked it up through straws ill-suited to the heavy clumps of fruit until their thirst had been quenched.

"So, how are you going to win her back?" asked Tariq, his sandals heavy against the paving, loose coins clanking happily in his pocket.

They drew up to the paan stall. It was shut.

"Shit, yaar, we missed it." He kicked the dust. "Go on, you were telling me how you are going to win back Jaya."

"I'm not," said Akash. "I opened up to Jaya, but I can't hold her back if I'm not what she wants. The best thing I can do is make this job work, build my life back into some semblance of normality. Who knows, maybe once Arjun's first swell of grief has eased, I can try to build a relationship with him. I need to prove to myself and Jaya that I can be a better man."

"What if what Jaya wants is for you to really chase her, prove your worth? Are you really going to give up this easily? That might not be what she wants, yaar."

"So, tell me, oh wise one, what might she want, since you're such a Romeo?" Teasing Tariq lightened his mood. If he were not to succeed in his quest for filial and romantic love, he had this friendship that had passed casually into a brotherhood.

They reached the beach, dark waters swirling with froth underneath the now blackened canopy of the sky.

"They want this!" Tariq ripped open his shirt, baring a scrawny chest. His perennial cough surfaced, giving him the look of a decrepit wannabe Don Juan.

"You idiot!" called Akash above his friend's raucous laughter.

He didn't see the group of men approaching behind Tariq until it was too late. Zahid Khan's podgy face loomed out of the darkness, flanked by his lapdogs. He was chewing tobacco, and spat into the sand at their feet. Grimy red spittle flew out.

"You two lovers out for an evening walk, I see?" he said, smirking. His wingmen tittered behind him, two fools desperate to impress their master.

"I guess you prefer threesomes," Akash drolly countered.

"Oooooooh," sang Zahid's bruisers in unison.

"What, you don't have permission to say anything meaningful?" said Akash.

Tariq drew the flaps of his shirt together and came to his side, his face wan, eyes large. Akash sent a message to his friend telepathically, desperate for him to understand. *Play it cool, yaar.* He could sense his friend's jittery movement beside him, like a bird stunned by a fall from a tree.

"You still haven't learnt from the last time we met." Zahid shook his head in mock consternation.

Tariq lay a pleading hand on Akash's arm. "Please. Let's just go." To Zahid, "We don't want any trouble, Zahid Saheb."

Akash shrugged him off. "No. It's about time we put an end to this once and for all."

Zahid rolled up the sleeves of his tunic. He was dressed as if he'd been to masjid this evening, yet here he stood batting for the devil. "What's that clanking I hear? A bulge in your pants?" He turned to his men. "For me, that would have an unmistakable meaning, but this dog is not so well-endowed." He walked up to Akash, menacingly close, glancing around to ensure there would be no risk of interference by passers-by, then motioned to his men. "Have you been stealing again? Let's do our civic duty, shall we? Empty their pockets."

The men approached Tariq first, turning him upside down, shaking him until his earnings fell to the sand. Akash reached out to help his friend and received a kick in his face. He nursed his jaw while Zahid's men dropped Tariq, leaving him in a groaning heap.

"Enough!" said Akash, bending down beside Tariq. "We are invisible to everyone, but you seek us out to cause trouble. Why won't you just leave us alone?"

"Because I don't like you. People like you are a stain on Mother India," said Zahid. He leaned forward, so the angry red veins in his nose were visible though the sun had long fled. "And because I heard about Janghir's offer to you."

Akash's head jerked up in surprise. There was an energy emanating from Zahid, at once alien and familiar, one that stemmed from envy and loathing, repurposed as resolve. He understood too late they should have run. One man, hooded eyes over a thin moustache, hands like a butcher's, pulled him away from Tariq. He held Akash firmly, while Zahid first tore at Akash's trousers, then his shirt, leaving him naked but for his underpants. A few crumpled rupees and Janghir Saheb's keys fell from his pockets. Akash balled his fists, enraged, ashamed, trying not to let his humiliation show.

"What's a battle between men without degradation?" said Zahid, quiet, psychopathic. He picked up the keys, smirking, and lobbed them through the air. They arched and landed with a clank.

Tariq whimpered, but Zahid blocked Akash's view with his bulk.

"What's this?" said Zahid, spotting the locket that hung around Akash's neck.

A vein in Akash's neck pulsed, insistent with wrath. "That's mine," he said through gritted teeth.

"I'll take good care of it," said Zahid, unfastening the clasp and shaking out the pictures of Arjun and Leela. "Let's face it. You're not really a family man, are you?"

He motioned to his brute, who pressed Akash up against a palm tree. The man looped one leg around Akash's so he was trapped, his arms pinned against the prickly trunk. Akash scanned the beach and recognised how alone they were. Even if the nearby sands weren't deserted, why would anyone intervene in trouble that was not of their making?

Zahid continued, enjoying his moment of power. "Look at my men here. So obedient. They know which side their bread is buttered. They're no upstarts. How unfair is it to them that the old fool Janghir—" He spat in the sand "—gives you two handouts? What does it say for sane business practice? No, no, not on my watch. It's time to teach you two a lesson. Let's see if Janghir wants you at his store once we've finished with you."

Akash struggled against his captor, pausing, gathering his strength and pushing forwards, to no avail. The man had an iron grip. The other man, heavy-set and sneering, straddled Tariq where he lay, positioning his weight on his friend's already heaving chest so he had no hope of escape. Tariq's cough rocked him with vengeance, and his face contorted as he tried to fill his lungs with air. Akash looked on, panic rising, wondering what Zahid had in store for them, wishing that he had his sack of belongings at hand, seeing in his mind's eye the blunt shaving blade they could have used to defend themselves.

"Stay calm, bhai. It'll be okay," said Akash, desperation seeping into his words.

Tariq's eyelids fluttered open, a hunted animal in the grip of a larger beast.

"It won't be okay," said Zahid. With his man still atop Tariq, crushing his chest, he began a rhythmic kick with his laced-up shoe, until the laces flew through the air, tapered ribbons of death, back and forth, back and forth. The sound of cracked bone, loose teeth. Tariq made no sounds, and Akash realised it was his own voice that cried out, insulting first, then begging.

"Bloodthirsty arseholes, you're like a pack of wolves!"

"Not his head!"

"Please, hurt me, hurt me. I'll do anything."

Zahid halted his assault. "You'll be my bitch from now on?"

Akash bit his tongue until he tasted blood.

"I thought not." He wiped the sweat from his forehead. "Your turn," he said to the brute on Tariq's chest. The man clambered to his feet, then changed his mind, dropping to his knees in the cold sands which cradled Tariq as he inflicted hardened knuckles at Tariq's head. Grains of sand dispersed through the air until Tariq's eyebrows were matted with it. It mingled with blood from cuts, gooey pearls of crimson on ashen skin illuminated by the rising moon.

Tariq went limp.

"Oh shit," said Zahid. He stepped aside, motioning for Tariq's aggressor to do the same. Akash's captor released his hold ever so slightly. It was enough. Akash tugged his arms, lashed out with an open palm, so his jagged fingernails caught the bruiser's eye. The man yelped, disarmed, allowing Akash to disentangle his leg and launch himself at Tariq.

Akash fell to his knees beside his friend, ignoring the scuffling behind him. The wings of Tariq's shirt remained open, his chest frighteningly concave.

"Tariq? Brother?" Akash cupped his friend's wet face in his hands. Elation flooded him for a brief moment when Tariq's eyes opened a fraction. "It'll be okay. I'll get help. Janghir Saheb..."

"No." His breathing was ragged and painful to hear. Blood oozed from his head. "They broke me...Sometimes we lose."

"Don't say that." Akash's throat felt like blades of glass. He couldn't eject his words. "Don't leave me alone."

"Promise me—"

"I won't promise you anything. I'm getting help."

Tariq shuddered, and Akash wrapped his naked body around him, burying his face in the crook of Tariq's neck as if they were lovers. When he drew back, he saw his friend's light had already flickered out and nothing remained except for the broken shell of his body.

Akash sobbed, rocking in the sands with his precious cargo. After some time, he looked around, and realised the men had gone. He pulled on his trousers and found the discarded pictures of his son and the baby. He wandered in a daze, repeatedly turning to look at Tariq's lifeless body. Eventually he stumbled across Janghir Saheb's keys, the metal like ice in his palms. He placed them in his pocket.

He returned to Tariq, his heart an open wound, buttoned up his friend's shirt with infinite care, and found his shirt on the dunes. He kissed his friend's cool forehead, then used his own shirt to cover his face. He imagined Tariq waking then, spreading his limbs into a star shape underneath his blanket as he did each morning, but there was no life left to animate him.

"You're too cruel!" he called out to the gods, under the sky that he and Tariq loved so much.

That night, he kept vigil next to his friend's corpse, chasing off the yapping packs of dogs that approached. He ignored the rupees scattered in the sands. Notes fluttered away on the breeze like monochrome butterflies. Coins bored into the sands to be found later by strangers. None of it mattered. Akash wrapped the cold and loneliness around him until deathly fingers embraced him. Then, he scavenged for some dry wood. He rubbed the wood together, the task as familiar to him as Tariq's gap-toothed grin, until there was enough friction to create an ember. He blew patiently on the wood and coaxed the sparks into a larger flame. A sombre procession brought him to the palm tree that had held him captive, mere feet away from where Tariq had suffered. He set the tree alight and was mesmerised by its orange glow, billowing smoke and crackling foliage. The fire kept him warm, a symbol of the life that had been lost, raging against the night sky and ominous moon.

# 38

**The time had** come for fresh beginnings. It wasn't that Arjun wanted to erase his mother, but he had begun to see the Red Room — where she and his father had spent so much time together, where she had died — as a tomb. That part of the house pained him, and he avoided it just as he avoided talking about his parents. Now he realised his failure to communicate with Muna had been driving a wedge between them and had even begun to taint his mother's memory. She gazed at him with displeasure whenever he passed her garlanded portrait in the living room, her almond eyes hard and unrelenting.

He had taken a few days off from the restaurant to clear his head, leaving the business in the capable hands of his right-hand man, although he had already begun to feel the lack of a woman's touch there. It was important to him to white wash the Red Room himself, to purify what had happened there. Maybe then he could move on.

Arjun pushed the bed, side tables and the desk into the middle of the room, covering them with a dust sheet. He climbed the ladder, opened the tin of paint and spread thick white emulsion onto the walls. The claret-red shone through, and he knew he would need to apply multiple layers for it to be gone. He sighed, but eventually the monotony of the labour became comforting.

He could hear the faint echo of the baby's cries upstairs. She had been missing her naps and Muna had grown tetchy. Geeta helped, but it hurt Muna when the maid was able to settle Leela, so she had become possessive and frustrated. The cries grew louder. A rattle at the door, and Muna stepped into the room. Leela gurgled and smiled at her father. Muna looked from one to another, and bit her lip. Tears threatened to spill.

"Can you take Leela for a minute? I need the bathroom."

Arjun climbed down off the ladder and set down his paintbrush. "Sure." He slipped into the ensuite to wash his hands, and then held out his hands to his daughter. She tumbled into them. Muna harrumphed and pushed past him into the bathroom, locking the door. He heard her sit down on the seat. She turned on the tap, and behind the door he thought he heard her crying. She emerged a few minutes later, red-eyed and downcast, watching him throw their chuckling daughter into the air.

"How about you take some time for yourself tonight? Meet with friends, go for a meal? I'll look after Leela. I don't need to be at the restaurant until Thursday."

She hesitated. "I'm too tired to talk to anyone."

"Then close the door and sleep, have a bath."

"I need to get out for a couple of hours. These walls are driving me crazy."

"So go out. I'll get Rajesh to drive you anywhere you want."

"That would be nice."

"Do it then."

"Thank you." She smiled, buoyed by the thought of a night without the baby. "How do you feel? It must be strange being in here. It looks strange in white. Maa was so stylish, she would find this boring."

Arjun watched as she fussed over the sheets covering the furniture, her heavy plait swinging behind her. A yellow patch of curdled milk from the baby sat on her shoulder. Once it would have repulsed him; now it made him love her even more. It reminded him of how much she gave of herself to Leela and to him.

"What's this?" said Muna.

She had opened a desk drawer to stack its contents neatly: a pad of paper, envelopes, a few postcards from his mother's trip to America many years ago. The police had searched in here after his mother's death and hadn't thought to return the items to their proper place, so now Muna rearranged what she found. She shuffled through glossy rectangles of his mother's favourite places from her US travels: Boston

Library, a misty San Francisco, Broadway. She then coaxed out a small blue envelope from it that had half-disappeared into the join of the drawer. It had been inscribed with the big S impression his mother liked to use. Muna swung around to Arjun, her eyes wide.

"It's for you."

There, in his mother's loopy handwriting—as if even the mere act of forming the letters possessed an innate freedom—was Arjun's name. Muna offered him the letter and then reached out her arms for the baby.

Arjun trembled as his slid his finger across the seal, bitter-sweet in the knowledge that this was most likely her final instruction to him, her final comfort. It was everything and not enough at once. He heard his mother's voice in his head, not his own.

> *My son,*
> *I didn't want to leave you so soon, but I am happy that you aren't alone, that you have Muna, Leela and your father. When you find this letter, you will know that it was my decision, and that your father comforted me in a lonely moment. It was not a burden I could ever have asked of you. You are everything to me, so why would I cause you pain?*
> *I think it would bring you and your father both comfort to reconcile with each other. His absence was, after all, my fault. I know better than most, that there's a wound that comes from secrets.*
> *Please forgive me for my mistakes. If I can ask anything from beyond the grave, it is this: live bravely. I know that you'll go on to do wonderful things. Know that you were always the most important thing in my life, and that I am only gone because my body demanded it.*
> *Maa.*

Tears sped down Arjun's face as he read. He folded the letter carefully, slipped it back into its envelope, and rubbed his fingers across the imprint of his mother's initial. Then he gathered his wife to him, with the baby held tenderly between them. He couldn't put it off any longer: he had to find his father.

In the early hours of the morning, Akash stirred from his uneasy slumber. Dawn had broken across the city, blanketing it in a red haze, bringing with it the full horrors of the night before. In front of him, the tree stump still smoked. Akash staggered to his feet, his skin clammy from the fever that had taken him in the night. Next to him, in perfect repose, lay his best friend. Tariq's shirt rippled in the breeze, and if Akash squinted, he could almost confuse the rise and fall for breath.

But that would be a lie. His friend was dead. Tariq's words reverberated through his skull. *Sometimes we win, sometimes we lose.* A sob caught in his throat. It was so unfair. Just when fortune had turned their way, when it looked like they could build something of their lives. He had tucked his shirt around Tariq's upper body and used the weight of his friend to hold the shirt in place. Now, he peeled back the material covering Tariq's face, and saw that his mouth had remained open and the blood had stopped flowing, making it difficult to close the orifice. He wept then with the passion of a child, for the blameless, hapless man, whose dignity had been stolen even in death.

After some time, when the waves of grief receded, Akash swallowed the needling pain in his throat and clenched his fists. Zahid and his henchmen had to pay. He owed Tariq that much. He knew who he must see, and yet he could not bring himself to abandon his friend's body, not when he was all alone, defenceless even in death. The city stirred and Akash could linger no more, so he crouched next to Tariq and whispered in his ear.

"I'll be back for you as soon as I can, bhai. You matter."

Part of him thought that the dead could still hear the living, at least until burial. Akash considered finding items to shield Tariq from prying eyes, but the beach was bare except for litter, and passers-by could mistake him easily for a sleeping drunkard. He turned to leave, and then swivelled back, his tone gentle. "You made these past years worth living, my brother."

He collected the fallen rupees he could find, some of which had been Tariq's, then began a brisk walk to the main road to hail an auto rickshaw. Nobody would blink twice at a shirtless man of his ilk, but Akash knew the reason for it and his pain and anger weighed each step down. He climbed into the rickshaw, and held on as the driver, opaque eyes showing the tell-tale signs of cataracts, bumped along the potholes and wove with vigour through the growing traffic.

Thirty minutes later, Akash stood in front of the gloomy police station he had left a few weeks previously. No journalists waited outside this time. He thought how different death was for the famous, and how similar. He shuffled up the steps, his adrenalin spiking, suddenly unsure whether he could trust the woman whose help he needed. Inside, the grey plaster reminded him of the Tariq's pallid complexion where he lay on the sands. He imagined cocooning Tariq's body in a chrysalis to preserve him. A man's voice startled him, tearing him away from his morbid thoughts.

"Can I help you?" Inquisitive eyes over a khaki uniform and handle-bar moustache.

"No." He corrected himself. "I mean, yes. Inspector Fortes. Can I speak with her?"

"Do you have an appointment?"

"No, but I have information."

He looked Akash up and down, taking in his state of undress. "Your name?"

"Akash Choudry."

"Wait here." The man strode away, into the recesses of the building.

Akash lowered himself onto a bench, his bare skin cool against an oak bench. He was tracing the circular patterns of the tree's life cycle in the grain of the wood when Inspector Fortes arrived.

"Mr. Choudry?" Her angular face was rounded out by concern. She held out her hand to shake his. Akash returned the gesture, taking comfort from her firm grip.

"Thank you for seeing me."

"Is everything okay?"

Such a simple question, and such a temptation to invent some fiction, to let the question float past as millions of people did on a daily basis, keeping their secrets for themselves. Except, Tariq was alone, and Tariq deserved justice, whatever the risk to Akash.

"My friend, Tariq."

She furrowed her brow. "I remember. You were concerned he would worry about you."

"He was killed last night."

Inspector Fortes nodded as if this was the most normal thing in the world to say. "Follow me."

# 39

**Only at art** class could Jaya unleash her truest self. Here, she was not judged, regardless of what she put on the page or the quality of her interactions. She arrived early this week, knowing Firoz would always welcome her. He buzzed her in, and she travelled up in the elevator to the studio, her mind whirring like the keys on a grand piano being played by a virtuoso.

"It's all ready?" said Firoz.

Jaya nodded.

"I'm glad, brave woman."

That morning, she placed a poster in bright red lettering in the window at Tara, inviting Akash to meet her on Friday evening. The poster read:

> To A,
> if you see this,
> meet me at dusk on Friday,
> there where the flowers died,
> J.

She knew how to play him. He was her husband, after all. It was her way of taking control, of testing him about the moments that haunted her most. Only then would she know if their marriage was worthy of a second chance.

She banished him from her mind as she helped Firoz set up for class, dotting easels around the place, setting out a bowl on the table and balancing the fruit there precariously for a still life session. Coconuts, guavas, bananas, mangos and grapes spilled out of the bowl. Then the click of heels behind her. She spun to see Firoz greeting a young woman in cobalt kitten heels.

Firoz opened his arms wide in a flamboyant gesture. "Welcome! This must be your first time?"

The woman nodded, creamy skin, flawless even under the unforgiving spotlights.

Firoz beamed. "I need to give the paint bottles a quick clean, but please, make yourself comfortable. Jaya is an old hand here. She can answer any questions. Why don't you take the easel next to hers?" He wandered off, his pert bottom bobbing up and down in his yoga pants, toned from years of exercise despite his age and penchant for caramel ice cream.

The woman, perhaps young enough to be Jaya's daughter, watched Firoz disappear, then turned to Jaya with a look of trepidation.

"Don't worry, you'll get used to him," said Jaya. "I've been friends with Firoz ever since I started coming here. Come, how about those two?" She motioned to two easels on the far side of the room. "The glare from the windows isn't too bad there."

"Thank you," said the woman. "It's my first time away from the baby. I thought doing some art would relax me. But it's been so long since I've done it, that I probably won't be able to do it at all."

"You'll be fine," said Jaya. "How old is your little one?"

"Eight months."

"Beautiful."

"Honestly? It's tough. I don't even know from one moment to the other if my breasts will cooperate. I'm feeding." She laughed, and Jaya found herself warming to her. "I'm Muna."

"Jaya."

They sat side by side during class, both immersed in the swirling colours, the stroke of their brushes, the spell-binding focus of artists in flow.

Firoz floated through the room with his characteristic exuberance, gesturing wildly when he witnessed novel touches emerging under the fingertips of his students, delightful and embarrassing at the same time.

After class was over, Muna helped clean away and beckoned to Jaya. She pointed to her work, a crude painting with hesitant lines, blotchy colours and fruit that bore no correlation to the bowl from which they had taken inspiration. "It's a start, right?"

"Yes, it's definitely that," Jaya joked. "Come and have some chai."

They collected their steaming mugs, taking pleasure from the scent of cinnamon and clove wafting through the room mingling with the smell of the acrylics. Muna looked tired.

"Are you okay?" said Jaya.

"Oh, I'll be fine. Just the pressure of being a wife and mother. You know how it is."

"Actually, I don't. I don't have children." It always felt shameful to say it out loud, like not having children amounted to a failure.

"I miss that. Not having the responsibility. I've not talked to anyone in months." They stood looking out from Firoz's window across the vast expanse of the bay. "Not properly. It's just me and the baby, and emotionally supporting my husband. His mother died recently, you see, and it wasn't easy."

"I'm sorry."

"I am too. You know, my mother-in-law was beautiful, clever, strong. And now, when I look at the jewellery and clothes I inherited from her—these heavy silks, and fashionable cut-out sari blouses, necklaces that sit like weighted ornaments around my neck—all I think of is the burden to be perfect. It feels selfish to say it, but I can't always be the strong one. Or the best mother. Sometimes I just want to sit in my pyjamas and not be elegant, or kind, or even clean." Muna pushed back her shoulders. "I'm sorry. I can't believe I blurted that all out to a stranger."

"I'm happy to listen if it helps," said Jaya. "It sounds like you've been waiting for a long time to get that off your chest." It did her good to think about someone else's problems for a change. "But if there is one thing I know, it's that nothing is perfect. I have no one, not really. And that, too, is difficult sometimes."

"I shouldn't admit this," said Muna, nursing her chai between her hands, "but I sometimes wonder what it would be like to have been single for longer. I married so young. I'd still pick the same man, but maybe I should have waited a bit longer."

"The time is never right. There are advantages to being single," said Jaya. She swept aside her introverted nature in an attempt to put the younger woman at ease. "I can close my door and no one will come in." She lowered her voice so she was not overheard. "I can take off my clothes and not worry that I am being judged. I can sit in my knickers and not have a man feel it is for his pleasure. But my question to you is, which is better: to be lonely or to be loved?"

"Aren't we lonely even when we are loved?" said Muna. "The path we take is ours alone. No one can accompany us the whole way."

Jaya slurped her tea. "I always wanted a family, children. It never happened for me." She wondered whether the child she had dreamed of, with inky eyes and bouncy pig-tails, had been born to someone else or whether she only existed in her thoughts.

"It's not always easy. My own mother died too long ago for me to have asked her the questions I now think about," said Muna. "It seems for women, everyone has a right to our bodies, and we last of all. Take the hospital room when a child is born. We become a map, a foreign land unconquered, the unknown. Hands grasp us, then they are all gone and we are discarded while strangers tend to the newborn."

"It's the same in every country," said Jaya. "For every woman, born rich or poor, whatever her age. Perhaps more so in India. We are going through growing pains. Isn't it always the women and children who bear the pain of that growth?" She thought of her own mother, and wondered how different she might have been if she'd been exposed to more influences outside the home. Would she have been more compassionate, less concerned with herself?

"What would the world be like if it were ruled by women?" Muna mused, deep in thought. "You know, my period started a few days ago. The first time since I became pregnant. And Leela, she's not sleeping and I'm constantly exhausted, and I know my husband is already thinking about another baby. There is something about death that makes us crave life. I couldn't do it," said Muna. "I couldn't tell my husband that my body is ready for another child, so I went to great lengths to hide the bloody towels, emptied the bathroom bin so he wouldn't catch me out and realise."

"Oh Muna. Surely you can just tell him you're not ready?" It was this subterfuge that caused the rot in relationships, Jaya was certain.

"And what would that say about me as a woman?"

"That you're human. That you have other dreams apart from motherhood." She set her cup down on the floor and noticed how most of the class had left, gone home to their loved ones. "How different we are. I would give the world to have had your journey. I have strong relationships but I crave the companionship of a romantic attachment. My sister would have been better suited to being alone than me. She is strong, self-sufficient. She doesn't care about gossip at the temple. Disapproval doesn't seem to touch her. Even at this age, I struggle with my lot. The world 'spinster' makes me want to crawl into a cave."

Muna rolled her eyes. "The gossip trap old women fall into, judging others so they don't have to focus on their own problems. I've never understood it."

"Not just old women, all men and women. We all talk. To understand but also to elevate ourselves above others," said Jaya. She paused, not wanting to reveal too much about herself. However much she liked this woman, she was but a stranger. She proceeded cautiously. Some secrets needed to remain intact. "My mother, even today, drops hints about how I wasted my beauty by not keeping a husband. As if without men, beauty is an unused tool in our arsenal."

"Reduced to an ornament or a trophy. It's sad when women pass those thoughts onto their daughters."

"It's what she's been taught," said Jaya, realising that her mother's failings were not all her own. Somehow, that made her mother's harshness easier to bear. "The truth is, I'm no less of a woman if I choose not to colour my hair or wear tight-fitting clothes. I'm no less of a woman because my life did not lead me to traditional milestones. I can still use my maternal instincts. I'm a great auntieji. My nephew tells me things he wouldn't tell his mother. And I embrace my femininity in other ways: work, my art, how I dress." She placed her hands on her waist, swishing her tulip-shaped skirt this way and that. "My body and mind are mine, and it should be okay, except it isn't."

"You had someone once?" said Muna.

Jaya looked out across the water and the twinkling lights in the distance. "Yes, a husband, a long time ago."

"He is still alive?"

"Yes." She strove to banish the wistfulness in her tone, and again, her mind flew to her plan, and she willed Akash to succeed with all her might. Talking to this stranger, who knew neither her nor Akash, gifted Jaya with permission to consider Akash's strengths. "I was drawn to his gentleness, the way he looks at the world, his love of literature, the way, all those years ago, he would lay out my toothpaste on my brush in the morning and fold his trousers on the chair. I loved him for the idea of what we could be together, what we could achieve. What drove us apart was his weakness for another woman. And not even her, really, more that he had given up on us. I couldn't accept that."

"Yet here you are, talking about him as if he still means so much to you."

"Maybe he does." She hugged the seed of her love close to her.

"Would you give him another chance?" said Muna.

"I don't know." There was something about the younger woman, a kindness and non-judgemental openness that loosened Jaya's tongue. "Long ago, in another lifetime, I did something terrible and sometimes I think I did it to drive men away. I couldn't trust myself not to give in to love, and I didn't want the pain of it. For a long time, I wanted to die. Now... now I'm a cold fish. My heart hasn't thawed. It hardened and I'm not sure it's capable of softening again."

"I think it has already softened." Muna scooped up the empty cups. Remnants of the chai sloshed at the bottom, speckles of grains and herbs clinging to the base like wet sand on the beach. "Don't be afraid to take your husband back if you love him. We all have the right to a happy ending of our own choosing."

# 40

**Anger interspersed with** Akash's grief. Soraya's death had been unavoidable, Tariq's senseless. The temptation to dull his pain with alcohol beckoned. He had ample money. He could steal from the store, but his morality forbade it. Besides, it would be no escape. Tariq had been the drinker. Akash knew from experience that precious little comfort could be found in the bottom of a bottle. It made the lows worse. It would compound his loneliness rather than alleviate it.

Instead, he stumbled into a temple, fuelled by anger, and rang the bell harshly, an affront to the cruel garlanded god before him. He was not yet ready to pray for the dead. His lips condemned. The prayer house did not unburden his spirit.

Only the thought of justice provided comfort. He and Tariq had survived so much together, and now, the idea of working for Janghir Saheb without his friend pained him. Even now Akash could feel Tariq's excitement at their prospects like the emotion was tangible, something he had bottled. He heard whispers of his friend's desires in his waking moments. It was why he visited Janghir Saheb in two minds about whether to continue working for him. The old man deserved the truth at least.

When he told the old man what had happened, his face twisted in grief as if he had lost a son, and it helped Akash to know that Tariq had more friends than he had realised. That others mourned him.

"The job is still yours, whether Tariq Bhai is here or not," said Janghir Saheb. "I know you do your work. If you need to see to any — business — you do not need to worry about me stopping you. I am an old man. I know death does not occur without its rituals."

"Thank you," said Akash. His loyalty to Janghir Saheb deepened then. He respected the old man, and realised that not everyone wielded power heartlessly, that some remained capable of empathetic responses to piteous circumstances.

The next day he bathed in the sea next to a bobbing reflection of Tariq, then bought a new shirt. He turned up to work although he felt a limb was missing, confusing the guffaws of a carpenter at the store for Tariq, hearing his friend in the spluttering cough of the electrician.

Akash was stocking shelves when Inspector Fortes arrived to take him back to the police station. The hours rolled past. He could not be sure how long he had been in the interview room. He had no watch, and no clock adorned the stark walls. He supposed the bare walls were deliberate, to disorientate the hapless occupants of this room. Cool air seeped into his skin, and it seemed to him the sun and moon might never shine again, because of all the atrocities they witnessed.

Across from him sat Inspector Fortes, eyeing Akash's statement over half-moon spectacles. "There is no detail you left out? Nothing you are hiding?"

"No." His gut told him he could trust her, but he couldn't be sure, not with men and women of the law. He thought of Tariq, alone and friendless.

"My men recovered your friend's body," said Fortes. "And this." She pushed his locket towards him.

Akash reached clumsy fingers for the chain and rubbed his thumb over the engraving, a ritual to calm his anxiety. He bowed his head, imagining Tariq on a cold stone slab. He wondered if his friend was nearby, in this very building. He remembered their early years together, and how they would scavenge for food, and Tariq would jump behind trees and buildings, over the top and ridiculous, drunk, determined to make him laugh. His grip on sanity loosened and for a moment he forgot Tariq had gone and his mouth twitched at the happy memory.

"I'm sorry for your loss."

The black cloud of sadness swept over him again. Akash focused on Inspector Fortes and glimpsed the woman behind the professional mask. She cleared her throat, closing the door on her natural empathy, assuming the mantle of her office once more. "We have collected evidence this morning from Zahid Khan's work premises. We found his boots in his home and have already matched Mr. Khan's boots to the imprints found on Tariq Beynon's face. Unfortunately, Khan and his colleagues absconded, but we will find them. It's only a matter of time. Until then, be careful. You have my card if you need me."

"I understand. Can I ask? The cause of death?"

"Collapsed lungs, presumably as a result of the pressure applied to Mr. Beynon's chest, exacerbated by pneumonia. The charge, once we catch the culprits, will be manslaughter."

Akash shuddered. Tariq must have been in such pain. He couldn't imagine the crushing pressure. "When can you release his body for burial?"

"Two, three days maybe. I need to be honest, I can't rule out that Mr. Khan and his colleagues come up with a plausible reason for their absence. If the courts believe them, and they can pay bail, they may be allowed to remain in the community until sentencing, and that can take a long time. But rest assured, we have marked these men as dangerous. They would be stupid to try anything else."

Fear crawled up Akash's spine at the thought of a vengeful Zahid being hunted by police yet still determined to punish him. He swallowed the bile that rose in his throat. The news didn't come as surprise. The rich had means at their disposal that erased even the biggest mistakes. He was thankful that Inspector Fortes had taken the matter seriously.

"You have my address at Janghir Saheb's store?"

"I do," said Fortes. "There's something else."

"Yes?" He resisted the urge to press his palm against the agitated strumming of his heart. Could it be that he had been implicated somehow?

"I received a call this morning. Your son is trying to track you down. He's waiting for you outside. My advice to you Mr. Choudry?" Kindness tinged with resignation emanated from Fortes' every pore. "When you find yourself alone, the best thing you can do is build bridges." She smiled at him wearily, intending to be encouraging. Little did she know that companionship didn't come easily in the craggy landscape of his life.

Arjun waited on the steps, his face an inscrutable mask. Akash squinted as he descended into the light, unsure of the best greeting. Words fought to tumble out of his mouth behind the prison of his teeth, but this time he needed Arjun to take the first steps.

Arjun nodded a hello. "Fortes told me you were here."

"Yes." It shamed Akash for this meeting to take place on the steps of the police station. He wished with every atom in his body that Arjun would be proud of him, that he could see his father doing an honest day's work, or surrounded by love he had earned. He stood still, waiting for a signal from Arjun. Their repeated run ins led to one conclusion: it was better to follow Arjun's lead. That was the only way he would be able to have a relationship with his son.

"I'm going to visit Maa's grave. Would you like to come?" said Arjun. His voice lacked warmth. Akash understood that this was a challenge.

He imagined Soraya's frail body under the earth, felt the cool metal of her locket against his chest. He couldn't refuse the opportunity to pay his respects and he didn't want to. "I'd like that."

"Follow me." A driver waited on the kerb in a shiny grey saloon that mocked the dust of the city.

Akash felt in his pocket for coins, weighing up whether to ask Arjun to stop at a shop. It pained him to turn up at Soraya's grave empty-handed. He knew the Muslim customs. He had slept by enough graveyards to know how Muslims sprinkled water on the grave to settle the soil. He had always seen this ritual as a way to pay homage, to quench the thirst of the departed. Incense sticks, too, were planted in the soil to ward off evil spirits or refresh the decaying air.

Father and son sat in the back-seat side by side, their hands—duplicates in all but age, long spindly fingers with short thumbs—

on their knees. Akash couldn't resist a sly look sidewards, capturing his son's profile.

Arjun's thick hair had the buoyancy of youth, achingly similar to Akash's own hair at his age. Arjun remained silent and brooding. At his feet, a carrier bag rustled, and Akash noticed a litre bottle of water and some sunflowers. Arjun had come well prepared and Akash was glad he didn't have to interrupt the fragile silence.

Finally, they arrived at the gated Islamic cemetery, where Muslims lay together in rows with simple stone markings regardless of their social stature. A peace reigned here. Sparse trees dotted the edges of the grounds, and an orange-beaked blackbird flew ahead of them as they weaved their way through the graves. Arjun's bag of goods rustled in the breeze.

All at once, he stopped and set down the bag. Akash fell in line with his son, conscious of the soil mingling with his sandaled feet. There, on a mound still raised, lay an intricate flower arrangement in freesias and lilies spelling out Soraya's name.

"Muna came yesterday," said Arjun by way of explanation. "The day before, the flowers here were stolen. Who does that?" He bent down to lay the sunflowers on his mother's resting place. No other grave was so adorned.

The fragrance from the flowers filled Akash's nostrils and momentarily cut through the bank of his pain, leaving him hollow. Soraya. Tariq. Zahid. Jaya. Arjun. It all melted into a cauldron of horrors filled with mistakes he could not undo. Arjun opened the bottle of water and poured it liberally into the soil, muttering under his breath. A prayer perhaps. A sacred ritual his father had no part in. Then he lit a match. A scratching sound and a flare of phosphorus that pulled Akash out of the void. Memories of Jaya came flooding back, the deathly dance of the flames on her skirt, his helplessness. Then as Arjun knelt in the soil where his mother lay, he remembered Soraya on her death bed: her fluttering eyelids, the bloodied dawn of her clothes.

He waited while Arjun placed incense sticks in the earth and offered him one. Then, he took a deep breath and crouched to lay his hand on her grave. He placed the incense where he imagined her feet might be. "Your mother was a remarkable woman."

"Yes, she was." Arjun's look stripped him bare. "That's why I brought you here. You'll think twice about lying to me at her grave."

"Why would I lie?" Akash asked, surprised.

"You didn't exactly tell me the truth when she was at death's door, did you?" said Arjun. "She needed me."

"That's just it. She didn't. She was strong. She knew what she wanted, and it wasn't you." The last words spilled out artlessly, a remnant perhaps from the time he and Soraya were lovers. He felt no possessiveness. He had merely expressed fact. Soraya hadn't wanted to die with her son at her side.

Arjun flinched. "Tell me then, Akash. What happened in my mother's dying moments? You owe me that much." He didn't wait for a response. He dusted his mother's stone with his hands, a loving touch, and a whisper to return. Then he scooped up the carrier bag holding his litter and walked away towards a withered bench.

Akash took a moment at the grave. "Our son is spirited, just like you," he said, not expecting her to hear, but talking to her all the same. Then he made his way to his son who sat, stern in a way that aged him, stiff as a board, bushy eyebrows over glowering eyes.

"I want to get to know you, to be a part of your life if you want. What can I do to convince you of that?" said Akash.

"Tell me, in detail, about my mother's last moments."

"The truth is a burden, Arjun. Be careful what you wish for," said Akash, lowering himself onto the bench. Still, part of him felt maybe this would do him good, unburdening himself of the secrets he had voluntarily kept. Perhaps their love of Soraya would bond them, even though she'd gone.

"I'm ready."

Akash traced the grain of the wood with his index finger, remembering. "She'd had cancer for some time. It was inoperable. She didn't want you to know. She said she'd been both mother and father to you. She wanted to protect you."

"How long had she known?" Arjun's voice trembled at first, but he steeled himself.

"Close to a year, I think."

"Why tell you, a stranger, when she couldn't even tell her own son?"

Akash shrugged, unsure. "I owed her. I abandoned them both. My wife, your mother. You. I think she didn't feel any guilt burdening me, abandoning me..." He grew quiet.

"Go on," Arjun urged.

Akash's eyes blurred as he retreated into his memories and the cemetery around him faded into nothing.

"I am a proud woman, Akash. My loved ones are settled and have no need of me. I don't fear death. I fear the loss of my dignity. I want to choose when I go. And the time is near," said Soraya.

He looked at her and the scales fell from his eyes. He saw a body that was brittle and frail, hair arranged in the best possible way to hide that it was thinning, inky blue shadows under her eyes. Desperation and bitterness flooded him.

"But what of me? Arjun? Leela?"

"What of you? Understand this at least, you silly man. You still have life left. Guilt has already consumed your best decades. Let this be a lesson to you to live, to find Jaya, to be a better man, a father to Arjun."

"How can you do this?"

"The cancer is eating away at me, Akash. I can no longer deny that. It makes my bones hurt. My lungs tire and it hurts to breathe. Sometimes, it's as if I can feel my organs rotting inside me."

He no longer wanted to hear how her body was failing her. It was unfair. He resisted the urge to rail against the universe.

"We all have choices. Please understand mine. Help me act on it." She hesitated. "I don't want to die alone."

It wasn't Soraya he thought of in this moment, but himself. He might love Jaya, but Soraya was the mother of his child. They were bonded. They had history. She was a supporter, a friend.

"There must be something they can do."

"I 've seen the best doctors. I wanted to live. But I can't hide from my fate. Life is fleeting. I have no regrets."

"Not even what we had?" A memory overwhelmed him and he close his eyes as he remembered a stolen moment together, the air heavy with heat while he made love to her in a tangle of sheets to the sound of rickshaws outside. He shook it away, immediately guilty.

*Jaya, forgive me. It is you I want.*

"Akash, I am not scared of death. It is the act of dying that I'm fearful of. I prayed for somebody to lighten my burden. And you came. An unlikely guardian, perhaps, but nevertheless someone to accompany me at my end."

She held something up, turning it in her hand. Akash's breath caught in his throat. This plan of hers felt so wrong, but how could he disagree with a dying woman's wishes?

"This is the knife I want to use. I bought it especially. It felt wrong to take one from the kitchen where I've cooked family meals," said Soraya. The blade glinted with sparkly malevolence in her palm. Its handle was a smooth ivory with gold markings. "I'll do it. You don't need to worry about a thing. I just ask that Arjun and Muna don't witness it, and that I'm not left alone."

"Let me come with you," said Akash, suddenly weary. "I'm tired. We can do this together."

Soraya's voice cut through the air in a sharp slash. "No! Arjun has only just been reunited with you. He needs you, even if he doesn't think he does. There's no running away this time, Akash. You need to face life. When Arjun is ready, tell him I didn't choose to leave. There are no winners with cancer. I'm not in a happier place. I wanted to stay here with him, with my granddaughter."

Later, when it was nearly time, Akash watched Soraya as she slept. A slight sheen of perspiration coated her skin. She instinctively turned her body towards him. He drank in the curve of her lips, the fluttering of her eyelids as she dreamt and remembered when they had been lovers. The hours passed and still he lay beside her, awake, her silent watchman. Dawn was Soraya's favourite time of day and it came too quickly, the golden light finding its way through the curtains he had opened while dark still reigned. Her eyes flickered open and held his. He fought the urge to run from the room, to call Arjun, to hide all the sharp objects he could find. He told himself over and over: it is what she wants.

She removed the knife from beneath her pillow and felt the cold, sharp edge of the blade. He pushed the blade aside and kissed her forehead, entreating her to stay with him and their son. She smiled, sad and resolute, and smoothed her hair. Then, with a cry of desolation, as the sun streamed through the curtains, Soraya buried the knife between her ribs. It was not the death she had hoped for; it was messy and he saw she struggled to hold onto the shreds of her courage. He looked away as her eyes flashed open in pain and red spilled out across her salwar kameez. Akash took her in his arms and wept.

"Thank you," he thought he heard her say, but he couldn't be sure.

She shut her eyes for the last time. The corners of her mouth were upturned.

Akash could no longer tell if she remained conscious. Wasn't hearing the last sense to leave a dying body, the last grasp of a soul departing this physical life? He whispered to her about their son, their youth and how proud he was to have shared parts of her life. He told her that she had changed him forever and that though they had never belonged completely to one another, she was a part of him. He stroked her face as watched his tears trace paths down her cheeks. He thanked her for Arjun and their grandchild.

When her body grew cold, Akash arranged Soraya on the bed. He ran his hand over her eyes to make sure they were closed. He couldn't leave the knife in her body. He clenched his jaw and removed it, taking care to be gentle though she was already dead. The knife fell from his trembling fingers onto the bed. Akash smoothed the sheet over Soraya. He blinked back the hot tears filling his eyes, then retrieved the locket and Jaya's letter. Afterwards, he returned to the bed to take Soraya's hand.

There, he waited for their son to find his dead mother, his mind a white-out.

# 41

**Dusk had settled** across the sky. Red and orange fingers bled into blue. How long they had been there, Akash didn't know. His voice was heavy with exhaustion and melancholy when he spoke. "You see, she wanted it that way. I've never met a braver woman."

"So she planned it? It wasn't an impulse thing? She'd planned it all along?" Arjun slumped on the bench.

"She knew she was dying. She'd had enough of the pills poisoning her body. She didn't want you to see her suffer. Your mother was proud. She preferred a warrior's end to her life."

"What, a knife in her abdomen? Couldn't there have been a better way? I saw her that morning. She looked like a victim, not a warrior!" Arjun's voice rose and pierced the quiet. "You could have saved her."

"No. You might have had another few days, a week or two maybe, but the end was close. Surely the autopsy report told you that?"

"You loved her?" said Arjun. The question was weighted, and Akash didn't know which answer his son would prefer. He decided to speak the truth.

"Not in the way you might think. Maybe once, a long time ago. Mostly, I was infatuated with her."

"Why didn't you find a way to tell me all this before? You must have realised I need to know," said Arjun. "Maa may have decided her fate but you were the executioner. I wish you'd died, not her."

A child's sentiment coming from a man's body, but one Akash could understand. He knew only too well the disorienting nature of grief. Still, here his son faced up to his demons when Akash himself had run. There was more of Soraya in Arjun than the boy himself knew.

"You think you were justified in withholding the truth of Maa's illness from me because she was dying anyway? Well, you were wrong! A few more days with her, a few weeks...who knows what you took away from me, from my daughter, from Muna? You stole those last moments from us. I wanted to be there for her, to close her eyes, to say *in a illahi rajauun*."

A swarm of birds left a nearby tree. The waves of emotion rolled between them. Akash reached out to touch his son's hand. Arjun snatched it away.

"I'm sorry, son." It made his heart sing to say the word. *Son. Son. Son.* Despite all the tragedy, he was not alone.

Arjun sighed. "She's gone, and the hole she has left is too big. I keep tripping over it."

"When a big tree falls, the earth shakes," said Akash, echoing Rajiv Gandhi's words after his mother's assassination.

Arjun stood, and fear clawed at Akash. He couldn't let this chance to make something of his relationship with his son dissipate. He garbled his words he spoke, "Why did you come to find me, Arjun?" The seed of hope still lived that his son might want to reconcile. "You didn't call Fortes to try to find me, you didn't bring me here, just to walk away. Why, Arjun? Did you come to insult a stranger or to embrace a father?"

"I came because Maa left me a letter and I needed the truth. I came to look you in the eye and to see what kind of man you really are. I think I know now."

A lonely ache accompanied Akash while he toiled at Janghir Saheb's store. When the day was done and everyone had gone home to their families, when a threadbare blanket, shared pots and their shaving blade was all he had to remind him of Tariq, he locked up, tucked the jangling keys into his pocket and pounded the streets. The moon hid behind a blanket of clouds. Akash couldn't resist. Jaya might have told him it was over, but he followed his feet to Tara Theatre nevertheless, as if pulled by an invisible thread.

It neared midnight when he arrived. The theatre was shrouded in darkness, actors and audience fled. He ran his fingers over the glass front. Perhaps this was his last pilgrimage to her before letting her go. He could not have what she did not want to give, that much was clear. He turned tired feet towards his empty home, already missing Tariq's counsel. Jagged red lettering caught his eye. He read:

> *I ♂ A,*
> *if you see this,*
> *meet me on at dusk on Friday,*
> *there where the flowers died,*
> *J.*

He froze, looking behind him, to the left, then the right. Could this be a joke? Maybe Zahid was out on bail, furious, had found a way to taunt him. But then, how could Zahid know about his Jaya? He considered the possibilities. If the note happened to be from Jaya, where could she mean? He struggled, jumping through their history as if it were a tape deck: his aunt's house, where they first met; her parent's neglected patio garden; a park, perhaps? Then he realised. It had to be where she had first seen him and Soraya, in the rose garden outside university, where their marriage had unravelled.

Where the flowers died. Only Jaya could know that. There could be no doubt it was his wife who summoned him. And he would go as a lamb to the slaughter. He yearned to have a happy ending, but there were no love songs or brightly-costumed dancers in sight. Whatever Jaya had planned, he was hers.

"You came."

"I came."

The clouds formed silver roads in the sky. The roses were not dead. They lived, as Jaya knew they did. It pleased her he had understood her little play on words, that Akash realised the turning point they had experienced here.

She had dressed carefully. She'd applied her make-up with precision, enhancing her eyes, making her lips appear fuller with a deep red. Then she wiped it away, surveying the clown that looked back at her from the mirror. Did he deserve her attempts to impress him? In the end, she wore her favourite salwar in emerald green, not because she wanted to look beautiful for Akash, but because she felt at ease in it.

Ruhi and Firoz were hiding a few yards behind her, shielded by a group of palm trees, but Akash didn't know that. Neither did he know about the pouch Ruhi had pressed into Jaya's hand moments before, the one that held her discarded wedding band. He thought she'd come alone. As if she would meet him, a fly in a spider's web, without seeing the colours of his remorse. She might love him still, despite herself, but she could make rational choices. Her plan hinged on it.

Akash stood before her, anxious, fiddling with his over-sized trousers, his shirt cuffs. She longed to touch his face, to trace the lines that made him. Her fingers itched, as if they had been given permission by the bonds of marriage. The stirring of dormant physical attraction upset her. She shrugged it off, suppressed it behind her still face.

"Won't you sit?" The bench, too, she remembered. He had kissed his lover here, many moons ago.

"Thank you." He sat, expectant, unsure. "You wanted to talk?"

"I want to test," said Jaya. She had to protect herself.

"Okay."

"For a woman, whether we marry or who we marry is one of the most important decisions in life."

Confusion flashed across his face.

"I had little choice in the matter. I might have been a romantic — then — but I knew what was expected. I was a commodity traded by my parents." She laughed, not with abandon but sadly. "I saw a photo and I believed you were a hero when you were full of flaws. I loved you like a god. That's what a good wife does. Until you broke our vows and exchanged me for someone you liked more."

"I'm so sorry for my mistakes," said Akash, sorrow painting his face grey. "I wish...I wish it hadn't happened. I wish I'd come back, even after the fire. Maybe we could have salvaged us. Facing you seemed the hardest thing in the world. Your father..."

"Yes, yes, I know. Again, the man in the driving seat. Don't be sorry, though. You taught me the way of the world. The truth isn't always beautiful but the need for it is. I need it today as much as I did then." Her voice trembled. So much rode on his answers. On her reading the truth in his eyes. "I am more powerful now. I have no fear. What can happen to me worse than what I've already survived?" Jaya lied. Her fear raged like a hungry beast. She quelled it.

Maybe if they could both break out of their prison of familiarity they stood a chance. She'd thought long and hard how to show Akash who she really was and who she wanted to be, and she had finally cracked it. First, she wondered how Soraya would have done it. And then she realised Soraya neither occupied the femme fatale role, as Jaya had attributed to her, nor the mother role. She was everything and nothing because she was herself. Could Jaya find love in the wreckage of her marriage? Could she have everything she wanted if she stopped doubting herself and him?

"I know why I'm here, Akash. When I love, I don't give up easily. That is my weakness, and maybe my strength. The question is, why did you come here? Why insist on trying to save our marriage when you hardly know me anymore?"

His eyes danced in the lamplight, pools of black she tried her best to fathom. "I've spoken to you in my head for years, Jaya. What I see now is more beautiful than I imagined."

"I will not be Soraya's replacement."

"I chose you. I'd choose you even if she was still alive." After all this time, she had never imaged their voices would ring out again in the same place. "She was an obsession for me. I wasn't ready for selfless love. What better way to guard myself than to go after the unobtainable, that which I never expected to keep? Finding an impossible partner meant that I didn't risk intimacy. I liked my freedom until it became a prison. And I will never, never hurt you again."

Jaya waved her hand impatiently. "Haven't you learnt already? There are no guarantees. We've been tested by time and distance, by tragedy and lust, and I still love you. The strongest loves exist in spite of faults. There is no perfect love. I need to be sure, though, that you're not in love with a ghost, Akash. I can't compete with that. How can I be sure?"

He rummaged around his neck. "This is the only thing I have of hers. It is yours if you want it."

She took the glinting necklace from him and saw it was a locket. She squinted at it in the streetlight, unclasping it to discover the miniature photographs of his son and a baby inside. It made all the difference he had offered this to her. His assurances went some way to appeasing her jealousy of the dead woman.

"Jaya?" He quivered, and she knew her power over him.

"Yes?"

"How can you love a man like me?"

The answer came forth, unencumbered, the easiest thing she had ever said. "Soraya interrupted our love story. You let her. But it wasn't just you, Akash. It takes two to love. And I'm ready. Did you ever think it wasn't about you? This is about me. My ability to determine what happens in my life. I'm in control, and I like it."

A silence grew between them while she collected her thoughts and tried to put them into some sort of order. She failed, and in the end, only her intuition came to her rescue, the feeling that if she didn't forgive him now, it would be she who suffered.

"Be warned, Akash, it's all or nothing. I won't be beholden to empty promises. If our love story is to be resurrected, we won't smother it behind closed doors and under tradition. We'll wear our scars proudly."

"I don't understand." His brow wrinkled and she was hit once more by the urge to touch him, to smooth it out.

"I have been suffocated by tradition. I want love on my own terms. If we're to save it, truth will be the oil of this relationship. The first time, I made up a person in my head you could never be. This time, we'll lay ourselves bare. Every flaw, every secret. We'll rekindle our love, but we'll live apart until I'm ready. I'll always have the freedom to do as I wish. I won't wash your clothes simply because you demand it, or cut papayas at dawn."

"I understand." His eyes were full of love and she almost couldn't stand it, the distance between them. She had to be strong, but still she doubted. Were they in love with the idea of love, or was this the real thing? She couldn't be sure without risking her heart again.

"I have witnesses here," said Jaya. The click-clack of Ruhi's heels echoed in her head as Ruhi and Firoz stepped out from behind the palm trees. They came to stand by her side, solemn as mourners at a funeral. "If you can agree to these vows of my choosing, we can begin again."

"Jaya, are you sure about this?" said Ruhi, her words a whisper masked by the night breeze.

Jaya coaxed her eyes away from the contours of her husband's face. She still needed to learn how time had changed him. "Sometimes we shut our eyes and fall. I've been falling for years. This time, I'll embrace it." She slipped her wedding ring, tired yellow gold, from the pouch. She held the wedding band between her thumb and forefinger, toying with it. "It's not happiness I expect. I expect a disaster. We won't go into this with blinkers on. Whatever the outcome, I'll be changed, and to change is to move forward. And maybe, just maybe," she addressed Akash, "you'll prove yourself to be the ideal husband. Not to my family or friends, but to me."

"Does this mean what I think it means?" He trembled.

She nodded.

He fell to her feet, kissing her shoes, there where her toes were missing. She bent, touching his bony shoulders, feeling her heart swell for the second chance her father had almost stolen from them. "Make no mistake. This is a vow we're taking. Ruhi and Firoz can attest to that. They will hold me and you to account if we deviate, if our love disappoints. This is your trial by fire, and if you falter, I will leave and I won't look back. There'll be no coming back."

Tears streaked down his cheeks and he looked up to the sky to mouth something Jaya couldn't understand.

"Do you have vows of your own to add?" said Firoz.

"No," said Akash, smiling through his tears. "Once Jaya's parents spoke for her. Now her words will bind us. It is enough. It is everything."

"Then you agree?" said Jaya.

"I agree, Jaya. We'll rebuild our lives and I'm yours for as long as you'll have me."

She handed him her wedding ring and the four of them stood, in a semi-circle by the night roses while Akash gently took Jaya's hand

and swivelled the ring into place. Her hand tingled where he had caressed it. Her breath caught in her throat while he pricked his thumb on a thorn, and used a drop of blood to mark her forehead, just under the hair line, with the ancient symbol of marriage.

She took a vine from the bush, wordless, and fashioned it into a ring for his finger. He extended his hand and it quivered like a leaf in the wind. The vine sat at the base of his hand, green, the colour of life. She wondered how long it would last. It soothed her to see how emotional he was, this man who had taken so much from her. She would have to learn to read him again, a new language, a new terrain.

# 42

**Akash could not** deny the pull he felt to the temple.
His faith in the gods ebbed and flowed, but he experienced it most in
grief and gratitude. This time, joy drove him to prostrate before
Shiva. Only when he approached did he notice the Shivaratri
celebrations in progress, marking the day Lord Shiva married the
goddess Parvati. Surely it had to be a sign from the heavens that his
rejoining with Jaya fell on the same day?

He rang the *ghanta* as he entered the temple. The bell
sounded out, reverberating high and clear across the temple, an
Om sound that beckoned him to a spiritual plane. Inside, he
joined the swaying throngs chanting *Om Namah Shivaya* and
offering flowers to a smooth cylindrical stone representing Shiva,
The Blue-Throated, who saved the world, whose cosmic dance
was the source of creation, preservation and dissolution. He
closed his eyes and, with every breath, sent a burst of gratitude
to the heavens.

Afterwards, he returned to sleep on the floor of Janghir Saheb's
store. He cradled his ring finger and its adornment to him, and a
wholesome sleep came to him that had eluded him for years.
Shadows did not haunt his dreams. He saw neither a burning Jaya, a
withering Soraya nor an accusing Arjun. His fears rested, locked
away by Jaya's trust in him.

His journey to this point had all been in search of love, and he
understood now that only by facing his past, reconciling with it,
could he build something of value. He'd survived his years on the
street by walking towards a mirage of his perfect love, when he he'd
perhaps had it all along.

Even now, Akash recognised he paled in comparison to Arjun, a man who had managed so successfully what he had failed at: marriage, business, raising a family. Perhaps his journey would have been easier, had he been able to buy love, to shower Jaya, Arjun and Leela with gifts. But, no. He had fallen prey to his vanities before, and he was determined to be the best man he could be for Jaya, to live up to the ring on his finger, to build a life of joy and companionship, make up for his errors in the past, and walk into old age hand in hand. Without the hope of love, everything paled.

They had been reconciled for one night and already his stomach churned at the thought of losing her, of never having his fill of her laughter and her touch. He'd believed she was dead for so long, that this seemed to him like a delicious, precarious dream that might disintegrate at any instant. They had plans to meet tomorrow. He wanted them to sit together in the fading light and reminiscence about the times they shared and the times they were apart. He wanted to find some meaning in it all. But first, there was work to do. He hadn't forgotten Tariq. Zahid was still free, and Akash wanted revenge.

Jaya had been looking forward to attending Firoz's class all day. Work had been tiresome, with endless alterations to costumes for Tara's forthcoming production. Jaya had cut, tacked and stitched, remaining patient with the performers. All the while she had willed herself here, to the quiet of Firoz's studio, the comfort of the canvas and the joy of the friendship that had blossomed with Muna.

Firoz greeted her with a smile as she arrived. He fizzed with enthusiasm and enfolded her in a hug.

"You see these pink pants? They're my happy pants!" he exclaimed. "I am so happy for you, Jaya. Last night—last night was beautiful. You cut out a piece of your past and you remade it to work for you. *That*, that is living."

She laughed. His enthusiasm was infectious. So often over the years he'd been the sunshine to her dark cloud. It felt good to have a reason to celebrate together. Still, nobody apart from her inner circle—Firoz, Ruhi and Akash himself—could know she'd reconciled with Akash until she had worked out precisely what that meant and how to tell her parents. For now, at least, her ring hung around her neck on the chain Akash had given her, suspended side by side with his locket.

She considered briefly how her parents might react to the news, whether they would be happy for her or horrified. There would be time to dwell later. She tossed the anxiety from her mind.

At the near end of the studio sat Muna, already using a pencil to draw fine lines on the canvas, biting her lip in concentration. Jaya crossed the floor to sit at the easel next to Muna, briefly wrapping her arms around the younger woman from behind as she passed. She flattered herself to think they might have passed as mother and daughter to the unknowing eye.

"Hello, you," said Jaya.

"Hi," smiled Muna, pretty in a mauve salwar kameez with blue beading.

"You look beautiful. Careful you don't splash paint on your outfit. Firoz has some aprons at the back if you need one."

"I'm okay. I inherited enough clothes from my mother-in-law not to have to repeat an outfit in my lifetime," said Muna.

Jaya picked up her palette and squeezed colour on to it.

"I guess I'm lucky to have inherited her things. She had no daughters."

Jaya picked up her brush and drew strokes, trying to replicate Akash's face. The image of him in the rose garden—the one she had seen for decades, of him entwined in another woman's arms—had been replaced by one of an older Akash renewing their marriage vow. She wanted to capture his face. She needed to expel his likeness onto the page just in case he didn't stay and she was left with nothing.

She leaned forward and the locket and ring dipped close to her palette. She tenderly held them before placing them inside her blouse. She smiled at Muna, content, before picking up her brush. "It's addictive coming here, isn't it? You can't keep away."

"I'm lucky Arjun doesn't mind me leaving the baby with him."

Jaya froze. "Your husband is called Arjun?"

"Yes, why?" said Muna, tilting her head to study her work.

Firoz paced nearby, greeting each and every one of his class.

Jaya's heart raced. "Your mother-in-law, was she called Soraya?" The locket hung heavy between her breasts.

Startled, Muna turned to Jaya. "How did you know? Have you been to the restaurant? Such a small world."

Jaya fumbled for the chain and slowly drew out the locket. The ring clinked next to it.

"What's that?" said Muna, her brow furrowed. She reached out her hand to touch the locket. "I've seen one of those before."

Other students traipsed through the studio, rustling bags, saying hello. Jaya was grateful for the bustle. She opened the locket and the air stilled around her as she offered it to Muna to look inside.

"Jayaji, why have you got a picture of my husband and baby in your necklace?" asked Muna, pale and quiet under the bright studio light.

"Because I followed your advice, Muna. I went after my happiness. And the man I love, the one I spoke of to you, he gave me this. He is Akash, Arjun's father, and the woman who stole my husband from me gave him this locket. She was Soraya."

Akash busied himself at the store, hauling out rubbish to the containers in the alleyway. The bins smelt like someone had pissed against them and he made a mental note to wash them when he had a quiet moment. He'd have to be careful not to damage his makeshift ring. He glanced down at his finger, his heart swelling with pride, matched only by Janghir Saheb, who was preening like a peacock at his shop's imminent opening. Inside, the aisles gleamed, stacked to the brim with canned and boxed goods, snacks of every description and even a fresh fruit and vegetables corner overflowing with guavas and mangoes, okra and onions, green beans and bulbs of garlic. If only Tariq had been here to witness it.

Akash made his way back inside. Low strains of Asha Bhosle from the tired CD player filled the shop. A low laugh curdled his contentment, sending fear darting up his spine. Akash turned, slowly, for fear his eyes would corroborate what his ears had told him.

"We've been looking for you. I should have known you'd be here. That the old fool would trust you after what you did," said Zahid, flanked by his brutes from the beach, looming large and menacing in the doorway.

Akash thought hard and fast. Was Zahid really trying to pin the blame for Tariq's death on him? He had to get away. He knew what Zahid was capable of. Akash's hands were empty. He had no weapon. The shop was deserted apart from him and Janghir Saheb, who was in his back office. The workmen had completed their jobs.

"I'm going to deliver you to the police. My friends there will see to it you will never harm anyone again, you scum." Zahid's bald head gleamed.

A movement in the corner of his eye gave him a glimmer of hope. Janghir Saheb emerged, upright and intent.

"I've called the police. They're on their way," he said.

"Good. The sooner this dog is locked up the better," said Zahid, edging his way towards Akash.

"Run, Akash!" shouted Janghir Saheb, lifting his cane into the air and running at the men, surprisingly agile for a man of his age. "Run!"

Akash did not need telling twice. He darted down the aisle, heading for the back exit, but at the last moment he circled back round, fearful for the old man. Rice and ready-made chapatis, tomatoes and cans of soda flew from the aisles behind him as the men gave chase. His heart beat thundered like the hooves of a horse, rattling in his chest. They were bigger, but he was faster. He had something to live for.

A crash behind him. He hurled a glance over his shoulder. There lay one of the henchmen amongst an assorted pile of groceries, a spray of flour in the air, his face grim. Akash rounded the last aisle, anxious for Janghir Saheb, already sorry for the damage that had been done, the misfortune he had attracted. The old man had cornered Zahid's other brute against the freezer. He groaned with every sharp hit of Janghir Saheb's cane, able but unwilling to strike his elder. Relief drove tears to Akash's eyes.

"Go! What are you waiting for!" shouted Janghir Saheb.

Akash nodded, unable to speak, his lungs burning. He jumped over the threshold and burst into the open, only to be nearly run over by a passing swarm of cycles. A young boy called out an admonishment in rapid-fire Hindi. Akash barely processed him. His gaze swept to the alley. He had to finish this once and for all. He knew what was in the bins. He launched himself towards the container, sensing Zahid hot on his heels, his steps heavy, determined.

"You can't escape me, dog. I told you once before you are my bitch. I can do whatever I want to you," said Zahid.

He was mere yards away, almost at Akash's back. A flick behind him, like a spring mechanism.

Akash veered round. He had found what he needed.

Zahid held a blade. It glinted in the sunlight.

Akash didn't want to die in this reeking alley. He looked down for the symbol of hope on his finger. *Help me, Jaya.* His thoughts reached out to her as if she were his goddess.

Zahid hurled himself at Akash, plunging the knife towards him.

For a second, Akash saw Tariq's dead face, his gap-toothed mouth wide open, imagined insects crawling into the orifice. Then he swung the plank of wood in his hand into Zahid, with force, seeking to do damage.

The knife scattered across the dirty paving, and still Akash did not stop. Sirens sounded in the distance. He cut through the air with the plank, landing on Zahid's bulbous nose, his portly belly, his back, his legs. The other man crumpled to the floor, moaning, bloodied, but alive.

Suddenly Fortes was there, her baton raised, yelling at Akash to stop. He let the plank fall from numb fingers. His world widened to the policewoman, Janghir Saheb, and men handcuffing Tariq's killers. Fortes dragged Zahid to his feet and carefully retrieved the fallen knife.

Fortes's voice. "Zahid Khan, I am arresting you for the manslaughter of Tariq Khan..."

A pause. Someone next to him. "Mr. Choudry. Mr. Choudry, it's okay now. We have them. We have them now, Akash. Can you hear me?"

Akash slowly focused on Fortes's face, let her words filter through. "Yes, I'm okay. Can I talk to him before you take him away?"

"Two minutes," said Fortes. She nodded to her man.

He hauled Zahid back into the alley. Zahid looked at Akash through swollen eyes, venomous even in defeat.

"You are going to pay for what you did," Akash quietly said.

"We'll see about that," said Zahid, spitting a gloopy ball of blood at Akash. It hit his shoulder, slid down.

"Are you more of a man because of your strength, because you crush the weak? Did no one ever love you?" said Akash, turning away. He had heard enough.

Behind him, Zahid was not finished. "You think you're worthy by just being born? What have you done? What have you achieved? You, the small man with illusions of grandeur."

Fury coursed through Akash's veins as he spun around. "You killed a man. You killed my friend."

"You deserved it," said Zahid.

"Well, that's our case signed, sealed and delivered," said Fortes. She laughed. "It's not usually that easy. Well done, Mr. Choudry." She shook his hand.

"Wait, wait, I didn't—"

Fortes motioned for her colleague to take Zahid away.

"Am I in any trouble?" Akash asked her. He looked down at his hands. They throbbed. Zahid's blood had spattered there. Jaya's ring hung by a thread.

"No. He is badly hurt, but he'll survive. You'll have to come down to the station, of course, but Janghir Saheb here told us everything. He saw Zahid use the knife. You have self-defence wounds."

Akash followed her eyes to the wounds on his arm, one in his leg. He hadn't felt a thing, but now they burned and he knew he was alive. He nodded, spent of emotion.

There was nothing left to say. Akash walked towards Janghir Saheb on legs that felt ungrounded, separate from his body. The older man grasped him as he would a son. Akash did not spare a glance for Tariq's killers. It was over. It was a new day.

# 43

**Jaya stood on** the beach waiting for him, as planned. She had promised she'd be there, but still Akash held his breath as he rounded the corner and only expelled it when he recognised her silhouette against the cloudless sky. The world grew quiet when he looked at her. The pain fell away. She wore Western dress today, his wife. *My wife, alive and well, and with me.* She had trained her eyes on the horizon, serene, a strong, honest woman doing nothing but holding his future in her hands. Akash's lips stretched into a smile, too wide, until he felt like a goon.

Excitement propelled him towards her. He yearned to hear her voice, understand her every thought, undo the pain he had caused. He wanted to tell her about Tariq, his kind, funny friend, and the justice he and Fortes had somehow engineered despite the odds. He longed to tell her about Arjun's invitation. How his son wanted to have dinner, how Jaya could accompany him, if she wanted. They could take this first step together towards being a family.

His excitement gained force as he crossed the sand towards her, ignoring back packers and sun worshippers. He had so much to share. He wanted everything now, to empty his thoughts into her head so she could understand how every fibre of his being was up to the task of earning her forgiveness, of being the most wonderful husband. *Slow down, Akash*, he told himself, *you have all the time in the world. Don't overwhelm her, you idiot.*

He touched her, and she didn't flinch. She turned to face him. His hot fingers ignited a trail of goosebumps down her bare arm despite the heat. Her expression didn't mirror his joy, and Akash's spirits dipped.

"Are you okay?" he asked.

"Yes," she said.

Her chest rose underneath the bodice of her dress as she took a deep breath. Up close, the shape of the dress reminded him of the one she'd burned in. He saw the flames for a moment, the freshly cooked samosas sitting unscathed on the work surface behind her, then blinked the demons away. Everything would be okay.

"Shall we sit?" he asked gently, and led her to the dunes.

They sat, side by side, their bodies carving moulds into the dirty yellow of the beach. Her skirt rose, travelling upwards. Pitted skin, light and dark, showed underneath. She watched him carefully and he sensed her anxiety. He met her challenge, neither gawping nor turning his gaze. He drank in the marks of their history, and reached out to trace them with his calloused fingers.

Jaya grasped his hand firmly, stopping him in his tracks.

"Wait, there is more." She took off her shoes, undoing the laces. Her choice of shoe stood out as unusual. Most women in India chose sandals. She peeled off her ankle socks. He understood then why her gait was unsteady, the reason for her limp. Sorrow weighed heavy within him as he pivoted in the sand to sit opposite her. The sun beat down on them, exposing, warming. He took her feet in his hands, kissing them with singular intent, feather-light caresses, uncaring about who might see them on the open expanse of beach. First, her right foot with its chipped nail varnish, and then her left one, with its stumps for toes. If only he'd been able to stop her. If only he had declared the love that was buried in him, underneath his immaturity and vanity, underneath the conviction that nothing untoward could ever happen to him or anyone he loved.

Jaya neither pulled away nor softened into his embrace. "Akash."

He let go of her and saw a seriousness in the planes of her face that he wanted to erase.

"I need you to hear me. These scars are nothing compared to the scars inside. I gave into an urge of annihilation. I lit the match; you left me to burn."

"Jaya, I tried that day. I couldn't break down the door. Your screams, I couldn't see you die."

She studied his face. "I believe you."

He shuddered with relief.

"But know this. Pain changes us. I lost my trust in myself and in others after you left. I pushed everyone away because they weren't you. I missed out on children. Even after the slow rehabilitation, when the raw wounds had closed, I carried my grief with me, a silent companion." She paused. "I need to tell you this. I searched for you initially because I wanted to see you broken. Then, I searched for you for closure. Eventually, I searched for you because I realised the old me had died but my love for you lived."

It pained him to hear this, but like her, he realised they needed to excavate their past to progress beyond it. However much his ego, small though it was, compelled him to defend himself, he refused. He had earned these arrows. He would not silence her.

She cut through his thoughts. "I won't let sorrow and guilt get in the way of us. We won't carry that weight. I understand now, there is no love without pain. It's proof of engagement, of being in the fray. There are never any guarantees of a happy ending. I need you to do one thing with me."

"Anything." He meant it.

"It is time." She bent to put her shoes and socks back on.

"For what?"

"To face my parents."

The market traders had packed away by the time Jaya and Akash reached her parents' house in Bandra. Jaya slipped her key into the lock and turned it. The door opened, and she took Akash's hand. He squeezed it, apprehensive. It irked her to see how he had attempted to make himself presentable this morning, combing out his coarse hair, shaving his patchy beard, as if an improved appearance would sway her parents' opinion of him. She knew how this would unravel. For so long, Jaya had dreamt of honesty with her parents, but now the moment had arrived, her insides twisted, nerves throbbing, heart rate heightened. It thrummed in her ear like a hummingbird's wings.

She had called Ruhi en route, her plea urgent through her old handset, her fingers determined, clumsy. "Meet me there?"

"Of course. You're going to tell them?" Ruhi's concern radiated across the sound waves.

"Yes."

"They won't like it."

"No." Beside her, Akash pretended not to listen.

"I'll be there in a quarter of an hour," said Ruhi.

"Don't prepare them."

"I won't."

The house smelt of samosas, hot oil and pungent vegetables as they entered. Jaya's stomach turned. Samosas still made her think of the day of the fire. She grasped Akash's hand tighter. She'd expected reluctance from him, but he matched her step for step. Her hand fitted into his larger one like a jigsaw puzzle. Her father looked up from the television, roused by their footsteps. He paled. Not a word of greeting.

"Minakshi!" he called to his wife.

Jaya and Akash waited next to Lord Vishnu's shrine, side by side, expectant and ready. The god watched them, his four arms suspended in time, his cloud-coloured visage unmoved. Her mother emerged from the kitchen, behind her a woman Jaya recognised from temple. She should have known her mother would never have taken it upon herself to cook independently.

"Oh!" said her mother, covering her mouth in surprise. She recovered quickly. "Kanthibai, I'm sorry, you need to go. This is a family matter." Her voice took on a tone of outrage. "And this is unacceptable of my daughter."

"This is very unusual, Minakshi," said Kanthibai, harrumphing. She waddled past, her stomach shaking underneath her salwar, like a snow-capped mountain preparing to avalanche. She ogled Jaya and Akash as she retrieved her purse, her tongue itching to wag as soon as she stepped outside. Ruhi darted through the open door just in time for the fireworks.

"I came as quickly as I could," she said, huffing with exertion, dishevelled.

"What's the meaning of this, Jaya?" Her mother puffed up her chest like a parrot's. "This man is dead to us." She surveyed Akash from head to foot, her lip curled, then directed a venomous glance at their joined hands.

Her father stood up, shedding his usually gentle demeanour. "I told you never to come back!" he bristled.

"That's just it. You took my choice away from me," said Jaya. Her father shrank. "I thought Akash had left. It broke me. But he came back. Twice. And I didn't know."

Ruhi reddened. She, too, had lied. The best intentions counted for nothing in the face of untruths.

"You honestly forgive this man, you stupid girl?" spat her mother.

"It was you who advised me to agree to this marriage the first time, mother, or don't you remember? Perhaps your outrage is really targeting me rather than Akash. A disobedient daughter is worth nothing, isn't that true?"

Her mother failed to register Jaya's sarcasm. "We brought you up to listen to your elders."

Jaya let go of Akash's hand and felt power pulse through her. "We sacrifice ourselves at the altar of family. But what if that family is not functional? What if your mother does not want to mother you? What if instead of freeing you she ensnares you in age old traps out of some corrupted sense of tradition? What if she is so resentful of the way her own life turned out that she supports those same traps by her silence and agreement? What if she wants you to shrink yourself for her own comfort?"

"A mother is only as happy as her unhappiest child," said her mother. The words reached out and slapped Jaya as if they had been a physical blow.

She stood her ground.

Her father stepped forward. "We love you, Jaya. We tried our best. We had no sons. We invested everything in the two of you. This man is not worthy of you."

"You're wrong," said Jaya. "We all make mistakes." Her heart broke as she looked at the man she thought had been her supporter. "You knew, Papa. You knew all along. You paid Akash's parents for 'a clean break'. My dowry as payment for hiding our skeletons. To keep the peace. Your peace. So you could distract from my scars by pointing to another ogre in the room." Her bitterness seeped into the air, causing discomfort. *Good,* she thought. *I am not a marionette. This is real.* "It's not Akash on trial here. It is you and Maa. It is India. Can

India continue to tolerate crimes against women? Can our parents and grandparents continue to be complicit?"

Her mother grabbed her arm. The nails dug into the bare flesh of Jaya's arm. Akash and Ruhi stepped forward, vigilant, ready to intervene. Jaya held up her hand, signalling them to stay back.

"You always had ideas above your station. Even as a little girl I had to beat it out of you. A doctor, a lawyer? Not my daughter. You weren't bright enough for that. I saved you. That marriage, being in the home, that's where you could have found your place, but you had to ruin that. You weren't even capable of that." Her mother nodded over to Akash. "You should be grateful we let you come back here. Really, what good are you to him? A broken, sad woman like you? You think I didn't know all those years what you were looking for in those newspapers?"

Jaya spoke quietly. "I'm not sure you've ever known a day of true happiness, mother." She bent to touch her mother's feet, then her father's. "This is what you want. Love as servitude, as duty, as pain. Can't it be more?"

Her mother threw her a look of disgust. "I'm warning you, Jaya. You'll never be happy with that...that vagrant."

"Enough. My choices are mine alone." Jaya turned to Ruhi. Ruhi was always there. "Can you arrange for my things to be collected?"

Her sister ignored their bristling mother and hugged her. "Where are you going?"

"I'll call you."

"I'll be waiting. You know my door is open."

"I know," said Jaya.

Ruhi's embrace grew in intensity. "I knew you could do it, my brave, kind sister." Ruhi stretched out her arms to include Akash in her embrace. He stood, awkward next to Jaya. It was time to go. "Be happy," she whispered.

Jaya blinked back her tears and took Akash's hand once more. As they stepped out of the only home Jaya had ever really known into their new life together, the garlanded statue of Vishnu smiled. Her spirit soared at the thought of a fresh beginning, an unblemished page for their new story. She flung her house keys onto the stairs as they left the familiar and the binding behind.

# 44

**Akash guided Jaya** back towards the beach. The sea washed away his fears. The vast waters reminded him the earth would continue to turn despite human fortunes. Why wouldn't it help Jaya, too? Their procession, hands linked, summoned grainy memories of the past, their walk looping around the flame at their wedding.

"Are you all right?" asked Akash. Jaya mirrored his step, silent and pensive.

"I will be."

He didn't insist on unpacking what had occurred. There would be plenty of time for that in the days that followed. Instead, he pulled her into his arms when they reached the beach, and she relaxed into him inch by inch with the fumbling awkwardness of a newborn foal.

"It shouldn't be this way, not yet, but in your arms I feel safe," she said, and he held her tighter.

Akash traced out the constellations for her: *Saptarshi, Kalpurush, Vrishabh.* Over the years the sky had become as familiar to him as wallpaper to a house-proud man. He intimately knew its every colour, its every form. He grew fearful when the customary shapes morphed into something altogether alien and monstrous. It couldn't be a bad omen, there was nothing left to fear.

He didn't know how to chase away his disquiet and so he repeated what he had told her before but she hadn't believed, hoping that the words would bring her comfort when she felt alone.

"I love you."

Her eyes were black wells of endless depth when she looked at him. She faced the sea, and her words floated away on the wind so he had to strain to hear her. "One thing I have learned, though it has taken me a lifetime to understand it, is never to regret love, in all its forms. My love for my sister, my love for my parents, however flawed, my love for my nephew and my friends, my love for you. That love never went away, though I was hurt. I feel the same about Soraya. Your love for her happened. You don't need to wish it away. It created Arjun. I am happy for you. Anything else would only harm myself." Had the tides been turned, Akash felt sure his bitterness would have eroded their second chance, a seeping poison. He accepted her graciousness with relief.

Eventually, Jaya tired and her head lolled against his chest. She had not spoken of where she might go and Akash avoided it, not wanting to misstep. The beach was no place for his wife to sleep. So he woke her, nuzzling her cheek with his cracked lips.

"Would you like me to take you to Ruhi or Firoz?"

"No. Tonight, I want to come with you."

"To Janghir Saheb's store? Are you sure? I don't own many possessions. It is not a home." Shame filled him at the thought of how little he had to offer her.

"I'm sure. It is yours." Jaya's eyelids drooped with weariness and protectiveness surged within him, as if she were a small child and he her father.

The night had cooled and she shivered. He took her hand and pulled her to her feet, and helped shake the sand from her dress. They strolled through the murky streets while Akash kept watch for a passing rickshaw. The city reeked of body odour and spices, of agarwood and tobacco, but when he leant his head on the clouds of her hair he could smell only coconut and sun.

When they arrived, Akash unlocked the shop and ushered Jaya inside, where she waited in the darkness for him to join her. She followed him through the aisles to the back room, where he turned on the light. Her eyes swept across his meagre possessions neatly stacked in the corner. She hesitated and he feared she regretted it all.

He set to work making a bed for her, unrolling the blankets, layering them so Jaya would be comfortable. He didn't presume that he would sleep next to her. The chair would suit him just fine. It honoured him to sacrifice his comfort for her.

She sat on the bed. "Come," she said, eyes downcast, shielding her emotion from him. It pulsed there, beneath the surface, anxiety and longing, too. She patted the bedding. Fear paralysed Akash. Clammy air weighed on him. He stood, motionless, until she beckoned him again.

He didn't need the perfect love story. Bollywood was obsolete to him, like a hothouse bloom in an artificial colour. He needed Jaya, the truth only she could offer him. She held his gaze in the harsh light, her tiredness forgotten as she unfastened the tiny buttons at her bodice, slipping her arms out of the capped sleeves and letting the material drape at her waist. His breath caught in his throat. He wanted to dart feather kisses across her body, but he held back. He wanted it to be perfect, not to sully her by making love to her in a back office. More than that, he wasn't sure if he was enough.

"I break everything I touch," he said.

She sought his eyes and forced him to hold her gaze.

Electricity shot through him as his body responded.

"You are my husband are you not?"

"Yes."

"Then touch me." The shadows played on her skin. The power was all hers, and she knew it.

He sucked in a ragged breath. He worried she'd find him repulsive. The years had changed him. He could not hide his yellowed teeth, his weathered skin that always seemed dirty, or the twisted sculpture of his skeletal frame. "Shall I turn the lights off?"

"No."

She unhooked her bra and lifted her hips to unfasten her skirt at her waist. Akash's breath caught in his throat, and, for a moment, he forgot everything but her. She beckoned him, and he pushed her skirt gently over her rounded hips, marvelling at the skin underneath. She lay there in all her vulnerability and splendour, and he'd never loved her more than in that instant.

He worshipped her then, as a man worships his wife, exploring her body until they were skin to skin, mouth to mouth, hot breath and damp skin, listening to the sound of her breathing as he pleasured her. They were no longer estranged but entwined, as if they would never part.

She healed him.

He sought to burn each touch and feeling into the reel of his memories. Their joining rung out with the clarity of a bell on a mountain-top church.

Afterwards, Jaya fell asleep almost immediately, her eyelids fanning her cheeks. Their bodies moulded together, two tarnished spoons cupped together perfectly. Akash cherished the warmth of Jaya's body, drank in her scent, the rhythm of her breath, the widow's peak at her forehead, every imperfection, and knew this was where he belonged.

# 45

**They woke in** the morning in a tangle of limbs as the heat of the sun grew over Bombay. Jaya cast a glance at her husband and smiled. A year had passed since they renewed their vows in the rose garden, but the sight of him in their bed would never get old.

"Morning," she said, barely opening her mouth to speak, aware of breath soured by the curry they had cooked and devoured for dinner the night before.

"Hi," said Akash, pulling her into the crook of his bony arm. His musty scent comforted her. However much she fed him, his body refused to reach a healthy weight, as if it was incapable of breaking the mould of his previous life as a homeless man.

She rose reluctantly to dress, pulling the light covers off him as Akash pretended to pout at her. His eyes consumed her with abandonment, elevating her to the level of goddess. There could be no doubt he wanted her.

She swatted him with her pillow, giving thanks for this happiness she never thought could be hers so late in life. "Get up, lazy. Arjun is expecting us. We'll be late for Leela's party if we don't hurry up."

Akash rolled out of bed and retrieved his shirt from where it lay folded on a chair. She watched him button it, pulling it over the curve of his back. He filled the empty spaces in her she'd thought she would carry to her grave. Their rented flat with its old walls, a stone's throw away from her sister's apartment, had become her haven. Akash, too, had found sanctuary here, though he had become used to living under the open sky. Together, they had carved out a small piece of it above their garden. Even with their broken past, they had somehow made a masterpiece of it all.

The twelve months since they'd been reconciled had flown by. Jaya was thankful for every misstep that had made her the woman she had become. Finally, a warrior, even on the days when the separation from her parents weighed heavily, though it felt good to be free from their moods and needs. Forgiveness lay within her reach, and one day soon, she would make that journey. Just not today: today belonged to her new family.

"Now look who's taking forever?" teased Akash. "Stop day dreaming, wife. I know how long it takes you to rim those beautiful eyes with kohl."

She threw him a scathing glance and checked the time before fleeing to the bathroom, his laugh ringing in her ears.

Forty-five minutes later they arrived at Arjun's rose-adorned bungalow, gift in hand to celebrate Leela's second birthday. The stone-clad building loomed against the sky. The guards called through their arrival. They approached as a pair, and Jaya knew the comfort of not being alone in a culture where being one was not enough.

Once, the thought of visiting Soraya's former home would have struck her as odd given the enmity she had borne the other woman for much of her life, but not anymore. The past year had eased her nerves about visiting this palace of high walls, which held so much history for them all. It would have been easy to be envious of the biological relationship Akash shared with his son, to allow her soul to be devoured by cobwebs of insufficiency, but in truth, this family gifted her with so much more than she had bargained for. Over time, she had begun to accompany Akash with eagerness to visit his son, buoyed by the open welcome she received and aided by both her easy friendship with Muna and her fondness for the child.

Today, excitement leaked out of every pore, as if she were an untightened faucet. A child's birthday was special, magical even, and Jaya cherished every interaction with children. They arrived at the door and Akash lowered the box he had been carrying onto the ground. It rocked at their feet and they heard a muffled meow.

"I hope she likes the present." His voice tingled at her ear.

"How can she not? Every child dreams of having their own kitten."

"You don't think she's too young?" He had been an absent father for so long that even now he second-guessed his decisions.

She squeezed his arm. "Stop worrying. Arjun wouldn't have said yes if he thought she was."

Arjun opened the door with a creak, a young man suited in solemnity, as ever, with his father's lips and his mother's haughtiness. His face broke into a smile when he saw her and Jaya reciprocated. In some ways, this man was more comfortable with her than his own father.

Arjun extended a hand to his father and kissed Jaya's cheek. "Leela's going to be so excited to see you. Her friends will be here this afternoon but all she could talk about this morning is the big present Dadabapa had promised her." A mewling sound erupted from the box. Arjun laughed. "Is that it?"

"You sure this is okay, beta?" said Akash, scooping the box into his arms.

"I'd wager she'll remember this birthday! Come, we'd better get that box open."

They took off their shoes and padded after him in their socked feet. Arjun led the way into the now familiar bowels of the house, along a twisty corridor and into a bright kitchen.

"Ah, there she is, my gorgeous granddaughter," said Akash, handing the box to Arjun before sweeping a giggling Leela in his arms.

"Dada!" said the little girl, her cheeks rosy with pleasure.

"Happy birthday, *beti*," said Jaya, placing a kiss on the girl's cheek.

Muna rushed to greet them, a vision in green chiffon. Not a line marred her face. "I'm so glad you came. Didn't Janghir Saheb mind?"

Akash leaned into her embrace, his arms still full of the child. "Oh, you know what he's like. Family first, always."

The smell of burnt onions and chilli hung in the air, burning Jaya's eyes. She blinked rapidly and opened her arms to hug the younger woman. "It smells delicious."

Muna laughed. "No, it doesn't, but we eat the restaurant food all the time. I wanted to do something special for Leela's birthday." She indicated the disarray on the worktops. "Please excuse the mess." Steam rose from a bowl of crispy okra curry alongside pickled aubergines and diced potatoes. The pungent scent of cumin and mustard seeds filled Jaya's nostrils.

"You must have been working since dawn," said Akash. His voice trembled and Jaya reached across to press his hand. He would never take the warmth of family life for granted. Seeing the world through his eyes gave her a new appreciation.

Akash set Leela back on the floor. He locked his eyes on Jaya's, perhaps for permission, she wasn't sure. She nodded, an imperceptible movement. "Are you ready for your present, little one?" He guided her gently to the box, tipping it onto its side. Out spilled the kitten, a fluffy ball of grey with a white bib.

Leela squealed and the kitten darted away, startled. Everyone laughed in delight, watching them interact, a game of to and fro between two tiny beings, before Muna excused herself.

"Food's nearly ready. Just a few more rotis to go," said Muna.

"Come. I'll help you," said Jaya. She rolled up the sleeves of the salwar kameez and tied the scarf in a knot at her hip to keep it out of the way. Then she approached the griddle already on the burner. She rolled out the roti and placed the powdery dough on the heat, working with nimble fingers while Muna cleared the disarray in the kitchen, pausing only to butter the finished rotis. Behind them, the men supervised Leela, sometimes encouraging, sometimes chiding as she learnt to play with the kitten. The griddle hissed and the stack of bread grew, and Jaya gave thanks for the little joys that had become part of her life.

After the party ended and the last of the children and their parents had gone home, Akash and Jaya took their leave, refusing Arjun's offer of a lift. They wandered past the outhouse in the gardens on the way out. It seemed a lifetime ago that he had found Soraya and received a beating at Arjun's hands, like it had happened in a parallel universe. Akash only had to close his eyes to relive it. But with the pain came the wheels of change which had reunited him with Jaya. He didn't want to close his eyes again; they were firmly trained on the present.

He kneaded Jaya's hand as they walked, lost in his thoughts, in the promise of the fulfilling relationships he had finally built with his wife, son and granddaughter. It was inconceivable to him that he had escaped his poor choices, that the gods were smiling on him.

"I'd forgotten my husband is such a dreamer," said Jaya. Happiness shone from her flushed cheeks.

"Sorry." His eyes rested on her face, the hair that escaped its bonds, the crinkles at the corners of her mouth, her delicate jaw and arched brows. "How was that for you?"

"Wonderful," said Jaya, squeezing his hand.

A cow herd had wandered into the road ahead, a mass of dirty white and tan. Traffic stalled to a halt behind the herd as even the most impatient Bombay drivers waited, to let the sacred animals pass. Akash placed his hand on the hollow of Jaya's lower back to guide her across the street, still lost in his dreams.

Too late did he see two boys on a motorcycle careening towards them. They scooted past the herd, helmetless, tyres kicking up dust, parcels teetering in the passenger's arms.

Time slowed and Akash stood frozen as the motorcycle swerved, travelling too fast to brake, realising he was shielded by Jaya's body.

Instinct kicked in. Akash pushed his wife with all his might.

Her face twisted in horror. She fell onto the road.

The motorcycle skidded, crashed into him, sending its riders up into an unholy trajectory.

Akash's legs crunched and he flew through the air as though in slow motion, his hand stretched out towards his wife. He landed in a heap, heard his bones fragment, old bones that had been worn down by the wrong nourishment, the elements, the years of drifting, the lack of love. Not even the bright sun of Jaya's love could make up for the years of neglect. Coldness enfolded him, bleak and black. Akash placed his hand on his head, and his fingers found the matted warmth of his bloodied cranium. He worried about Janghir Saheb's keys. Were they still in his pocket? He called out to Jaya, his thoughts disjointed. What did he need to say to her?

"Jaya?"

A flurry of footsteps. She entered his field of vision. He blinked, frustrated he couldn't see clearly. She blurred, like an under-exposed photograph. She leant closer, and he could smell the coconut lotion she used on her skin. Her breathing was raspy like she had been running. Her posture looked defeated, shrunken shoulders, a retreat into her core.

"I'm here." Her voice comforted him like a blanket on a cool night, enveloping him with love.

The shadows next to her confused him. They grew taller, found their forms. He recognised them and his heart sang. They had always shared his happiness. Of course they would be here today.

"You're here," said Akash. Tariq and Soraya nodded, expressions gentle, not joyous like he would have expected.

"Help is coming, Akash! Arjun will know what to do. Don't leave me." Jaya sounded like she was crying but he couldn't work out why.

"But I'll never leave you." His words came out jumbled. He wanted to tell her how much he loved her, but his mouth wouldn't form the words. He loved her. No Bollywood fanfare or pity for life's knocks, just all-encompassing love. He tried to caress her face, but his hand did not obey his command. He needed a rest. He closed his eyes.

"Akash, Akash, please! Look at me! Stay with me."

She sounded desperate, his Jaya. He wanted to tell her about Tariq and Soraya holding his hands. How loved he felt. She buried her head in his chest and it hurt, like a little bird landing on a broken branch. He wished he could be stronger for her. She was so strong, his Jaya. He needed to tell her how proud he was, but Tariq and Soraya, they didn't want to wait. He had to go.

"I'll always find my way back to you," he said, and he believed it.

He was so cold. His eyelids fluttered shut, and his final thought escaped him, leaving a ghost of a smile on his dead lips.

## THE END

# BOOK CLUB GUIDE

**1.** What are the main themes of the novel?

**2.** Who is your favourite major/minor character?

**3.** Which symbols are used in the novel and what do they represent?

**4.** Which character did you relate to the most and why?

**5.** Which character did you most hate?

**6.** Which familial/romantic/platonic relationships are the most nourishing in the novel?

**7.** What role do religion and culture play in the story?

**8.** What motivates Akash to get his life in order?

**9.** How did the structure of the book affect the story?

**10.** Which character did you relate to the most and why?

**11.** Could the story have taken place anywhere?

**12.** How does Jaya learn to cope with her trauma?

**13.** Was Akash wrong to sleep with the older Soraya as they said their goodbye?

**14.** What was your favourite moment in the book? Your least favourite?

**15.** How do the characters grow in the course of the novel?

**16.** At what point does Jaya make a breakthrough in achieving happiness?

**17.** At what point in the novel is Akash truly selfless for the first time?

**18.** How did you feel about the ending?

**19.** Would Akash and Jaya's relationship have survived into old age?

**20.** What surprised you the most when you were reading this book?

**21.** If Jaya and Akash had each chosen different love interests, then how might the story have ended?

**22.** How do you imagine the story continues for Arjun?

**23.** Did the novel challenge your perspective in any way?

# INTERVIEW WITH THE AUTHOR

**Q. Which book have you read has most influenced your life?**

**A.** There are too many that have left their mark to choose only one. Some books are like friends, and I get cross if people borrow them and don't bring them back. Ones that have changed me include: *The Well of Loneliness* by Radclyffe Hall, *The Handmaid's Tale* by Margaret Atwood, *The Bell Jar* by Sylvia Plath, *Half of a Yellow Sun* by Chimamanda Ngozi Adichie, *The Road* by Cormac McCarthy, *Book of Lilith* by P.K. Tyler, *Extremely Loud and Incredibly Close* by Jonathan Safran Foer, *The Night Circus* by Erin Morgenstern, *To Kill a Mockingbird* by Harper Lee, *The Kiterunner* by Khaled Hosseini, *American Gods* by Neil Gaiman, *We Need to Talk About Kevin* by Lionel Shriver, and poetry by Simon Armitage and Carol Ann Duffy. I'm going to kick myself later, as there are so many more, amongst them books for children. Have you read *Goodnight Stories for Rebel Girls*?

**Q. If you could spend time with a character from this book, whom would it be? And what would you do during that day?**

**A.** A night with Soraya at her restaurant—without Arjun—would be great. I'd have so many questions for her. But for me it has to be a toss up between Inspector Fortes and Firoz. Fortes doesn't get a lot of page space but how does woman like her hold her own in the Indian police force? She must be formidable, but she hasn't lost her empathy or her sense of humour. Then there's Firoz. Firoz is a balm. He's fun and non-judgmental and so at ease with himself. What a joy. We'd drink chai, he'd show me the yoga moves I need to get the cricks out of my back, and we'd laugh until the stars came up over his atelier.

## Q. What does your writing day look like?

**A.** I try hard to stick to a writing routine. For me that means rushing about like a whirlwind as soon as I wake and getting the kids to school. Then it's me and the baby. I make a cup of tea, put some music on and work in the living room while the baby plays or naps nearby. I've learnt to make use of every minute. Right now, he needs me close. Soon, I'll be able to use my desk in the office at the bottom of our garden again. It's filled with inherited furniture: my father's heavy oak desk with its crumbling varnished surface, and the worn burnt leather sofas I grew up with. I 've hung up canvasses of Zadie Smith holding a copy of *On Beauty*, and another of Twiggy. Strong, creative women to surround myself with. I try not to get swept into social media but the news is my real vice. I write until the kids are home from school, and tend to be fairly relaxed about squeezing in another writing window when the kids are home. Some ideas and moods need capturing immediately or they escape me.

## Q. Does a big ego help or hurt writers?

**A.** I was born in London but am of Indian heritage. There's this thing that shy Indian women sometimes do in Bollywood movies: they hide behind the fabric of their sari. Sometimes, that part of my identity is strong. I don't enjoy the limelight. But I trust in who I am and what I can do. I think that's important. In all walks of life, not just writing, self-doubt is a game-killer. Does Soraya arguably achieve more than Jaya because she is self-assured? Jaya learns eventually that self-love is what she needs to transform her life. On the flipside, an exaggerated sense of self-importance blinds you to your flaws. Like most things, balance is key.

## Q. Does writing energize or exhaust you?

**A.** Thinking about writing—when I am longing to get to my desk and life intervenes—exhausts me. It feels like inertia. There is something unpleasant about it. But writing itself, it energises me. Writing is breath. It is infinite possibility. It is a sanctuary away from the 24-hour news cycle. I write to untie the knots in my head. It is the ability to explore my thoughts without rushing and without worrying about their impact (that's for the publication stage). It is a comfort and I'm very grateful to be able to do it.

**Q. You are running the 100-yard dash with a new writer. What writing or publishing wisdom do you offer?**

**A.** I'm not a runner, so after the race is over, and I have peeled myself off the floor, I would tell the writer that writing is not a sprint but a marathon. Everyone runs their own race, but there are helpful things you can do along the way. Find your writer tribe: friends who are encouraging and understand the joys and frustrations. Start a blog. The blogging community is saturated but blogging isn't always about being read. For me, it was central to toughening up my mindset. Blogging teaches you the discipline of writing regularly and forces you to be brave enough to publish your words. Find your gurus. There have been so many for me along the way: Julia Cameron, Susan Kaye Quinn, Chuck Wendig. Most importantly, finish your projects and seek feedback. As long as you are moving forward, a word, a skill, a rejection even, you are winning.

**Q. What can we expect next from you?**

**A.** I'm signed with Evolved Publishing for three literary fiction novels. My pace for novels tends to be about one a year. My next novel, *Hidden Colours*, tells the story of a circus performer and a journalist in Berlin. It's about grief and chance, and about race and fixed viewpoints. I'm at the point in the process when the web of connections is becoming clear. It's exciting. I also try to submit two short stories a year to anthologies. Depending on my success rate, you can expect to read those too! To be the first to hear about my books, sign up for my newsletter at:
**http://nillunasser.com/mailing-list/**

# Acknowledgements

Thanks to my team at Evolved Publishing for believing in this book and bringing it to life, especially my editor Jess for your guidance and friendship.

I am grateful to my critique group for your wisdom, and here I must single out Pav for your generous advice and tattoo-laden brilliance. Thanks also to my first readers Amira, Meg, Tess and Phillip for your time and vital insights, and to Zahra and Azhar for sharing your wisdom though you are far from home.

I cannot express enough gratitude to the online writing communities, which I fell into by accident. Finding you in many ways was like coming home. You spurred me on. I owe you more than I can say.

I cannot forget Vera and Evemarie, my Stuttgart family, and the conversations we had around the kitchen table, together with the books on your shelves, which initially sparked my interest in feminism. You lit a fire.

Lindsay, my creative sister, thanks for going to bat for me. Snatched moments with you buoy me.

Thank you to my parents for teaching me to love well, and for encouraging me to paper my path with my own views and dreams.

To my children, thanks for your patience when mummy disappeared into her dream world or was chasing a deadline. Remember you can do whatever you set your mind to.

Finally, to Jan, the calm to my storm. Without your faith, encouragement and good humour, this book would have remained the whisper of an idea in my head. Thank you for being you.

# About the Author

Nillu Nasser is a writer of literary fiction novels. She also blogs and writes short fiction and poetry.

Nillu's short story 'Painted Truths and Prayer Beads' was published in May 2016 in *Mosaics 2: A Collection of Independent Women*. Another short story 'The Tombstone Man and the Coming of the Tigress' was published in June 2016 in *UnCommon Origins*, an anthology of short fiction. In 2017, 'Tombstone Man' reappeared in *UnCommonly Good*.

Nillu has a BA in English and German Literature and an MA in European Politics. After graduating, she worked in national and regional politics, but eventually reverted to her first love.

She lives in London with her husband, three children, and one angelic and one demonic cat, though she secretly yearns for a dog. If you fly into Gatwick and look hard enough, you will see her furiously scribbling in her garden office where she's working on her next story.

**For more, please visit Nillu Nasser online at:**
Personal Website: www.NilluNasser.com
Publisher Website: www.EvolvedPub.com
Goodreads: Nillu_Nasser
Twitter: @NilluNasser
Facebook: NilluNasser

# What's Next?

## HIDDEN COLOURS BY NILLU NASSER

Watch for *Hidden Colours,* the next literary fiction from Nillu Nasser to release in late 2018. For more information on this book, please visit Nillu's page at www.EvolvedPub.com or sign up for her newsletter on her author website at **www.NilluNasser.com**.

~~~

Each evening, nestled in Berlin's Treptower Park, the immigrant circus comes to life. Ellie is passionate about the circus, Germany's flagship integration project—not least because she is in love with Yusuf the acrobat—but her editor wants her to head up a campaign against it.

When Yusuf fled Syria, he lost everything. Now the circus, with its middle-eastern flair, is the only home he knows. When the lights go on, the refugees dazzle their audience, but off-stage they can't escape the traumas of their past and the far-right radicals that dog their every move.

One night, Yusuf interrupts his acrobatics to chase two young boys. The resulting violence shines a spotlight on the refugee estate, and swells the tide of public and media opinion against the immigrant circus.

As tensions rise and with the circus at risk of closure, Ellie must convince her readers that we can have compassion for those we fear or Yusuf will be forced to uproot again.

# More from Evolved Publishing

**FANTASY (Adult)**
THE SUNDERED OATH by Ciara Ballintyne:
*In the Company of the Dead (Book 1)*
*On the Edge of Death (Book 2)*
THE AMULI CHRONICLES: SOULBOUND by Kira A. McFadden:
*The Soulbound Curse (Book 1)*
*The Soulless King (Book 2)*
*The Throne of Souls (Book 3)*
*Shadow Swarm* by D. Robert Pease


**HISTORICAL FICTION**
*Galerie* by Steven Greenberg
*Fresh News Straight from Heaven* by Gregg Sapp
*Broken Path* by Ruby Standing Deer
SHINING LIGHT'S SAGA by Ruby Standing Deer:
*Circles (Book 1)*
*Spirals (Book 2)*
*Stones (Book 3)*


**HORROR**
WRITER'S BLOCK by A.K. Kuykendall:
*The Possession (Book 1)*
GODSKNIFE by Timothy C. Ward:
*Godsknife: Revolt (Book 1)*
*Godsknife: Abyss (Book 2)*


**LITERARY FICTION**
*The Atheist and the Parrotfish* by Richard Barager
*Carry Me Away* by Robb Grindstaff
*Hannah's Voice* by Robb Grindstaff

*Turning Trixie* by Robb Grindstaff
*Behind the Open Walls* by Lanette Kauten
*Cassia* by Lanette Kauten
*The Daughter of the Sea and the Sky* by David Litwack
*A Handful of Wishes* by E.D. Martin
*The Futility of Loving a Soldier* by E.D. Martin
*Yours to Keep or Throw Aside* by E.D. Martin
*All the Tomorrows* by Nillu Nasser
*Hidden Colours* by Nillu Nasser
THE DESERT by Angela Scott:
    *Desert Rice (Book 1)*
    *Desert Flower (Book 2)*
*White Chalk* by P.K. Tyler


## MEMOIR
*And Then It Rained* by Megan Morrison
*Girl Enlightened* by Megan Morrison


## MIDDLE GRADE & YOUNG ADULT (Crossover)
FRENDYL KRUNE by Kira A. McFadden:
    *Frendyl Krune and the Blood of the Sun (Book 1)*
    *Frendyl Krune and the Snake Across the Sea (Book 2)*
    *Frendyl Krune and the Stone Princess (Book 3)*
    *Frendyl Krune and the Nightmare in the North (Book 4)*
NOAH ZARC by D. Robert Pease:
    *Mammoth Trouble (Book 1)*
    *Cataclysm (Book 2)*
    *Declaration (Book 3)*
    *Omnibus (Special 3-in-1 Edition)*


## MYSTERY / CRIME / DETECTIVE
DUNCAN COCHRANE by David Hagerty:
    *They Tell Me You Are Wicked (Book 1)*
    *They Tell Me You Are Crooked (Book 2)*
    *They Tell Me You Are Brutal (Book 3)*
*The Last Meridian* by Joe Hefferon
*Hot Sinatra* by Axel Howerton

## ROMANCE / EROTICA
COLLEGE ROMANCE by Amelia James:
*Tell Me You Want Me (Book 1)*
*Secret Storm (Book 2)*
*Tell Me You Want Forever (Book 3)*
*Destined for Genius* by Amelia James
*Let It Ride* by Amelia James
THE TWISTED MOSAIC by Amelia James:
*Her Twisted Pleasures (Book 1)*
*Their Twisted Love (Book 2)*
*His Twisted Choice (Book 3)*
*The Twisted Mosaic – Specail Omnibus Edition 1-3 (Book 4)*
*The Devil Made Me Do It* by Amelia James
THE SUGAR HOUSE NOVELLAS by Pavarti K. Tyler:
*Sugar & Salt (Book 1)*
*Protecting Portia (Book 2)*
*Dual Domination (Book 3)*
*The Sugar House Novellas – Special Omnibus Edition 1-3 (Book 4)*


## SCIENCE FICTION
THE PANHELION CHRONICLES by Marlin Desault:
*Shroud of Eden (Book 1)*
*The Vanquished of Eden (Book 2)*
THE CONSPIRATOR'S ODYSSEY by A.K. Kuykendall:
*Imperium Heirs (Book 1)*
JAKKATTU by P.K. Tyler:
*The Jakkattu Vector (Book 1)*
*The Jakkattu Insurrection (Book 2)*
*The Jakkattu Exodus (Book 3)*
*Two Moons of Sera* by P.K. Tyler


## SUSPENSE / THRILLER
ELOAH by Lex Allen:
*Eloah: No Heaven (Book 1)*
*Eloah: No Hell (Book 2)*
*Eloah: No Religion (Book 3)*
*Fracture Point* by Jeff Altabef
*Shatter Point* by Jeff Altabef

TONY HOOPER by Lane Diamond:
*Forgive Me, Alex (Book 1)*
*The Devil's Bane (Book 2)*
*Enfold Me* by Steven Greenberg
THE SYNDICATE-BORN TRILOGY by K.M. Hodge:
*Red on the Run (Book 1)*
*Black and White Truth (Book 2)*
*Kubrick's Game* by Derek Taylor Kent
THE OZ FILES by Barry Metcalf:
*Broometime Serenade (Book 1)*
*Intrigue at Sandy Point (Book 2)*
*Spirit of Warrnambool (Book 3)*
THE ZOE DELANTE THRILLERS by C.L. Roberts-Huth:
*Whispers of the Dead (Book 1)*
*Whispers of the Serpent (Book 2)*
*Whispers of the Sidhe (Book 3)*
*Kill or be Killed: Under Cover* by Linda Kay Silva


**YOUNG ADULT**
CHOSEN by Jeff Altabef and Erynn Altabef:
*Wind Catcher (Book 1)*
*Brink of Dawn (Book 2)*
*Scorched Souls (Book 3)*
RED DEATH by Jeff Altabef:
*Red Death (Book 1)*
*The Ghost King (Book 2)*
THE KIN CHRONICLES by Michael Dadich:
*The Silver Sphere (Book 1)*
*The Sinister Kin (Book 2)*
UPLOADED by James W. Hughes:
*Uploaded (Book 1)*
*Viral (Book 2)*
DIRT AND STARS by Kevin Killiany:
*Down to Dirt (Book 1)*
*Life on Dirt (Book 2)*
STORMBOURNE CHRONICLES by Karissa Laurel:
*Heir of Thunder (Book 1)*
*Quest of Thunder (Book 2)*

THE DARLA DECKER DIARIES by Jessica McHugh:
*Darla Decker Hates to Wait (Book 1)*
*Darla Decker Takes the Cake (Book 2)*
*Darla Decker Shakes the State (Book 3)*
*Darla Decker Plays it Straight (Book 4)*
*Darla Decker Breaks the Case (Book 5)*
JOEY COLA by D. Robert Pease:
*Dream Warriors (Book 1)*
*Cleopatra Rising (Book 2)*
*Third Reality (Book 3)*
*Anyone?* by Angela Scott
THE ZOMBIE WEST TRILOGY by Angela Scott:
*Wanted: Dead or Undead (Book 1)*
*Survivor Roundup (Book 2)*
*Dead Plains (Book 3)*
*The Zombie West Trilogy – Special Omnibus Edition 1-3*
WHITEWASHED by Adelaide Thorne:
*The Trace (Book 1)*
*The Integer (Book 2)*

9 781622 537853